MW00526919

The Many Mother's of Ivy Puddingstone

"A new Randy Susan Meyers novel is always a cause for celebration! Her novels are beautifully written and full of warmth, wit, and wisdom. I'm a devoted fan!"

–LIANE MORIARTY, *New York Times* bestselling author of *Big Little Lies* and *Nine Perfect Strangers.*

"Randy Susan Meyers returns with a timely and exciting story of womanhood, family, and coming of age set against the turbulent background of the 1960s moving through to the present. Meyers delves into the untold strength of mothers and the unfathomable choices they face—and will have readers whipping through these pages."

–PAM JENOFF, *New York Times* bestselling author of *The Orphan's Tale* and *The Lost Girls of Paris*

". . . a powerful story of the fraught bond between mothers and daughters. Against the backdrop of the explosive events of the 1960s and '70s, idealist Annabel struggles to balance her passions with parenthood. The perfect solution: send her daughter, Ivy, to a childhood Eden—a house in Vermont where Ivy will live with six other children and a rotating cast of mothers to govern them. However, when tragedy strikes, the families must face the dark side of their do-gooding. With a deft hand, Randy Susan Meyers seamlessly weaves in the issues of the day in this beautifully crafted novel that questions what we're willing to sacrifice in our attempts to right the wrongs of the world. I fell in love with both Ivy and Annabel in this story, which manages to be both heart wrenching and heartwarming. A gorgeous novel that's not to be missed."

–JENNIFER S. BROWN, *USA Today* bestselling author of *The Whisper Sister*

"Would you live apart from your children if it meant you could focus on creating a better future for all children? *The Many Mothers of Ivy Puddingstone* explores this question from the points of view of a mother and daughter who each give the reader their side of the story in compelling scenes that will bring back memories of the '60s and '70s for older readers as well as portraying the effects of their early choices in contemporary settings. There are no easy answers here; social justice, familial love, and acceptance are works in progress in Randy Susan Meyers' wise depiction of good people trying to do their best in a turbulent era. As I closed the book I wanted to go visit Puddingstone and the Roundhouse to see where the characters put their ideals into motion, and to think deeply about how things went wrong. This is a thought-provoking novel from an accomplished storyteller."

—ALICE ELLIOTT DARK, author of *Fellowship Point and In the Gloaming*

"Meyer's meticulously researched novel paints an evocative picture of 1960s activism, with its dichotomies of sacrifice and thrill, intelligence and naivete, service to others and to ego. Annabelle Cooper, like so many in the movement, brims with altruism—both for her children and for humanity. But when idealism collides with reality, good intentions are cold comfort as the collateral damage mounts. A smart, clear-eyed, incisively written novel about the tension between saving the world and caring for those we love."

—JULIETTE FAY, *USA Today* bestselling author of *The Half of It*

"Randy Susan Meyers depicts the raw, fraught love between mothers and daughters with brilliant insight as she follows Annabel and Ivy within an extended chosen family committed to activism in the turbulent social movements of the twentieth century. The political and personal are one in this riveting, explosive saga loaded with a fierce and tender love that must ultimately encompass a daughter's rage--and a mother's guilt."

–LYNNE HUGO, author of *The Language of Kin*

"The hardest parts of growing up can be accepting that our parents had lives before we were born—and that their very best intentions in raising us have led to pain and anguish. Randy Susan Meyers explores these facts of life against a backdrop of political and social activism that asks us to question our motives, values, and longings. Meyers takes us across the decades and deep into the hearts of her dazzling cast of characters with her signature storytelling, compassion, and insight."

–ELIZABETH BENEDICT, author of *Rewriting Illness: A View of My Own* and *The Practice of Deceit*

The Many Mothers of Ivy Puddingstone

by Randy Susan Meyers

Published by

köhlerbooks™

3705 Shore Drive
Virginia Beach, VA 23455
800-435-4811
www.koehlerbooks.com

The Many Mothers of Ivy Puddingstone

Randy Susan Meyers

VIRGINIA BEACH
CAPE CHARLES

BOOKS BY RANDY SUSAN MEYERS

The Murderer's Daughters
The Comfort of Lies
Accidents of Marriage
The Widow of Wall Street
Waisted

For Jeff, who owns my heart.

Above all, be the heroine of your life, not the victim.

—Nora Ephron

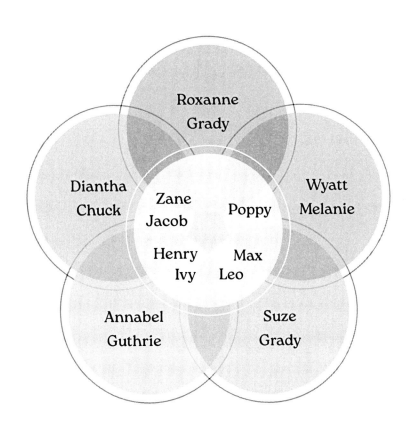

Prologue

❋

Ivy

JANUARY, 1984

Dealers-Choice Granola

Once upon a time, I belonged to a tribe of kids who ran free. Too free.

I grew to hate and love many things while living in Vermont those years. The umpteen words for pot drove me crazy even before I hated smoking, smelling, or seeing the substance. I'll never miss the choking odor of patchouli oil, the flavor of brown rice, or the sight of stir-fried vegetables drenched in tamari sauce.

I hated the word *screwing*. In truth, I hated all references to sex. Roundhouse, our commune in Vermont, practically made a nun out of me. And I'm not sure if I can use these words in a college admission essay, but don't they tell you what Roundhouse did to me? Freedom of expression was sacred there.

I almost began to hate art because my mother personified creativity. I missed her so much during my years at Roundhouse that sometimes my love for her turned to hate, but I could never sustain the emotion. I treasured her cataclysmic and vivid paintings; good and evil came alive with her oils and watercolors.

Our path to Roundhouse began well before I was born, the year my mother Annabel turned eighteen—when one makes the bravest and the clumsiest decisions—often at the exact same moment.

Roundhouse still occupies my dreams—sometimes, in my sleep, Poppy and I laugh as we paint chains of outsized daisies around the massive barn, splayed old brushes spattering our skin purple and yellow. In my nightmares, my brother and I race in endless circles, searching for the grown-ups.

I imagine the joy of the follow-your-passion days—as declared by the grown-ups—when the seven of us choose our paths for the day. Poppy and I once spent an entire passion day coloring our nails with magic markers, rolling our hair in giant curlers, and beautifying ourselves in filched makeup. We jumped in the pond each time we finished a new look, scrubbed our skin with sandy dirt, and then began again.

The mothers hated that one.

The grown-ups christened our children's community *Roundhouse*. They believed Roundhouse would fulfill their dream of a children's utopia, but neither the word their dream nor utopia ever described Roundhouse before or after.

The house in Boston where I was born and spent my youngest years and where they remained after they sent us to Vermont, Puddingstone, was a nod to the quarries from which our house sprang.

They loosely modeled Roundhouse—very loosely—on a kibbutz in Israel, as per the memory of my father, who had once lived in one for three weeks; they built us an ersatz kibbutz minus the discipline, set routines, and soothing nightly visits from parents.

Roundhouse's name was a nod to Joni Mitchell's "Circle Game." Irony flooded me when, at sixteen, I learned that Joni had placed her daughter for adoption.

My brother and I still crack up when we talk about that choice.

Our grown-ups swore their fondest wish was for us to be raised free. We were to be cuddly lambs gamboling in the meadows. More often, we resembled Norwegian lemmings, animals with a ferocious survival instinct who turn on creatures far beyond their size.

Other times, we became a pack of orphaned puppies, depending on each other no matter how much we might growl. Like most kids who don't trust their parents, we protected members of our clutch even if we occasionally nipped at each other.

According to their original statement of purpose, still bound in the red and purple leather journal handmade by my mother, our parents planned an idyll where nature would nurture us. Fresh air! Organic vegetables we grew with our own hands! Milk from the cows we raised from calves!

Neither cows nor calves materialized, and plucking disgusting bugs off the few vegetables that grew became automatic. I longed for the Green Giant string beans with almonds my grandmother served alongside her roasted chicken—something else I craved. Poppy and I papered our room with ragged-edged advertisements torn from magazines. We woke to Chef Boyardee holding a can of his ravioli, staring at us with grandfatherly beneficence while our dealers-choice granola waited in the kitchen.

Our parents suspended their choices on claims of wanting us to be free of hang-ups.

Once, I believed Roundhouse came about because they knew true freedom to follow their dreams meant choosing between them or us, and we lost the coin toss. They didn't want to become hung up on the twisted cords of familial connections as they pursued their politics and passions.

Hung up. Hang-ups. More words I learned to hate.

Marching, getting arrested, and saving the world left little time for pushing us on playground swings and helping with homework. Maybe my parents considered themselves as having sacrificed for the cause; I believed they forfeited us.

When I was born, my mother was very young; I don't think I was ever as young as she was. But our path to Roundhouse began the year my mother Annabel turned eighteen—well before I was born—when one makes the bravest and the clumsiest decisions—often at the exact same moment.

When I hit fifteen, I told myself freedom, to them, had been just another word for sleeping with each other in any combinations that struck their fancy without any watchful children inhibiting their bed-hopping.

If that were true, they could have avoided sending us to Vermont if they'd read Victor Hugo's words—*no one can keep a secret better than a child.*

But I couldn't hold that belief. Imagining her and the other women slipping in and out of the arms of varied partners made me want to throw up. Sacrificing themselves on the stake like Joan of Arc in the name of freedom was easier to imagine than them having sex with each other.

I decided they were too humorless to have that much fun.

My father referred to Roundhouse as "parenting with intentionality."

The grown-ups planned to parent us in shifts, just like they took turns cleaning the toilets and cooking meals according to the elaborate chore chart on the kitchen wall. Imagining their enthusiasm took no effort on my part. When it came to Roundhouse, they probably believed that with the right chart, parental responsibilities could come down to a weekend or two per month—less with artful trading—and a few full weeks each year. However, as it played out, schedules for when they came to see us became as loose as their work commitments were iron-clad.

My singular goal became getting my mother alone when she came for her childcare weeks—an impossible dream; my brother affixed himself to her as though they were magnets of opposite polarities. And then, when I wended my way between them, I still competed with the other six Roundhouse children, all desperate for her artsy-craftsy, intense-when-in-the-moment version of mothering.

All the kids craved attention from the women of Puddingstone traveling from Boston to Putney. We also reveled in holding the spotlight of the men—the fathers—but they didn't make or break us like the mothers. We liked impressing the fathers and were dazzled by their building, fixing, and braininess feats, but they weren't the mothers.

We wanted to suck in Melanie's calm warmth, laugh at Suze's

humor, and imitate Roxanne's haughty glamor. Diantha, our permanent house mother, was a victim of familiarity. We could ignore her.

But only the presence of Annabel, my real mother, allowed me to relax my hypervigilance and act out the way kids need to. Mom offered me her totality of love, but only when she was there—and most of the time, she wasn't.

She made everything fun: mud pies became impressionistic art, weaving yarn God's Eyes brought magical mysticism, and our plays became fodder for political interpretations. Most importantly, we cracked her up.

Her ability to be fantastic made me even angrier at being separated.

Early on in the experiment, our grown-ups thought they could be a friends-with-benefits version of parents, the first generation to have children without the struggle—all the while holding fast to the belief that they offered us utopia.

Once upon a time, I tried to figure out if we were the victims of a failed experiment or the best of loving intentions that lacked actual parameters.

—*Ivy Pascal's College Admission Essay to Pratt University in 1984*

Part One

❋

Freedom Summer

Annabel

The volunteers merely dropped in for a summer, then went home to question America. Some would spearhead the events that defined the 1960s . . . Others, spreading ideals absorbed in Mississippi, would be forever skeptical of authority, forever democrats with a small d, and forever touched by this single season of their youth.

But first, they had to survive Freedom Summer.

—Bruce Watson

Chapter 1

❀

Annabel

Why Pray When You Can Knit?

My parents planted the seeds of radical change in me with less than zero intention. By the time I reached eighteen, those seeds had grown into vines thick enough to choke out the merest whiff of injustice.

My mother and father believed an overnight camp, a mere hour's drive from our home in Rhinebeck, would be better than hanging out with my friends on Montgomery Street. They nodded with approval at Camp Wonder's brochure, which promised that spinning clay bowls and learning the breaststroke would be side by side with civic virtue, integrity, and moral values.

And, of course, as I got older, they hoped the bonus would be that an all-girls overnight camp would keep me from fast boys.

My virtuous, hard-working folks believed the Unitarian Universalist camp's beliefs would resemble those of our Good Shepherd Church. However, by the time my father realized the staff clung closer to folk-music-Christian—his description—than traditional service-driven Catholicism, that train had left the station.

I began camp at the age of twelve. By thirteen, I'd given up greed, substituting begging for candy with chanting "Trick or Treat for

UNICEF!"

At fourteen, while friends practiced makeup techniques meant to capture the interest of the boys in town, I honed my art by painting fields of waving daisies to cheer up the walls of the depressing local senior center in the basement of Good Shepherd.

At fifteen, while my sisters practiced going ever lower while dancing the limbo, I joined my mother and her friends in scrubbing and repainting a nursery school in the poorest section of nearby Poughkeepsie.

At sixteen, almost seventeen, I unearthed a copy of *The Red Record* deep in the stacks of Rhinebeck's small-town library. After sobbing and struggling through Ida B. Wells's accounts of lynching and other racial murders, the axis of my world spun to civil rights. I bought and then wore out Pete Seeger's album, *We Shall Overcome.*

I declared myself a free-thinking Unitarian and boiled my life's goal down to their three mantras: *love radically, serve gratefully, and wonder daily.* Thus, a year later, as a college freshman in Boston, I vibrated with surety when I stumbled upon a flyer seeking volunteers to register voters in Mississippi. As I filled out the forms, I devised plans to convince my parents to sign the consent portion. Being only eighteen, I still needed their permission.

Over Easter weekend, I began my campaign, starting with my mother. She expected her daughters—I was the youngest of the four sisters—to welcome the marginalized and care for the sick, needy, underprivileged, widowed, orphaned, abused, and vulnerable. Those who were last should come first. Camille Cooper taught her children that Christianity translated to mercy, forgiveness, love, praying for our enemies, and, most of all, action.

Camille never prayed to keep a poor child warm when she could knit him a sweater, so to persuade her, I'd aim straight at her belief in active purpose.

After Easter dinner, alone with my mother in the kitchen I'd cleaned till it sparkled, I clutched my Mississippi Freedom Summer

Project brochure so hard that it wrinkled while presenting my dream. I emphasized the word *nonviolent* in the Student Nonviolent Coordinating Committee, SNCC—and then pointed to the artwork of Black and White hands clasped together. I made it sound like I'd be ladling soup to the poorest in America.

My mother nodded in approval.

My father required different tactics.

"Daddy, I don't know what I'll do if I can't go to Mississippi! Helping these people is my calling. I feel a burning in my heart! Look at what my friends are doing—drinking and racing off in cars with boys they barely know. I don't want any of that, Daddy. I want to be decent like you and Mom."

My father, a flinty fiscal conservative who gave everyone a fair shake if they did the same, had hands as hard as the wood he chopped, but he held a gooey core for his four daughters—especially me, his baby.

Like my mother, he chose a varietal of Christianity he deemed formed in the tradition of charity and valued practical measures.

My pitch highlighted the nursery school, the reading curriculum, and practical projects that would resonate with both of my parents. Registering voters would mirror Mom holding book drives at Good Shepherd Church and Daddy helping drivers stuck in the blizzards blanketing the Taconic Highway every winter.

My parents sent me off with a wad of traveler's checks and a stern warning to hide the billfold. I nodded and hugged them both tight before brushing away every bit of advice they gave.

Two months later, during training at the Western College for Women in Oxford, Ohio, Freedom Summer trainers shared graphic details about the coming dangers: bloodthirsty men traveling in packs, the KKK fomenting unwarranted arrests while delivering beatings and hanging men from trees. They whispered the word *rape*; they pounded desks and lecterns while warning us of lynch mobs and burning crosses. It seemed that fewer of the White volunteers took their counsel as much to heart as the staff wanted. Some eyes glazed over in the stifling heat of the crowded lecture rooms, while others widened in terror at our imagined future.

We practiced self-defense on the green grass of Ohio, learning what to do if we were attacked. Roll up in a ball. Don't let your legs stick out—those legs could be broken with one stomp. Watch for cars without license plates and cops without badges.

The trainers worked to push my lifetime learning of going to the police for help out of me. They warned us to keep the shades down at night and never stand in a lighted doorway.

They instructed newcomers with cars to remove the dome lights to avoid being illuminated, to check their cars for bombs every morning, to learn all the roads in and out of town, and to memorize the danger spots. The staff warned us to vary routes when driving—and never let a stranger pass them on the road. That car might block our path forward—a warning of impending violence. Most importantly, the trainers repeated daily, never go anywhere alone.

Our introduction to the reality of the Klan was hard and ugly, as our trainer shared from a pamphlet titled *Why You Should Join the Ku Klux Klan*, emphasizing why Jews, Papists, Turks, Mongols, Tartars, Oriental, Negroes, or any other person the Klan considered foreign to the Anglo-Saxons should not apply for membership or, it seemed, for human rights. The Klan recruitment posters they shared, with masked White men, crosses, and licks of flames haunted me.

A tall, spare Black supervisor from California read the words NAACP executive director Roy Wilkins had given at a press conference following the brutal murder of Medgar Evans in his driveway the previous summer. "There is no state with a record that approaches that of Mississippi in inhumanity, murder, brutality, and racial hatred. It is absolutely at the bottom of the list."

After training, SNCC assigned me to Greenwood, Mississippi,

where I'd teach the ABCs at a church—a choice that offered my parents the reassurance they craved when I called. I made summer school sound as safe as ladling soup.

Chapter 2

❀

Annabel

No Patent on Adoration

W e'd been on the bus from Ohio to Mississippi for ten hours nonstop—two drivers taking turns steering and sleeping—when we pulled over to a spot I later learned was about twenty minutes outside town.

Our supervisor, Clay, who had three years on most of us, stood at the front of the bus. "I want you to climb out quietly, stand with your backs against the bus, and take a deep breath. Then, cross your arms and hold hands with those beside you. Without speaking."

He held a finger to his lips to emphasize silence and gestured for us to rise and follow him.

Irene, who sat next to me but had shared little, stood and faced the aisle, with me mirroring her every move. "Why do you think we're leaving?" I whispered as softly as possible toward the back of her head.

Without turning, she put up her hand in a stop signal. Irene, who'd spent most of the ride reading and writing and little of it talking to me, already seemed smarter and superior—I didn't dare say another word. The girl standing in the seat across from her met my eyes and winked. I placed a hoped-for friendship in her gesture.

The humid June air felt like a slap of wet laundry. We lined up wordlessly, facing a thick tangle of unfamiliar trees, watching Clay for signs of what to do next. He crossed his arms and held the hand of the second supervisor, Herb, who'd exited the bus last. Herb's pressed blue shirt with the sleeves rolled up almost matched Clay's. They became mirror images in dark and light, Clay with close-cropped dark curls only a few shades darker than his complexion, Herb's freckled skin already reddened from the heat.

"Lord, make me an instrument of your peace: where there is hatred, let me sow love; where there is injury, pardon; where there is doubt, faith; where there is despair, hope; where there is darkness, light; where there is sadness, joy," Clay recited.

"*Baruch atah Adonai, rofeh hacholim*," Herb said. I recognized his words as Hebrew from the interfaith services held at Camp Wonder. "Help me to endure the suffering and dissolve the fear, renew within me the calm spirit of trust and peace."

Clay again nodded at us, and we brought ourselves together in a line of white and brown linked hands.

For the first time in my life, I felt part of a greater good; for the first time, I felt great fear.

We shuffled into the small SNCC office, crowding the room to the point where the whirring fan became nothing but decoration. Carol, a remarkably tall woman with an electric presence, introduced herself as the director of the Greenwood SNCC office and then presented all the staff members. Other than Herb, the entire team was Black, introducing me to a shaming surprise: I'd never thought of leadership as other than White and Christian.

During her instructions, Carol emphasized the dangers facing us, but judging from the hope shining around the room, most of us floated on a cloud of how good we were and how we would save the world.

Plus, we were exhausted from the trip; beds were more on our minds than rule-following.

That evening, I became a guest of Mr. and Mrs. Harris and their three sons. I shared a small back room with Irene, my distant seatmate, and Helen, in a room the Harris's younger sons had given up for us. They now slept with their brother in an even smaller space.

Guthrie Pascal, a guy from New York—the city, not upstate like me—spread his sleeping bag on the open back porch. He was the fourth volunteer living at the Harris house.

Mrs. Harris politely avoided sentimental connections, presenting sustenance with neither fuss nor noise. I became desperate for her approval.

Within five days, Guthrie and I showed ourselves as those who worked hardest to show appreciation for our bed and board. He woke before dawn to clean out stalls and pig pens, working quietly, never trying to take on the showy farm tasks like milking their cow or feeding the chickens.

At dinner, when everyone placed the last fork on the table, I jumped up, ready to scrub. I furtively followed my roommates around the three small rooms to which we had access with a sponge and dust mop, fearing Mrs. Harris would resent the girls' careless blindness.

I'd imagined the three girls in the Harris house would bond as closely as the girls in my summer camp, but our enthusiasms collided more than they matched. Neither Helen, a tightly wrapped Connecticut girl from Barnard College, nor Irene, who I learned was a scary-smart New Yorker who'd be a Wellesley senior in September, seemed uninterested in anything but the job in front of them. They appeared particularly incurious about me.

Irene devoted every moment to the adults she taught civics and history to. Late into the night, she bent over her books, flashlight beaming, her dark brown eyes almost invisible behind her thick glasses.

We'd learned in Ohio—and now saw daily—the deliberation with which Mississippi made decent education unattainable for Black citizens and then made that same education a requirement to pass the test for voting. Irene seemed intent on singularly changing the paradoxical nightmare. Helen cotaught with her; Irene's vast book knowledge, married with life experience, put White Helen in the role of Black Irene's assistant—a system they both embraced.

They left me out of their symbiotic relationship, making me only a distant admirer.

My zeal for Freedom Summer exploded—so much so that my devotion to the Greater Love Baptist Church summer school class I taught uncovered my long-buried desire to become a nun, a saint, or both. I became enthralled with the children, who ranged in age from six to ten years old, as I planned a future devoted to serving God and the needy.

Until I fell for Clay.

When he wasn't registering voters, Clay advised us, always using respect and humor. Most of the young men of Freedom Summer orated; Clay spoke without embellishment, always made sense, and he listened. Kindness laced his California cool. An easygoing manner belied his blazing intellect, which made for a killer combination.

I didn't hold the patent on adoration; everyone looked up to Clay. During our first community church supper women from the congregation handed him the best bits of glazed meatloaf—the end pieces—the coldest sweet tea and the plumpest biscuits. Irene pursed her lips when she noticed my gaze settling on Clay, giving an invisible shake of her head before walking to the table where Helen held a seat for her among the volunteers who I'd labeled *the brain trust*—a mix of Black, White, Jewish, and Christian ministers-in-training. They intimidated the heck out of me.

A curvy woman, her face lit up with gold rose-shaped earrings, grinned at Clay with what looked like flirtation, though she had to be at least fifty. "I bet they don't bake biscuits like this in California."

"Only in my mother's kitchen," Clay said before taking a big bite. "Did you make this, ma'am?"

The woman smiled and bobbed her head with pride. "You're eating a cherished family secret there."

"I don't think I'll tell my mother how much I loved this particular biscuit." He wiped his mouth with a red-checked napkin. "Unless maybe you want to share the recipe? I'll ask her if she wants to try Mississippi-style."

"Maybe I could write it out for you . . . if you'd like to meet my daughter. But I don't want her running off to California." Her laugh's subtext whispered *how about I help you find a lovely house when you marry her?*

"My mama's heart would break if I ever left our town for good."

She winked. "Maybe she'd feel better if she came here to visit. Anyway, I better go set up my pies."

"I'll be watching to see which ones you bring out."

"You'll see a mess of pecan and Mississippi mud pies—but pass them by. The heat's never good for them—look for my Lemon Ice Box Pie."

"Gonna put on my glasses, ma'am."

Once Clay stood alone, I moved toward him. He would resemble a young, glorified version of my father if Daddy were Black. Like my father, Clay possessed sharply planed features and hands toughened by work, though in Clay's case, the labor took place on his parents' walnut farm. During one training session, Clay said farming formed his beliefs and reading sharpened them.

"Hey," I said in a weak attempt to connect.

"Hey to you. How was your first week of teaching?"

"I love it! The kids are great." *I love it? The kids are great?* How much more like a gushing schoolgirl could I sound?

"And how are they great?" he asked.

"They're so enthusiastic. I've never worked with children. My only job was after school at my father's auto shop. When you pump someone's gas, the customers don't jump up and hug you."

"That sounds about right. You wouldn't want some old guy throwing his arms around you. What do you like best? I mean here, not pumping gas." He held up a finger to signify *wait*, looked around, handed me his plate, and then pulled over two wooden folding chairs and a glass of sweet tea for each of us.

"Okay," he said. "Now, what do you like about the school?"

"Watching them. Their faces light up when they get all their spellings right or when I give them a big fat A+ for doing their numbers. Most of all, I love to watch them draw. I'm studying art—I've done art forever—but I'm only learning now how much kids are pure naturals. They don't worry about anything being right—they're simply involved in the process . . . in expressing themselves. They make me remember why art is so important. Though sometimes I worry I'm not doing enough to match why I came."

"What do you think you need to accomplish? Why are you in Greenwood?"

His question surprised me. Wasn't the answer obvious? "Aren't we all here for the same reason? To register voters?"

Clay shook his head and gave the faintest smile as though he were about to school me. "Registering voters is the mission of the Freedom Project, but everyone has a different justification for coming." He ticked off reasons on his fingers. "Savior complex. Anger. Some are nearly saints, and some are trying not to be sinners. And others?"

I leaned in, fascinated by Clay's every word, though I'd have listened if he'd recited the alphabet.

He shrugged. "They want it on their resume when they try to enter Heaven. And, of course, it all depends on whether you're White."

I left the comment hanging. "What brought you here? Why do you think I came?"

"The first thing I know about you is that you're smart. Look how fast you turned the question back on me. What brings you here?"

I broke off a corner from a biscuit I'd held for the longest time. Before popping it into my mouth, I answered. "I believe in 'love radically, serve gratefully, and wonder daily.'"

"Ah, a fellow Unitarian. So, how do you link that to being here?"

My heart raced at our connection. "Love for your fellow man can be trivial, something you give lip service to on Sundays," I said. "Or you can stand in line to improve everyone's lot."

"So, you're a soldier for Christ?" he asked.

I recoiled, afraid he thought of me as a thin-lipped do-gooder, a church lady packing Bibles for Africa. "A soldier? Why can't I be Joan of Arc?"

"Didn't they burn Joan of Arc?" Clay crossed his arms and smiled. "Let's hope you don't meet that particular goal. Honestly, Annabel, only White people are here to provide service to humanity. But the rest of us?"

I nodded, ready to catch his words and secret them away to examine later.

He swept his arm toward a cluster of Black men and women. "We don't have the luxury of rescuing humanity. We're fighting to save our families and ourselves. Don't get me wrong; I'm grateful for your help. We all are. But you're just peeling back the evil done by other White folks. So, in a way, you're not providing aid. You're making amends for the sins of others."

Before I could react to his swift analysis of me and my Whiteness, the round-faced woman and her sparkly earrings reappeared carrying a plate filled with three slices of pie—all for Clay. She narrowed her eyes with suspicion and insinuated herself between us, making her back a weapon to cut me off from him.

Chapter 3

❀

Annabel

JUNE 1964

Didn't They Burn Joan of Arc?

Overnight, my stomach began somersaulting when I saw Clay. Fantasies of wearing a wimple and habit while kneeling at the altar to marry God disappeared. Clay replaced Jesus, though he radiated distance and caution.

I mined myself for admirable qualities that might appeal to Clay. Lovely and compassionate girls surrounded us; neither beauty nor kindness alone would make me stand out, so instead, I took notes, wrote meeting minutes, and moved the chairs into circles for discussions—and then moved them back again when the meetings ended. As my mother had taught, I listened ten times as much as I spoke.

After overhearing Clay and my housemate Guthrie talk over each other as they compared thoughts about their passion for science fiction, I borrowed Guthrie's copy of *Fahrenheit 451.*

My goal became twofold: being the most committed volunteer in Greenwood and improving every facet of myself. I slept with shreds of cloth wrapped around my curls so they'd bounce just so and put a dab of oil on my eyelashes each night to make them grow. On my first free afternoon, I snuck into town to buy a lemon, sneaking into a private corner of the backyard to squeeze it into a glass of water and comb it through my hair, hoping to go from dishwater blond to golden yellow like my mother. I woke first in the house to have ample time to wash and prettify. After ironing the tablecloths and napkins that I'd scrubbed the previous night, lightening the load for Mrs. Harris, I used my extra time to iron my blouse.

I imitated my mother by never complaining and working twice as hard and three times as fast as anyone else.

Neither Clay nor I could ignore the sparks that flew when we lingered in the church after meetings. Conversations that began as polite chat about colleges—he'd be a senior at NYU in the fall, I'd be a sophomore at the Boston School of Practical Art—became whispers of dreams and music and poetry. Our smoldering attraction ignited, even as he tried to push it away.

Within a week, we had a conflagration.

He'd once again stopped to wash up at the church pump in the dusky courtyard on his way to a SNCC meeting in town. I'd once again lingered after school and wandered outside when I spotted him.

We sat almost knee to knee on a low stone fence.

"This is the prettiest time of day," I said. "The light is so soft, almost like Cape Cod."

"Did you go there often?" he asked.

I laughed. "Hardly. That's a long drive from Rhinebeck—we did it for one summer trip. My father can't hardly take any time off from his shop."

"It sounds like my dad and his walnut farm."

I liked the idea of finding similarities in our fathers. The thought relaxed me into forgetting the world around us, and without thinking, I leaned against him.

He pulled away, searching the empty church lot for stray eyes. "We have to be careful," he warned, though my head had scarcely grazed his shoulder.

His words marked the first time he'd acknowledged we'd inched toward being *we*.

"Of course." My voice sounded far too fervent, even to my ears. "But isn't this what we're fighting for?"

Clay laughed. "We're fighting to register voters. Not to thrill White girls with a kiss from a forbidden guy."

"Is that what you think I'm looking for? A thrill? Getting kisses is easy." I walked away from the hard-packed area where cars parked, embarrassed by Clay's thinking. I wanted to hide in the branches of an overgrown sweetgum tree.

He followed me. "Trust me, I don't doubt it's easy for you."

"But I rarely accept an offer."

"Why?" he asked.

I pulled up the insouciance my mother and sisters threw around so well. "Because few are worth the trouble."

"Sounds smart. And we can't make it worth the trouble for either of us," Clay said. "Cause no woman—certainly no White woman—merits hanging for."

My stomach plummeted. I'd swum out of my depth, trying to play a sophisticated woman. I was barely a girl on the playground when it came to boys. My nonchalance and cuteness disappeared.

I plopped down on the crunchy grass, pulled my skirt over my crossed legs, and put my head down in my hands. "We have to stay far from each other."

Clay nodded. "That's the Lord's truth."

Tears fell, embarrassing me. I swiped them as fast as they came, hating myself for crying. Clay was the one in danger. Just being here talking to me was a sin to the Klan—and the Klan was everywhere. SNCC training warned us repeatedly against the threat of romances in the field.

He sank beside me, pulled out a handkerchief, and wiped my face clean. "I should run away this minute, but I don't want to. Damn. Damn. Damn. My parents would kill me. The girls here—the sisters, not the White ones—would have both of us on a spit."

Memories of Irene's pursed lips remained, though she could afford to eschew romance—she wore a small engagement diamond on her left hand.

I pushed away my girlish thoughts. The work accomplished by Irene, Helen, and the rest of the brain trust outshone me by miles. They taught and registered voters all day and then spent hours each night writing up theses on the Mississippi Democratic Party.

They most decidedly did not spend time preparing their hair for anything but cleanliness, whereas I would soon earn a master's degree in coaxing my hair down from the frizz wrought by the Southern humidity.

"So why are we still sitting here?"

Clay put a hand under my chin and tipped it up. He stared, and I stared.

"I have no idea. Maybe I'm a sucker for the Joan of Arc type. Your utter devotion to the good fight and worthy cause."

I couldn't tell if he was genuinely being sardonic or covering his want with seeming sarcasm.

"Everyone here is devoted to the cause," I said.

"You're so damn voracious. And I'm about to be so stupid."

The unspoken fizzed between us. Along with being dumb and greedy, we were both so pretty and forbidden—those qualities, stirred with our burn to save the world, made for a lethal combination.

Clay put his arms around me and brought his lips to mine. Though not my first embrace, his lips meeting mine felt like my first kiss. A universe of tenderness and want exploded. I never wanted to leave.

We were the first people in the world to ever kiss like this. I knew this.

Clay lit me up like he held a torch to my skin, and I knew, I knew, that I did the same for him.

We pulled apart. "We'd best go," Clay said. "You leave first."

By evening, just speaking the name of my beloved filled me with something so vast and intense that I believed that force heralded God's plan. Clay and I would bring forth children who'd represent a new world. A better world.

I believed in us so fiercely I'm surprised I didn't spend that night writing our future wedding vows.

Chapter 4

✳

Annabel

List Your Next of Kin

I plotted to find time with Clay as though leading a war, always starting with finding ways to stay at church after school ended. That day, once the children left and I'd cleaned the classroom, I dove into chores around the church. Reverend Daniels, an imposing man in stature and speech, smiled with approval when he caught me scouring the old kitchen to operating room standards.

I knew if the reverend, as starched in personality as in his shirts, suspected I lingered to catch Clay on his walk home, he'd put me on the next bus out of Greenwood. I played the part of a saint who loved scrubbing while trying not to show up Marlene and Joe—the other volunteers at the church school. Not that I could compete—Marlene, a recent graduate from Spelman College, wove magic tales for the children about the plans she'd made to rebuild America. Her stature rivaled that of members of the Supremes, while Joe, muscled though compact, could throw the kids so high in the air he was a walking, talking carnival ride.

Clay didn't show up on any precise schedule, but after three weeks, my surety about his appearance stopped wavering. A girl could tell when a guy cared—even the stoic ones. Even the guys who had to watch for the watchers.

Like all couples since time began, Clay and I took up habits; Adam and Eve probably had routines. After our first embrace, our daily church visits became routine.

My days had become familiar with habits and schedules, some imposed, most chosen.

At night, stifling heat took over the farmhouse kitchen, pressing down on the cot where I slept, the single window barely allowing a breeze. My morning walks to the church meant batting away never-ending tribes of mosquitos. Students hungry for lessons, eager for the books, paper, pens, and crayons I offered filled my steamy classroom. Each of the fifteen in my class clamored for attention.

"Look at my picture!"

"Did you see how fast I ran?"

I'd never been happier.

As I waited for Clay, I polished the pews, washed the schoolroom floor, and scrubbed the bathroom—a most precious space, as available bathrooms for Greenwood SNCC volunteers, especially our Black volunteers, were rare and needed. I broke up my self-appointed tasks with trips to stare out the window. I practiced our happiness to come, hoping that later if we could guarantee our solitude, we might steal a kiss.

I peered through the softening late afternoon light, praying to catch Clay walking up the road straight as a soldier despite the bulging knapsack filled with practice tests, pencils, and books strapped to his back.

God answered my prayers. The Mississippi sun covered Clay with a honeyed shine, giving his hair a halo and flashing on his high school graduation ring.

When he bent to wash up at the water pump, I hurried to the kitchen, returning to the Greater Love Church's spare anteroom just as he entered, shiny from his washup but frowning.

"I saved this from lunchtime." I held up cornbread I'd kept warm, the neatly cut slice sitting prettily on a yellow plate dotted with cornflowers, and then brought it to the oak table by the window seat.

Butter ran into the cornbread's steamy crevices. "Trust me, hiding this took some doing. Bible study met today."

Clay lifted his lips in a small, forced smile. "You want me to eat when I'm on my way to dinner? Heck, Joe's cooking tonight." He lived in a bunkhouse with ten other guys, including my coworker.

I broke off the best part of the cornbread, the crispy corner, and held it out. "I'm betting you'll find room for those overcooked beans and hot dogs waiting for you."

He swallowed my offered taste in a second. "Don't forget the potato chips."

"No doubt you'll all eat your weight in grease and salt. My mother would ask if you guys knew what a vegetable was."

"And my mother would say, 'Oh, he knows all right. He's just too pig-headed and lazy to cut a carrot.'" Clay lifted the plate from the table and sat on the wide window seat.

"No crumbs on that," I warned. "Reverend Daniels will have my head."

"Someday, I'll take you on a proper date."

Mississippi heat thickened and pressed. I drew my thick curls into a high ponytail, tying it up with a rubber band I carried for that purpose. "I'll put on lipstick and a swirling taffeta skirt."

"My shirt will be ironed so stiff and be so bright with bleach your eyes will pop."

I took a nibble from the cornbread he held up to me. "You're that good with an iron?"

"My mother is."

"Will she like me?"

Clay cocked his head as though measuring me for a new dress. "She'd try, but you'd scare her half to death."

I shivered. The week before, someone had tossed a bottle stuffed with a rag soaked in kerosene at the house where Clay stayed. The small rocket missed, setting only a patch of dry grass afire, small enough to extinguish with a few buckets of water. He'd dismissed my concern by joking about how White men couldn't throw straight.

By now, I understood why SNCC instructed us to list our next of kin and have our pictures taken with an identification number across our chests (so the police or coroner could identify us in case of death) before coming to Mississippi.

Two weeks earlier, police had dragged a pregnant Black woman down the street to prevent her from visiting the courthouse to register to vote. Nobody had seen her since; her mother told Clay to stay clear of their house.

I moved the empty cornflower plate to the side and rested my head on Clay's shoulder, careful not to let our sparks turn to flame. We couldn't tempt the omnipresent menace surrounding us.

After minutes, he nudged me. I couldn't keep my fear strong enough to be the one to push away—and though it shamed me, I relied on his strength born from experience.

"We wait," he said. "September will be ours. I plan on visiting Massachusetts before school starts." Clay studied me. "Will your mother like me?"

We joined hands when I turned to face him. "She'll be scared for us, just like your mom, but she'll like you."

I hoped I spoke the truth. My parents didn't say a word when my oldest sister dated a Colombian guy for two years, but I didn't know how far their belief in equality stretched.

He crossed his arms across his chest. "How about your dad? Would he like me?"

I fought to be honest. "My father respects hard work and honesty. How could he not like you?"

We looked at each other and laughed, knowing we were building fantasies and pushing away the reality of how little our parents would want to see us together.

"What was your day like?" I asked.

Clay sighed. "Been putting off telling you. A woman grabbed me as I walked down the road. Old as dirt, but strong enough to hurt when she poked me. Boy, she had a bony finger. 'People been talking about you,' she said. 'Stop hangin' with that White girl.'"

My stomach dropped. "But we're so careful."

"Even the trees have eyes around here. 'Never underestimate an inch of how much White folk hate us. Don't be acting the fool.' That's what she said." He took a folded paper from his back pocket and handed it to me. "I've been a fool, all right. Where I live in California isn't that different. The whole country is inches from this horror. I better start memorizing the subtext."

I unfolded the ragged sheet. Each time I saw a copy of the Mississippi literacy test, I fought against voicing my impotent rage, which only showed me to be naïve, unworthy of Clay and every member of SNCC.

Already, I was planning a lifetime of fighting the system with Clay and for our children.

The literacy form represented a formidable barrier to voting in the state constitution, though fear of being lynched, shot, or set afire topped everything. The paper felt evil, containing words that pried the romantic stars from my eyes. But Clay repeatedly urged me to read it anew, forcing me to see his world, each time making me concentrate on another piece of the test.

"Could you pass?" Clay's easygoing voice couldn't mask the challenge in his question.

I shuffled through the three pages once again. The so-called 'literacy test' should have been labeled *Fuck you for daring to be a citizen.*

Question 18. Write and copy below Section ___ of the Constitution of Mississippi. (Instructions to Registrar: You will designate the section of the Constitution and point out same to applicant.)

Question 19. Write in the space below a reasonable interpretation of the section of the Constitution of Mississippi which you have just copied.

Question 20. Write in the space below a statement setting forth your understanding of the duties and obligations of citizenship under a constitutional form of government.

Words I'd heard during training stuck in my brain like the adhesive you can never get off the bottom of a jar. The trainer's syrupy Southern voice and the friendly freckles dotting her light brown complexion belied her ability to lay the truth straight as a ruler. "The White clerk decides who's literate. They test us with complicated technical passages while White folk get elementary things to explain—"

"Can't forget Mississippi's 'grandfather clause.'" The wiry cotrainer bit off his words. "That was a kiss to the White folk of Mississippi. Anyone whose ancestors registered to vote before the Civil War qualifies without taking the test, which means all Whites and none of us. And if poll taxes, literacy tests, and all the other treats don't keep us out, there's getting fired, eviction, and losing credit. They think our very breath is theirs for the taking. Violence waits for every Black man, woman, and child in Mississippi. Slavery only ended in the narrowest sense."

The so-called rules were as crooked as someone tying my arms behind my back, taping my mouth, and then placing steaming stew in front of me while whispering, "You won't starve if you just eat."

Seven days a week, Clay helped folks in Greenwood prepare for their tests, hard workers who, along with studying, planted and hoed, cared for children, cleaned other people's messes, and cooked giant meals for volunteers.

Clay let them grumble out their demons to ensure they didn't carry their nightmares to the courthouse, but he didn't allow himself but a minute to scowl at the end of his day.

Compared to folks around here, I spent my days surrounded by rainbows and puppies and came of age like a princess annoyed by a pea.

"What should we do?" I asked.

"First thing we do is cut out these visits."

Chapter 5

❊

Annabel

Don't Travel Alone

I hadn't seen Clay for three days.

He hadn't come by the church, though I hadn't stopped looking for him. I continued to use chores as excuses to remain at Greater Love after school, hoping the reverend wouldn't notice how often I drifted to the window while dusting or sweeping.

On Saturday, during my free morning, I hunted for art supplies for my students. SNCC only provided basic waxy crayons and pads of thin paper; my planned project required Crayola, not the cheap imitations that cracked with the slightest pressure.

I dressed for the trip to Woolworths Five and Ten in a manner meant to attract the least attention. Gratitude toward my mother washed over me while walking down Howard Street. She'd forced the dressier clothes into my suitcase, half-warning and half-explaining as she made room. "You need to be ready for any situation, Annabel."

My mother's prescience didn't shock me—whenever the world turned upside down, her wisdom played in my mind. In sixth grade, when my first period came on during a math lesson, unwanted, unexpected, and accompanied by nauseating waves of dull cramps, my mother's imagined wisdom told me what to do. I raised my hand, received the nod to visit the bathroom, and walked out rigidly, holding my legs together as best I could.

The red stain in my underwear had leaked through the white cotton to my yellow flowered skirt, making a rusty mess visible everywhere. Weighing getting in trouble versus humiliation, I walked out of school without permission and hiked the three miles home, knowing my mother would approve. "Always watch out for yourself," she counseled all her daughters. "Other than me and Daddy, nobody else will."

Faith in my mother's advice meant not being tagged as an agitator while shopping for materials to make books with my students.

Clay's warning echoed as I hunted Woolworths for art supplies for my students. Eyes followed me everywhere. I nodded through Woolworth's aisles, fighting the bubbles of discomfort brought on by each tentative head bob offered by fellow shoppers. I kept a pleasant expression on my face while I gathered supplies. Clay and I would never walk into this store together, much less hold hands with our children by our sides like the family ahead—Clay scolding our son for touching stuff, me kneeling to wipe chocolate smudges off a cheek.

Even wearing my Peter Pan-collared shirt covered with delicate rosebuds, folks narrowed their eyes as they inspected me as though the core of my Clay-loving heart showed right through my prim Saturday blouse.

SNCC leadership repeatedly warned against traveling alone, but I craved unaccompanied time, surrounded by the comfort of crayons and paper. So I marched along in my disguise of sweet and pretty, ignoring watching eyes, protected not by starched cotton but by my white skin.

On Monday, I arrived at school ready to introduce my kids to their new assignment: making an alphabet book based on heroes from freedom and civil rights struggles. I'd planned this since my second week in

Greenwood—horrified by the lack of early readers and how the ABC books highlighted Dick and Jane, whose sole nonwhite references were the black splotches on Spot, the children's dog. For the older students who were already readers, I presented the project as a lesson in bookmaking.

Between my research and the help of the reverend and his wife, I'd come up with twenty-six men and women from A to Z. Clay and Guthrie had helped by poring through every book at SNCC headquarters and the library at the older kids' Freedom School during their rare moments of free time.

Mrs. Harris let me read two precious magazines that she had unwrapped from layers of newspaper. Though *Negro Heroes,* Volume 1 and 2, were just what the school needed, no amount of begging made a dent in Mrs. Harris's refusal to let the books leave her sight.

"When my sister moved to Chicago years ago to become a teacher, she sent these to us. We read them to the boys every night, and now we're saving them for our grandbabies." Mrs. Harris stirred a pot of pea soup as I diced ham to add. "You want to read them—with clean hands, where I can see you—fine. Copy out what you need. But these don't leave the room, and neither do I."

After dinner, I'd spent hours copying from the magazines, word-for-word, picture by picture, while Mrs. Harris repaired shirts and pants from her mending basket. Then, I'd gathered all my material and sketched the twenty-six hero's images, printed names, and wrote two or three sentences below each using the thick paper I'd bought.

Now, the children worked together, coloring in the images, printing the first letter of their person's name on top, and tracing the words. I tried not to appear too prideful watching the children bent over their desks, but in truth, my and their satisfaction spilled all over the place.

As my mother had preached, I used art to reach a practical, meaningful place.

The only place I'd cheated was on the letter Z—using Zora Neal Hurston's first name, underlining the Z in Zora.

I moved from child to child, their heads bent in deep concentration over their paper, helping them trace the letters I'd sketched in pencil the night before. The children took ownership of their heroes, each declaring that theirs was the best.

"Henry Flipper beats Wilma Rudolph," seven-year-old Georgie yelled at his twin sister Addie. "He was the first to graduate West Point."

"Big deal," she said. "You don't even know what West Point is."

He stuck his tongue out. "Do too!"

"Who's gonna make the cover, Teacher?" Shelly, my favorite, asked. Having favorites was wrong, but when Shelly squealed each time I brought out paintbrushes, she scooped out an extra slice of my heart.

"Good question, Shel! Who wants to make the cover?"

Fifteen hands shot up as though I pulled a lever.

"Wow," I said. "Okay. Everyone can draw one. Our book will have more covers than any book in America."

The children cheered so loudly that I didn't see Reverend Daniels and Guthrie enter the class until they were almost on top of me.

The reverend's white button-down appeared brighter than usual next to Guthrie's soot-covered T-shirt. I turned cold. Burnt cork appeared to cover Guthrie's shoes; he smelled of smoke and kerosene.

I pressed my hand to my chest as my heart slid down. "What happened?"

"Firebomb. At the Dell farm." Guthrie's words spilled out staccato. "Clay and I were working with the family."

"Clay," I whispered. I hadn't seen him since he'd cut out our visits. "I'll go help."

Reverend Daniels face hardened. "That boy can watch out for himself. You're not going anywhere except to help Guthrie get the children to a protected place."

Guthrie touched my arm. "Don't worry. The Dells are safe. Clay's helping with the cows."

"Enough talking," the reverend said. "They could be coming here next. Annabel, go up the hill with Joe and your classes. Their parents will expect to find them up top."

The *they* who could be coming needed no explanation. The Klan's threat pervaded Greenwood. Nor did the reverend have to mention why being up the hill—where we'd see anyone approaching—was necessary.

"Guthrie can go with Joe. I'm staying here in case anyone shows up."

Anyone.

Reverend Daniels pointed a rigid finger. "There is no time for—"

Guthrie held up a placating hand. "I don't like it either, but we gotta take the kids out now. I brought two guys with me. Big guys. The three of us will take the kids while Joe and Annabel watch the church."

The reverend frowned, shook his head, and marched out.

Chapter 6

❋

Annabel

You Got Another Name, Annabel?

Oppressive afternoon heat melted into a steamy early evening as I paced the road by the parking lot, watching for Clay far longer than watching made sense. Nervous volunteers walked by—word passed fast—returning earlier than usual from their day registering voters. Everyone obeyed the rules and traveled in pairs.

Clay never paid enough attention to SNCC's traveling directives. Maybe I'd broken the rule on Saturday, but I was in plain sight, strolling the aisles of Woolworths.

And I was White. Hate the truth as I might, I lived inside that bubble of reality.

Frustration rose as I pressed my lips in irritation at Clay's taking on his tasks alone, swearing he got twice as much done without dragging along some neophyte.

The wooden windowsills held a high shine; nevertheless, I swiped them with an oiled rag, staring out, working like a robot until a chugging engine and tires hitting gravel announced a car creeping from the shadowed road into the dirt-packed church lot.

A wide-shouldered man, almost hidden by his oversized hat, stepped out. A gun hung from the holster on his hip. He marched to the door like a colossus striding across his continent.

I reached for a blue work shirt hanging from a hook by the door. I didn't know whose shirt it was, but instinct told me to hurry and cover my bare arms. My sleeveless cotton dress felt no more protective than a girlish slip.

"Hey, little lady." The sheriff stepped into the small church foyer. "Who might you be?"

I swallowed twice, trying to get saliva into my sandy throat.

The man hitched his pants as he loomed over me. "I asked you a question, girl."

"Annabel," I managed to say.

"You got another name, Annabel?" He stretched out my name, rolling it around in his mouth as though weighing whether to take a big juicy bite from the peach my syllables offered.

"Cooper." Hearing my strangled voice, I took a deep breath, mustered more assurance, and tried a do-over. "Cooper. Annabel Cooper."

"Well, Annabel Cooper, you one of those White girls imported from up North to live here with the colored folk? You sharing a house with them, right? The Harris people down on Ramper's farm?"

The sheriff identified the Black families by the names of those on whose land they share-cropped. I nodded, not wanting to give a bit of information he didn't force from me.

"Speak up, gal."

"Yes."

"Yes, what?"

"Yes, I am living with the Harris family."

My pride in using the family's proper name disgusted me. How could I take pride in such a simple act? My mother's likely words rang—*Pride goeth before a fall, Annabel.* As my imagined mother rightfully chastised me, I longed for my father. The sheriff would never intimidate him.

"They got some sons?" The sheriff folded his arms across his chest. "This Harris family."

My stomach dropped clear down to my feet. "I guess so."

"You guess so? You blind, girl?" He smiled at his joke. "Seems like you can see. You ever notice those Harris boys come home late at night with a pile of them voter registration papers?"

"No, sir."

"No, you don't see them, or no, you don't see them with them papers?"

Joe opened the church front door and then came out. His face revealed that he'd been listening. Joe, who I only knew as an agreeable guy fast with a joke, crossed his arms over his chest, perhaps trying to match the sheriff's stance. But Joe's muscles were no match for the decades of brawn covering the sheriff. "Registering voters isn't illegal."

"You Annabel's lawyer, boy?" The sheriff laughed and looked at me. "Why would you need a lawyer, Annabel Cooper?"

I shrank back, drawing closer to Joe, mortified at being thankful he was White, ashamed for grasping at that truth's safety. Too many truths crowded in as my disgust at wanting the protection of my skin collided with my panic.

"We have a friend of yours downtown, gal. He's asking for you. Says you're ready to vouch for him. Is this true?"

"Who?" I caught Joe's eyes, but he had no more experience than I at handling Mississippi sheriffs.

"Says he's a dear, dear friend. He speaking the truth, this fella? You best of friends with a colored boy named Clay?"

I felt as useless as a ten-year-old waiting for my mother and father to rush in and rescue me, but nobody was coming. Clay might be hurt. Needing me. The situation must be awful or very strange if he had asked for me. He should and would turn to one of the SNCC leaders for help, as they had the lawyers to call.

But my parents would always come through no matter what I needed. Maybe Clay wanted their help.

"Where is he?" Joe asked.

"You wanna come along, boy? You involved in this here best friendship?"

I shook my head. "Stay here. You'll need to talk to the others." Joe bunked down the road from the Harris's.

The sheriff looked at Joe hard, all pretense of asking rather than ordering gone. "You best come along with Miz Cooper and me. What's a boy like you doing down here, anyway? What's your Christian name?"

Joe pulled himself up to his barely-scraping five-foot seven-inch height and faced the sheriff. The older man came closer, towering over him, likely outweighing him by half again, his hard stomach jutting into Joe's chest.

"Joseph D. Bernadino."

"Bernadino, eh?" The sheriff unhooked the baton at his hip and waved it toward Joe and me. "You two walk right out and sit in the car. Backseat." Sharpness replaced threatening playfulness. He frowned when neither of us moved, then poked Joe in the stomach with the wooden stick.

"Come on, boy. Both of you get in the car. Your colored families gonna have to do without you for a night. Let's go. Nobody asked you agitators to come down here. Time to answer some questions."

"Where's Clay? Are you taking us to him?" My voice sounded like it belonged to a squeaky cartoon mouse.

"Sure are, girl," He pushed the wide church doors open, not bothering to shut them behind him.

I turned my head, hoping the reverend had miraculously returned through the back entrance and would now appear.

The sheriff's meaty hand pressed on my shoulder. "Face forward, prisoner. March."

"Prisoner?" I stumbled as the sheriff pushed me to walk faster.

Joe stopped short. "What the hell?"

"You gonna get in that car peacefully or force me to drag you?" The sheriff touched the gun hanging from his side. "You resisting me, Mr. Bernadino? How about you, An-na-bel?"

His stony eyes reflected how much my bouncy lemon-kissed curls, freckles, and cornflower blue eyes meant jack to him.

Remembering the lessons drilled in during orientation, I cleared my throat. "Joe. Just do what he says."

Joe appeared to wrestle with his conscience. I prayed he wouldn't give in to any cowboy crap. His chest went in and out a few times as the sheriff tapped his gun. Then, after one last attempt to look tough, Joe began walking toward the car.

The sheriff pushed me into a cell crowded with six White women, including Helen, with whom Irene and I shared the bedroom at the Harris's.

An unfamiliar woman slept in a curled ball, emanating fumes of alcohol and the stench of needing a bath. All the others in my cell were fellow volunteers.

Eleven Black women, from teens to grandmothers, jammed the next cell. I recognized some of them from SNCC meetings and church. Some stood. The older ones sat on the splintered benches, some with crossed arms; others, motherly types, draped protective arms over the younger ones.

Amid the eleven stood Irene, my other roommate, who laced her fingers in a fierce grip. Our eyes met for a moment, and then she looked away.

Everyone in my cell wore worry like a veil, while most of the Black women hid theirs.

I curled my shaking hands, fingertips stained from ink. When I asked for a phone call after they jammed my fingers into the inkpad for prints, the man in uniform snorted and shook his head.

"Do you even know where you are, girl?" Those were his only words before tossing me into the steamy cell.

The moment he left, I pressed close to Helen. "What's happening? Have you heard where Clay is?"

Helen clutched her upper arms tight enough to strain the back of her blouse and then slowly shook her head.

"How about Guthrie?"

"No idea. He wasn't at the house when they took us."

"How about Mr. and Mrs. Harris?" I shook, imagining them locked in cells. "Their sons?"

Helen tightened. "I don't know. I suppose. Lower your voice."

I rose and pressed close to the adjoining cell packed by the Black women and girls.

"Has anyone heard about Clay?" I directed my tremulous question through the bars. "Clayton Williams?"

For a few minutes, the women remained silent, inspecting me sideways.

Stupid. I was so stupid.

I gathered myself, remembering the danger they faced compared to me. My parents expected me to call three times a week. Without contact, my father would fly down and march to the church to claim me. Once he reached the jail, the lawmen would treat him with the deference given to a White Christian man, even one whose daughter they'd consider a whore.

Speaking lower and softer, I whispered this time and added respect. "Sorry. I don't want to make things any worse." I pressed so close to the bars that the sour iron odor filled my nostrils.

None of the women spoke; one of the volunteers from the SNCC office twisted the thin cotton fabric of her flowered skirt. Finally, Irene choked out a few words. "Then don't. Keep quiet. We must worry about ourselves, Annabel, not you."

I lowered my voice to barely audible. "When the sheriff came to Greater Love, he asked about Clay. Do you have any idea what's going on?" I whispered.

Irene shook her head and backed away.

One of the younger girls tipped her head in recognition. "You're one of the teachers, right?"

I nodded. "Yes. For the little kids."

"My little brother goes to your class. Johnny Bailey."

I pushed out a smile. "Johnny's a sweet little guy."

"Yeah, he likes you all right."

"What's your name?"

"Milly."

The other women followed the conversation with suspicious expressions, two standing on either side of Milly. "Quiet, girl," an older woman warned. "Both of you. Don't want any more trouble than we have."

I turned to the tall, spare woman. "Why are we in trouble?"

The woman raised her eyes to the heavens as though praying for strength. She recognized my stupidity. "You? Probably because you know Clay." The woman said the word *know* with quotation marks surrounding it. "Us? Cause we're not White."

"What happened to Clay? What did he do?" I twisted the tail of my borrowed shirt first to the left and then to the right.

"Do?" The woman glared. "That good boy didn't do anything except try fighting for our damn legal rights. And get sweet on you. That's why he's gone. That's why he's in the wind."

"Gone? Gone where?"

"You think I'd tell you if I knew?" she whispered. "Nobody'd be surprised if they killed him. Nobody'd be surprised if you're the cause."

Chapter 7

❀

Annabel

JUNE 1964

Only a Fool Wouldn't be Cautious

A week vanished. Privacy disappeared. Any piece of clothing we could remove without revealing sensitive spots became curtains we held up around the toilet until overflowing sewage from clogged pipes forced us to use them as emergency mops. We took turns resting on the few wooden benches by leaning our heads against the wall as a week vanished.

Swallowing solid matter became impossible. I existed on water and softened bread crusts while the others gobbled the dry jelly sandwiches and unrecognizable stew making up our meals.

I fell into a waking coma.

I slept.

I woke.

Little felt different between the states of being.

Only one reality faced me: "Nobody'd be surprised if they killed him. Nobody'd be surprised if you're the cause."

On the eighth day, some of us escaped the overflowing slop buckets, mosquitos, vermin, and gag-inducing food as our parents paid the finally proffered bail—*some* meaning the White girls. Only us White girls deserved the surety option.

Greenwood-style justice offered the Black women in the neighboring cell a trip to a local prison farm. I prayed SNCC would somehow look out for Irene. For everyone.

My parents flew to Mississippi as fast as they could book a flight and drove straight from Greenwood Municipal Airport to the lawyer recommended by SNCC. Guthrie's release coincided with mine. His parents handled his case with more nonchalance than mine, with his lawyer-father hiring the same attorney we used but hiring him via phone and overseeing the details from his legal firm in New York City.

Guthrie, my parents, and I shared a long leather couch in the lawyer's office, with the receptionist offering Fanta soda and butterscotch drops.

After visiting the lawyer, my parents bundled me into the closest, cleanest motel, where I fell into a thrashing sleep, crying when I woke and refusing to leave when they planned our flight home.

"You go," I said. "I'm staying."

They approached me with trepidation, as though not recognizing me—and how could they? When they asked me questions, even ones as gentle as "Would you like a cup of tea?" I stared as though hearing an unfamiliar language. Who cared if I drank tea?

Cyclones of emotions overshadowed everything.

My crushing love for Clay, lost.

The bliss of teaching children who soaked up books and art, lost.

Becoming a vessel for justice, lost.

I'd accomplished only one thing: causing trouble.

"Please take me to see Guthrie," I begged the third time they tried to coax me home. "I need to go with him to the Harris's." I sank to the carpet and threw my arms around my father's knees.

My dramatic gestures and nonstop tears painted my parents with terrified expressions, and after days of watching me cry, living on air and sips of water, my parents reluctantly gave in. They brought Guthrie to join the Annabel-must-eat brigade; he stayed for breakfast, lunch, and dinner, while almost nothing passed my lips.

By the next day, worries about my shrinking body overcame their fear of Mississippi; my father steered the four of us in the rented Chevy Impala as Guthrie gave directions to the Harris farm while I sat rubbing repetitive circles on the leather seat.

Mrs. Harris stood on the porch, arms crossed and eyes stern as though she'd been waiting, though we'd had no way to notify her of our arrival. Undecipherable emotions emanated as she walked down the two narrow steps. She remained rigid when I tried to hug her, pushing me to arm's length.

Guthrie stayed close, a silent sentry.

"I heard the car coming and wondered . . ." Her words drifted off as she blocked entry to her house.

"I need to talk to you, Mrs. Harris." I tried to appear calm and show the woman I'd bring no harm, though how I'd accomplish that was anyone's guess.

"It's good that you're safe, Annabel. And you, Guthrie. But you can't be here." Mrs. Harris turned to my mother and father. "You're Annabel's parents."

"Gordon and Camille Cooper," my father said.

"Take her away, Mr. Cooper." Mrs. Harris clutched her elbows. "We're working on bringing my sons home. Having you around makes everything worse. Please. Go."

"Do you know where Clay is?" I asked.

Mrs. Harris stepped back until she stood on the first of the two steps leading to the narrow wooden porch. "No."

My mother placed an arm over my shoulders. "Sweetheart, let's go. Mrs. Harris can't have you here."

"Are you scared?" I asked Mrs. Harris. "Do you want us to go because you're scared?"

My mother tugged me toward the car. "Only a fool wouldn't be cautious at this point."

I pulled away. "I can't leave."

"Listen closely," Mrs. Harris said. "Clay would want you to be safe. He'd want my family and me safe. You being here makes everything a thousand times worse."

My father tipped his hat. "Thank you for your time, ma'am. We appreciate all you've done, including making a home for these two." He held out his hand.

After a moment, she accepted and shook. "You're welcome."

Then my father nodded his head, first at me and then Guthrie. "In the car, kids. We're putting this good woman and her loved ones in danger."

"Your father's right, Annabel," Guthrie said. "Let's go."

Nobody understood. I wanted Clay. I needed to find him.

"Thank you again, Mrs. Harris." Guthrie slipped a folded piece of yellow-lined paper from his back pocket. "Here's my parents' information—their phone numbers, both home and work, and address. You can always reach me this way. If you ever need anything . . ." He trailed off as though unsure how to complete the offer. "Anything at all. Please. If you can, contact me if you learn something."

Mrs. Harris nodded, her hands shaking as she took the paper. She tightened her lips, her need for us to leave shouting despite her silence.

The next day, my mother begged me to fly back to Rhinebeck with her and my father. "You're too young for this." She grabbed my hand, showing an emotional side she usually kept under wraps. "We let you come here with the understanding that someone would be watching over you."

"Who?" I asked. "Did you think you were sending me to summer camp? I'll be in my second year of college soon. How will you trust me there if you don't trust me here?"

"Trusting *you* isn't the problem," my father said, waving his hand as though encompassing the entire town. "These people—how do they call themselves Christians?"

"All groups contain honorable and dishonorable, sir, though the bad seems to tip evil here." Guthrie tucked his hands into his pockets.

"Right," my father said. "That's why Annabel should be coming with us."

Guthrie placed his hands on my father's shoulders as though they were exchanging roles. "Your daughter and I have something in common. Something big. We aim to dedicate ourselves to changing the balance between evil and good."

"Son, you're far too young to understand what a pledge like that entails. Plus, it's hardly reassuring regarding my daughter's safety."

Guthrie didn't argue about his youth or sincerity. "You and I share something else, Mr. Cooper. I'm planning to keep Annabel safe. And I'll keep that pledge."

Through my blur, I recognized Guthrie's words as more than comradely interest, but I didn't care, as they seemed to be working. I didn't know how or why my parents listened to Guthrie's reassurances. Perhaps they understood they'd only get me to leave Greenwood if they used physical force. Maybe they hoped Guthrie would take my mind off Clay.

"I'll call every day," I promised.

"She'll be protected." Guthrie again cited the expensive secure hotel an hour outside Greenwood—where we'd sleep in separate rooms— paid for by his parents, who'd wired him another large sum of money. "My parents are committed to SNCC and to helping Annabel. I'll protect her."

Guthrie talked and talked and talked as only the son of a lawyer could. He emphasized the legal protection SNCC would provide, although even I knew that was a massive stretch of his imagination. They put faith in Guthrie's years on me; in September, like Clay, he'd be a senior.

In the battle between their concern about leaving me and their worry about me falling apart in Rhinebeck, they put their trust in Guthrie, his parent's money, their connections, and—as they later told me—his obvious adoration of me.

❁ ❁ ❁

My parents allowed me only a few weeks to remain in Greenwood, and we used every hour. The first night on our own, we sat in the SNCC office tracing circles on a map, invoking a ten-mile perimeter for searching and dividing it into segments. I sketched a portrait of Clay, using the permanence of India-ink to make it last—which also meant I couldn't make a mistake. Stroke by stroke, Clay came to life on the paper. I didn't have the luxury of assorted pens, thin or thick; I couldn't choose the right instrument to cross-hatch his dense close-cropped curls or properly shade his distinctive square chin. Nevertheless, with his face engraved in me, my sole instrument brought him to life.

Rather than asking permission, I waited until Guthrie and I were alone in the office to mimeograph dozens of copies, afterward gently waving them, trying to clear the pungent sweet smell of the ink. Guthrie looked over my shoulder at the damp pieces of paper that created an eerie, sad display of paper Clays.

"I keep thinking I'll turn the corner and see him," Guthrie said.

Lost as I was in self-recrimination, I forgot Guthrie and Clay had formed a bond—both planning law careers, the indulged only children of their family, and both rabid fans of Philip K. Dick books. The two had spent time after Sunday meetings debating Dick's portrayal of capitalism as they drank the icy Cokes to which they were both addicted.

"I know. Sorry if I've been . . ." I stopped, sifting through a zillion descriptors for myself, with childish, self-involved, and clueless heading the list.

Guthrie laced his fingers at the back of his head. "I joined you for both of us—I never expected caretaking. I'm fine."

I nodded, blinked away tears brought on by his kindness, and began making packets for our Clay search. Copies of my sketches, written-out questions, pens, and notebooks filled our backpacks.

Two weeks had passed since the sheriff took me away.

Knots of sorrow and dread kept me from eating. Sleeping felt like disloyalty; wakefulness stayed until exhaustion stole me away, and foreboding accompanied every step.

Chapter 8

❃

Annabel

Swamps and Rolling Hills

Far sooner than we wanted, the senior staff in the SNCC office distanced themselves from our project. Carole never outright forbade our search—she even allowed Guthrie and me to use desk space—but within days, she'd warned us to stay away from the church and not to draw attention to ourselves.

We walked the streets much of the day, questioning anyone willing to talk—but no answers came. Mirages appeared and disappeared with each conversation. Most Black folks glanced at the picture and pulled away; a few gave a gleam of trying to help as they whispered ideas.

"Maybe I mighta seen him down by Avenue N."

"Check with the Bell family down by First Baptist."

White folks warned us to stop our foolishness.

"You all should l go back North if you gotta a brain in your head."

"He's missing, huh? Well, whaddya know about that?"

They all pursed their lips, whether they squinted or opened their eyes wide. Nobody of any color wanted us around. We kept an eye out for police uniforms, slipping on and off the streets each time we spotted one, my terror of another lockup butting against my need to find Clay.

Midafternoon on the Wednesday of our second week of searching, we returned to the SNCC office to regroup, wilted, thirsty, and hungry.

"Hey, you two." Carole stepped out of her small cubicle. Her duties supervising the Greenwood office kept her terse and moving; most often, we saw her only in passing. "We must talk. Follow me." She tipped her head at Anthony, the administrative manager, indicating he should come with us.

Once inside the cramped meeting and supplies room, Anthony laid out cold bottles of Doctor Pepper, a local favorite that neither Guthrie nor I liked. We sat across a wooden library table marked with the dings of a thousand children.

"We got some good news." Anthony swelled with the chance to be important. "This will—"

"We hope it's good news," Carole interrupted.

"She means we think it's verified, but there's always a small probability—"

"We have to mention every contingency, Anthony."

Guthrie and I clutched our sodas, looking back and forth between the two. Even I, who'd paid zero attention to office politics, could see that Carole hated Anthony.

"We got it," Guthrie said. "What's up?"

Anthony folded his hands on the table as though he were either forty or four. "Clay's parents have been in touch."

Carole shot him a look I couldn't interpret. "This is important, Annabel. Guthrie. You must stop asking about him."

I held my soda tighter so I wouldn't bang it and shatter the glass against the table. "Clay said that?"

She nodded once. "Clay told his parents he wants you two to stop poking around. Word got back that you and Guthrie are raising dust all over town, and he's afraid you'll end up hurting people. He's afraid for the Harris family and for Reverend Daniels. You need to leave."

"And he told you to deliver this message?" I tried to reconcile the cold terse words with the sort of message I'd expect from Clay.

"Every day you're playing detective puts everyone in danger." Carole's dark eyes drilled into me.

I leaned forward. "Where is he?"

Carole brought her chair closer to the table. "He's staying low. And you're a distraction. All the noise you're making diminishes people's willingness to get involved with us. Do you understand? Poking around makes folks less likely to register. There's plenty enough fear around without you stirring up more."

"But Clay—"

"Clay told you to go home. You have his wishes." Carole leaned forward and patted my hand for a moment. "I'm sure he cared for you—but the last thing in this world he needs right now is you."

"Is he in trouble?"

A long-suffering sigh escaped her lips. "What the hell do you think?"

Guthrie pushed his chair away from the table. "Let's go, Annabel. Time's up. If Clay worries about you, he won't worry enough about himself. The only way you can help him is to let go."

We drove to the hotel in silence. I wasn't a complete fool; I understood they needed to button down operations and concentrate on registering voters. Still, I was desperate for a way to contact Clay when summer ended.

I didn't know his parents' first names. His last name—Williams—was as common as water. He'd described his hometown in California but never named the place. Or I'd never listened well enough to remember.

Where was Clay?

Carole said he was safe, but the women in jail had it right.

He was in the wind, and everyone would let him stay there.

My eyes were open. Nobody wanted me here. I'd made trouble for Clay, for SNCC.

A chill passed through me as I sat in the steamy car.

Three Freedom Summer volunteers from CORE—the Congress on Racial Equality—were also missing.

Their names reverberated in my head, a loop of barely controlled hysteria.

James Chaney.

Michael Schwerner.

Andrew Goodman.

Names invoked in whispers and screams.

In the wind.

I dropped my pencil, startled by a gentle knock. After a wakeful night, I'd been up since five, staying in bed, sketching memories of Clay in my black and white notebook.

"Guthrie?" I called out.

"Yes. It's me. May I come in?"

"Sure." We had copies of the keys to each other's rooms. I closed the notebook and pulled the blanket up over the old T-shirt of my father's I wore. My sisters and I loved sleeping in them—the family joke was that we all bought him new packs for Christmas and then stole the old ones that he'd worn to the best sleeping softness.

Guthrie held a hotel coffee cup, a copy of the *New York Times* tucked under his arm.

His reddened eyes and messier-than-usual thick dark hair alerted me to trouble.

After handing me the coffee, he sat on the bed beside me, quiet momentarily, and stared out the window at the brazenly bright day. The Mississippi sun assaults you. There's no escaping the arrogant glare.

"I'm just gonna tell you."

"Clay!"

He took my hand. "No, not Clay, but bad. They found the station wagon."

I understood instantly. *James. Michael. Andrew.* Their car.

Guthrie adjusted his black glasses, pushed them higher on the bridge of his nose, and then put the newspaper where we'd both see the story. I leaned on his shoulder and read the headline. "Wreckage Raises New Fears Over Fate of the Missing Men."

They found James, Michael, and Andrew's burnt station wagon buried in a swamp. James, Michael, and Andrew were missing.

Their bodies might be anywhere.

The FBI searched.

The *New York Times* put it far more poetically than made sense, telling readers that lawmen searched through "the swamps and the rolling red hills."

Lyrical words. Perhaps reporters thought that made the truth easier to swallow.

Three young men.

Like Clay. In the wind.

The story hollowed me.

Whatever reassurances Carole had given, I only heard one voice.

Nobody'd be surprised if they killed him. Nobody'd be surprised if you're the cause.

My cup shook. Guthrie removed it and set it on the nightstand by his side. "You're going to be okay."

"I love him."

"I know. And I'm sure he loves you, but he has to love himself and his family more."

Guthrie held me as I wept. The scent of the night still clung to us. The clean laundry scent of the sheets rose with the musk of muddy coffee and Guthrie's dried sweat.

His blue shirt grew dark and wet with my tears. "Shhh," he crooned while holding me.

I fought a sudden sweet ache of wanting him closer. He inched his lower half away, trying to conceal my effect on him. Still and silent, we breathed together, our only movement his hand making small circles on my upper back.

Using some magic of gentleness, without breaking our spell, he moved his hand down my arm, stroking first the soft cotton of my sleep shirt, then running his palm down my bare flesh. My breath caught when he traced the line of my hip.

"Is this okay?" he asked.

"I'm a virgin," I whispered.

When he pulled his hand away, I drew it back. "No. Don't stop."

Accepting Guthrie's caress was wrong and wicked, but I hungered to be touched. *Now, now, now.*

Clay inhabited me.

Guthrie held me.

Clay had evaporated.

Guthrie took care of me.

The comfort of Guthrie's tenderness overtook my shame. I devoured the intoxication of forgetfulness that laced the sweetness of our kisses. I caught his fire and met him, disappearing with grateful hunger when he pulled off my shirt and touched me in wonder as we signed a silent pledge with our bodies.

Chapter 9

❋

Annabel

JUNE 1964

The Last Mississippi Meal

Guthrie and I ate our last Mississippi meal on a bench outside the Greyhound Bus station: chips, nuts, and apples. We didn't want to eat in a segregated restaurant.

I shook out the remaining pistachios and split them open one by one, licking the salt off my fingers, now stained red from the dye used to color the pistachios, counting off all the ways I'd failed Freedom Summer.

I'd disappeared from the school kids' lives without a word. Not one person registered to vote because of me.

The entire experience became all about me—my shiny romance, the children loving me, and what a saint I'd considered myself because I dusted well. Reality slapped me again. The simplicity of salvation was a myth; I couldn't make a change simply by existing.

I practiced not crying as I watched for the bus. "How do we walk on the side of justice?"

Guthrie picked up his Coke and held it to the back of his neck. Not an inch of shade protected us. "Start by finding patience. Soft running water will eventually wear away the rocks."

"Am I the rock or the water in your scenario?"

"That's part of the discovery you face."

"How very Zen you can be." I wasn't sure what being 'very Zen' meant, but the phrase sounded right. Guthrie took my hand as we waited silently until the bus pulled up. When it arrived, he loaded our suitcases as I climbed the stairs to find seats.

I turned when I heard a squeak. The driver had swiveled in his seat and stared. The Supreme Court banned interstate travel segregation in a 1947 ruling, but adherence to the policy remained jagged.

The driver appeared weary. When I settled in the next to last row of the nearly empty bus, he rolled his eyes as though a battle with a White girl he recognized *as one of those* types was so much not what he wanted. I raised my eyebrows to convey, *come on, buddy. Is this worth it?*

I visualized the scene unfolding in his mind as Guthrie stepped up, walked down the aisle, and sat beside me. Police. Dogs. A schedule screwed for the rest of the day.

The driver shook his head and started the engine. I pushed away the pride that rose, knowing the outcome if Clay and I had been the ones choosing seats.

Guthrie and I spent almost two days traveling home, passing through a swath of Mississippi after boarding in Indianola and traveling endless miles on the highways of Alabama, Georgia, North Carolina, Virginia, and Delaware before hitting New York.

We exchanged the stories as we rode, ones we'd have previously shared if we'd met during normal times. Summer camp and his parents formed his beliefs—his camp connected to the Federation of Jewish Philanthropy; thus, I learned he was half-Jewish, though neither his German-Jewish mother nor Scottish-Catholic father put much stock in religion beyond celebrations that included food or presents—preferably both.

Guthrie taught me the difference between cultural and religious

Jews and the many gradations within each subsection: Reform, Conservative, and Orthodox. Then he explained Bar Mitzvahs, the ceremony when one becomes of age, responsible for one's actions, and can decide for themselves how they would like to practice Judaism; to his parents, it meant him coming of age ethically when they expected him to be a part of the side of righteousness.

Plus, see above—presents and food.

Like me, Guthrie's parents raised him to participate in actions that helped the world, though his parents skewed more to political actions and social justice than the Christian charity of my mother and father.

For instance, his parents named him in honor of Woody Guthrie; his father venerated the folksinger, seeing the man as someone who spoke up—whether for Dust Bowl migrants or working to break the color barrier well before those actions were popular.

"Woody managed to escape the stew of prejudice he was raised in. I think his father might have been in the damn KKK. He was a self-made man," Guthrie said.

"Sounds like your parents admire that tenacity."

"Yeah, but on the other hand, my father's a lawyer who ping-pongs between dedication to pro bono work for places like the NAACP and his private practice for corporations." Guthrie shrugged. "He and my mother like nice things. They give new meaning to the word cognitive dissonance. My bar mitzvah audience held, to quote Marion Montgomery—who my parents love—paupers, poets, pirates, and more than a dash of millionaires."

I worked hard to picture the solemn synagogue service with him starring in the ritual that elevated him to this quasi adulthood. The following dinner and dancing at a fancy hotel sounded more exciting than any wedding I'd attended.

For a dreamy moment, I imagined belonging to a Reform synagogue.

"And your family?" he asked.

"My parents expect their daughters to nurture their aptitudes and find matching moneymaking trades. They told us to be each other's best friends, though it didn't always play out. Kirstie tortured me because I knocked her off the perch of being the youngest, and thus most adored, child. She swore my moneymaker would be a job as a stripper."

"She was jealous. You're a beauty."

I waved away his words. "None of us got credit for being pretty." I cleared my throat and imitated my mother's throaty voice. "'*Helvete*! Being beautiful won't fill the bankbook, provide kindness, or help anyone. Beauty is as beauty does.' *Helvete* means hell. That's her favorite swear word." My mother's ethereal blond beauty hid her Swedish practicality.

Guthrie told me of summers spent in a kibbutz in Israel, where he learned the value of fighting in mind and spirit and how the desert-toughened kibbutznik was the Jews' answer to the Holocaust.

After we exchanged our family histories, Guthrie wove the history of hard-fought freedoms and independence movements from Gandhi to Sudan, to our country, choking with anger as he related the horrors the Cherokee experienced on the Trail of Tears. He knew everything and cared about everyone. He spilled over with stories and knowledge.

Being drawn to Guthrie while aching for Clay bewildered me.

Both were brilliant. That trait turned out to be my romantic Kryptonite.

Clay offered lessons slowly, appearing to measure my readiness, while Guthrie loved the sound of his voice and theories, which should have been annoying but instead felt like I was gathering presents.

Where Clay reminded me of my father, holding his counsel— doing more and talking less—Guthrie examined the world through conversation.

Our closeness grew during the long bus ride. Guthrie would soon be a senior at Harvard; we'd be in the same place, him in Cambridge, me in Boston. Our interest in each other crept beyond friendship and politics.

I reminded myself that Clay had told me to leave. Carole and Anthony didn't follow up with any messages telling me to wait or that he'd contact me. I might not know his hometown, but he knew mine. Finding the Coopers of Rhinebeck would take only one call to a phone operator.

The bus pulled into the dreary unloading platform at the Port Authority in New York City. Mississippi was gone. "How do I forget him?" I said quietly.

"You don't have to. And you have to know that you can care about more than one person. I'll never ask you to forget Clay."

Guthrie walked me to the mammoth post office building on 8th Avenue, where my parents waited, before he took the subway to his parent's apartment on the Upper West Side.

I spotted my parents before they saw me. They sat in their station wagon, windows rolled up, doors locked, and air conditioning probably on high—one of the rare luxuries my mother indulged in. She swiveled to find me, undoubtedly anxious to whisk me back to Rhinebeck.

As Guthrie kissed me goodbye, I worried I'd transferred my unresolved love and passion for Clay to Guthrie as though it were an emotional bank deposit. The possibility rang dishonest, even wicked, but when I'd offered some portion of the idea to Guthrie on the train, he'd countered with *bashert*—the Yiddish word for "meant to be." Guthrie believed we were meant to be, and I believed in Guthrie. A siren song of inevitability entwined us.

On the fourth of August, Guthrie borrowed his father's car and drove to Rhinebeck after calling first to ask if I'd read the day's newspaper.

I had. My parents raised us to finish the *New York Times* seven days a week.

When Guthrie called, I sat on my bed, clutching the front section. *Bodies believed to be those of three civil rights workers missing since June 21 were found early tonight.*

My mother sat beside me, smoothing the rosebud-covered spread she'd stitched years before. "Come on, sweetheart. Please give me the paper. I'll save it for you. Let me make you tea with honey."

But my mother couldn't coax the paper from me—I wouldn't let go until I'd scratched every word into my brain.

"They didn't print their names until the twelfth paragraph." I lifted the paper to read aloud. "*The missing men were Michael H. Schwerner, 24 years old, and Andrew Goodman, 20, both white and both from New York City, and James E. Chaney, 21, a Negro of Meridian, Miss.*"

"That's so very sad."

"Sad? Sad? It's not sad, Mom; it's tragic. Their deaths are sins. What if that had been me? Would you call it sad, then?"

"Don't talk like that." My mother snatched the paper from my hands. "That would never happen to you. You have no idea what they were doing or why the sheriff arrested them."

"What were they doing? Why the sheriff arrested them? How can you say that? What if that sheriff had raped me? He thought I was sleeping with Clay; only being a White girl kept me alive, not that I was a good girl! How do you not see that?"

"That's not what I meant," she said.

I ran to my parents' porch to wait for Guthrie.

I threw myself onto the wicker rocker and clutched my knees.

The women in the jail cell had spoken the truth. I knew that in my bones. Clay's gentle romancing of me probably signified his death knell.

We had to change this country or die trying.

And I had to grow the hell up.

Part Two

❊

Boston

Annabel

The artist must elect to fight for freedom or for slavery.
> *—Paul Robeson*

Chapter 10

❋

Annabel

When LBJ Canonized Mickey

"'Those who notice nature will never be bored.'"

My Drawing Nature 101 instructor nodded several times, his red bowtie askew, his middle-parted hair standing on end from his habit of raking it between sentences. "Ah, didn't Rachel Carson say things beautifully? We will miss her. Offering nature in art will never go out of style. Now. Let's see what you've noticed."

I concentrated on allowing the charcoal to lead me, curious how my voice could transform the rocks, moss, and broken terracotta scattered on the table. Within a short time, my drawing morphed into a river flowing over a place at the bottom where Clay might lie.

Guthrie and I arrived in Boston in September—him a senior at Harvard, me in my second year in The School of Practical Art. Practical Art was a studio school, a college my parents hoped would hone my creativity into a career in commercial art.

I convinced my parents to let me drive up with Guthrie, who rented a U-Haul in New York City, filled it with his belongings, and then came to Rhinebeck, where he loaded my things. My parents had already driven their four daughters to colleges dozens of times, with added trips for Sonja, my changeable sister who'd enrolled at Berkeley for art history, McGill for sociology, and then to her final destination, George Washington in DC, where she graduated with a degree in liberal arts.

My mother repeatedly mentioned Sonja, using my sister as her Ghost of Christmas Future parable that I must avoid. "Your sister squeaked by. She could have ended up waitressing with some useless degree in ceramics burning a hole in her back pocket. Use your talent for practical purposes. Plan now. If you don't know where you want to end up, you'll find yourself on the road to nowhere."

I held back from asking my mother which colleges offered ceramics degrees or reminding her that my talented sister sculpted extraordinary copper, bronze, iron, and steel pieces—she'd never been near any road to nowhere.

My father took his affinity for mechanical things and built the number-one auto repair business in the Hudson Valley. My mother powered her skill in weaving, knitting, and embroidery into a cottage industry—every small-town New York store catering to tourists offered her Scandinavian-inspired blankets and tableware.

When applying to Practical Arts, I'd planned on following my mother's ordination to learn the art of sketching advertisements and finding the perfect métier that spelled paycheck, but Mississippi had altered my compass. Now, I swore to jump off a cliff before painting polite watercolor landscapes sold in gift shops across the Hudson Valley. Not with the growing horrors our county faced.

President Lyndon Baines Johnson chose Walt Disney to receive the Presidential Medal of Freedom.

Men died trying to register voters; LBJ canonized Mickey Mouse.

My mother must have sensed me slipping away from my role as her doppelgänger; she scoured Rhinebeck Library's newspapers for jobs for commercial artists and glued them into her letters with the heading "Inspiration!"

I ignored every clipping as I dug into the school library and discovered protest art. Diego Rivera's murals attacking the church, capitalism, and the ruling class left me breathless. Why hadn't Jacob Lawrence's *Migration of the Negro* series, his *Harlem* series, made him a household name? I lost hours examining the art of the suffrage movement, captured to immortality by Emily Ford's *The Factory Acts: They Have a Cheek. I've Never Been Asked.*

My focus shifted from drawing willowy women in evening gowns to capturing images from Mississippi.

I emulated Guthrie's surety of purpose—his dedication to ideals offset my parents' hammering about using one's drive to prosper.

When we weren't being purposeful, we were in bed.

For all intents, we lived together—thanks to Harvard's blind-eye policy about seniors and their bedrooms—becoming adept at occupying Guthrie's single room. When not falling into bed, we dug into our work. I devoted myself to illustrating struggle. He dedicated himself to graduating at the top of his class and to the newly formed SDS—Students for a Democratic Society.

When the *Harvard Crimson* quoted a statement Guthrie had labored on, he read the student newspaper aloud as we ate pizza in his room, his pride almost hitting me in the head. "*A new group on the Harvard campus—Students for a Democratic Society*—blah, blah, blah . . . here's the part where they quote us: *Our quest is for a political and economic order in which peace and plenty are used for the widest social benefit, a participatory democracy in which people are given the means to control their lives.*"

I nodded. "Impressive."

"Does it come across as too intellectual?"

"Just intellectual enough?" I laughed until the sight of his hungry eyes told me how he intensely he anticipated my answer. I squeezed his knee. "Hey, you're Harvard guys. We expect no less."

"What about this?" He ran a finger down the page. "Listen— *Projects range from campaigning against Republican Presidential candidate Barry Goldwater to setting up a local community center, from discussing domestic problems to studying the conversion of military production to peacetime purposes.* How does it sound?" Guthrie asked.

"Lofty. Admirable. Though maybe a bit broad," I suggested.

He tensed beside me on the narrow bed.

"But sometimes these things are complicated to understand," I hurried to add, "if someone isn't on the ground. Like how hard it is for me to describe Freedom Summer."

Guthrie took off his thick-rimmed glasses and pinched the bridge of his nose.

I lifted my laced fingers to my lips, wondering what Guthrie expected me to say.

"I'll give you some papers to read," he said without looking at me. "We're building a complex new political system."

"That's not something you could explain in an article." I wondered if when my mother admired my father's efforts—which she often did— she sometimes tucked her tongue extra-firmly in her cheek.

"Certainly not by a college reporter." Guthrie breathed out as he came back to himself. Square-shouldered, but not Tarzan-broad, and of average height, I swore he expanded, appearing almost massive when blown up by the genius of his thoughts. "Though she was cool with us and vice versa."

"Was she cute?" I asked.

He put a finger under my chin and lifted it. "Not even in the same dictionary as you."

My art classes flew through a blur of stages and techniques, from Life and Rendering class to Techniques to Advertising Design 1, and then Representational Painting to Color, Color, Color. Outside classes, I went further afield, dipping my toes into pop art while self-studying political art and posters.

Pot entered my life. Smoking pot didn't transform my world—it barely enticed me—but weed built a wall between who we considered *them* and *us*. In our growing movement, some veered political, some spiritual, and lots headed straight for fun, but everyone recognized the messages in the music that overtook us. Guthrie and I rotated between Dylan's albums (his) and Joan Baez's (mine).

By the spring of 1965, SDS owned Guthrie. His dedicated followers repeated and recited every word he uttered.

And we all counted the time until the march against the Vietnam War in Washington planned for April 17. The day before the march, we rode nine hours on a crowded bus, crashed at a high school friend of Guthrie's, and arrived at the White House early the following day with picket signs.

The crowd swelled to sizes beyond our dreams. Songs and chants drowned the small group of Young Americans for Freedom and the self-proclaimed Nazis wearing uniforms and swastika armbands.

Blue paint dripped from the sloppy *Peace Creeps Go Home* sign held by the raging red-faced Nazi clone, while the YAF guy raising the banner reading *Pink Colleges Turn Out Yellow Reds* looked like he'd taken a wrong turn on the way to church.

The latter placard would have benefited from my expertise. I imagined the letters painted pink, yellow, and red, sparked up with a traditional flag background.

My heart skipped when I spotted the SNCC banner floating above the crowds as we approached the grounds of the Washington Monument. I nodded as Guthrie estimated the size of the crowd, trying to hide my desperate search for Clay. Lately, when I spoke Clay's name and Guthrie took my hand, I sensed agitation along with his comfort.

I knew that Guthrie wanted me to be over Clay. He'd deny it, but his tight jaw and pressed-together lips gave the truth away, so I buried my memories and rarely spoke Clay's name. When I couldn't breathe from needing to say his name, I returned to my dorm room.

Under the bed in my room, I kept a blue suitcase. Hidden below piles of artwork were my drawings of Clay—the original and the mimeos from the ones I'd drawn in the notebook while crying in Greenwood. I'd tried adding a new sketch, imagining him with minuscule changes—a haircut, wearing a tie—but I couldn't. Clay had frozen in visual time the day I went to jail.

Now, aware I'd lost track of the speech booming around me on the National Mall, I concentrated on listening to Bob Moses on the podium; he'd been a presence in Mississippi. I recognized the sincerity in his slightly halting words as he connected the government's refusal to enforce civil rights in the South with the escalation of the war in Vietnam.

When Paul Potter, founding member and president of SDS, rose to speak, Guthrie stood straight as Potter enunciated every inchoate thought forming inside us. "Most of us grew up thinking that the United States was a strong but humble nation that involved itself in world affairs only reluctantly, that respected the integrity of other nations and other systems, and that engaged in wars only as a last resort . . ."

I moved closer to Guthrie, humbled by the crowd and Potter's words. I saw Joan Baez standing off to the side, her simple white sheath bisected by her guitar strap, her glossy dark hair pulled back. Guthrie brought my hand to his lips, kissed my knuckle, and kept hold as though we had made a pact to save the world with our hands.

Beatific commitment shone on the faces of all those around me.

My people.

I returned from my Easter break in Rhinebeck exhausted, tired of fighting my parents' warnings about my future. Now, back with Guthrie, I sat across from him, trying to capture his hands with charcoal, sketching the workman-like, thick-knuckled hands that belied his Manhattan-Cambridge-Harvard life.

I'd seen the same hands on his father when we joined his parents for a Passover seder—my introduction to everything from matzo to Hebrew to parents who viewed their son as a gift from above. They hung on Guthrie's every word as he described the gathering in Washington; my parents called my life a Peter Pan existence.

"You'll have to grow up someday," my mother warned on my last night home, axing away at the beliefs she considered naive and more self-righteous than righteous. "Sooner rather than later, *fina du*. Nobody spends their life surrounded by people who have all the time in the world to examine their navels. Wait until you finish college and have to earn a living. Then you'll understand." My mother's use of *fina du*, Swedish for "beautiful you," held the ton of sarcasm she meant, as she once again reminded me how much beauty isn't enough in this world.

My father tried to soften my mother's approach. "Honey, your tender heart is a gift. But you can't take care of the world if you can't care for yourself."

I fumed, wondering how much they believed one had to choose between caring for oneself and working for peace and justice.

"How about Joan Baez?" I asked. "She's helping while creating music that changes the world *and* making a ton of money. Why can't I do that with art? Why can't you believe in me?"

My mother gave me a look that said, *Really? You're gonna be Joan Baez?*

No, I didn't think I'd be Joan Baez, but artists marked movements toward freedom, whatever the métier. "Look at Marisol, the Artists' Suffrage League, Diego Rivera. No matter what you say, I'm not spending my life drawing kittens for Hallmark."

Now, I took a breath and tried to sort out my mood, examining Guthrie's fingers as he flipped the pages of a thick textbook. His mother and father paid for his single room at Harvard—they could afford the luxury. They didn't worry whether he'd devote himself to money in the future.

His parents could afford not to worry. They couldn't imagine their son in a scenario without a healthy bank account.

I roughed up Guthrie's sketched fingernails to make them appear more ragged. He bit his, a surprising habit that helped me see his confidence wasn't without holes. "My parents are scared of you."

"Because I'm Jewish?" he asked without looking up.

"Why is that your first response?" I reached over and pushed down his book, forcing him to look at me.

"Well, is it?"

"They think you're terrific." I had no idea just how terrific they thought he was or if they cared if he was Jewish. But I knew what they did care about.

"Whether you went to our church or were a Martian, they'd ask the same two things. 'Is he planning to marry you, or is he just having a good time?'"

"Not a good time—a great one. And what's your parents' other question?"

"Where is he going to practice law?"

"On Mars." He patted the space next to him on the bed. "Are they afraid I'll drag you to the moon?"

"They want all their daughters to live within driving distance forever and ever."

I worked overtime practicing honesty with Guthrie, unable to imagine how lying could connect us, though I gave myself a pass about the times I got lost in thoughts about Clay.

That I might be turning into the woman my sisters had urged upon me made me shudder. They warned me not to tell Guthrie about our parents' bullshit worries, practically screaming their advice when we gathered on the porch: "Never talk about marriage, children, or any future with a boyfriend," Kirstie had said. "That's the kind of pressure that makes them disappear."

"Guthrie's loss," I'd said.

My sisters had pretended to gag at my show-off assurance about Guthrie's love; his love felt encased in a future permanence.

Life became safer when a guy loved you more than you loved him. My mother passed that wisdom on to me; unlike other beliefs, I held on to this one.

That security made it easy to say anything.

Almost anything. Clay's name stayed off my lips. I only visited the hidden room in my heart where Clay lived at night while Guthrie slept.

Some afternoons after classes, I walked to the Boston Public Library's main branch, where I searched through the phone books of the entire country. On each visit, I picked another town in California or another borough in New York City, searching for Clay and Clayton Williams.

I kept a list embedded in a sketching notebook. Someday, I'd call every number. Or, I reassured myself, Clay would one day call me. Rhinebeck still had only one Cooper listed in the phonebook. The story I told myself about why I didn't share my library habit with Guthrie went like this: I was working out my need to find Clay. Burdening Guthrie with my worries made no sense—what harm was I doing with my searches?

Guthrie took off his glasses and turned to me. "They want you to stay within driving distance, huh? Tell them that's a damn nice wish and one I plan on honoring."

Just like that, I realized that someday Guthrie and I would marry. And I'd keep looking for Clay. But not in a lying kind of way.

Chapter 11

✤

Annabel

SEPT 1965

A Thousand Crusted Pots of Chili

Guthrie entered law school, and I became a junior. Harvard Law School's housing options did not lend themselves to romance; thus, the time came to take the next step.

In 1965 ordinary folks slipped on engagement rings, while couples like Guthrie and me shared cheap apartments, considering our choice an ideological statement as much as a romantic one. I got jazzed up nerves thinking about telling my mother and father, but my plan to live in unwed sin barely registered for them, with my sister Vivienne's French boyfriend dragging her off to starve in Montparnasse.

My parents barely noticed that Guthrie and I could have been crowned the SDS poster children for political couples of September 1965. They didn't worry about Guthrie these days. They might judge us as blind for thinking a whirlwind of protest could change the world, but his future held the law. Camille and Gordon convinced themselves our devotion to political causes was a youthful stage, a rite of passage, so they indulged us as we humored their hopes in our work being a "stage."

Guthrie and I trekked through grungy apartments in student ghettos tucked into the neighborhoods of Brighton and Allston. Our potential homes housed roaches, chipped bathroom floors hosting god-knew-what, flimsy locks protecting peeling linoleum, pock-marked walls, and cracked windows. Guthrie's parents would contribute the amount they now paid for Harvard housing and no more—their way of letting us know how much they disapproved of their son devoting himself to anything other than studies and politics.

On our fourth apartment-hunting day, we stood on a sloped, uneven wooden floor in a kitchen forgotten by time and sponges. The stove showed memories of a thousand crusted pots of chili and remnants of dinner past. The showerhead hung at an angle that would only work if we bathed on our knees, yet it worked better than the faint drip from the sink faucet.

Guthrie was tired of the hunt. "Settle for the best of the worst," he urged. "I can fix things."

"Really?" The idea of Guthrie holding a hammer didn't compute.

"Don't underestimate me. And stop looking for the impossible."

I ignored him using Gandhi-style noncompliance, refusing to stop looking until I found at least a facsimile of a decent apartment, somewhere better than a hotel for roaches and rodents. I doubted Guthrie had a minute to repair anything. Remembering his stories of growing up in New York City luxury apartments, I distrusted his claim that he possessed handyman skills beyond calling for the building superintendent.

If we settled for the best of the worst of these horrible apartments, my father and mother would be there in seconds to put every detail in order, but I didn't want my mother reminding me how much better we'd do when Guthrie and I had professional jobs with a full-sized paycheck or my father judging every swing Guthrie took with a hammer.

"Honey, we know you have a giant heart," my father said each time I came home. "And you'll always be able to volunteer."

My parents were Rhinebeck's king and queen of the volunteers—first in line for everything from lake waterfront cleanups to raising money for a senior center. I shuddered at the thought of joining that life.

Guthrie and I divided our time between school, bed, apartment hunting, and political meetings for weeks. I walked beside Guthrie at marches, despising the yelling and chanting of slogans. When parading, I only mouthed the words. I panicked at being loud and bringing attention to myself during demonstrations, shrinking from the police lining the streets.

Fear of the law had followed me from Mississippi, but I fought my anxiety and never missed a march. Each protest brought an opportunity to scan the streets for Clay. By now, searching was an almost autonomic response.

I craved behind-the-scenes roles. Creating advance posters and protest signs mimicking Peter Max's art challenged and soothed me. Guthrie drove me crazy when he suggested my work was too splashy, expounding on the superior dark art of the 1930s Communist movement. Nevertheless, I became the creative go-to for Guthrie's SDS chapter, while purists in my art history courses accused me of weaponizing art.

In truth, while Guthrie put a price above rubies on his law courses and applied every lesson to his political efforts, his valuation of my work seemed minimal. Arguing my point was impossible; he denied everything, swearing that I confused his passion for the law with a lack of enthusiasm for mine. Guthrie's ability to drown me in word soup presaged well for his law career.

Guthrie might be careless with his words, but his rock-solid love never wavered.

What the hell became my attitude toward his inattention to our future housing. Like a gracious queen, I forgave his careless dismissal of all things domestic. While my dorm mates chose to worship the pretty boy-type charm of Paul McCartney look-alikes or the rough-trade appeal of Jagger, Guthrie's commitment to building a just world was what attracted me,

Chilly November air blew my hair into a storm of tangles as we stood in Harvard Yard. We hugged ourselves against the wind as a large crowd gathered to protest the escalation of combat troops being sent to Vietnam. Guthrie scanned the crowd for I wasn't sure what. My mind wandered to our recent housing contenders, imagining us in the varied imperfect choices.

My fear rose as we became hemmed in by the unexpected number of people assembling. SDS had sprung into action as the death count of Americans and Vietnamese rose. I clutched my thin navy peacoat tight as the crowds shouted, "Bring our troops home," so loud that my heart thumped in the rhythm. One, two, then dozens of guys climbed trees and began shaking the branches.

Another group gathered to face us off, screaming "Communists" and "draft dodgers" at our crowd. A muscled man in a hard hat picked up a rock and threw it toward the trees; our guys answered with lobbed acorns and rocks thrown like missiles.

Both sides went wild, shouting "murderers," "fascists," "pinkos," and "faggots," at each other, crowding closer and shaking their signs as though wielding cudgels.

Moments later, a wedge of police approached.

I tugged at Guthrie's jacket before he ran toward the car as I tried to pull him back. "We should go."

"Don't worry. I have us covered. We have lawyers here. Take this." He handed me a red bandanna. "In case of tear gas."

"I can't stay here," I shouted over the rising din. "Meet me at the Co-op. Guthrie tried to mask his moment of disappointment at the terror that law enforcement still awoke in me, but I could see his dismay.

I left anyway.

The group shouted "warmongers," as I slipped away. My cowardice disgusted me—but still, I escaped, running off from a few local cops while our country rained bullets and napalm on children in Vietnam.

I hurried toward the giant bookstore across from the Harvard Yard exit, putting space between me and the police flanking the demonstrators.

Trips to Harvard Square always ended at the Harvard Co-op, the only business with bathrooms open to the public. I entered the building through the hidden side entrance on Palmer Street, climbing steep stairs to visit the not-so-clean, but thankfully available, bathroom tucked away on the second floor.

Afterward, I studied the patch of the wall outside the women's room we used as a community bulletin board sans the corkboard, bending to read a flyer outlined in earthshaking cobalt blue letters.

Politics Aren't Just for Marches
Choose Intentional Living!

We're looking to expand our group in Mission Hill. We are seeking a like-minded couple who believes that justice begins at home. We have a rambling house with room for couples with kids (we already have some) or those without (but who love them.) No dog allergies, please!

Find out about our intentional community—Puddingstone— our extraordinary home, where we're raising everything from our consciousness to our children. You must be fervent about fighting for freedom and civil rights, stopping the war, and loving vegetables. Poker, softball, and spaghetti-sauce skills are a plus.

Call Diantha. Tear off a tab below.

I'd call my mother for her spaghetti sauce recipe tomorrow. I fished out my tiny red address book and scribbled down the number, a seedling of hope settling as I checked every digit I wrote against the pinned paper.

Three times.

A sense of destiny engulfed me, the sense of my future hitting so hard that I unpinned the flyer from the wall. I now understood the

meaning of the first Yiddish word Guthrie had taught me: *bashert.*
Meant to be.

After promising myself that I'd return the flyer if I didn't like the place, I folded it in quarters and buried it deep in my bag. I didn't want competition for my fate.

Arguing with Guthrie about ethics wasn't on my list of things to do that night.

Chapter 12

❀

Annabel

How Important is Cleanliness in Your Life?

Four days later, we met the folks of Puddingstone—me wearing a garnet corduroy baby-doll dress I'd sewn and then embroidered with orange thread and shiny good intentions. Guthrie wore his constant explosions of brilliance. Once again, I noticed how his parents raised him to value his opinion and his complete lack of shyness about sharing his thoughts.

Depending on my mood, I could resent or admire his self-confidence, but at the moment, I worked on ignoring the bits of leaf gathering on my tongue, courtesy of the chamomile tea we drank from rough brown mugs.

Within ten minutes of arriving, Diantha, the woman I'd called, introduced us to her husband, the three other couples, four children, one floppy mutt, and one baby in the belly. Though I'd grown up with two parents, three sisters, two dogs, and a cat, the thought of living with this panoply of unrelated people overwhelmed me—but being part of a home dedicated to political action brought shivers of hope.

I focused on differentiating the crowd. As we shook hands, I repeated each name aloud and silently. Using my father's tricks for remembering his customers' names, I vowed to ping myself with their particular facts throughout the day.

Diantha twirled an exceptionally long brunette braid. She sat with her husband, Chuck, who was intense, dark-haired, and as wiry as Diantha was muscular and broad. I barely avoided being run over as their sons Zane, age three, and Jacob, age four, rushed in and out of the room like human race cars. Diantha worked in the Boston City Hospital emergency room; Chuck wrote advertisements for a local sneaker brand. Or perhaps he supervised copywriters.

A lot went on in a short time.

Waves of blond hair trailed down the back of angelic-looking Melanie, who resembled a Pre-Raphaelite painting brought to the present day. She leaned on her boyfriend Wyatt while cradling her early pregnancy belly and spoke with modest pride about opening a daycare center. Wyatt, the prettiest one in the room, could model on the cover of a romance novel. However, he managed a food co-op.

Suze and Grady were joined by Mac, age four, and Leo, age two. Suze, whose broad, warm smile showed off jumbo-sized teeth, had recently finished her MFA and wanted to be a writer. Quiet Grady sported a beard and mustache and carried three pencils in his breast pocket. He studied engineering postgraduation and repaired bikes.

Roxanne and Quinn had no children, though Bowtie, the dog, leaned against Quinn. Roxanne worked in a gallery and looked the part with her hair twisted in a severe dark knot. Quinn, a carpenter, resembled a grown high school AV squad member.

By the time all the introductions had been made, I knew I was the youngest in the room.

The many personalities swamped me, while Guthrie, who'd grown up as an only child in a spacious Manhattan apartment, appeared to be at ease. When I reached for his hand, he responded with a reassuring squeeze.

They peppered us with questions: "How do you demonstrate your commitment to justice?" A softball for Guthrie.

"On a scale from one to ten, how important is cleanliness in your life?" I lied as I noted the basket piled with toys, clothes, and shoes as though someone had performed a sixty-second cleanup. A truthful *ten* might seem rigid, so I said *seven*.

As they grilled us, I assessed the effortless coolness surrounding my potential roommates. I took in as many details as possible during Diantha's casual tour, following her braid and the loose tunic swinging above her ample hips. We traveled in a pack, everyone pointing out the parts of Puddingstone they loved best while I silently reiterated their qualities in an attempt to keep them all straight.

Melanie (*Angel! Daycare! Pregnant!*) took us to the broad back porch, where a wicker swing topped with tapestry cushions swayed as it oversaw the oversized-for-the-city backyard. Colorful ribbons flew around a maypole. Unraked leaves decorated the back lawn just as they had the front.

"We don't rake until spring." Melanie tossed a gray tweed shawl over her shoulders, the dark color contrasting with her pink cheeks. "Nature's mulch."

Wyatt (*Handsome! Food co-op! Handsome!*) shook his head. "Hard to understand how people take the protection away, leaving those blades of grass and plants shivering all winter."

My parents handed rakes to my sisters and me as the first leaf drifted down. What would they make of this brittle carpet of leaves crunching underfoot?

I swore we wandered through a hundred bedrooms, but there were only nine. One waited for the chosen couple; they designated another a guest room and one a quiet room. According to Suze (*Writer! Chiclet teeth!*), it was a rare week someone wasn't crashing at the house.

Evidence abounded for the need for a room dedicated to quiet.

The three children's bedrooms were allocated by age. Zane (*Child of braided Diantha!*) and Leo (*Son of smiling Suze!*), three and two, slept in the bright yellow room. Rainbows arced across one wall. Red wooden boxes held everything from blankets to teddy bears. The floor hid under clothes, toys, and god-knew-what scattered everywhere.

An empty, sheetless crib topped by tiny patchwork quilts waited for the next baby in another room with a dark blue starry ceiling.

The older children, Jacob (*son of braided Diantha and skinny, sneaker-writer Chuck!*) and Mac (belonging to *smiling Suze and bike-man Grady!*), lived in a smaller room overlooking the backyard, drenched in light. The walls were painted with handprints, and strewn clothes covered every surface.

The adult bedrooms merged into a compilation of beauty, distinction, and posters, some so messy I worked against making a face.

I longed to own the velvet quilt the color of evergreens, the marble-topped antique dressing table, and the four-poster bed in Roxanne's (*Tall! Angled! Arty! Sarcastic!*) and Quinn's (*Unassuming! Friendly!*) room. Perhaps because they were childless, their room shone with jewel-box perfection. The room captured the painterly Roxanne, while Quinn seemed like a visitor until Roxanne mentioned that Quinn had built the bed.

Suze and Grady's mattress lay on the floor, covered with Indian bedspreads overlaid with stuffed animals. Giant sunflowers on orange fabric covered the windows.

We sped up; Diantha and Chuck's room surprised me with an eclectic mix of mahogany and satinwood Victorian furniture, filmy lace curtains, and a wedding ring patchwork quilt. Well-worn flannel shirts and an oversized fisherman sweater hung from the bedposts.

Stray toys dominated the kitchen, the playroom, the bedrooms, the bathrooms, and the library.

Ease, acceptance, and happiness emanated from every corner, whether messy or orderly.

We circled the house and returned to the living room, a tidy oasis. The room signified a cease-fire from chaos, whether by design or in preparation for Guthrie and me, I couldn't guess.

The fireplace took up almost an entire wall. Peace signs, in at least ten iterations, covered the mantel. A world of art modalities spoke for peace: painted squares, copper, ceramic, child-made, and twisted pipe cleaners.

My desire to add my fingerprint of peace itched, my fingers already holding the imagined needle embroidering a rainbow of colors.

Puddingstone could be our home. I pushed away the messy parts—the floor begging for a good sweep, the dog hair on the couch—and concentrated on the array of political books covering the end tables, the handcrafted wooden candlesticks, the pots Suze had thrown, and the giant Raggedy Ann and Andy sitting on the steps as though guarding the children.

Guthrie and I would occupy a bedroom overlooking trees and a grape arbor.

Here, I could realize the dream of marrying art with justice and find my great passion.

Chuck (*Sneaker guy, Diantha's husband*) described Mission Hill as being perfectly fluctuating-stable. The Irish-majority enclave had grown more diverse over the past few years. Folks of every color and culture bought houses and rented, including a growing influx of students who never left.

Unlike other Boston neighborhoods, here, many locals stayed put, however grudgingly, making room for the new people while injecting their own brand of humor. Chuck bragged about belonging to the Mission Hill Men's softball league, boasting how their team—Steve's Warriors, representing a local bar—had been nicknamed "The Bomb Tossers" for their politics.

The men in the house clearly revered the born and bred.

"Maybe we're outliers for our politics, but after the games, we drink our beers sitting next to the guys who might march on the opposite side of the street." Chuck nodded and stared into the distance, perhaps engulfed in self-admiration.

Thick black glasses overtook Chuck's thin face and delicate features. Zane and Jacob appeared cloned from their father, neither holding a trace of their mother other than having her dense hair. Diantha looked capable of anything, from her broad shoulders to the sturdy plait halfway down her back. Black-haired Chuck and his boys looked like they'd blow away in heavy wind, while Diantha could withstand a year of back-to-back hurricanes.

"Do you all belong to the team?" Guthrie asked.

"Angling for a spot?" Chuck threw a pretend pitch. "We start practicing in March."

"Ready for tryouts." Guthrie took a mock bat swing. "Any time, any place."

I raised my eyebrows and cocked my head. Guthrie had buried his sports interest from me.

"Fair warning: come March 21, sun, rain, or snow, we practice," Wyatt added. "Sweatshirts on, we grab our bats."

"And leave those bats all over the house," Melanie said. The sharpish words surprised me from the angel of the house. Her corn-colored waves sprang free, her eyes seemingly painted by God to match a Cape Cod summer sky. The seamlessness of the golden skin covering her gentle curves, toes to brow, radiated wholesomeness. Even pregnant, she epitomized innocent beauty. I could imagine painting Melanie as a gauzy nude but never naked.

Wyatt knocked movie star gorgeous out of the park. Coppery brown hair shot through with strands of blond and flowed around his planed face while his amber-green eyes studied your soul.

When *Life* magazine published a sensitive spread on communes, Wyatt and the ethereal Melanie could be the stars.

I reached for Guthrie's hand.

"And then, of course, there are all the women on your team." Suze slapped her hand against her forehead. "Oh, wait! There are no women on the teams." She twisted her curly ropes of black hair and then passed Leo from her lap to her husband's arms. Grady's smile also exuded warmth, which, combined with his already thinning hairline—balanced by his beard and mustache—made Suze and Grady the least intimidating people in the house: not beautiful, not handsome, just right.

"But we are allowed to cheerlead, right?" Roxanne, she of a Lauren Bacall voice, possessed that dangerously wicked kind of beauty that made me shiver with jealousy. A scary Modigliani of a woman, all sharp angles ready to cut.

"Change is incremental," Chuck-the-sneaker-guy said. "Do you know what it means that guys like us are on the field with the locals?"

"Yeah, babe. You're a regular Jackie Robinson." Diantha rolled her eyes.

"Ah, put away your jealousy, Di. I don't see you breaking barriers with the local women."

"News flash! We don't drink with them; we hang out at the playground on the top of the hill." Diantha punctuated her sentence by plunking her feet on the giant coffee table made of an old wooden wire spool. "Trust me. Those women are stronger than any of your heroes living at a bar."

Guthrie and I wandered back to the trolley in Brigham Circle. We walked the perimeter of Mission Hill in less than an hour. It seemed like a town within a city and a traditional neighborhood in flux.

Neatly trimmed bushes in front of a triple-decker building rushed the season with a covering of outdoor green-and-red Christmas lights, while a second-floor apartment featured Indian bedspread curtains of orange and yellow. The playground swarmed with children of every hue—an unusual sight in Boston.

Evidence of the old Puddingstone quarries showed walls and buildings built from the smooth gray stone. Bars popped up everywhere except the streets around the massive Basilica of Perpetual Help, or Mission Church, as Guthrie told me was the local name. The triangle of the church, playgrounds, and bars sang a siren song; I wanted to belong to something smaller than the overwhelming streets of Boston and Cambridge, where I'd been.

Harvard Square outsmarted me.

Kenmore, where my school and Boston University were located, lacked a sense of permanence or cohesion. The quilt of stores and restaurants appeared drab instead of welcoming.

The student ghetto of Allston depressed me with the omnipresent scent of beer.

Between the house on Alleghany Street and the pugnaciousness I sensed in these streets, I felt that my corner of the world might be in this mixed-up world of Mission Hill.

Chapter 13

❄

Annabel

DECEMBER 1965

Is There a Market for Such Downcast Paintings?

Guthrie and I packed our books (him: more than seemed possible), art supplies (me: fewer than I wanted), clothes, flotsam, jetsam, and sentimental items and moved into Puddingstone at the end of Allegheny Street.

We were now a couple within a group of couples, spokes on a spinning wheel. By December, I learned my first lesson in communal living: satisfying a group often meant satisfying nobody. My commitment to Puddingstone's ideals held firm while my patience with individuals thinned—especially in regard to piled-up dishes and dust thick enough to make grimy angels on the floor.

Thus, preparing for my parents' first visit a few weeks ahead of Christmas induced a terror about how the house and my roommates would look through their perfectionist eyes.

The day before their arrival, after finishing my classes, I hurried home to clean, scrubbing as though auditioning for the role of a scullery maid. I knelt almost inside the tub, scouring the ancient rust ring that had probably begun forming in 1895 when farmers built the house.

"Hello?" Diantha stuck her head in the bathroom, eyebrows raised, sardonic expression firmly in place. "Are your folks planning to take baths after dinner?"

I considered raising my middle finger, but it, like all my fingers, was covered in foaming Ajax.

"Give her a break." Our poster boy, Wyatt, appeared at Diantha's shoulder, an empty oversized backpack hanging from his square shoulders. "I'm heading to a meeting at the food co-op. Need anything?"

Diantha stroked the end of her braid as she thought. "Let's stock up on oats. I'm trying out a few granola recipes."

After giving her order, she waved Wyatt off and returned her attention to the bathroom. He winked and gave me a supportive smile; I sent him a silent thanks with my eyes. If Diantha had her way, every soul in the house would follow her commands, including when to clean. Diantha's whims held more sway than anyone else's, except when Wyatt ruled through his benevolent beauty stature.

"Why not let your family see the real us," Diantha had insisted during the previous evening's house meeting when I begged everyone to pitch in for my parents' arrival. When her grin reached a rare wideness, broad enough to show her deep dimples, I realized her playful side peeking out.

"Like masses of dishes piled in the sink? We practically have a triple decker going." Suze noticed our clutter and chaos but appeared to float above the mess, never wanting to get her hands in the greasy water. She shook a cigarette from a communal pack of Pall Malls lying on the oversized kitchen table.

Nobody could stand Pall Malls—the most intense of the unfiltered brands—so the Puddingstone smokers chose them as the carton they chipped in for each week. Lessening resentment about who cadged more from whom and cutting back on smoking was the purported goal, but all it served, in my nonsmoker's estimation, was to make the habit easier.

"Should we include the clothes stacked in the laundry room for the tour?" Chuck asked his wife, Diantha, who replied by kicking him.

"Dirty, clean, or both?" Melanie smiled as she moved her chair close enough to Wyatt to plunk her feet in his lap. His thumb rubbing her instep mesmerized me, making it impossible to concentrate on the conversation.

My cleaning was a source of entertainment.

"Come on, all of you. Wanting to organize and unclutter makes sense for Annabel. Her parents aren't used to anything like this place. You should see their house." Guthrie squeezed my shoulder. "Gleaming doesn't begin to cover it. I don't know how they do it. I mean, they own an auto repair shop."

"Sounds gritty." Roxanne still wore her black sheath from her day at the gallery, though she'd kicked off her stiletto heels. "Amazing they can keep the house spotless."

I frowned. "My father's business isn't in the house. We live blocks away. And he scrubs with Lava soap before he leaves work. Ever seen it? It's like Ajax for hands. Removing grease isn't that difficult."

"And? What's your point?" Diantha rose to put on water for another pot of tea. "Mom and Dad are dedicated to sanitizing? They'll faint at the sight of dust? Should we buy some Lava and scrub the kids?"

The conversation continued round and round. It drove me crazy when we devoted more energy to dissecting the merits of instant coffee versus the perked kind than how to prevent a highway from isolating the neighborhoods of Roxbury, Mission Hill, and Jamaica Plain from the rest of Boston.

I joined Stop the Highway the week we moved into Puddingstone and promptly had to battle Guthrie, who believed efforts to promote the antiwar movement far outweighed neighborhood issues. Skirmishes over making the bed soon followed. His dorm room never awakened the nascent hausfrau in me as did our Puddingstone bedroom.

Guthrie declared bedmaking a middle-class affectation, though only when I asked him to shake out the sheets and smooth the comforter. When I was the one who made the hospital corners with crisp linens, he seemed to very much enjoy slipping into the well-made bed I provided, his complaints of bourgeois behavior evaporated.

Whether we argued over the relative importance of civil rights vs. the Vietnam War vs. the Southwest Corridor project, I swore all Guthrie's arguments began with "How can you even compare—"

Now, bent over the tub under Diantha's mocking eyes until she drifted away, I glared at her back and didn't try to think of a single excuse for my cleaning mania—or, as my mother and father would describe it, normality.

Ultimately, I took the easy road and cleaned every room in the house other than the adults' bedrooms, the kids watching in bemusement as I lined up their toys.

My mother stuck her head into my bedroom, peeking without stepping over the threshold. "Nice."

I heard the word as *quelle horreur!* despite the perfect order.

"Come in, Mom. Dad. Really." I acted like a five-year-old, excited to unveil my school project.

My father looked around the room, appearing desperate for something to comment on. He ran his fingers over the shelves lining the walls under the windows and then tapped the wood.

"Terrific workmanship, here. Smooth. Nobody's going to get splinters from this bookcase. Did Guthrie build this?"

If I could have, I would have lied. *Yes, Daddy! Even though he's an intellectual law student from New York City who leads masses of students in political actions, he's, of course, quite the builder.*

But lying had never been my talent. I could pull off sins of omission, but not outright dishonesty.

"Um, no. Wyatt put them up. Before we moved in." I didn't add that he built them after hearing me wonder where we'd store our boxes and boxes of books.

"Wyatt? The good-looking one?" My mother smiled as though sharing a secret with me.

"No, Mom. The woodworker one. Guthrie is the good-looking one."

She raised her eyebrows. *Sure, honey. And I'm the queen of England.*

"This is what I want you to see." I pulled my parents to my low oak dresser, straightened an already aligned vase holding a single red zinnia, and then pointed at the framed painting on the above wall. "I did that in class and entered it into the school-wide watercolor competition. And I won. First place."

Mom moved close, peered, and then backed up to study the painting from afar.

"They hung it in the Practical Arts entry for four weeks." I clenched my fists as she stared.

The painting's almost garish bright right side drifted to a gloomier left panel. Women filled two side-by-side jail cells—one with White girls and one with Black girls and women. Cartoonish yellow and pink sundresses underscored the White girls' innocent belief in their release and futures. The Black women's dark blue dresses hung limp. Their expressions hid all emotions, but an undercurrent of shaking rage seeped out.

At least, that's what I'd aimed for when I attacked the canvas.

My father put an arm around my shoulders. "You've been a magician with a brush since you first held one."

My mother tipped her head and continued staring.

"What do you think, Mom?"

She backed up and sat on the hand-crocheted bedspread covering the bed. Made by Camille and now patted by her. Within a few minutes, my mother managed to take ownership of the room. "Sit for a moment."

I took my place next to her. My father leaned against the doorjamb.

"So," Mom said, "what will you do with this painting?"

I tried to parse the exact meaning of *do*. "Exactly what I did. I hung it."

"But what is the piece for?"

"I made it for class."

"But why this? What was your impetus?"

"For . . . it's for . . ." I reached for words that would convince her, but of what? My talent? My usefulness? Her question stopped me. I couldn't find a reason to be entitled to the air I breathed. "For resistance. I'm making protest art. I'm expressing the horror Black women in the South live through daily. While we, the White girls, dropped in and dabbled in their pain."

"That's a wonderful sentiment, sweetheart. It's uniquely you, Annabel. But how will you monetize pieces like this? You can put them in a gallery, but is there a market for such downcast paintings? How will you bring this unique talent to the world?"

My father sat on my other side. "You must consider every path you take. Nobody should move through this world without the ability to put food on the table and a roof over their family's head."

"You're not planning on Guthrie underwriting your work, right?"

My mother, suddenly Rhinebeck's Betty Friedan. I remained stiff and still.

She patted my hand. "Winning prizes isn't enough." Beauty wasn't sufficient unto itself—nor was talent, the Cooper family motto.

I squeaked out the words clogging my throat. "Aren't you proud of me?"

"Of course!" she kissed my forehead. "We are always proud of you. God blessed you with many gifts. But you must take a good, hard look at everything you do—what you accomplish with these gifts is what matters."

Once again, Camille and Gordon brought me to a hard stop.

What would I do with my one and only life?

Chapter 14

❂

Annabel

A Broom in One Hand and a Paycheck in the Other

T he next night, I lay on Roxanne's giant bed, hands under my hips, pretend-pedaling a bike with fury as I used the old high school gym exercise to get rid of my angry energy. I'd tamped down a million words while working to please my parents during dinner. Roxanne and Suze nodded the way friends should as I recounted the evening in excruciating detail.

"They think I'll be lining up jobs painting seascapes for hotels or drawing puppies and blue-eyed children for Hallmark the minute I graduate." As I biked my final imaginary lap, I panted between every sentence and then collapsed.

Suze held up the *Boston Globe*, alternating tokes from the joint we passed and dramatic readings from the Help Wanted section. "Here's another excellent opportunity for women!" She cleared her throat. "*Barmaid-Go-Go Girl Dancer. Apply in person at 10:30. Mornings.*"

"Your parents would be so very proud." Roxanne jumped up, tied her shirt under her breasts—an old blue button-down of Quinn's—and began dancing a frantic frug. "Imagine this on top of a bar."

"Go-go too racy?" Suze asked. "Here you go: *Housekeeper. Live-in.*

No drinkers! No smokers! $150 per month."

"Let's see." I sat up, drew in a long toke, and then poked a finger at one ad after another. "Secretary? Receptionist? Shopkeeper? Every job on the women's side of Help Wanted means servicing someone. Where are the ads for hookers? Might as well keep it honest."

Suze stabbed the newsprint. "Hey. We have the go-go dancer."

I pretended to lift a phone's handset to my ear as I spoke in a nasal voice. "Wiggle your behind or answer the phones, ladies. Preference, please?"

Roxanne inhaled deep enough to get stoned for a week. "I'm sick to death of my options at work."

Suze flipped the newspaper pages. "I thought you liked the gallery."

"Me too." The mattress bounced as I flopped on my stomach and held my chin between my hands. Roxanne's job managing a Newbury Street art gallery sounded enticing, though I had no idea what she did. I'd imagined everything from putting on shows to discovering new artists.

"*Manager*'s just a glorified word for sales and reception. What they like is scrutinizing my ass. Four years at the revered Art Institute of Chicago and the gallery owners pay me for wearing and looking good in a tight dress." Roxanne said the school's name in faux admiration, as though quotation marks surrounded the name. She usually presented her work as glamorous and necessary—Quinn's extra-strong weed had extra-loosened all our tongues tonight.

"If wiggling around a gallery is the best Roxanne can do—Miss Prestigious Art Institute—what hope do I have when I graduate?" I flung a dramatic arm across my brow.

Suze grabbed an Oreo from the bag we'd secreted upstairs, hiding the purchase from the Puddingstone food police team of Diantha and Melanie. "Think of this while you whine—less than fifty years ago, we couldn't have voted in the last election. Less than fifty years!"

We inhaled cookies while pondering that truth. Suze loved spilling current and historical facts like a walking, breathing encyclopedia, but lately, her conversation contained an unending barrage of women's history. She swore that joining the men putting out *The Phoenix*, a nascent alternative newspaper, churned up her growing rage.

"The Position of Women in The SDS," Suze's first article, had come out three weeks before. Guthrie seethed about the piece but went especially batty when he saw the elements of my illustration that ran along with it: a long-haired woman at a copy machine—her mini skirt riding high on her thighs—handed a mug of coffee to one mop-headed guy while supplying pamphlets to another.

After I framed the original and hung it in the hallway entry, Guthrie went ballistic.

The guys in the house quietly rolled their eyes at the sketch as they passed by, letting Guthrie speak for them. The women were ready to light candles beneath it.

"Like it or not, you're looking at my first published art," I'd reminded him. "That's huge for me."

"You're denigrating what we do."

"That's what you think? Writing about how men belittle women will denigrate perpetrators?"

"Now we're *perpetrators*, Annabel? For god's sake!" He'd stomped out without waiting for an answer.

"Guthrie still snarls when he walks past my piece," I said, nibbling another Oreo.

"Men. They dream of us with a broom in one hand and a paycheck in the other," Roxanne said. "And wearing a black negligée. And all the while, nothing changes for them. We get hired, our pile of work grows to impossible heights, and they keep looking for their maids, their prostitutes, their mothers, and cooks all rolled together like a Swiss roll cake."

"I ask Grady to watch the boys, and he tells me why he's too busy to 'babysit.' I tell him, 'Nobody babysits their fucking kids.' He shakes his head and smacks the damn papers he's grading on his hand as though they're writing an updated constitution. He's a postgrad student, for god's sake, not a fireman running into a burning building."

Suze held her hand out. "Pass me that joint."

We waited as she took a drag deep enough to scorch her lungs. "At work, they hold up copies of *Playboy* and then pretend to hide them when I walk by. My new nickname is 'Tight-ass Suzie,'" she said in a choked voice as she worked to hold the smoke in as long as possible.

"They're idiots. They're angry that your article attracted so much attention they can't ignore you. What's happening now?" Roxanne asked me. "After the five thousand letters you got?"

I laughed at Roxanne's exaggeration, though she wasn't far off. Despite *The Phoenix* being a recent addition to the Boston newspaper scene, Suze's piece had detonated a landslide of mail.

Men wrote that "Suze should be grateful to serve coffee to the soldiers of the SDS."

Men insisted that "America should send SDS men and women to Vietnam and Russia, where they belonged."

Men wondered—in the most intellectual of terms—"whether this was the fight they should be fighting. After all, you must agree that we must prioritize civil rights and Vietnam."

Women very much did not agree. The idea of waiting in line while the more worthy and deserving got parity didn't wash anymore; we were ready to make the damn line wider.

Women wrote in response to Suze's article with thousands of words equaling a giant howling scream that boiled down to "Yes!"

Suze received typewritten letters that went on forever, brief cards on heavy stock, handwritten notes on fancy stationery, and penciled encouragement on yellow-lined paper.

I'd copied the best lines, saving them as I considered the ethics of making them into a collage.

Soaring quotes from the past washed through some letters—those I included in my current project. I worked in five shades of blue, bleeding into each other, using calligraphy for the stark words I couldn't forget, like, "Those who do not move do not notice their chains," from Rosa Luxemburg

When the men in the house saw me working on the image, they couldn't hold back a grin or chuckle; even Quinn, the sweetest in the house, smiled ruefully.

And then Guthrie had come behind me one night as I shaded colors, leaned down, and kissed my neck. "Baby, you have a bit of studying ahead of you about the actual meaning of downtrodden."

I removed the pencil clenched in my teeth. "I didn't see you holding a machine gun in battle before you began protesting the draft."

None of the Puddingstone men knew us as we knew them. As in any hierarchy, the ones below studied those above, while the opposite rarely occurred.

They didn't understand why Suze never left the house without her mother's Oberlin College ring hanging around her neck on a long chain. They didn't know history sparked from the number twenty-eight embedded in a golden O. Suze's mother had raised her with bedtime stories of how she chose to attend Oberlin because it was the first college in America to admit Black students, way back, and in 1835, the first to grant bachelor's degrees to women in a coeducational program.

I waited for Suze to answer Roxanne's question. Now that we'd been awoken—first by Suze's article, then by our men's reactions—what would our next moves be?

We three felt slightly guilty about our tight threesome. But Diantha lived in her passionate world of motherhood, natural grains, and homeschooling rights, while Melanie spun between her daycare center, a food pantry, and a shelter for homeless families.

But make no mistake, Melanie and Diantha wanted us in the fight even when they weren't there.

Suze laced her fingers and smiled. "NOW. They need us."

"Now?" Roxanne asked. "Yes, of course now."

"No. *N-O-W.* All capitals. The National Organization of Women is practically brand new. People attending the Third National Conference of the Commission on the Status of Women established it in June with a statement of purpose. *The purpose of NOW is to take action to bring women into full participation in the mainstream of American society now, exercising all privileges and responsibilities thereof in truly equal partnership with men."*

"You memorized it?" Suze's brain awed me.

"If they can do it, I can memorize it. My next article will be about NOW."

The three of us fell back, lying on Rozanne's beautiful quilt in a hazy circle of love and weed.

"Sign me up," Roxanne said. "With indelible ink."

Chapter 15

✳

Annabel

JANUARY 1966

The Great Puddingstone
Monogamy Debate

Nobody missed a house meeting without a hell of a reason. These weekly gatherings were the lifeblood of our house, though sometimes the battle to reach consensus made me wish Guthrie and I lived in some clean, cozy little apartment on our own. Everyone felt that way at some point.

During our Monday evening kitchen table meetings, we argued about everything, from how we shared cars to brands of wine to which political actions we'd support with the entire weight of Puddingstone. Between the posturing and polemic, unless the stars, moon, and sun aligned, we spent hours shouting over each other.

Only hospitalization emergencies justified skipping a house meeting, though nobody would miss this week's summit—not with sex on the agenda. *Week Four: the final round of the Great Puddingstone Monogamy Debate,* promised everything from sexual tension to raised voices, anger, and soul-searching deliberation.

We'd already chewed up millions of words about getting into each other's beds—I'd had to choose the most salient to put on paper as the official house recorder. Guthrie and Diantha, in a rare alliance, were on fire. They cloaked their desire to switch partners in rhetoric, taking turns as the chief-anti-monogamists-in-charge, expounding as they surreptitiously drank in Wyatt and Melanie, the golden couple of Puddingstone.

Guthrie's desire for Melanie never surprised me—who wouldn't want her? She was sweet—certainly sweeter than me. As I grew more strident, her seeming pliancy (emphasis on 'seeming;' I sensed iron underneath the velvet) and girl-next-door beauty with a touch of sexiness, third trimester-pregnant or not, was honey to a fly.

Wyatt knew he embodied Hollywood handsome—I'd learned that over the past few months—but despite being a god, kindness infused him as it did Melanie. All the children in the house gravitated to them.

"Freud considered monogamy as an oppressive sexual norm, a source of neurosis for both men and women," Diantha said.

"In 1915." Melanie placed her hands on her belly. "By 1930, he said modernity couldn't exist without monogamy."

God save anyone in the house who forgot about Melanie's Mensa-level brain. The men always did.

"Why bring another possible area of conflict into the arena?" Melanie exuded thoughtful openness as she cocked her head. Suze pinched me under the table.

"What are you talking about?" Diantha frowned. "Do we have conflict in *the arena*—the bedroom—now?"

"Are you using the royal *we*?" Melanie tapped the side of her head. "Never mind. Pregnancy brain."

Melanie clearly didn't want to argue; her exhaustion showed, and arguments with Diantha could last for soul-crushing hours.

"I agree with Mel. We have enough things to fight about in the house without adding sex," I said.

Guthrie winked and then squeezed me around the shoulder. "Fight? We want to make love, not do battle."

After shaking off his hand, I choose between my colored pens to represent the increasing heat of the conversation. Purple seemed about right; we hadn't yet reached red status. I kept the official notes of our meetings, illustrating them as though I were a combination court reporter and artist.

"Not funny. Why put our relationships at risk?" As I spoke, I sketched a profile of quiet Quinn, his heavy brows set with the weight of the decision.

"Sleeping around is a lousy practice in a house with children." Suze fiddled with her Oberlin ring, hypnotizing us by pulling it back and forth on the gold chain. "And rife with complications."

Guthrie rocked on the back legs of the kitchen chair. "Sexual liaisons occur in nearly all socially monogamous animals. Lions mate with as many as fifty females daily during mating season."

"Someone has big dreams," Chuck said.

"Exactly how does this apply to us?" Suze asked. "Southern night monkeys are thoroughly monogamous. The male monkey spends his time watching his babies. The gray wolf prefers to mate and bond with one partner at a time. So, which are you? Do you fancy yourself the monkey, the lion, or the wolf?"

I held back a laugh as I sketched a quick Suze drawing, adding masses of hair tumbling around her narrow face. Guthrie and Suze were like a tennis match—armed with facts, numbers, and history for every meeting.

"The most basic argument against monogamy is this: affairs are unavoidable." Guthrie took a long drink of cold coffee. "No instinct is more powerful than sex. Men are evolutionarily wired to pass on as many genes as possible."

Suze threw her head back and aimed smoke rings at the ceiling. "Bullshit."

"I take it you don't agree." Guthrie righted the chair and placed his hands on the table. "Okay. Give me your point of view."

Suze sliced a sliver of brownie from the pile on a blue glass plate. She only ate morsel-by-morsel, as though a portion divided into twenty pieces could never hit her thighs. Suze despised her pear-shaped body; I thought she resembled a deliciously sardonic Mother Earth. Grady watched Suze closely. All the husbands except Guthrie, his overconfident parent's son, walked the fine line.

"We've been trading Guthrie-anointed ideas for a month," Suze said. "We don't need another lecture on men's genetic drive to spread their sperm, otherwise known as 'Here's another excuse for getting laid.'"

"We can fend off jealousy by bringing in a cultural way to manage our earthier desires. Fewer fights. Lower divorce rates." Guthrie never backed down.

"Why stop there?" Suze asked. "Maybe having more sex with more people can end famine! War! Racism! How about you consider this unassailable fact? Despite Harvard men screwing like wolves, women aren't yet allowed to enroll at your precious institution."

Guthrie leaped from his chair. "What kind of reasoning is that? You know that—"

Suze put up her hands as though warding him off. "Don't give me any crap about Radcliffe. I'm tired of men on the left using intellectual garbage to talk women into doing their bidding."

Guthrie took a deep breath and sat. "Have you considered how discussing the monogamy parameters can help the women in this room?"

Let it go, Guthrie; I scribbled in cramped, illegible letters in the margin of my notes. *Just let it go.*

"No. We haven't thought of that. Because we know your idea won't push women—us—further. It sure as hell won't get us into class with you." Roxanne removed a pack of Marlboros—she never allowed Pall Mall's flecks of tobacco on her tongue—from Quinn's flannel shirt pocket. I penciled her sinewy shape and signature dark topknot as she lit it.

"Here's my point of view, Guthrie," Roxanne continued. "We can agree to screw like monkeys in the jungle, but until it rains rubbers from heaven, Quinn and I are staying in our beds."

I put down my pencil and raised my hands, palm out. "Whoa, we're not deciding that folks have to sleep with each other, are we?"

Laughter broke the tension, and we decided to vote. At one in the morning, monogamy officially lost. However, the minority opinion (Suze, Roxanne, Melanie, and me) pushed so many codicils that jumping beds would require an act of God.

Our men, though, it seemed, had a deep maternal curiosity, forcing Melanie, a week later, at the next meeting, to announce that pregnancy made the idea of sex with anyone but Wyatt—and at this moment, even with him—unthinkable. Though she appreciated *all* the polite requests for her company, "No thank you. And please stop asking."

Within a week I politely refused Chuck, Wyatt courteously turned away Diantha, and the issue appeared to melt away. Diantha spun Wyatt's rejection into a newfound belief against open sex. She took up the banner for purity, motherhood, and apple pie, but nobody was ready to start another debate to change the guidelines once again. Official Puddingstone rules still allowed for bed creeping.

I thanked God the dilemma had ended, grateful that I didn't have to spend every free minute imagining sex with a rotating cast.

But an idea planted throws out sprouts. When I folded laundry before beginning dinner the next day, I imagined adding partner-switching to balancing school, political work, interacting with my many housemates, and being a quasi-mother to the children of the house.

Maybe it was my cycle, or perhaps it was the curiosity of only having ever slept with Guthrie, but I reminded myself that sex beyond Guthrie could only bring trouble. He might not offer the holy-love-floating-above-earth feelings Clay had engendered, but Guthrie was my rock. Maybe our initial blaze dimensioned, but our deep pull to each other never stopped.

I might have been numb the first time we slept together, but Guthrie's adoration pulsed hard enough for both of us. I absorbed his need as though standing in a field, arms out, letting an electrical storm pass through me. Where I'd worried that we'd begun with one-sided strength and passion, now I knew we braced each other. When he collapsed after leading the charge for one more assault against the war, I could put him back together.

He swept me from crushing shame—if someone had killed Clay, the fault was mine. I carried that guilt everywhere. Guthrie witnessed this and still loved me.

Heart-hurting glitter had disappeared with Clay.

I didn't expect it back, and that was okay.

Guthrie loved me, and that he didn't steal the depths of my soul brought comfort. Both of us found passion in work. We had room for loyalty, pleasure, and commitment.

The phone rang as I stacked clean white T-shirts on the kitchen table.

"Don't wait for me, baby," Guthrie said. "There's a big emergency, so I'm crashing at the office. I'll explain tomorrow. Love you madly."

SDS emergencies occurred often. Contrived or real, this one? SDS crises could involve anything from planning a life-saving demonstration to an argument over strategy that mattered not one whit to guys wanting to stay and bullshit all night.

Still, I didn't make a squeak of protest. A quiet night sounded perfect. It was my turn to cook but without pressure to perform. Diantha and Chuck's date night had coincided with Melanie leaving to visit her parents in New Hampshire. Cooking for only Suze, Grady, and Wyatt felt like a free pass to a leisurely dinner. I was on babysitting duty, and the children were happy with anything if I promised to sneak them a cookie for dessert. I enjoyed playing the role of the good aunt who'd spoil them with crayons and sweets.

I stirred tomato sauce with a wooden spoon as I stared out the kitchen window. The older boys—older being relative since Diantha's Jacob and Suze's Mac had only recently turned five—ran through the fenced yard. Fresh snowflakes made it into a fairyland. The boys twirled in circles as the pine trees lining our property became frosted with white.

The little ones, Suze's three-year-old Leo and Diantha's ridiculously self-confident and capable four-year-old Zane played peacefully in the kid corner of the kitchen, humming as I sang "Crazy" along with Patsy Cline.

Midstir, Wyatt came up behind me, leaned over my shoulder, and inhaled. "Something smells mighty good."

I turned and offered him the spoon. He tasted the sauce and sighed. "You know how to cook, babe."

Babe. The word heated me. Guthrie called me *baby*, which sorely lacked *babe*'s sexy cowboy single-syllable edge.

He tipped his head toward the radio. "Country?"

"I picked up a taste for it working in my dad's shop. Who doesn't like Patsy Cline?"

"Gotta agree with that. I don't hear the great Miss Cline around here often enough." He opened the fridge, took a beer, and held it up. "One for you?"

Glancing at Zane bombarding Leo with stuffed puppies, I shook my head. "Better not."

I flamed my way through dinner. When Wyatt sweet-smiled at me, blood raced through the center of my being. I turned all my rising hot sugar on Zane and Jacob. They were easy-to-please kids.

Leo concentrated on his goals, including zipping his mouth against unwanted food. Grady served Mac more meatballs as Suze coaxed Leo to try a quarter teaspoon of peas, to no avail. Between wiping up spilled milk and cutting up the honeyed apple pie I made for dessert, neither Suze nor Grady noticed the growing inferno that Wyatt stoked in me.

How Suze and Grady didn't get scorched, I'll never know. When they weren't feeding the kids, Grady chattered about his bike shop, and Suze planned articles aloud, both ignorant of the sexed-up bluebirds flying above their heads.

❁ ❁ ❁

When quiet and privacy finally reigned that night, ignoring all the intricate agreements and guidelines decreed by the Puddingstone monogamy convention rules, Wyatt crept into my bed using the old-fashioned method of chemistry.

He removed a library copy of *The Golden Notebook* from my hands, pulled down the strap of my white nightgown, and ran his cool fingers from my bare shoulder to my forearm. His streaked hair fell on my cheek as he bent to kiss me. I brushed his hair back and returned his embrace.

Beautiful Wyatt. All our beautiful young men with their newly long hair, walking proud, doing good. Our men.

Glowing moonlight snuck in through the window and outlined him with silvery light.

Guthrie entered my thoughts; I pushed him out.

Wyatt and I drew together and began a silent, searing race, as first he lifted me on top, then tumbled over, bringing me with him. And then he loomed above.

He held my hands high over my head, staring until the intensity forced us both to turn away. As first I and then he reached a shattering climax, he released my arms and buried his lips in my neck.

Afterward, we lay side by side, fingertips touching.

I rose on one elbow and traced the planes of his face. Finally, I pressed the middle of his upper lip as though saying, "Shh."

Without a sound, we tacitly made a pact to keep our moment locked, agreeing wordlessly that no house meeting would pound, analyze, or examine our night.

We kissed once more, and then he left.

Neither Wyatt nor I ever spoke of our encounter, not to each other, not to Guthrie—and I'd bet my right arm he never told Melanie—and most decidedly not to anyone else.

Our memories would be safe. They'd never lie in a dry husk on the kitchen's scarred oak floor, broken open by another endless tsunami of words.

Nobody would know.

Chapter 16

❋

Annabel

JANUARY 1966

Pregnancy Math

Scratchy paper rustled under my naked behind as the doctor rummaged between my legs. I closed my eyes against his invasion, shutting out the sight of his bullseye of a bald spot and the stupid poster taped to the ceiling. Who among doctor's office decorators thought pregnant women wanted to stare at Benjamin Bunny?

News of the day, Doctor Inwood: conception doesn't equal an emergence of latent desires to surround oneself with Beatrix Potter.

I wanted screaming abstracts. Bloody reds slashed with purples, edged with green, contrasting with sunny yellows, splashing into fiery oranges— now that would please me. I built the paintings behind my eyes.

Obstetricians should put cautionary posters on the doors to their offices: *Warning! Last stop before cartoons and bunnies.*

Knocked up. Pregnant. With child. A member in good standing of the diaphragm failure club. Science had confirmed what I'd suspected: conception was official. I'd called the doctor's office for my test results before the exam, forestalling the possibility of them reaching the house and giving away my secret.

Telling Guthrie terrified me. I performed pregnancy math for the thousandth time and then threw away my calculation. No formula covered this problem: not algebra, calculus, or basic math, though I tried to formulate an algorithm. If you sleep with X one time and sleep with Y ten times, who will be the father of Z?

When the doctor finally pulled the tortuous cold metal from between my legs, I breathed ragged gulps.

The nurse placed a calming hand on my wrist; her uniform loomed when I opened my eyes to smile in thanks. Pink and blue bunnies jumped over the nurse's breasts; her wide hips strained more cotton-tailed creatures to their breaking point. The future waved in the shape of bunnies wearing fuzzy shades of pastel.

I'd not come far at all. First, you played with your stuffed Easter bunny, then you got a bra, and then boys in your sixth-grade class came up behind you and ran their fingers down your back. "Annabel belongs to the Bunny Rabbit Association!" they'd shout after snapping your strap.

Only after talking to my older, wiser sisters did I learn the Bunny Rabbit Association stood for "She's wearing a bra!"

B-R-A.

Then Playboy Bunnies emerged. I'd barely blown out the candles from my twelfth birthday cake when Hugh Hefner breathed life into his bunnies and overendowed cottontails entered the zeitgeist. Overnight, girls craved hourglass figures.

Doctor Inwood patted my knee. I clenched my fists to keep from knocking away his pawing hand. Dozens of cartoon rabbits hopping on the chubby nurse continued to mesmerize me.

"Everything looks perfect." He peeled off his gloves and handed them to Nurse Bunny Breast.

"Thanks." I tried visualizing the obstetrician's view of *perfect*. Shiny pink labia? Plump uterine walls ascertained through Doctor Inwood's magic medical touch?

"So, dear, do you have any questions? Is your husband in the waiting room? Maybe he wants to join us. Nurse, why don't you bring him in."

I surreptitiously twisted the opal ring my mother had given me on my sixteenth birthday so only the band showed. Despite all my rebellion against the status quo, I was embarrassed to have no mark of respectability. No engagement ring. No wedding band. "It's only me today."

"No problem." He squeezed my ankle, conveniently located above my foot opportunely wedged in the metal stirrup, making it the perfect height for yet another touch. "Someone's got to bring home the bacon. Get dressed, mommy, and nurse will show you to my office."

Stirrups, I finally understood, were installed to keep us from kicking doctors who insisted on touching, touching, touching us. They pinned us down so we couldn't punch them, these patronizing pompous asses promising that using a diaphragm would prevent pregnancy as though a dome of rubber could save our lives.

I left the doctor's office laden with pamphlets about formula, courtesy of Mead Johnson, manufacturer of Similac formula, prenatal vitamin samples, and a sickeningly pastel pink, yellow, and blue booklet titled *Hello, Mom!* I walked to nearby Kenmore Square in a daze, jealous when I saw the crowds of students, especially those from Practical Art, worried about nothing more than their next test.

Going to my class held little appeal. All I could think about was everything. Like telling Guthrie. Who'd care for my baby while I was at school? I envisioned dropping my infant in my mother's arms—competent, unflappable Camille, and then laughed.

Along with Kotex, sanitary belts, and a clear explanation of the facts of life, my sisters and I all received the same unique addendum to her maternal advice when we got our first periods: "If you get pregnant, you're the mother. You're the one taking care of that child."

My mother didn't hesitate to explain that she'd done her time, done it well, and she'd be damned if she'd return to the starting line.

Perhaps I could join the invasion of women—and a sprinkle of men—seemingly unchanged as they strode around Boston wearing baby-filled backpacks. I could carry the baby to class on my back, taking her out for feeding and changing and then letting her nap and coo from behind.

With my three sisters and me, a girl felt inevitable.

Guthrie and I hadn't even faintly dreamed about babies yet. We never sat in the light of a flickering candle imagining the enchantment our son or daughter might bring, nor had we tried out names. Emmeline! Fredrick! Pablo! Marie-Denise!

I didn't spend my childhood rocking dolls, never mopping up after the messy Betsy Wetsys passed down by my sisters. If I wanted, I could have fed and changed a small army of plastic babies, but instead, I insisted my mother hide them. I hated the scary round eyes staring up at me, the liquid leaking out of their butts, and the open mouths demanding food and water.

I leaned against a parked car and stared at the red, white, and blue Citgo sign that Bostonians worshipped. My Drawing II class had begun ten minutes earlier, a course meant to develop our technique and style.

I did not want to go.

Creepy Marcus, who sat at the drawing table beside me, maintained that his oh-so-personal technique just happened to mirror R. Crumb. I despised Crumb with his hyper-sexualized Amazonian-sized women depicted satisfying odd and scrawny men.

Sitting next to scraggy Marcus forced on me the sight of him sketching Crumb-style mountainous females, their breasts bulging from tight tops, their microskirts cinched with wide studded belts.

March wind sliced through my thin coat.

Fuck.

I curved my hand around my stomach, the automatic protective gesture rising from a genetically coded movement meant to ruin my life.

Nausea rose at the thought of an afternoon of giant-breasted faux-Crumb women. Or maybe it was the alien inside me.

I walked to Copley Square, got on the E-line train, and headed home, where I slipped in the rear door and raced up the back staircase to my bedroom. After shrugging on a flannel shirt that Guthrie had flung over the doorknob, I pulled on my oldest Levi's. How long would they fit before I'd have to wear shapeless caftans?

I dragged out a sketch pad and charcoal.

My future had taken a hard left turn. Motherhood terrified me. Babies belonged to Camille. Diantha. Suze. Newly minted mom, Melanie. The champs. The naturals.

Not me, not now, not at twenty. Options played out, but despite my terror at being pregnant, finding my way through the labyrinth to an illegal abortion petrified me.

Stories of postabortion horrors abounded, from sepsis to hemorrhages. I'd witnessed the before and after of a roommate during my freshman year; her uterine perforation forced a hysterectomy.

Somewhere in my hazy thoughts of *future*, perhaps visions of motherhood lurked like a mist I never expected to hold. Maybe, if pressed, I'd say, *Yes. I will be a mother someday—just not this day.*

With five curved lines, I illustrated a pregnant woman lying on her side, seen from the front. Using softer lines, I sketched an infant in utero. I leaned my sketch pad against the window, facing where Guthrie would see it upon entering the room.

Then I lay on the bed and stared.

My paper baby looked sad. Anxious.

I woke the moment Guthrie turned the knob to our bedroom.

"Jesus Christ." In case I hadn't heard, he repeated the words. "Damn."

He got my sketch message straightaway. Harvard-smart, that man.

"Damn, damn, damn," he repeated.

I stared at the ceiling. "Right. Damn, damn, damn."

"Shit!" Guthrie fell beside me, barely lit by the waning light. He closed his eyes, crossed his hands on his chest without speaking, and finally turned and placed a hand on my stomach. "Fuck it. Don't worry. We'll work it out."

Damn, damn, damn. Maybe Guthrie was a miracle.

I turned on my side and slipped a hand under the blue denim work shirt that was his uniform at class, searching for the soft T-shirt warmed by his body heat. "Deal. I'll grow it; you see about the working it out."

He placed his large hand over my cotton-covered one. "Will your parents be happy?"

"Not at all. Yours?"

"Doubtful." He tapped his chest. "Remember me? The only child? The anointed one? Impending fatherhood colliding with my first year in Harvard Law School is hardly their dream."

Perhaps saying *law school* without specifying *Harvard* broke some Ivy League law. "I suppose we'll have to tell them," I said.

"At the very least, before he's born."

"Or she."

"It's a riddle, this gender thing." He leaned over and kissed my belly.

"'Tis." I ran my fingers through his almost black hair.

Images of Guthrie's parents padded into my mind on tiny feet. His father, dark and thick-built—Guthrie mirrored his father in practically every way. His mom, tall and thin, with planed cheekbones and honeyed hair, could pass as Wyatt's mother as much as Guthrie's. For that accident of genetic fate, I was grateful.

He gazed at me and my belly with wonder, tearing up for the first time since I'd known him. "I thoroughly love you. And now we'll have someone new that I'll love just as much. I will do anything in my power to keep us safe. We're making a family, baby."

Guthrie, my lion, ready to fight an entire country to do the right thing, went to my dresser top and rummaged until he turned, holding a rarely used tube of lipstick. Intent on his task, he came back to me and knelt. As I watched, he outlined his lips, imitating his mother perhaps, or me from my rare times using my Cover Girl Rose.

I gaped in curiosity and wonder until Guthrie lifted my shirt and covered my still-flat belly with a hundred kisses.

The next day Guthrie surprised me with a two-pound tin of Louis Sherry chocolates in a pink container, the box decorated with garlands of forget-me-nots and leaves, the sentimental gesture so unlike Guthrie that we embarked on a weekend of diaphragm-free sex.

Practical Guthrie replaced Tender Guthrie the following week. Pencil and legal pad in hand, he worked on a budget at his desk while I sat on the bed sketching in soft pencil. I looked up as his chair scraped on the wooden floor.

"Verdict?" I asked.

"The truth in black and white." He showed me long columns of figures scratched on a legal pad. "Numbers never lie."

"Yellow." I pointed at the pad. "The truth in black and yellow. And numbers can lie. Haven't you heard of the three types of lies? Lies, damn lies, and statistics."

"I know you're nervous," he said. "I've been reading. Hormones are messing with your brain. Statistics may lie, but not numbers. What is, is. My parents give me just enough for us to get by, along with paying for school. Your parents don't even pay for your college—you're building a ton of loans to pay back. We'll save money and interest if you take a leave next year."

"Guthrie!"

He looked into my widening eyes, placed the pad on his desk, and raised his arms. "Temporary! I promise. We can't afford your school, a babysitter, and rent. You can finish out this year, and then next year, when the baby's born, you'll be able to do your art at home."

Do my art at home.

As though playing with crayons.

Do my art at home.

As though caring for a baby required nothing more than an occasional diaper change. Guthrie scarcely noticed the constant needs of the already born and very present Puddingstone children running around the house like a pack of clumsy bear cubs. Wyatt and Melanie's baby, a little girl they'd named Poppy, wailed half the night; we'd never sleep if Melanie weren't considerate enough to rock her in the downstairs playroom with the door shut.

Anxiety and rage fought for primacy. I pressed my lips together until I gained enough control to stay quiet.

He took off his glasses and peered at me with concern.

"I didn't say you should drop out. I'm just looking at the practicalities. We didn't plan this. I'm not mad, at least not at you! But damn that manufacturer. No warnings came in that box, right?" he asked for the hundredth time. "Not one?"

We'd discussed the fallibility of my diaphragm until I never wanted to hear the words birth control failure again. When Guthrie suggested filling it with water to see if there were any pinholes, I threw the thing out, burying the rubber deep inside the trash, and smashing the plastic clamshell case into tiny pink shards.

Guthrie's words became a cloud of noise as he explained how being unmarried had advantages. I could apply for and receive food stamps without a wedding ring! Maybe even welfare, he suggested. He pelted me with words. "All the research—"

"Welfare! My parents would kill me."

"Are they planning to feed and clothe the baby and us? If not, they don't get a vote."

"Why isn't the only vote mine?"

I waited for him to bellow. Instead, he looked at me with a patronizing patience that I found worse than any explosion.

Chapter 17

✱

Annabel

Scary Habits of Welfare Workers

Guthrie ignored my protests, bringing up his food-stamps-welfare idea at the next house meeting. As we argued amid the smoke of a thousand cigarettes, we drew gender lines even more sharply than during the Great Monogamy Debate.

The men considered going on welfare a juicy way to stick it to a broken system, while Suze, Diantha, Melanie, Roxanne, and I knew pretending to be poor disrespected women in real need.

Diantha filibustered about how the house arrangement wouldn't weather an inspection—nor did she want to be scrutinized by the system. The names on the deed were hers and Chuck's, not ours. Chuck changed his vote when she pointed this out, and welfare went down.

Food stamps, however, received a thumbs-up.

Everyone agreed there was no need to mention this to any of our parents.

Wyatt made sure to mention that his precious co-op accepted food stamps.

Et tu, Wyatt?

I almost threw up when Wyatt put in his two cents. Of course, everything made me want to vomit these days, but no matter how much everyone tried to convince me that I deserved food stamps, the idea made me shudder. Nobody had forced precious Melanie to register for food stamps.

Wyatt and I had avoided each other's eyes since I announced my pregnancy, but now I sent him a giant side-eye of *Fuck you, buddy.*

The Mission Hill welfare office, housed in a long, faceless gray building resembling a jail, echoed with the footsteps of angry women. Hours spent waiting in line, filling out forms, and answering questions designed to make me feel like complete crap for needing help left me hungry, thirsty, and humiliated.

The Department of Welfare should have just perched a crown of thorns on my head and finished the deed. Whether we wanted food stamps or welfare, they questioned us with shivs. Every hurdle and hoop required to receive a few food stamp dollars seemed designed for maximum degradation.

"Are you looking for work? Daily?"

"Are you living with the father of your baby?"

"Is he looking for work?"

"Are you planning on using contraception after your baby is born?"

Without coaching in what to say, I plucked my answers from the air.

"Do you agree to HLA testing if we or the father question paternity?"

Of course, I said, having no idea what HLA meant, but I almost hoped they'd insist on the test and end my worried questions. More likely, just asking the question represented the latest budget-cutting measure brilliance from the government: thinning the herd through mortification. And what if the answer was Wyatt? I could throw up at the thought of the troubles that would bring.

I could throw up anyway as I shuffled from line to line. For the first time, I experienced the smallest measure of the humiliation heaped on the Black people of Mississippi attempting to vote. I understood with my heart, not just my brain, how those with even a fraction of power use it to keep people powerless.

My cheeks blazed as I walked out of the municipal building on Tremont Street. *Fuck you, Guthrie.* I begged for food stamps while he marched around the halls of Harvard wearing his badge of brains.

Exhaustion and a case of hunger shakes almost overcame me as I walked down the granite steps, wooed by Mike's Donuts from across the street. I'd taken note of the bins filled with muffins, doughnuts, and crullers visible through the steamy windows earlier. Melanie and Diantha would call the treats baby poison.

One, just one, would be my reward, I'd promised myself, for whatever lay ahead and for suffering the daily doses of brewer's yeast and yogurt Diantha foisted on me. Maybe I'd have two doughnuts. Perhaps a doughnut and a cruller. Images of a sugar-crusted cruller had kept me going while lying through answer after answer.

"No, I do not live with the baby's father."

"Yes, I do look for work daily."

Guthrie had promised they wouldn't check on this, that they used that energy to catch women receiving full benefits, not food stamps alone.

"And when did you become an expert on the habits of welfare workers?" I asked.

"Trust me," he said.

So, I did, as I had no other choice. My inconvenient truth about Wyatt kept me from wanting more confrontation with Guthrie.

Only once! We'd only slept together that one time!

I soothed myself with that number daily.

Once.

Statistics promised Wyatt would not be the father.

"No, the baby's father does not provide support."

The questioning woman, prim in her lacy blouse, had looked at me with wary eyes, cocking her head as though reading through my skull to uncover my plan to sell my food stamps on the corner to buy heroin before turning a trick or two.

"What should I wear?" I'd asked Suze and Roxanne that morning. They went through my closet with an eye toward proper welfare wear and then, brooking no complaints, agreed on the still-unworn maternity top my mother had sent—the pink cotton maternity smock my mother designed and sewed just for me.

Blue, white, and deep pink bunnies taunted me as they danced across the fabric.

I wore the bunnies to Welfare, letting them swing across my not-yet-very-big-at-all belly, and now I crossed the street to bring them to Mike's Donuts.

Older men and mothers with small children filled the tables at Mike's. I ordered my long-awaited cruller with a cup of tea. Coffee nauseated me these days, yet I missed drinking the stuff, angry every morning as I averted my eyes from Guthrie's cup.

"Thanks," I said to the frazzled woman who slid a steaming white mug and paper plate across the counter.

I looked around at the filled tables, choosing a seat next to a woman breaking off chunks of a doughnut and placing it in front of a toddler. I imagined Diantha snatching it away to replace it with some wooden baked goods she concocted. The woman and I smiled in recognition—her already a prisoner of motherhood and me on my way.

I removed the *Boston Globe* from my shoulder bag and opened the *Help Wanted* section, trying not to groan as I glanced down at "Women Wanted."

Miss Curley at Valle's in Newton offered a cascade of waitressing opportunities.

The woman across from me grinned. "You're looking for a job? Now?"

I covered my stomach with a hand. "Does it show?"

She tipped her head at my shirt. "Normal women don't wear that many rabbits."

"I'm looking more passively than actively."

"What in the world does that mean? I'm Mary, by the way. And this is Valentina." She pointed to a woman placing two cups of coffee on the round Formica table.

"Annabel." I smiled at the two friendliest faces I'd seen in hours.

Just looking at Valentina's freckled, round face made me less heavy-hearted. She reminded me of Pippi Longstocking if Pippi had morphed into an adult Black woman. Mary's short blond hair also framed a freckled face, though a fair and angled one.

"Finding work while pregnant, passively or not, would be pretty hard," Valentina said. "You're hardly a boss's dream."

"I can't go back to school next year. I'm having this baby in October, so I need a job I might be able to do for a few months."

"What sort of job do you think that might be?"

I shrugged. "Color me clueless. What's available for women without training or a degree?"

"Cleaning houses?" Mary asked. "Stripping?"

I pointed to my stomach. "Is there a niche for pregnant strippers?"

Mary picked up her mug and tipped it to Valentina's. "Can't help you with the stripping, but we have an underground cleaning service. Though if you tip them off," she pointed to the Welfare building, "we will have to kill you."

Chapter 18

❋

Annabel

Tiny Wild Beasts

Mary and Valentina couldn't spare any cleaning clients, but they sent me mending from the women they worked for. My hands ached from the previous night's stitching as I crept out of bed, Guthrie snoring, praying that everyone in the house still slept at five. The longer I lived in Puddingstone, the more time alone became gold. I tiptoed past Melanie and Wyatt's room, not wanting to wake the ever-squalling Poppy.

Dear Lord, please let our baby be quiet! I couldn't imagine Guthrie pacing to quiet an infant as uncomplainingly as Wyatt.

Sunrise brought a sweet, cool breeze on this last day of May. Masses of pink Lady Slipper growing under the oak tree soothed me as I carried my weak tea to the porch. I missed the tulips. During one of their wild pack runs, the kids had trampled every single one.

I planned to meet Valentina and Mary at Mike's that day. Guthrie didn't respect what he called *your doughnut shop buddies* anywhere as much as he regarded Roxanne, Diantha, and Suze. Just how he pronounced Mary and Valentina's names made his judgment obvious, as though I spent my time at a Tupperware party.

None of the men in the house would admit their snobbishness.

They wanted—desperately, fervently, with almost a sexual longing—to make friends with their local neighbors, but at the softball field, not the welfare office. Unlike the guys drinking and slapping each other's backs after running bases, Diantha, Melanie, and Suze had formed a playgroup with the neighborhood moms, taking turns watching each other's children.

Watching each other's children never earned the political respect of men throwing balls.

The playgroup had met at the house yesterday. Fourteen kids packed the downstairs playroom. Tumbling block towers forced me to dodge them as I weaved to the kitchen. Rather than cute preschool freedom in action, I saw tiny wild beasts.

I tried to imagine my child screaming her head off or crashing into our knees as though adults were no more than moving furniture, but I couldn't see it. My visualization brought only a sleeping baby in the wooden cradle built by Wyatt, the one that Wyatt and Melanie would pass on to Guthrie and me.

Despite burying my head in my pillow to drown out Poppy's nightly wailing wakeups, I held tight to denial. Not my baby!

After one more breath of spring air, I tiptoed back to the kitchen, put away the dishes piled in a haphazard mess in the drainer, and then washed and dried my teacup. If I hurried, I could get the first shower, thus gratefully skipping the step of scrubbing out the hairs and dirt left by the previous bather.

The relative quiet of Mike's Donuts calmed me, as did the company of Valentina and Mary—my friends were entangled in the center of Mission Hill activism, though Mary was the quietest rabble-rouser in the neighborhood. Valentina and Mary brought me great stories of political and cultural struggles, ones Guthrie had never heard. And then, of course, there were the doughnuts.

According to Mary, third-generation Mission Hill long-timers didn't need us new people to teach them about dissent. These people had stayed despite race-baiting realtors working their asses off to get people like Mary to sell their homes and move to Whiter areas of Boston and the surrounding suburbs.

It was those remaining native Mission Hillers who made room for the new people—sometimes grudgingly—whether those moving in were expatriates from Alabama, like Valentina, or college do-gooders like me. They folded us into their bars and softball teams, albeit with, as Mary admitted, plenty of racial, ethnic, and hippie jokes and eye-rolling behind our backs.

As the local men took turns buying rounds at the bars, we treated each other to Mike's baked goods. Valentina plunked a cinnamon twist in front of me and a jelly doughnut before Mary. I liked trying a new kind every week; Mary never veered from her choice. Stability mattered to her. Her husband painted houses, but they turned to food stamps to feed their six children when the work dried up. When their funds disappeared, Pete moved out, wink-wink, and Mary applied for welfare.

Of course, welfare checks alone never got anyone through hard times. When the bad weeks hit, Mary's nails got raggedy; her chapped pale hands turned rough and red from the Spic and Span she used to scrub other people's houses.

Valentina's husband had died early in the Vietnam War, leaving her with three young sons. Her friendship with Mary grew from sharing cleaning clients until they became best friends cast in iron when Mary rented Valentina her downstairs apartment. Seeing pale, freckled Mary and brown, freckled Valentina sitting on their shared porch drinking their nightly whiskey and soda disguised in Mary's stoneware coffee mugs became as ubiquitous as their kids shouting as they played ball.

"Take a look at this." Mary shoved a rolled-up paper across the table.

I smoothed out a mimeographed flyer. Handwritten angry slashes of letters read:

Join WAW (Women for Adequate Welfare)!

Thursday, June 1st at 3 p.m.

We are tired of having our checks cut off without warning or investigation because of malicious gossip and lying officials!

We are tired of hostile social workers and supervisors!

Join us at the Mattapan Welfare Office.

I bit into the doughnut as I read the flyer, almost shuddering with pleasure as the sugar and buttery flakes hit my tongue. Puddingstone meals consisted of cardboard, liver, and vegetables these days. Wyatt, Diantha, and Suze foisted *Let's Have Healthy Children* by Adelle Davis menus on the entire house, with particular attention given to the nutrition renegades—me, Guthrie, Quinn, and Roxanne. The four of us snuck out for hamburgers and loudly passed M&Ms to each other during the house meetings.

"Another demonstration?" I asked.

"*Another* one?" Mary pressed her fingers to her lips for a moment and then took a deep breath, using her 'Are you an idiot' voice. "We should demonstrate every day the way they treat us. We should scream at those shitty bureaucrats and smug politicians all day long. You should bow down to WAW, Annabel."

"Did you join yet?" Valentina looked over her owlish glasses at me.

I avoided the question by biting another hunk of the cinnamon twist.

Women for Adequate Welfare never rose to the same level of importance as SDS—not for me, not at Puddingstone. Mary and Valentina revved me up about WAW, and then Chuck and Guthrie pushed my concerns away once I was home. They waxed on about attending to more meaningful work. Nothing else registered for them, and they wanted the same for all of us. End the war; end the draft. They gave more respect to Grady's campaign to replace cars with bikes than they did WAW.

I cared about Vietnam. And sure, I respected bikes. Then, when I sat with Mary and Valentina, I saw the war at home, where the guns—virtual and real—were aimed at poor women. Women in totality, of course, but poor women most of all. And most significantly, non-White poor women.

When I paid for groceries with food stamps, resentful customers stared at me with judgmental eyes. Women on welfare and women who used food stamps were constant and unprotected targets. Guthrie wouldn't use them, claiming that some mysterious supermarket beings could construe it as fraud. He had to protect himself! Wasn't he going to be a lawyer, after all?

I stopped asking him to shop with them and dropped the topic; mostly, I thought his words were bull. Where was his future lawyerness when he'd marched on Washington?

A sharp burn of shame overcame me for having not signed up for WAW yet. People working in the welfare office looked at me as though I smelled like garbage, the same as they did with all the other women, but I knew my stint with food stamps was temporary. A messed-up realization hit me. I might sympathize with the other women standing in line, but I stood apart from them in my heart, considering myself a visitor from a better place. One with a lawyer-to-be almost-husband who came from money. One who'd grown up with everything she ever needed.

I played at being poor.

"I'll mail in my registration today."

"Yes, you will," Mary nodded at the done deal and took a giant bite of her second doughnut. For a tiny woman, she consumed an enormous amount of food.

"Don't worry. I'm practically at the post office right now."

"Whoa! It's not that easy. Do you take food stamps? Do you complain about the mean folk at welfare? Signing up in support isn't enough. You're coming with us to Mattapan," Mary said. Pack for overnight. We'll probably be sitting in."

"Unless they give right into our demands that afternoon." Valentina chuckled. "I guess that will be right after they serve us a nice lunch of filet mignon."

Chapter 19

❋

Annabel

We're All Ma'am to You

Guthrie drove us to the welfare office on the first Friday in June. The gray clouds blanketing the sky matched his mood, his worry filling the car. I sat in the front passenger seat of the old Ford Falcon, one of our two shared Puddingstone cars, while Mary and Valentina were in the back. The configuration felt weird, though I couldn't imagine any other seating arrangement.

He pulled into the open bus stop before the dirty, yellow-bricked welfare office on Blue Hill Avenue. Carved above the door, I read the exact foreboding words chiseled into the Mission Hill Welfare building.

CITY OF BOSTON
OVERSEERS OF THE
PUBLIC WELFARE

"Here we are." Guthrie turned to me and lowered his voice as though that could prevent Mary and Valentina from hearing him. "Are you sure about this?"

"Are you directing that to all of us or just your wife?" Mary asked.

I turned around and glared at her. "We're not married."

"That's a whole other discussion, huh?" Valentina laughed. "Makes it easier to get welfare, doesn't it?"

"We're not getting welfare," Guthrie said. "Just food stamps."

Now I glared at him. My cheeks burned at the insult he didn't know he'd given. "*We're* not getting anything," I said. "I'm the one standing in line at grocery stores."

"You're also the one who's over five months pregnant."

"We're not off to war, Guthrie. You can hold off on the worried guy stuff." Mary opened the car door.

"Why don't I go in with you?" Guthrie squared his shoulders, entering full political mode.

Valentina put her hands out in a no-can-do gesture. "Sorry. Invitation only."

I squeezed Guthrie's arm, annoyed yet touched by his concern. "We'll be fine. I promise."

"Do you have enough to eat? Read?"

I held up a green canvas backpack. "I have everything I need."

He drew me in for a kiss and an extralong hug.

"For Christ's sake," Mary said. "She's not going to war. Worst case, she'll get a sore ass."

Guthrie squeezed my hand and whispered. "Stay safe."

I pressed back, slipped inside, and joined the others milling around the lobby. There were mothers with babies and students, evident by their backpacks. The crowd skewed female and non-White.

Snacks covered a card table someone had dragged into the space. Taped to the wall above the food, a cardboard sign with block letters read:

WAW DEMANDS

1. No denial of aid based on hearsay evidence or malicious gossip. There must be investigations before checks are cut off.
2. Removal of police from all welfare offices.
3. Welfare workers must be available every morning to talk with recipients—not just one day a week.

4. Welfare workers must respect clients and treat them as equal human beings. Workers must have the power to make decisions quickly without running to supervisors.

5. There must be boards set up in each office who can act on emergency demands and policy statements without waiting for the long appeal process.

6. Welfare mothers must be appointed on all policy-making boards for welfare.

7. All mothers should be able to save as much as they can for their children's education—and each dollar should be matched by the welfare department—so that our children won't be on welfare too.

8. Mothers should be able to earn $85 a month and to keep 70% of the amount above $85. There should be no deductions of this money mothers earn.

9. There should be a campaign to change the image of the welfare system. 99% of recipients are honest and responsible.

The youngest participants, especially the young men, sat cross-legged on the floor, but most of the women had pulled the mismatched seating scattered around the lobby to a central point. I counted about thirty folks.

Special treatment for being pregnant seemed unlikely, or at least at a premium, as three other women displayed protruding bellies, all but one larger than mine.

The three of us claimed chairs and then surrounded the seats with our survival items: books, magazines, and cards. Mary's overstuffed knitting bag surprised me. I'd button-holed her into a softball type, having watched her play in women's pickup games atop the hill.

And, of course, there was food. We lugged a cooler with egg salad sandwiches and cut carrots along with the apples, peanut butter, and Chips Ahoy.

Laid out on the community table was a cornucopia of foods forbidden to me at home.

Sleeves of Oreos!

Five different brands of potato chips!

And, be still my heart, Bugles Corn Chips!

Seeing my favorite childhood snack induced a pregnancy craving so intense that I almost tore the ugly red and yellow Bugles box open. How many hours had my sisters and I spent putting them on our fingertips, pretending the snacks were our long nails, and then biting them off one by one?

I placed a wistful finger on the unopened box.

"Go ahead. There's no time like when you're pregnant to say yes." The woman beside me smiled and put a giant bag of apples on the blue card table. "I feel like I'm being let out of church and straight into hell."

I patted my protruding belly. "I guess I'll be taking this innocent down also."

The woman laughed and rubbed her stomach, though hers was flat. "With you. Though I'm not showing yet. And yeah, I know I gotta eat plenty of these." She tapped the corner of the overflowing apple bag. "But man, I want those." She sighed and pointed at the object of her desire, almost sighing at a box of Twinkies.

"Oh, my god!" I stared at the picture of cylinders of spongy yellow cake with bright white cream oozing out. "I will if you will."

We smiled like naughty schoolgirls and plucked out a wrapped Twinkie each. Before peeling off the cellophane, I tipped mine toward her and toasted. "To being very bad."

"Back at you." She peeled off the wrapper and sniffed the treat. "Mmm. Notes of caramel and vanilla with a trace of radical protest."

"I'm Annabel."

"Rochelle."

Rochelle's tiny body appeared more like a child's than likely to hold a child, but her knowing round eyes belied any hint of immaturity. "This your first time at a WAW thing?" she asked.

I nodded. "Yes. You?"

"Veteran. What brings you to Blue Hill Ave.?" Rochelle spoke like a native, saying *Ave.* instead of *Avenue*.

"First, my friends over there." I pointed at Mary and Valentina in a group with three other women, gesturing with their hands as though disciplining the words flying from their mouths. "They brought me along. Second is being considered a criminal for getting food stamps. You?"

Rochelle finished the last of her Twinkie and wiped her mouth with a tissue before answering. "I grew up here. Now I see my friends who need help treated as ignorant criminals, not even smart ones. My husband and I live in Cambridge, but this is still home. I teach art in a school nearby."

She tilted her head toward a small yellow-clad woman in the corner. "That's my mom, Josephine, but she likes to be called Josie. Fighting White power is a family business, though Mom can't be all hate-the-Whites-all-the-time. My husband's White."

"Mine too," I said. "We've got something in common."

Rochelle laughed. "I'm planning to like you."

"I'll try not to screw that up."

The women and the smattering of men spent the following hours eating, gossiping, and arguing about politics as we moved from our core groups, forming and reforming into new gatherings. As staff walked through the lobby to leave, we waved and wished them polite wishes of "Have a good evening."

One stomping woman, wearing the expression of an angry bulldog, sneered as she headed to the door. "I hear a whole lot of noise for a silent sit-in."

"Peaceful doesn't mean silent, ma'am," Mary said. "This is a peaceful vigil."

Bulldog lady shook her head in disgust and left the building to the sound of rising laughter as we toasted Mary with our Styrofoam cups of juice and soda.

A fiftyish man, overwhelmed by his rumpled brown suit, the last to come out from the inner sanctum, counted us aloud, watching as though taking snapshots with his eyes. He locked the door to the office, rattling the doorknob ten times more than needed to ensure the lock held. "Your little games aren't going to work, ladies. Trust me. Director Crane won't be coming."

Rochelle's mother, Josephine, tipped her head and smiled. "Eventually, he will. And when he does, we'll be here."

Brown Suit smiled the nastiest possible smile at Josephine. "Not if I have anything to say about it."

Josephine, small, muscled, and exuding surety, crossed her arms. "In the end, you won't."

"Won't what?" He sniffed and then ran a finger under his nose.

"You won't have anything to say about it," Josephine said.

"Watch out for yourself, Miss. And while you're at it, watch your damn mouth."

Rochelle joined her mother and the group leader, Billie Johnson. Where Josephine appeared to weigh no more than one hundred pounds, Billie towered above everyone in the room and outweighed most of us with pure muscle.

"Does my mother look like a *miss*, sir? She's ma'am to you." Rochelle swept an arm around the room. "We're *all* ma'am to you. Well, except them," she said, gesturing to our male fellow protesters.

"Keep it up." Brown Suit squinted his eyes, perhaps to get one more snapshot. "Just keep it up."

Chapter 20

✺

Annabel

School Yourself

We stayed the night. Shocking nobody, the director of welfare never showed.

I woke before dawn. Who could sleep past sunrise while slumbering in hardwood chairs or sleeping bags on the floor? Lucky me—the command had allocated camping cots to those pregnant or over seventy. The cots, canvas stretched over metal rods, fit the definition of cold comfort.

After visiting the ladies' room—which a group had scrubbed the previous night after discovering how far it stood from their standards—I stumbled to the food table, where I built a breakfast of peanut butter, crackers, and an apple.

Mary rose and nodded. "Coffee?" she mumbled.

I shook my head in the negative.

"Damn. I can't be responsible for my actions without caffeine. Pray there's Coke left."

We'd already put the place back in order when the welfare office workers trickled in. Some offered an imperceptible nod of what looked like support; others sneered. Most avoided our eyes, refusing to acknowledge our chirpy greetings.

Clients took our flyers, most furtively. Questions from the braver women broke the monotony.

Boredom mixed with a sense of unease as hours passed without any sight of the director. I huddled with Valentina, Mary, and Rochelle, the four of us forming a clique. Josephine stopped by while completing her room rounds, staying to watch Mary's winning streak as we played poker for Oreos.

"Guthrie must be going crazy," I said. "Maybe I can use a phone to call home."

Josie grunted in disbelief. "Are you kidding? They're only letting us access the bathrooms because they're afraid of what we might do if they didn't."

"Yeah. A bunch of animals like us." Valentina tugged at the bottom of her blue cotton smock. "Even a pregnant White girl like you won't be allowed to touch their phone."

"That's not what I meant." Layers of sweat popped no matter how much I wiped my face with Guthrie's handkerchief.

"Sure, sugar," Valentina said. "But you *are* White. You don't see the barriers screaming at me."

"School yourself more. I have this conversation with my husband every other day. I love him, but his Whiteness protects him more than he knows," Rochelle said.

Embarrassment covered me, but I recognized the cold truth. I couldn't claim to understand what Valentina, Rochelle, Josephine, or any other Black man or woman faced, certainly not because of the one ride I'd taken on the Freedom Train in Mississippi.

Our vigil crowd climbed to nearly fifty as we allowed in more people. The stifling air thickened, the closeness and rising heat increased, the overripe fruit became more noticeable, and our need for showers increased.

Folks passed food and drink orders out the window to kids willing to run to the G&G Deli if we tipped enough.

I fanned a now limp *Redbook* magazine, hoping to relieve the heat.

"What's the next step if this director doesn't come?" I asked nobody and everybody, not caring if I showed my novice status, finally schooling myself in the business of a takeover, a business I'd always left to Guthrie.

Valentina laced her fingers. "The meaning of vigil is waiting them out."

"The food keeps coming, so no worries." Mary pointed to a bag emblazoned with the Simco's logo being pushed through a window by a young kid. Hot dog grease darkened the paper.

Now, with all the forbidden sweet and salty in the world available, I longed for a big plate of Diantha's stir-fried vegetables.

The doors leading to the central area of the welfare offices opened. The officious man who'd confronted us the previous night, wearing the same baggy brown suit and holding a battered briefcase in his right hand, gestured with his left for us to stand back as though we held rifles. The women peering out from behind him tugged at heat-wrinkled blouses.

"Okay, ladies. It's time to pack up. The office is closing for the weekend." He nodded at the list of demands taped to the wall. We'll pass on your ideas."

Josephine rose from a chair and joined Billie Johnson at the door. "What's your name?" Billie asked.

The man hesitated, perhaps worried he'd be the next one called out in a WAW flyer.

Billie put out her hand. "Billie Johnson."

He returned the handshake with apparent reluctance. "Larry. Larry Malone."

"We're not leaving, Mr. Malone. Not until we have a chance to talk to the director."

"I'm afraid that won't be happening, Miss Johnson."

"Mrs. Johnson," she said.

"Excuse me?"

"Mrs. Johnson. As in married to Mr. Johnson

"Sorry." He cleared his throat. "That won't be happening, Mrs. Johnson."

"Why not?"

"You'll have to take my word. My staff is leaving, but I'll wait while you all clear out."

Billie nodded assent and turned to Josephine, who brought out an oversized canvas bag." You can pack up after my staff leaves," Larry Malone said.

WAW folks closed ranks by the door, blocking the entrance. Josephine carried the bag to the door and removed a thick chain. Two women looped it through the door handles and snapped a giant brass lock.

"I'm sorry, Mr. Malone," Billie said. "But you've just invited your staff to join us for the rest of the vigil. Perhaps you can give the director one more call."

After heated words, Malone led the welfare workers back to their desks or wherever they gathered.

We spend the next hour in a quiet, steamy-hot tension.

Seventy minutes later, an amplified voice blared from outside. "Director Crane just drove up. Unlock the entrance."

Billie went to an open window.

The growing crowd spilled onto the street when the sidewalk couldn't contain it.

"We prefer to speak in public," Billie called.

"If you want to talk to the director, let him in," a short White man in shirtsleeves insisted.

Billie leaned out. "This is a community matter. I'll be coming out with representatives."

The man held up his bullhorn again. "Open the doors."

Something crashed from outside.

Three workers from the office ran to the windows. A bulky woman wearing a sloppy ponytail pushed Billie over, leaned out, and shrieked to the street. "Help! A social worker is dying from a heart attack.

Josephine looked at Billie. "I'll see what's going on."

Billie nodded. "We're checking on the situation," she yelled out.

Hulking policemen rushed up with bullhorns. "We're coming in," one roared. "Stand back."

Bystanders blocked the police officers coming toward us. Screams and swears roared as cops and community folk collided.

Officers kicked in the windows before Josephine or Billie could order the chains removed. One headed straight for Billie, smashing the butt of his gun on her head. She crumpled, blood streaming. An older cop raised his club and whacked a young man to his knees, continuing to beat him after he fell.

I covered my stomach and backed away, flattening myself against a wall as police poured in. The cops pushed aside anyone they could reach, throwing Mary to the floor as they raced with bolt cutters toward the door.

Seeing Rochelle caught in the melee, tangled up in the crowd, I grabbed her arm. The two of us huddled in a corner behind a table.

Nobody fought or struggled; police swung their clubs, snapped the door chain, and entered full riot mode, pulling those in the vigil and welfare workers out the door without regard. Only the man in the brown suit walked out unimpeded.

Valentina hurried to Mary, bringing her to where Rochelle, I, and now Josephine stood.

"Follow me." Josephine opened a far back door and led us down a set of musty stairs leading to a basement corridor. Dirty yellow linoleum brought us to swinging doors that opened to an alley filled with trash cans.

We snaked down the narrow passage, turned left, and followed the path until reaching a street-level exit at the end of the municipal building.

With one hand in Rochelle's and the other on my stomach, we trailed Josephine as she wove through the chaotic crowd. Sirens screeched as police cars and ambulances careened down the road.

I stopped momentarily and stared as people poured out of houses and stores, emptying trash cans and throwing debris at police wielding clubs and pointing guns.

Mary turned and glared at me. "Stop rubbernecking and move!"

I spun around and kept going, bringing up the rear with Rochelle. "Where are we going?"

Rochelle panted as we ran. "My aunt lives about ten blocks away. Just be glad I'm pregnant. Worrying over her kids is the only reason Mom ever runs from trouble."

I covered my stomach with my hand.

Chapter 21

✸

Annabel

SEPTEMBER 1966

The Women's Section

Three months later, on September 4, 1966, a day shiny with the bluest, brightest, clearest sky ever to hold up the sun, I fell in love and learned the terror of a connection so engulfing your center explodes and obliterates you, rearranging every cell into this new being you've become: a mother.

Ivy became my drug of choice. My guts twisted when she cried. I wished I could graft her onto me, not wanting to let go for even a moment those first few weeks. Only Ivy-centered goals registered: soothe her, feed her, clean her, hold her.

All the terrifying paternity possibilities that haunted me disappeared as I convinced myself that the pregnancy math was on my side.

I inhaled Ivy's otherworldly milky scent, the newborn fragrance that one can only remember, never replicate. Sweet newness radiated in an aura of miraculous olfactory molecules.

Possibly, that alone explained those who birthed baby after baby.

Maybe the inevitable loss of infatuation with her scent explained my current state six months later, stuck inside by sleet, diapers, and the impossibility of steering a baby carriage down rutted streets in the snowy early March Boston brought.

I was no longer in thrall to Ivy's every scent molecule—though my oft-bathed baby smelled better than most whiffs of Puddingstone. All odors overwhelmed me: onions frying, rice cooking, dirty children, diapers, fresh joints, and stale weed, weed I couldn't use, seemed embedded in everything. Homemade herbal shampoo, pine needles, flowers, the vanilla Melanie dabbed on daily, sweet sandalwood, and patchouli incense also blanketed me.

Even the pleasing smells wearied me.

I was pregnant again.

Morning sickness, caring for a baby while growing another, and ten million other things wore me to a nub of irritated fatigue. Guthrie rarely stood still long enough to receive my full range of complaints, making me even testier. Ten minutes before, I'd shoved Ivy at him, grabbed the newspaper, and locked myself in the tiny downstairs bathroom: the only guarantee of private space in our house.

As I considered the possibility of hiding forever, I studied Confidential Chat, a popular column in the women's section of the *Boston Globe*, made up of readers' opinions, recipes, and household hints. As I read the same letter for the third time, I worried about my daughter's future. Who would write these two sentences? I grit my teeth once more at how the *Boston Globe* confined what they considered female" issues to the ghetto of the "women's section."

I studied the page as though the answers might float from the newsprint, the complaints of this woman sharing her beliefs simultaneously mesmerizing, baffling, and enraging me:

Satisfaction in doing housework is gone—this is why women are bored at home. Hanging out sheets whiter than anyone else's once made you the envy of the neighborhood, but everyone has bright laundry now.

Was she angry that better products had democratized the ability to have dazzling sheets? Did she miss how being the queen of laundry in her imagined competition of flapping sheets on lines?

No one pats you on the back for having the shiniest floor— it's no credit to you with all the detergents, waxes, floor scrubbers, and polishes available! Remember when each woman in the neighborhood could claim her role? Mrs. J ironed smooth as glass; Mrs. G's mustard pickles puckered every mouth! But with all the packages and cleansers available, so goes our enthusiasm for our chores! Glory and competition have gone by the board.

And the *Boston Globe* placed this crap smack in the middle of the page.

A surge of nausea rose. I threw the newspaper aside and fell to my knees in front of the toilet. After heaving up almost nothing, I collapsed cross-legged on the tile.

Guthrie banged on the door as though I'd murdered someone. "Are you done? I'm late!"

Ivy screamed from hunger from the other side of the wood. Or wetness. Or whatever the hell. Did babies get bored? Existentially angry? God knows I did.

I remained still, a necessity until all danger of vomiting passed. "Put up water for tea. And toast a piece of bread. Super-dark."

"I gotta leave, Annabel!"

"You can't make a fucking cup of tea and toast?" I hated him.

"I'll put the water up and bread in the toaster. Then I'm putting Ivy in the playpen. Do you hear me?"

I said nothing.

He clattered around the kitchen; soon, the front door slammed.

Ivy bellowed as though her world had ended.

I struggled up from my sentry post at the toilet, counting how many days remained until the end of this new pregnancy, desperate for every minute. I dreaded giving birth, petrified at the prospect of caring for a newborn while chasing a fourteen-month-old.

I wanted to bargain for more than the eight months left to carry this baby inside my womb, this period when mothering required only biology.

I wished I'd never believed in any form of birth control. Stupid, stupid me, thinking breastfeeding would prevent pregnancy.

I wished I'd never had sex.

I longed for freedom from Ivy's screeching as much as I'd yearned to be cemented to her before.

Freedom and autonomy never seemed paramount until it disappeared.

I held my baby close, worried my thoughts might poison my milk.

Replete and now content, Ivy gurgled when I placed her on the fuzzy blanket protecting her from the none-too-clean carpet—a carpet wearing the constant collective grime of sixteen people—a rug that only became debris-free when I dragged the fucking vacuum out.

I should have said "ten thousand" when Diantha asked where I stood on a one to ten cleanliness scale. Now, I seethed and swore as people tossed crusty pans into the sink as though magic cleaning fairies floated down from heaven to scrub them.

Guthrie explained in excruciating political detail why it didn't matter. Coming up with politicized arguments about grimy wool carpets came as easy to him as starting the car and escaping from me, Ivy, the mucky bathrooms, and the cigarette smoke I batted away from our baby.

Escaping cigarettes. Yet another useless endeavor.

My battles had turned ludicrously personal. I'd moved from battling for voting rights, marching to bringing the troops home, and fighting for adequate welfare to begging for help changing diapers as I battled nausea.

Almost four-year-old Leo wandered into the playroom from his afternoon nap. The other kids were all at various forms of daycare; he'd refused to attend his. I imagined Ivy kicking her heels at leaving me, and the doors to my jail tightened.

Suze's typewriter clattered upstairs as Leo followed me, as though Suze had clipped catnip for children to my jeans to ensure her freedom to write.

Plucking a solution for time, I knelt before him, staring into his determined little face. "Keep Ivy happy for thirty minutes, and I'll read *Busy, Busy Town*."

Leo's eyes disappeared into his cheeks with his huge grin. Adults hated reading the billion-word book aloud as much as the kids adored hearing it. I grabbed a timer near the playpen and wound it to ding in half an hour. He'd recently entered a rule-following stage; he'd watch the minutes click by as he waved lumpy hand-crocheted dolls in front of Ivy.

I carried a drippy metal watering can from one spider plant to another. Full-grown lush plants, delicate seedlings, and limp cuttings hung from hooks and shelves everywhere, chipping paint, staining wood, and stealing my attention and time.

Guthrie had bought me two colossal spider plants early in my pregnancy with Ivy. Now, such a profusion of baby spiders hung from the ground-zero plants that our sad mama spiders, leached of chlorophyll, seemed about to give up life for their future plant babies.

I overidentified with my spiders, imagining myself as a dried shell once our second baby fought its way out. Guthrie thought me crazy when I told him, but I knew pieces of my mind littered Beth Israel's maternity ward.

My likelihood of finishing school felt remote. Puddingstone's under-ten-year-old population would soon reach seven. I rubbed my belly. Adults: ten, children: seven weren't terrific odds.

We shared childcare in haphazard ways. Suze used a nursery school and me for her out-of-the-house time. When Diantha needed time, she took her kids to the drop-in babysitting center in the sneaker factory where Chuck worked. Melanie appeared determined to keep Poppy in a backpack forever, dragging her to the daycare center where she worked, which welcomed bringing babies to work.

As Suze had warned, the men called their time with the children "babysitting."

Brown tips at the end of the baby spider plant curled in. When the tiny knobs formed on the underside of the baby, I planted them in new little pots and then hung them, where they'd wait for *their* babies to come and produce the next generation. And so on. The circle of life would smother me as it did them.

Caring for the plants had become my persona. At first, I liked being considered Annabel with the green thumb, but soon I also became Annabel good at making soup, scrubbing floors, and good with children—all bullshit. I wasn't gifted and beloved with the children, not even in the same stratosphere as Melanie, a natural magician of motherhood. My day-to-day cooking registered as adequate.

I would admit to deserving an A+ in cleaning.

But I was the youngest, least employed, and least matriculated, so it became convenient to mythologize me as Mary Poppins.

I plucked the final spider plant shoot from the mother plant, walked to the trash, and buried the green baby. Deep. I wouldn't put it above Diantha to notice the stripey newborn's bright avocado color and fish it out, only to drop it in front of me later that day. Perhaps she'd call an emergency house meeting to hang me.

After the spider baby execution, I read to Leo while rocking Ivy. Never had my daughter fallen asleep without me holding her. When her eyes finally closed, I put my finger to my lips to keep Leo quiet, tiptoed to the crib, and lowered her to the small mattress.

Once back downstairs, I gathered the colored pencils I stashed in a kitchen drawer and dragged out the blue oak tag on which I'd drawn a grid. I'd hidden the stiff paper from the kids' grubby hands, placing it behind the piano, which the kids used as a pounding board.

I instituted many previous chore charts, but this would be my masterpiece.

No more spinning wheels that assigned tasks without follow-through; no more raggedy jokes of charts that the men in the house ignored like a kicked-off sneaker. Accountability, baby.

This system ran on points, with values allotted to each job. I stole the idea from *Ms.* Magazine and made it my own. Everyone chose their jobs—no more dreading dishwashing if that was one's nightmare—and completed their points due by Sunday night.

Scrubbing bathroom without a tub: 15 points.

Scrubbing bathrooms with tubs and showers: 20 points.

Shoveling snow under one foot deep: 20 points (with a point added for every six inches).

I stared at the number. Men rushed to shovel the snow. Such a brawny job! In the initial house meetings on the topic, they insisted on giving shoveling a higher score, the unspoken being that the chore required muscles! Stamina! Someone with a cock willing to work in the cold? What a hero!

After a moment of staring, I erased the 20 and replaced it with a 15, giving the men something to fight about where the woman could give in with grace. I wrote the names of everyone in the house across the top of the grid, then covered the oak tag with a plastic overlay on which we'd enter our points with a grease pencil, erase, and then repeat the next week, ad infinitum.

Everyone needed to complete chores that added up to eighty points per week. (The women wanted one hundred; the men sixty.)

I imagined Guthrie begging me to complete his points or him building a (clumsy) series of shelves, having learned the basics of carpentry from Wyatt and Quinn. Starting and finishing a massive project at the end of the week and wrapping up eighty points in one Sunday would be a male thing. I pictured Guthrie and Quinn hammering away, hanging shelf after shelf until our home looked like a bookstore.

Guthrie had tried to claim organizing and political work as a chore. Diantha had yelled, "Screw you."

I loved her for it.

During the previous week's house meeting, we'd hammered out job-point ratios as though attending the Geneva Convention. Eventually, the men deemed cooking meals as valuable as changing car oil but refused to consider adding childcare to the chart.

But we planned a surprise for our men.

I drew one final line and wrote *childcare*. Above, in the box value, I wrote *20 points per hour*.

The conversation that would ensue almost wrote itself.

Childcare. When the men saw the word and began steaming and pontificating, I'd plunk down a manifesto introducing childcare as a movement issue, a platform we'd finished at midnight the previous night while sitting around Valentina's kitchen.

Months earlier, eight of us had begun holding women's rights meetings: the Puddingstone women, plus Mary, Valentina, and Rochelle. We gathered at the only man-free house, Valentina's, where first we uncovered our scars, from rapes to the insults of segregated Want Ads to the daily torment born by Valentina and Rochelle as Black women.

We began by working on a women's manifesto.

For us. For our daughters. And for our sons.

We'd finalized our platform the last week, pregnant me drinking chamomile tea, which never quit tasting like honey-covered weeds, while the rest shared a bottle of our ever-ubiquitous Gallo Red Wine.

The government's thumb pressed on our throats. We couldn't even get bank credit without our husband's signature. Oh, wait! No husband? Tough luck for you.

Women were the designated scrubbers of men's toilet stains.

Childcare was the yoke we carried.

Rape in marriage wasn't rape.

Rape outside marriage was barely rape.

Illegal abortion accounted for an estimated 17 percent of all officially reported pregnancy-related deaths, and that number underestimated the truth by miles.

No more separating the personal and political. The personal *was* political.

Our declaration demanded that equality meant sharing household work and communal childcare. Each Puddingstone man would receive a mimeographed copy of our document, our manifesto. We considered our work poetry for a new day.

Surprise, guys!

We'd insisted women could do whatever men did. Fuck that, we'd declared at our meeting, high on wine, weed, and righteousness and a burgeoning belly full of surging hormones for me. Time to flip the script and have men step up and value cooking, cleaning, and burping as much as they worshipped political debate and softball.

If men never entered the damn kitchen, we'd never get out.

For the first time, we used politics as a weapon in our war at home. By distributing the manifesto, our men would come on board, or we'd publicly tag them as misogynists.

No more waiting in line for our turn.

Chapter 22

✤

Annabel

Did You Spend My Blouse Money?

"You paid what?" I asked.

Guthrie's new suit burned straight through my retinas to my brain. My words held the complaints of a thousand days of repressed self-righteousness, replete with self-pity and rage: I, who'd sacrificed, cleaned, cooked, and been his concubine while he'd pursued his law degree.

"Are you kidding with that question?" Guthrie turned to the right and left, admiring himself in the mirror from every angle.

I wanted to throw the Fisher Price van at him, hindered only by my position sitting on the bedroom floor, surrounded by the detritus of another day choked with kids. The tiny humans of Puddingstone—including our two-year-old Ivy and six-month-old Henry—spent their hours strewing possessions like drunken soldiers on their daily campaign to overtake their masters, us, their parents, and most especially the mothers, as we tried to corral and desavage them.

My mood lacked levity these days.

My fingers tightened on the plastic van. "Do I sound like I'm kidding?"

"We're living on the money from my parents. We owe them," Guthrie said.

I kept myself from shrinking as he swelled, readying for battle. "We owe them a suit?"

"What did you think I would wear to my cousin's wedding? Overalls?"

"I thought you'd wear the suit gathering dust in the closet. I didn't expect you to drop a hundred and fifty dollars at Brooks Brothers. I'm making a dress to wear."

"All you need for a dress is a yard of what? Silk? Velvet? You can hardly sew me a suit, right? Do you want me to wear my college graduation suit? That piece of shit? Are you nuts?"

"I'm not asking you to wear your great-grandfather's rags. Your graduation suit's still fine."

"Christ. That suit was secondhand when I bought it." Guthrie's face reddened further. He took off his glasses, a familiar gesture when he got furious. "Every penny we live on comes from my parents."

"Your parents' money—which they can damn well afford—barely covers our share of the mortgage and food. If I didn't sew like a pioneer woman—" I stopped. I hadn't been to the bank in over a week. "Did you spend my blouse money?"

Blouse money represented the million hours I spent embroidering the blouses I designed, made, and sold.

"*Your* blouse money? Since when do we have yours and mine? Do I call my parents' money *my* money?"

"You do when you march into Brooks Brothers without talking to me. Do you know how many pieces I sewed to pay for that suit?"

"This suit isn't just for the wedding. A Brooks Brothers appearance will get me through interviews that will change our lives." Guthrie squared his shoulders as he appreciated his reflection.

"What interviews?"

"Graduation is only two months away. I'm going to line up a slew of interviews with the top firms. And how I look is as important as my degree." His voice rose and deepened. "What's this inquisition about?"

I crossed my legs on the ancient rug Guthrie's parents had given us when they redecorated their Upper West Side apartment for the umpteenth time. "Aubusson," Penny had whispered as though the word meant something to me. I translated the hushed tone to mean "expensive." Now, I sat on Guthrie's parents' rug, listening to him parrot their words.

"Lower your voice. If you wake the kids, I will have to kill you. I'm talking about you spending the money I made, stitch-by-stitch, with these pinpricked fingers." I wiggled my fingers in illustration, grabbed a fabric remnant lying on the rug, and threw it at Guthrie. "Do you know how many blouses I had to embroider for you to buy that suit?"

After Henry's birth, I stopped repairing clothes for Mary and Valentina's clients and dug into the sewing skills that I'd learned from my mother to earn money from home. An upscale store in Beacon Hill loved offering handmade clothes by local artists, now including the one-of-a-kind creations on which I stitched *Annabel-Made* in bright purple and red on every tag.

If I considered my per-hour wages, I'd jump off the roof. Instead, I counted my worth in per-blouse earnings. I completed the intensive part of the work, the needlework, during the meetings I attended most every night while the children slept.

Bedtime was Guthrie's favorite time to watch them.

Our Boston Women's Manifesto—held up coast-to-coast as the measure for personal equality—remained in the realm of philosophy, solemn nods, and lip service. Movement men rarely denied their women outright, but, in the end, they still considered us *their* women as though our rights were theirs to give. We'd only won the intellectual battle, the war of words.

When you fought for every clean mug and plate, eventually, every skirmish flattened you enough that the entire world could walk on you.

I spent my free time at the Boston chapter of the National Welfare Rights Organization meetings, usually with Mary, Valentina, Josie, Billie, and sometimes Rochelle. In the time left, I continued fighting the crazy highway expansion plan in Jamaica Plain and Roxbury, where the city would divide us into the haves and have-nots, each on opposite sides of the road.

Suze and Roxanne joined me in the People Before Highways fight. "Fuck you, Confidential Chat," we said as we traded baking brownies and leading Girl Scout troops for saving the world.

Suze, Roxanne, Rochelle, and I formulated plans for our true dreams in the minuscule moments left between kids, sewing, marching, and political work, drawing logos, and writing mission statements for Sojourner Graphics, our women-run graphic design and printing firm, where we'd plow the profits back into rights for women.

Our men smiled at our pipe dreams; we stuck up our middle fingers when they turned their backs.

"I didn't use your blouse money. My mother sent me a check for the suit, a purchase that will more than pay for itself. Okay? Do you know what I'll make at a downtown firm?" Guthrie asked.

I put my hands behind my back and leaned back, digging my fingers into the rug's coarse wool fibers. We might not have discussed particulars, but in the fuzzy future of my imagination Guthrie worked in a legal collective. Civil rights. Labor law. That would be his bailiwick while I served the movement with Sojourner Graphics.

"Downtown? That's what you want?" I asked.

He shrugged off the rich blue suit jacket, stepped out of his trousers, and sank beside me. Guthrie's comfort with seminudity and full nudity annoyed me beyond reason. He'd begun lifting weights with Chuck; his muscled body seemed designed to contrast with and highlight the puckered, angry red skin crisscrossing my stomach.

Every man in the house annoyed every woman. Every man, even gentle Wyatt, had been raised in a world where women measured their moods and desires. I knew Guthrie's state of mind the moment he entered the house. I read the molecules surrounding him and sniffed the essence of his temper. Was he in a feminist-appreciative mood or carrying the beliefs of an ancient Greco-Roman warrior?

Women knew the aura of their men within moments, just as dogs smelled danger. One flick of an eyebrow, a millimeter of a mouth turned down, a moment's tightening of a hand on a knob, and we knew to take care.

Guthrie exhaled with impatience as he tossed the trousers on the bed. "I don't need this now, Annabel."

My father said almost those exact words when faced with my mother's questions.

I.

Don't.

Need.

This.

Now.

Well, when the hell will you "need this," Guthrie?

As always, I swallowed the words, but something broke, and I spoke. "When the hell will you need this, Guthrie? When is it my turn not to *need this*? Do I get to tell Henry I'm not in the mood when he cries? Should I tell Ivy I don't need this now when she's sad or mad?"

"Stop. Just stop." He rose and began stepping into the jeans he'd dropped on the floor earlier. "You keep going and going and going. So, I bought a fucking suit to look for a job. Who the hell supports us? *Me.* Only me. Your blouses won't pay for anything but rice and beans, so would you just shut up about who does what? In the end, it's me, Annabel. And my guess? It will always be me. We have little kids. Learn to live with it and worry about Ivy and Henry."

I took the crumpled jacket from the bed; the fabric felt like money. Making sure to use the sturdy wooden hanger on which it came—something Guthrie would never remember—I straightened the jacket and pants and placed them in the closet.

Guthrie put a hand on my back. "This won't go on forever."

I stiffened and moved from his touch. "We have no idea what my forever is. Your life has a thousand possible paths."

He hissed out a give-me-strength breath. "As does yours. When the kids are older, when they're in school, you can go back. You can go back at night right now."

"Right now? With Henry still nursing and Ivy attached to me like a damn barnacle?"

"I wish you could hear yourself. All you do is whine. We're on a journey." He ran his hand down my hip. "This is just the beginning, baby. Everything I'm doing is for us, including the suit. I'll earn enough downtown that we can fight the fight. We're going to let their money fund us. This suit is a down payment on the struggle."

Guthrie could talk the paint off a wall.

"We face an enormous amount of work, baby. Nixon's bullshit on ending the war? He's ramping it up and taking money from everything except rockets. We'll have a man on the moon before we have more civil rights. We need money to fight the fight. You don't understand."

"Our cost of living is almost nothing," I said. "We don't need a lot if we watch our spending."

"Be patient. Let me explore our options. Give me credit, okay? I know what I'm doing."

Every fight led to him listing my deficits: my impatience, unhappiness, whining, and lack of appreciation, immediately followed by my counting off Guthrie's problems: his lack of understanding, stubbornness, and overbearing sense of self.

In meetings, people praised my strengths: my humor and caretaking. Then I came home, and Guthrie detailed my deficits. He always wanted me, but which Annabel he craved, I didn't know. I feared that the Annabel he lusted after was the terrified baby he met in Mississippi.

"Good with the bad, girls." Each night, my mother had plopped us four girls in our oversized tub and offered the teachings of Camille:

* Always know what you want.

* Pick your work as carefully as you pick your husband. You'll spend as much or more time with that as you do with him.

* Glitter wears off, girls. Always. You'll have to take the good with the bad in every marriage. Even your wonderful daddy. Learn what you want and how to get there by yourself.

*No one else in the world will care for you as well as you can.

My mother planted her beliefs before we could read or write. Had I already failed in making Ivy and Henry strong and self-sufficient? More importantly, how was I making this world a place where they could be free *and* safe?

Protests had surged after the assassinations of Martin Luther King and Bobby Kennedy—riots, strikes, and protests included the bombing of a San Francisco police station, the Stonewall Riot, the Days of Rage in Chicago, and the recent violence in Coachella at what should have been a United Farm Workers celebration. I couldn't imagine what kind of world my children would come of age in.

I wanted freedom for my children; I wanted them to grow up in a just world, but the events we might need in order to reach the place we dreamed of terrified me. My fear ran at a constant burn as I watched for signs of a coming inferno.

Chapter 23

✿

Annabel

APRIL 1969

Secret Fairy Cookies

A month later, rage boiled in every corner of the movement, and Harvard was no exception. Nearly a hundred students had pushed into University Hall the previous night, forcing out deans and administrators and occupying the building. Then, SDS pinned a list of their demands on the door of President Pusey.

The Cambridge police and Massachusetts State troopers arrived at dawn and removed the occupiers inside, including Guthrie, using clubs and mace, arresting two hundred. Standing outside, I didn't know if Guthrie was one of them.

Chaos reigned all around us. Having brought the kids here was madness.

A growing crowd shouted loud, bitter slogans at the cops and state police, terrifyingly robot-like in their full riot gear. I backed away as rocks and fists flew, searching for Guthrie.

Helmets sparked as the sun hit the metal. Military boots worn by police formations trampled the protesters who fell.

Cops threw canisters of mace. Screams filled Harvard Yard.

I ran with Henry squealing as he bounced in the backpack and Ivy shrieking in terror from her seat in the flimsy umbrella stroller.

Gasping for breath, I stopped and turned when I arrived at the bricked edge of the yard.

The scene resembled a field of war.

I stood on the outskirts of the screaming crowd, realizing the danger of my situation with Ivy and Henry as the clash between police and students exploded.

Guthrie could buy ten new suits; I didn't care. Now, only his safety mattered. And at this moment, wherever he was, he'd tell me to take the kids far away. I avoided the Harvard Square T stop, just half a block away, fearing angry crowds. Instead, I walked to the stop where I'd find the number 66 bus that snaked through Cambridge, Allston, and Brookline till reaching Mission Hill and Puddingstone, slow, but God willing, safe.

The following Sunday morning, we sprawled in the living room. Guthrie's black eye had barely faded. I'd be lying if I didn't admit that seeing him wearing his tough-guy politics came with a frisson of a turn-on. The rolled-up sleeves of his worn blue work shirt showed angry scrapes on his forearms where police had dragged him along the pavement. Somehow, he'd managed to slip away without being arrested.

We took turns reading aloud snippets from newspapers and magazines. Adults and kids ravaged piles of cookies and Mike's Donuts as our nutritional philosophies fell to the sharp edge of excited nerves.

I leaned against Guthrie as I held Henry tight. Ivy traced Guthrie's injury as she sat on his lap. "I'm kissing your boo-boo again, Daddy." She planted tiny kisses all down the red marks. "All better?"

"Yes, sweetheart. Thank you." He placed his cheek on Ivy's head and squeezed her tight. "You're the best nurse in the world."

"We're even radicalizing the *Harvard Alumni Bulletin.* Listen to what they wrote." Wyatt cleared his throat and read aloud. "*The police riots of Chicago last summer were a Damascus for the young people of this country, a radicalizing experience that cannot be understated.*"

We hung on every word. "... *one of the results of the 'police riot' during the Democratic convention—Daley's Folly—is that it has hampered the effective use of police against students for generations to come. Everywhere today, the reaction of students to the police is completely emotional.*"

"That's a positive, right?" Melanie asked. "They're writing that as a good thing?"

"They're trying to be fair but not come across as radical. Let him finish reading." Chuck waved his hand, motioning Wyatt to continue.

"It's a long article. You should read it all, but here's the most relevant part: "*Accepting the use of police as an imperative, such an action carries the obligation to rationalize it to an offended community. In this, the administration failed.*"

Chuck nodded. "Harvard. What did anyone expect from an institution founded on paternalism?"

Guthrie grabbed the magazine and held it up. We all saw the angry red fist on the cover. "We're nothing but cannon fodder. Their draft deferments? Bribery so the privileged stay quiet while Nixon's precious Silent Majority burn Vietnamese kids alive." He pulled Ivy closer, making a protective circle around our daughter as I choked on crushing love for him, for Henry in my arms, and for Ivy in his.

Jacob, the oldest of the kids, tugged on Chuck's sleeve. "Are you gonna keep the children from being burned, Daddy?"

Fury laced our bed that night. Guthrie and I made love as though the world might end.

Guthrie's talk of working at a downtown law firm evaporated. He'd worn his Brooks Brothers suit interviewing at every top law firm in Boston. Many offered; he accepted none.

He chose his lesser suit when meeting with the Greater Boston Legal Assistance Project—GBLAP—and accepted their offer. When I mentioned his month of playing up to power lawyers, he dismissed my words with a laugh. "I was only researching the other side."

Now, five months into his new job, he'd solidified his position as Puddingstone's resident political expert, replete with the glory of his Harvard degrees, and having turned down four Brooks-Brothers-style jobs, the cred of working at GBLAP, and his solid SDS standing.

During our house dinners, the men jockeyed for power. Though none of us knew what Chuck did at his semi-hip corporate job at the sneaker factory, he owned the role of speaker for the working class. Wyatt took a different moral high ground, lecturing us on values via fruit and nuts from his food co-op perspective. Grady and Wyatt shared wood worshipping with Quinn, our resident carpenter. Among the men, only Quinn chose not to sing his own praise, though his skills shone throughout our house.

They rode the high of their importance in the movement. As more self-aggrandizing kicked in, they pushed us to revisit the monogamy question to remove the impossibly weird and convoluted rules. Conceivably, the men were bored with their too-familiar wives and quasi wives; perhaps they felt youth slipping away as they crept closer to thirty with Chuck and Diantha in the lead at twenty-nine. Everyone recognized the current stipulations were designed to keep us in our beds.

As the men opined, we women rolled our eyes and talked among ourselves in knots of two and three.

"Maybe," I said to Suze as we walked around Jamaica Pond early on a breezy Saturday morning with Roxanne, "our men are simply men. Whether they're marching against the war or counting beans at some accounting office, guys cheat. The only difference here is that ours are looking for a free no-blame pass."

I glanced at the periwinkles popping up around us. May flowers always seem hopeful and pushy.

"Should we be grateful?" Suze asked. "At least they're upfront and honest about their desires."

I snorted as she hopped over goose poop. "You must be kidding."

We remained quiet momentarily, letting the rising wind provide our soundtrack. The question of fidelity rose and fell like the sun. Like hormone levels. My cravings waxed and waned. Being tugged at by children all day made the idea of sex feel like one more chore to add to the list until my cycle switched and burning desire rode over the chore chart. But when I snuck down to check for Clay later in the updated White Pages at the main branch of the Boston Public Library, a jabbing hunger for sex struck.

Sometimes, lightning exploded in my solar plexus when I saw husky Quinn sanding wood, his bulging shoulders pushing against a tight white tee shirt.

"Are you at all interested?" Roxanne asked from my right side when I mentioned it.

We met each other's eyes and laughed.

When we reached the boathouse, we sprawled on an open bench. Suze and Roxanne lit cigarettes, and I pulled a pack of butterscotch lifesavers from my pocket. We pondered Roxanne's question while crunching and smoking. Unlike her, I never had the patience to suck a lifesaver to a thin sliver.

"How are you going to vote?" Roxanne asked.

Suzie took a long drag and blew out a perfect circle of smoke. "Damned either way? Yes, and we're fucked—"

"Quite literally," Roxanne said. "Voting no equals pouting men."

I stretched back and put my hands behind my head. "I'm tired of the whole topic," I said.

"Half the time, I'm sick of sex with Grady." Suze shrugged when we turned to her. "But then the other half the time, I'm horny. Come on. You know what I mean."

"Possibly," Roxanne said. "But do we want to walk that slippery slope?"

"Wanna make a sex chart, Annabel?" Suze asked.

The three of us cracked up so hard that runners passing by couldn't help but smile at us.

"What the hell," I said. "Maybe I should make this Guthrie's early Christmas present."

"Hannukah," Roxanne corrected.

"Fuck it," Suze said. "Happy Mother's Day to all five of them."

Nerves showed the night of the second monogamy vote. Chain-smoking, refilled wine glasses, and beer cans popping while we decimated a platter of doughnuts reflected our mood as much as our stupid, nervous jokes.

Outside the walls of Puddingstone, none of us brought up our discussion about bed-swapping. The fact that talking to Rochelle, Mary, or Valentina about this was impossible should have informed me that shame coated sharing the possibility of switching partners.

All the men but Wyatt argued for looser rules, though nervousness from everyone permeated the air. Wyatt remained quiet. Diantha and Melanie stayed on the side of the current standards, with the iterations of "how to sleep with thy housemate's partner" requiring everything but filling out forms in triplicate. Suze, Roxanne, and I changed our opinions every other minute.

With my third glass of wine, I looked over all the men. Did I want him? Him? Him?

When I got to Wyatt, I thudded to a hard stop. I stared at his honeyed hair, hating its similarity to Ivy's. But my daughter's hair also resembled Guthrie's mother's. Ivy's green eyes didn't match Wyatt's blue. Hers were sharp like pine needles, like Guthrie's father's.

"I'm reaching the point where I don't care," Roxanne said. "Isn't it still cheating when we call it a fancy word?"

"We're not talking about cheating," Chuck insisted. "Cheating presages secrets, and secrets ruin families. We're talking about the opposite: openness."

"So, we make an announcement when we're about to perform a

partner switch?" Suze laced her fingers and gave everyone a good-girl smile. "During? Before? After?"

"Not a stupid question," Guthrie said. "Only by being thorough now can we relax our standards after."

"Relax our standards?" I reached for one of the doughnut scraps left and chased it down with a sip of Guthrie's warm beer.

"You know what I mean," Guthrie said.

"You did sound a bit professorial." Quinn stood, shuffled, and took on a new persona. After pushing back his thick brown hair, he straightened an imaginary tie and pulled at pretend shirt cuffs. "So, will the jury please note when Annabel Cooper indulged in a bedtime ritual with Quinn Saunders, she'd signed, sealed, and delivered her full consent, said consent delivered on . . ." Quinn glanced at the oversized UNICEF calendar Guthrie's parents sent each year. "October 27, 1969."

We voted for a trial run.

"Are the kids all for-absolute-sure asleep?" My heart raced as we readied for bed the following week. I marked the occasion by trading what I usually slept in—Guthrie's old T-shirt—for the closest thing I had to a racy option: an ancient black full slip. Nudity wasn't happening.

I wondered if it was too late to take my *yes* back.

"Every single one." Guthrie held up his hand in the scout's honor position. "I checked all the rooms. Even Henry's snoring."

"That's a miracle," I said. "Are you sure-sure?" Our son, who seemed to possess zero sleep needs, stayed awake chattering nonsense to his teddy bear collection for hours some nights.

"Absolutely. Okay?"

After examining his face for signs of lying, I believed him and nodded.

A soft tap sounded moments later, and Guthrie opened the door with a crack. He gave Quinn what must have been their secret decoder signal, and he entered.

Quinn's robe covered boxer shorts. His barrel chest gave him a friendly Santa look while his massive work-scarred hands were sexy as hell. When he removed his glasses, he looked nineteen rather than twenty-nine, while I probably appeared more forty than twenty-three. I'd spent my day creating homemade playdough, chasing kids, cleaning, cooking dinner, embroidering six blouses, and writing the meeting minutes for two groups.

"You look beautiful." Quinn slipped into bed, making an Annabel sandwich.

"Are you talking to Guthrie or me?"

They laughed as though I'd cracked the funniest joke in history.

I tried dredging up the sexy feelings from when I'd agreed to this earlier in the week, the hours earlier contentment I'd felt when Guthrie brewed me a steaming cup of Constant Comment tea laced with brandy, and the happiness he brought by putting the kids to bed without requiring anything from me.

I felt like a pinball machine when they took turns working to turn me on, the prize being who made me explode first. Finally, I drifted away, soft fantasies playing through my head, floating from Wyatt to Clay until I piloted myself to cruising on automatic.

We were reaching the stage of getting down to serious business when the door squeaked.

My stomach dropped.

I pushed Quinn away, instinctively pulling the sheet up to cover us.

"Mommy?" Ivy opened her mouth and then closed it, curling her lower lip into a portrait of analysis. At three, she already possessed some preternatural ability to bore into my soul with her gaze.

"What's wrong, Pudding?"

"Why is Quinn sleeping with you and Daddy? Did he have a scary dream?"

Guthrie and Quinn turned to me. Inventing stories for children who stumble into their group sex must be listed under mommy's side of the parental job chart.

I ran through the reasons that would make sense to Ivy and sound innocent if repeated to someone like my mother-in-law.

"Mommy lost her earring," I said. "It was one of my very favorite ones. Quinn is helping us find it."

"How come it's dark? Where are his glasses?"

"Some people wear glasses mostly for far away things and take them off for close-up," Guthrie said.

"Also, I eat so many carrots that my night vision is extra-extra good." Quinn pulled the sheet so high only his head showed.

Ivy appeared more confused. "Better than in the light?"

Pivot. The only answer.

"Honey, did *you* have a bad dream?" I asked.

She bunched her flannel nightgown and twisted the red-dotted fabric into a fat knot. "I guess so."

"Okay, wait outside the door for just one tiny minute, and I'll be right out. And then, you know what? I'm going to take you to the kitchen for a no-more-nightmares-cookie!"

Ivy opened her mouth in shock. "We have cookies?"

We did, though I'd have to climb to the highest cupboard to uncover the hidden stash in the lobster pot, where we buried the noncarob, nonhoney sweets for those moments when we got stoned into the sugar zone.

"Magic fairy cookies—secret ones. Fairies can't let children see them, so you'll need to wait in the pantry and cover your eyes until I call you into the kitchen."

Chapter 24

Annabel

MAY 1970

Soft Cheeks Pressed into a Gritty Sidewalk.

A funereal quiet hung over the house. After the Kent State massacre the previous day, May 4, 1970, a day we'd never forget, it became clear we weren't dabbling in political change; we were at war with Nixon, the Republican Party, and the National Guard.

We gathered in the living room, needing the sustenance of closeness and food, as though we sat shiva or attended a wake, though nothing could fill the void of horror opened by the shootings.

We sprawled over the couches, stuffed chairs, and giant floor pillows. Only crumbs remained from the platter of brownies Melanie had baked in a daze.

The previous night, we'd debated how much to tell the kids, with opinions ranging from nothing (Melanie and Diantha) to everything (Roxanne) to somewhere in between. In the end, we chose openness tempered by reassurance.

"They need to know the world we brought them into and why we're working to change it," Suze had said, reaching the conclusion that we all eventually agreed with. "They must understand why we're always at meetings, working so hard, and that living together is more than taking turns shoveling snow."

Now, Melanie read from the *New York Times* as we huddled together.

"*Alison Krause, 19.*" Melanie lit a candle as she said each name. "*Sandra Lee Scheuer, 20. Jeffrey Glenn Miller, 20. Willian Knox Schroeder, 19.*"

Four flames flickered while we stared at a screaming girl kneeling in front of a body lying on the ground in Ohio. The grainy photo burned into my eyes. I saw any one of us there, any of our children.

Henry climbed into my lap as Ivy leaned her head on my shoulder. They'd transformed from babies to kids at almost four and five.

Melanie settled beside Ivy, holding Poppy tight and clutching Wyatt's hand. Poppy and Ivy were rarely apart; even though they were attached to Melanie and me as they were now, they wanted to be close.

Zane, Jacob, and Mac piled into their favorite yellow beanbag chair, crumbs and milk spills covering their T-shirts and jeans. Leo lay on the rug with his eyes closed. We were all gut-punched. What war would our kids be drafted to fight?

Despite Zane and Jacob holding the coloring and features of their parents, Diantha and Chuck, and Mac and Leo walking and talking like Grady and wearing Suze's thick dark hair, the four melded into being the boys. The kids on the street already called them the Puddingstone boys; they were the ones who ruled the neighborhood games.

After a moment of silence, Guthrie picked up the newspaper and read it to us. "*Four students at Kent State University, two of them women, were shot to death this afternoon by a volley of National Guard gunfire. At least 8 other students were wounded. The burst of gunfire came about 20 minutes after the guardsmen broke up a noon rally on the Commons, a grassy campus gathering spot, by lobbing tear gas at a crowd of about 1,000 young people. In Washington, President Nixon deplored the deaths of the four students in the following statement . . .*"

Guthrie scanned the paper before continuing to read aloud. Grady's hands, chapped from the steel wool he used to remove rust from old bikes, swiped away tears. Nobody chided Roxanne for chain-smoking around the kids.

"For god's sake," Guthrie said. "And now here's Nixon blaming it on dead kids: *This should remind us all once again that when dissent turns to violence it invites tragedy.*"

"Is he fucking kidding?" Roxanne pressed her palms into her temples. "Word soup. Bullshit."

Chuck slammed his fist on the table. "Nixon might as well have pulled the trigger."

"Nixon did this?" At eight, Mac continually tried to make sense of the world, especially when his school world collided with what we taught them.

"He didn't *actually* shoot them, dummy." Jacob, who was as emphatic as his father, Chuck, answered. Also eight but taller and more self-confident, he took the role of leader of the children. "My dad means metaphorically speaking."

Diantha threw a soft pillow at her son. "Metaphorical is a great word. Dummy isn't."

I opened my mouth to expand on Diantha's words but then stopped to form my thoughts. I honestly had no clue how to process this for the children. I agonized about us exposing them to this horror.

I worried about how the things they saw and heard affected them. When we hid something, I still fretted—the awful night Ivy had walked in while Quinn, Guthrie, and I attempted our threesome haunted me. I assumed we were only the tiniest bit successful in protecting our seven kids from the world we chose to live in.

We should stop. I knew this, but before I could say anything, Guthrie continued.

"Blah, blah, *of the Ohio National Guard, said in a statement that the guardsmen had been forced to shoot after a sniper opened fire against the troops from a nearby rooftop and the crowd began to move to encircle the guardsmen . . . They were under standing orders to take cover and return any fire.*" Guthrie took a deep breath. "Here's the money shot."

Making the kids leave now was impossible, but watching Ivy and Poppy wait for the next sentence just about killed me. They were only four.

"Listen." Guthrie read the following words slowly. "*This reporter, who was with the group of students, did not see any indication of sniper fire, nor was the sound of any gunfire audible before the Guard volley.*"

"Jesus. They want to kill us," Diantha said.

Wyatt sent a warning look to her as he tipped his head toward Poppy.

I held Henry, my baby, closer. Fifteen years from now, when he left for college, was a million years away, but I'd been in Mississippi only six years ago, and hadn't those years flashed by?

The time when Henry and Ivy left for college would sneak up and hit us in the chest.

What would I have done to change the world for them?

Between kids, making blouses, cleaning, and cooking, all I had extra time for was meetings and more meetings and then one hundred more. All we did was chew up words. Sojourner Graphics existed only in discussions and dreams.

When would I do things?

Our children were so tender, so loved. We feared for their safety; what about mothers in Vietnam, worrying about napalm scorching the flesh of their children?

I'd treated the children in Mississippi as props for my good works. Those precious little children were the sons and daughters of people in the firing line, not my damn projects.

Clay became my magic beau, a character in the gothic romance novel of my life.

"*A platoon of guardsmen, armed—as they have been since they arrived here with loaded M1 rifles and gas equipment—moved across the green and over the crest of the hill, chasing the main body of protesters . . .*"

Melanie rocked Poppy as though holding an infant.

"*The guardsmen moved into a grassy area just below the parking lot and fired . . .*"

The National Guard killed two boys and two girls for protesting, just like Guthrie and I had so many times.

Would this still be the world if my children had children? Rationality demanded we stop this madness.

Guthrie had been arrested at two demonstrations, rescued only by the long reach of his father's money and connections. But no amount of money could stop bullets.

We needed to fight and protect the children.

The words Guthrie read sounded like sad poetry of war.

"*As the guardsmen, moving up the hill in single file, reached the crest, they suddenly turned, forming a skirmish line and opening fire . . . students dove to the ground, crawling on the grass in terror . . . a student crumpled over, spun sideways, and fell to the ground, shot in the head.*

"*When the firing stopped, a slim girl, wearing a cowboy shirt and faded jeans, was lying face down on the road at the edge of the parking lot, blood pouring out . . .*"

I saw the faded jeans we wore, imagining Melanie lying on the ground, blood seeping from her, staining her golden hair. Her soft cheeks pressed into a gritty sidewalk.

Guthrie breathed heavily and took a break from reading. "Next is the statement by the commander of the troops. He says no warnings or official orders were given."

"It's all bullshit." Quinn, our designated quiet, calm one, appeared as though he'd shatter from fury. "This can't go on."

"*There are many unconfirmed reports of gunfire from various sources,*" Guthrie continued. "*We are asking for every possible appropriate investigation, which we shall undertake to pursue to the limit.*"

"Meaningless empty words," Quinn said. "I can't stand feeling so much hate." Roxanne made quiet shushing sounds and rubbed his shoulder.

"What are you going to do, Mama?" Ivy whispered. "So we don't get shotted."

I pulled my daughter closer. "Don't worry, Pudding. We're all sad and mad right now. But by tomorrow, we'll know what to do," I promised.

Ivy put her thumb in her mouth and reached for Poppy's hand across Melanie.

Chapter 25

✾

Annabel

The Venn Presentation

Diantha and Chuck were the last to walk into our next house meeting the following week. She entered first, clutching a 9x12 brown envelope fastened with string. Chuck followed, plunking a stack of folders on the kitchen table.

"I have an announcement," Diantha said. "An announcement and a concept. First, the announcement: I'm wealthy. My family has money. Family capital."

Judging by her words, I guessed she was wildly wealthy. She, who shared everything, didn't punctuate her announcement with a number nor modify *wealthy* with words like *sort of* or *kind of.* Putting it in the realm of "family capital" told the story.

I always figured Diantha for money—after all, she'd bought the Puddingstone house—but at the time, real estate in Mission Hill sold far below market price, even for Boston, where few homes were highly valued.

"Why is this relevant now?" Guthrie, as always, was ready to examine and analyze every word.

"You know, D, the co-op—"

Melanie tugged at Wyatt's arm. "Not now," she said.

"Wealthy Rockefeller or wealthy 'my parents bought me a car for graduation' wealthy?" Roxanne asked.

Diantha held up her hands for everyone to stop. "The important thing isn't my family; it's what Chuck and I plan to do with our money that matters. We bought a wonderful old farmhouse in Vermont—for all of us—for our children's future."

"That sounds incredible," Suze said, "but what—"

Diantha again held up her hand. She leaned back and reached for the tea Chuck set before her. "I know you'll have a million questions, but first, let me share my concept. I only ask that you rent the idea even if you're not ready to buy it."

I tried not to look into Roxanne's eyes, fearing we'd burst out laughing. Diantha's infatuation with the drama of her life never failed her.

"My proposal is based on my thoughts about us as parents." Diantha brought the tips of her fingers together before continuing. "The plan is something for us to meditate on.

"Do you mean literally?" Roxanne loved to poke a pin when anyone became too full of themselves. "Because I'd fall asleep from boredom. Trust me. I've tried."

Diantha nodded then cut a large slice of zucchini bread, taking a bite with slow deliberation before answering.

Again, Roxanne and I met eyes—both of us thinking, I'm sure, that Diantha might be meditating on the bread.

After patting her lips with a cloth napkin, she folded her hands. "No. I don't mean TM, though transcendental meditation would certainly help. Here, I use the word *meditation* to connote deep reflection."

"And we will think deeply about what exactly?" Guthrie ignored the reference to transcendental meditation. He automatically zoned out whenever Diantha talked about yoga and meditation. She held that breathwork, mindfulness, and whole grains fed the soul. Unfed souls, she believed, couldn't change the world, preaching how the brutality of red meat promoted voting Republican and racism.

Guthrie's exhaled breath told me what he thought of Diantha's theatrical presentation. My Guthrie presented himself as the busiest man in the world. I'd thought his time would open once he finished school, but instead, he added hours by taking every board seat the world offered. The few nights he made it home by seven, he walked in as though expecting a parade.

"Rent this idea," Quinn said. "Before we hear what you and Chuck have planned, let's return to the beginning. Satisfy our curiosity so we can concentrate on what's next. Where does your family money come from?" Quinn asked.

Finally, someone found the guts to ask the question

Wyatt extended his long legs and propped them on a nearby stool. "Come on, D. Put it out there. Where does your fortune come from, why did you tell us today, and, after we know that, what do you want to do with that wealth? In Vermont, it seems."

"How do you know the three are connected?" Diantha stretched her arms up and out, more than comfortable in the limelight.

"You brought them up together. And you, my friend, more than any of us, do not bring things up lightly." Wyatt pulled a cigarette from the group pack of Pall Malls. He sometimes buried a dig inside innocent-seeming words. Just then, he'd called Diantha humorless, which was both fair and not. The woman possessed great qualities, including generosity and boundless energy, but a comedian, she wasn't. Diantha treated life with ultraseriousness. But I didn't think that equaled humorlessness.

Diantha rose, swung her heavy braid to her back, and walked to stand beside Wyatt. With a grand gesture, she pointed. "*Tada*!"

"Tada? You get your wealth through Wyatt?" Melanie's look of confusion appeared genuine.

Diantha raised her eyebrows and pointed again. "Behold the Aetos family fortune in the flesh."

"Are you playing a game?" Quinn asked.

"She's giving you a clue. Two clues." Chuck tipped his head toward Wyatt.

I examined Wyatt head to toe.

Head to *toe*.

"Eagles," I said. My Rhinebeck education had subjected me to a bit of everything.

Aetos. Diantha Aetos. I remembered my seventh-grade mythology class.

Aetos Dios, a giant golden eagle, was Zeus's messenger and animal companion.

"Eagle sneakers?" I tapped Wyatt's left foot with my right one. "Eagle sneakers are your family business?"

"Guilty," Diantha said.

Eagle sneakers covered the feet of half the kids in Boston. And Wyatt. I glanced at Chuck's feet. Eagles. No doubt, Eagles littered the boys' bedrooms. I tried to wrap my head around this information.

Wyatt looked at his feet. "Congratulations, Diantha. Your family makes a hell of a comfortable sneaker."

Roxanne put down her empty mug. "While I reserve the right to discuss growing up in the Aetos sneaker family—in the greatest of detail, as my curiosity is steaming—"

"Why are we always more curious about rich people?" Guthrie asked.

Melanie leaned into Diantha and squeezed her arm. "Roxanne is trying to say, 'Tell us your idea.' That's the important part, right?"

Diantha smiled at her with gratitude. "Here's the nutshell: our devotion to the kids collides with our dedication to the movement."

Suze nodded. "True."

"We should render the same commitment to our kids that we do to our meetings and political work. I don't want my sons growing up like we did, hiding under desks thinking that will protect them from a nuclear attack." Diantha paused and twisted one of her many rings. Jewelry was her weakness.

I didn't want my kids worrying about bombs at all.

"Be specific. Please." Suze drew her thick hand-knit shawl closer around her thin shoulders and picked up her knitting needles and a skein of mustard-colored yarn.

Diantha rose and walked to the sink, leaning against the porcelain as she took the floor. "Like I said, we bought an enormous farmhouse. It has a huge old barn built for exploration, surrounded by acres and acres of land, a large pond for swimming, and a big meadow for us to host our softball games." She turned to Chuck and winked.

"Love you, babe," he said.

"The land is green, the house is red, and the view stretches for miles. I want to raise our children, all our Puddingstone children, there. I want to preserve their childhoods as we work to save this country." Diantha returned to the table, looking nervous as she awaited our reactions.

"You want us to move to Vermont?" Guthrie gave a crooked frown. "That's a pretty impossible thing to ask."

"But is it?" Diantha laced her fingers and leaned her chin on them, remaining quiet momentarily. Then, with all eyes on her, she stood, walked into the playroom, and returned with a large white posterboard clutched to her chest.

"I hid it behind the piano." Wearing a grin so wide her dimples popped, she held up a Venn diagram with five circles overlapping one in the middle.

"Here's my dream. Our children will become the center of our world ever more while we work to build a safer future for them. All of us, with no exclusion for nonbiological parents, provide a place of wonder. They attach to all of us as parents and benefit from our many circles. They live in Vermont; we knit them a security sphere, both from here and there. We have two wonderful homes, and we're twined to all the children and each other."

She nodded at Chuck, who passed out a folder to each couple.

"My initial thoughts are all here: possible schedules, schooling, and how and why I'm open to living in Vermont full time, acting as the permanent 'house parent' while you all come on rotations and, of course, as often as doable. We can build a paradise."

Diantha could be dramatic, but at the right moment, she could inspire earthshaking hope with just the right words. I remembered my admiration when first meeting her, seeing her ability to shape a world. A jolt of possibility surged.

She could be a pain in the ass, but her devotion to her kids never wavered. Of all of us, she and Melanie were most content in the company of the kids. Even as I recoiled at the thought of sending Ivy and Henry away, planning on rejecting the plan without a moment's thought, I saw Diantha and one or two of us on a beautiful wide porch overlooking miles of green, the children spinning around a new maypole, far away from stray bullets and showers of hatred.

For too long, I'd been torn about everything in my life.

Ivy and Henry vs. building Sojourner Graphics.

Guthrie vs. Sojourner.

Housekeeping vs. Sojourner.

Work that earned money vs. work that fed my soul.

Work that earned money vs. work that would change the world for our children.

All children.

What if we could balance our jumble of needs and wants?

Diantha reached for her large manila envelope. She undid the string wrapped around a paper disk and removed a bundle of photos. "Take a look. I don't want to prejudice anyone, but this is a slice of heaven on earth. Where else could we possibly want our children to be? It will take years of planning, but we can do it. I know we can."

Part Three

❁

Going to Vermont

Ivy

The fundamental condition of childhood is powerlessness.

—Jane Smiley

Chapter 26

✳

Ivy

Barbie and GI Joe

My mother squeezed my hand as we walked from the Trotter school. My brother Henry hung on her other side.

"I can't believe you won't be back here next year." She must have said those words a hundred times, but they really sank in that day. Now that eight was practically a spit away, my sense of time seemed sharper in a way that brought me no joy.

I looked back at the modern brick building. Not coming back sounded awful. I loved the William Monroe Trotter school. Being a goody-goody and an early reader made me a pet of my teacher and the principal, Mrs. Johnson. Plus, I had friends who didn't think me weird for living with so many other families—not like the kids on my block.

"But we might?" I took back my hand and wiped it on my skirt. Fizzy, hot rain surrounded us, and sweat coated my skin. "We might come back, right? "

My mother gazed down at me and curled her lips in, showing she would weigh her words. Her sweetie-pie face was hard to make sour, but her eyes gave her away. Right now, she wore her upset-trying-for-happiness face. "I know this for sure: we're planning the best life for you kids. Roundhouse will be wonderful. Fantastic things are waiting for you in Vermont."

I remembered all the weekends we went to a vast spread of grass with far-apart buildings and running in dizzy circles of freedom with the other kids while the adults hammered and painted—but no matter how many words my mother used, I couldn't understand why they'd send us there for always.

Henry and I shot out and escaped the car the moment our mother parked, running upstairs to the room we shared with Poppy, anxious about what might be gone from our shelves and drawers. Our mothers—and sometimes dads—emptied more of our spaces daily as they prepared for our move to Vermont.

Poppy attended a different school; otherwise, she and I remained inseparable. She had no siblings, so Henry became her brother, and the three of us followed the older boys. The two pairs of brothers, Zane and Jacob, and Mac and Leo, lived for battles with swords and guns, no matter how many peace signs we dutifully made for the mantle.

Of course, our grown-ups forbade toy weapons, but the boys got them by trading with kids in the neighborhood. Plus, our grandparents filled most of our wishes on birthdays and holidays. They loved balancing our parents' constant moral lessons.

The older boys in Puddingstone were as different as they were alike—Jacob was the smartest, Mac the sweetest, and Leo the most imaginative. Jacob read books while his brother, Zane, acted out the roles of a pirate, cowboy, and, lately, a Shaolin priest when we acted out Kung Fu episodes with our neighborhood friends.

And Zane was the top dog in the house and on the street.

My mother followed us upstairs and stood in the doorway. "Start choosing stuff for your backpacks, puddings. You don't want to have to rush your choices."

"I don't want to go to Round Vermont alone, Mommy," Henry said.

"Honey, you'll never be by yourself! You'll have Ivy and Poppy and all the other kids."

"But who'll take care of us?"

Gratitude for my little brother washed through me as he asked the questions that crowded my brain.

My mother sat on Henry's bed and held out his favorite stuffed dog. "You'll want this in your pack. Do you know who'll take care of you? *Everyone.* Diantha will always be there with you and Chuck a lot of the time, and the rest of us will take turns being with you. But Diantha won't leave."

"Vermont is a stupid idea," I muttered. "Stupid, dumb, retarded."

"Don't say retarted," Henry said.

"The word is retard, not *retart,* retard."

"She's calling me a bad word." Henry looked ready to cry. My brother was softer than oatmeal.

"Both of you, stop now. Retarded is an awful thing to say, Ivy, and I never want to hear it from either of you. We never make fun of people." She drew us close and hugged us tight. "I know you'll miss me. Daddy and I will miss you like crazy. We'll be like peanut butter without jam. We're gonna have giant holes in our hearts."

"So why are you sending us away?" I squeezed my eyes to keep from crying.

"First, we'll be with you plenty of the time! We're not sending you away! We're sending you *to.*" She slid off the bed, sat beside me on our shaggy rug, and took my hand. "To green and healthy and magical. We want everything fun, exciting, and wonderful for you while we work hard to improve everything here."

"So nobody shoots us," Henry said. "Like in Kent." My brother acted like the college was a country—the land of Kent.

"Nobody's going to shoot you, Henry. Not here, not in Vermont, not anywhere. That's why Daddy, I, and everyone in the house set up Roundhouse. To help bring peace and justice all over the world."

When Jacob read *Superman* comics aloud, and Superman said "Truth, Justice, and the American Way," I mixed up the characters with my parents. I imagined our grown-ups as superheroes saving America and the world, and even back then, I was ashamed of being jealous that America and the world got all their attention.

"Okay, turtle doves, let's make some progress choosing your most special things. You have two weeks to decide what you take the day we leave and what Diantha will bring up beforehand." She snuggled us momentarily and then got up, blowing us kisses from the doorway.

I reached under my bed for my backpack. My mother had made new ones for each of us. A month before, all the mothers and kids had visited about a hundred fabric stores from Harvard Square to Downtown Boston to a place called Dedham. My bag was purple, the deepest purple I could find. Mom had scattered yellow flowers all over, using embroidery thread so bright they blasted my eyes. To make it cheery, she'd said.

I didn't want to hurt her feelings by telling her I liked silver stars more, so I smiled and hugged her.

My mother made Poppy's bag of actual poppy-decorated fabric. Marimekko fabric, Suze had said at the store. Her lifted eyebrow signified expensive, but Melanie bought it anyway.

Jealousy spiked each time I spotted the sophisticated-looking bag with red abstract poppies sprawling over the white, black, and pink fabric.

My mother designed and sewed appliqués of puppies on Henry's backpack. He loved every dog in the world.

Zane and Mac, almost as inseparable as Poppy and me, had insisted on matching Kung Fu fabric, a choice that Zane's mother, Diantha, hated. Suze told her to be happy that Melanie talked them out of the khaki green spattered with guns.

Everyone said Melanie had the magic touch.

Jacob had examined bolts of cloth, looked at his mother, Diantha, and pointed to a sturdy navy. "That works."

Leo had picked a bolt studded with images of motorcycles. "Those are Yamahas," he told everyone in the store.

Suze rubbed his head. "You, my son, are a fountain of just about everything. Someday, I expect to attend your presidential inauguration."

Then she turned to her Mac, her other son. "The only question is which of my boys ascends the throne first."

We all thought Leo was her favorite, just like we believed Jacob was Diantha's and Henry was my mother's. Poppy, of course, had supremacy with both her parents.

As I stared at the purple backpack I was supposed to fill, I thought of the conversation I'd snuck to hear the week before when Mary and Valentina drank coffee in the kitchen with Mom and Suze. That's when I learned that people other than me questioned the idea of Roundhouse.

"I'm sorry, you two, but your plan still sounds crazy." Mary had taken a cigarette from the house pack. "No matter how many times you explain it."

"I know. You can't imagine it, but—"

"I can't imagine it because I don't think there's a stupider idea in the world. Who sends seven kids to the woods with one, shall we say, somewhat intense woman?" A chair scraped as someone moved away from the table.

"We're not sending them barefoot into the woods to forage for food; they're going to a virtual paradise. Away from the firestorm America has become. With the rest of us taking turns being with Diantha."

"Firestorm," Valentina scoffed. Nothing's burning; just the usual history of the world unfolding: war, famines, poverty—and with none of you in this house in the battle zone."

"Maybe, maybe not." Suze shrugged. "Maybe you just don't see what's going on around us. Every adult in this house is fighting for something, and we don't want the kids to become collateral damage."

"Valentina sees everything," Mary said. "She feels it firsthand. You're all going insane. Aren't there enough problems with DSS taking away peoples' children without you giving up yours? Oh, my lord. Are you crying, Annabel?"

"Ignore me." My mother's teary voice had scared me.

"What is it?" Suze asked, her own tears forming.

"I don't want them to go." The sound of her now full-on sobbing made my stomach hurt. "I don't want them to leave. But how can I protect them here when we might get arrested tomorrow?"

Suze grabbed my mother's hand and brought it to her lips.

Valentina showed no pity. "They need you even if you're out at meetings every night. Why can't you do your kids' community thing here? Let Diantha stay home and take care of them in Boston."

That sounded smart to me.

"I don't want to take something great from them just because I'm sad. I don't want to lose them."

"Oh, honey," Mary said. "The thing they should never lose is you."

I should've run into that kitchen and screamed, "listen to her, Mom!" But even then, even with my heart breaking, I never wanted to appear disloyal.

My father came home early. Before supper, he came upstairs and told Henry and me to get ready—we were going out for a surprise.

"What kind of surprise?" I didn't trust anything with all the changes, not with parents packing, Melanie canning fruit as though we were going to a desert, and Mom, Suze, and Roxanne making one art box after another. My stomach hurt when I saw all the activity. And now my father was home from work early. The world had turned upside down.

"Is it a good surprise?" Henry asked our father.

"Why would I take you for a bad surprise?" Dad placed his hands out wide and pretended to be shocked. "Put on your sneakers; we're off to Brigham Circle."

Most Mission Hill stores were in Brigham Circle, so I became hopeful. Dad held our hands as we walked down the street. He discussed every car we passed, ensuring we knew the VW bug wasn't as great as everyone thought. He said we should buy an American car, but not a Ford since they break down so much, talking with so much seriousness you'd think someone might call on Henry and me to repair one any minute.

I acted interested, waiting to find out about the surprise. I crossed the fingers of the hand not entwined with Dad's, praying to hear the words I hoped for: *Here's your ice cream, kids. Celebrate! We're not sending you away! You're staying with us.*

"Hold tight, kiddos."

We walked across the big street, Tremont, and then down the other side of Parker. Dad proudly tapped the outside wall when we got to a flat-sided row of bumpy rock houses. "See this?"

Henry bobbed his head twice, always wanting to please Dad and Mom.

"This is puddingstone from the quarries that were once here." My father continued to pat and stroke the rock. "Men dug up this rock and built everything from these small houses—which they made for workers to live in—to the Mission Church."

We nodded with the appreciation he wanted.

"Workers broke their bodies to dig up this stuff while rich men made money." Dad placed our hands on the cool stone. "Do you understand what I'm saying?"

"Rich men don't treat poor men good?" Henry wrinkled his face as he tried to figure out my father's words.

"They do not. Wars come because rich men want money."

"Is that why we have the Kent war?" Henry asked.

"The Vietnam War," Dad said. "But Kent State happened because of the Vietnam War. Colonialism caused the war. Rich countries boss around poorer ones and don't let them make free decisions."

As Dad kept talking, we nodded until Henry patted the house and ended the stream of words. "Is this our surprise?"

"No, kiddo. I'm trying to explain why we're fighting so hard to help people. And how you kids are helping by going to Vermont."

"Us living in Vermont helps poor people?" Henry asked.

Answer him, Dad.

My father nodded slowly. "In a way. Mom and I can concentrate better on what we must do when we know you guys are safe and happy."

I looked up at my father. "Please don't send us away. We'll be good and never fight. We'll be quiet so you can concentrate. I promise."

He pressed his lips together and then sighed so deeply I worried I was in trouble. Instead, he knelt and hugged me.

"Ivy, baby, this is not about you being better. You and Henry are perfect. You're always here. And here." He tapped his chest and then the side of his head. "You're always on my mind."

After squeezing me again, he stood and took our hands. We returned to Tremont Street and headed toward Brigham Circle and the stores. When we passed the Parker Hill Library, where we went all the time, Henry announced, "Puddingstone!"

Dad winked and swung our hands till we got to the church. "Puddingstone!"

I searched for more gray stone. When we got close to where the trolley went, I looked to the left at the stone wall behind the Giant Value Supermarket.

I clapped. "Puddingstone!" Dad, Henry, and I hugged like we'd discovered gold in the street.

We skipped into Fermoyles Drugstore, which sold everything from cough drops to books with the cover torn off. Mom said they tore off the covers so the store owners could sell them cheaper. Otherwise, they'd trash them, which made no sense.

"Here's the surprise, kiddos. We're gonna buy whatever the heck you want. Anything." He looked like he'd cry, which terrified me. My father never cried.

Henry picked his treats fast as though this unusual offer might end any second. He grabbed a Mars bar, a wooden paddle with a ball attached by a rubber string, and his favorite food in the world: a box of Cracker Jack. I bet anything he'd eat every piece before we even got home.

I clutched a giant bag of M&Ms while I walked up and down the row devoted to girls' things, unable to decide between Holly Hobbie and the Sunshine Family paper dolls. When Dad came up behind me and said, "Get them both," life felt upside down.

After we finished picking out surprises, Dad took us around the corner and bought us ice cream sundaes so big that he had to finish Henry's and mine.

Mom pretended not to see any of it when we got home. Not even Barbie or GI Joe.

How bad was the world facing us that she let Dad pack us off with so much forbidden stuff?

Chapter 27

✳

Ivy

AUGUST 1974

Just Like Three Orphan Annies

We took off at dawn on the day we left for Vermont. Henry, Poppy, and I rode in my parents' car; everyone else crowded into Diantha and Chuck's van.

I'd jammed so much into my purple backpack that I had to hold it closed the whole ride to keep my stuff from tumbling out. I'd stuffed all I could into my pack to make sure I had my treasures the minute we arrived.

Hidden at the bottom was my mother's red leather address book. My mother would kill me if she found out I had taken it.

Why would you do that, Ivy?

For an emergency, I answered in my mind.

I didn't know what emergency I feared, but the word was everywhere at school.

"In case of emergency, get down!"

"Line up if there's an emergency!"

"When the fire bell rings, act as though you're in a real emergency because that just may be true."

When Poppy and I slept over at our friend Maura's house down the street, we sneak-watched our favorite show, *Emergency!* In just one hour, a car with a family inside rolled over a cliff, the father died, the mother and son broke bones and bled from their heads, and then in the next part, a rattlesnake bit someone, and they almost died, and then somebody else had a heart attack.

I could imagine a thousand bad things happening in Vermont, a place with hills, lakes, and cliffs. Hospitals were far from the house, the giant barn scared me, and the pond froze in winter, but you could still fall through.

When I pictured living in Vermont, I felt like I did when my Grandpa Mike took me on a roller coaster that he called the Cyclone: sick and never-ending. My mother's address book was my insurance policy. Whether I flipped to the *P* for Pascal or the *C* for Cooper, I could call for help. Both sets of grandparents and my aunties were right there in Mom's pretty writing.

On top of the address book sat my pinkish violet tin, my new treasure box, the one my father had given to my mother before I was born. Inside, I'd crammed a picture of my parents, a tiny lavender china cat with gold-tipped ears from Grandma Penny, a charm bracelet I'd snuck out of my mother's drawer, and five skeleton keys that Grandpa Gordon had collected for me.

Next, I'd stuffed in my other essential things. I'd slid *Peter Pan* in sideways, a book from when Grandma Camille was little, illustrated with old-fashioned pictures. A plush tiger that felt like real fur took up most of the space, along with the giant bags of M&Ms I'd saved, Barbie, and my paper dolls.

The rest of my books were in my trunk. I didn't trust them going up early with Diantha.

After what seemed like a hundred hours, Daddy turned the car down the long, winding road that led to the sprawling red house and giant barn. The buildings sat like blocks in a bowl of green and trees. A rocky creek led to the pond and a meadow, from which everything was visible, and no other houses could be seen for miles.

We arrived first. While my parents unloaded food, Poppy, Henry, and I tiptoed in and out of the house as though we'd never been there. Rooms and rooms led us in dizzying patterns.

"We're just like three Orphan Annies," I whispered, as though the grown-ups had banished us to an orphanage like the cartoon my father read us on Sundays.

We darted around the barn a little bit, but the old tools hanging everywhere in the gloom seemed like monsters, so we returned to the house, where I saw a carousel picture I hadn't seen before, but I recognized that my mother had painted. Below the riot of colors were the words they'd used to name the house: *And the seasons, they go round and round—Joni Mitchell*

We were supposed to call our new home *Roundhouse.*

Moments later, when the van arrived, the house filled with grown-ups, kids, and a massive amount of everything in the world. The grown-ups carried everything into the house, leaving our suitcases and trunks in a pile in the hall.

Diantha stood at the entrance, giving orders to everyone. "After you pick rooms—when I say you can—you'll bring up your stuff. Big kids help little kids," she told us.

My mother and Suze laid a huge blanket on the lawn and set out coolers with cookout treats. Wyatt and Quinn set up the brand-new porch swing they'd built. The cover, made by my mother, had swirls of blue, the exact color of a robin's egg we'd found during our first visit to Putney, Vermont.

The grown-ups talked and talked and talked about the extraordinary life we'd have in Roundhouse. We kids ignored their rush of words as we concentrated on eating platefuls of rarely served food—hot dogs and hamburgers grilled by Chuck and served on fluffy white bread rolls, chips, brownies, blondies, and chocolate chip cookies—not one of them made with carob.

Unless we counted the potato salad and the tomatoes for burgers, there wasn't a vegetable in sight. We ran in circles, Poppy did cartwheels, the older boys sailed Frisbees over everyone's heads, the grown-ups laughed at Henry's stupid jokes, and I watched it all with my head in my mom's lap as she stroked my hair.

We played softball; captains Roxanne and Quinn chose teams while my father set up a volleyball net. My mother and Melanie painted our faces, Suze taught us how to make daisy chains, and Grady checked all the bikes in the barn for safety while Chuck and Wyatt roped off a swimming area in the pond.

That day, the world became a carnival, and I prayed for the bubbly joy to last forever.

A few hours later, Henry, Poppy, and I waved as all the grown-ups except Diantha and Roxanne disappeared. The car and van vanished, reappeared, and dissolved as they snaked down the winding road.

Roxanne was the only woman in Puddingstone without kids. For years afterward, I made up reasons they chose her to stay with Diantha and us for the first two weeks, but the truth never appeared until I became an adult: they were making it easier for the other mothers.

Once everyone left, the boys raced around the Roundhouse land, marking their territory. Henry ran after them and then caught up in seconds. He always ran faster than any of us.

"Jacob, watch Henry," Diantha called from the porch. She and Roxanne sat side by side on the hanging swing, drinking beers left from the cookout.

Roxanne stood and shaped her hands into a megaphone. "Nobody goes near the creek without a grown-up!"

Diantha shook her head. "Disagree. If there are two of them, that should be sufficient."

"Two kids can drown at the same time." Roxanne turned sideways to face Diantha. "We made the decision weeks ago."

"I didn't agree then, and I still don't." Diantha whipped her thick braid over her shoulder.

"This isn't a one-woman show," Roxanne said.

"But I'm the one who will always be here. The boys are ten, eleven, and twelve."

"But Henry is only six."

"We have to build their internal responsibility."

"I'm going to bring this up at our next meeting."

"Of course. But until then, everyone will have to trust me." When Diantha noticed our eyes glued on them as though watching a play, she came over to where we perched on the edge of the porch off to the right. "Girls, don't blow your chance to get first dibs at picking a room."

"We're allowed?" Poppy asked.

Diantha took a pen from her nearby notebook and tapped Poppy on the top of her head. "Permission granted."

We raised our eyebrows at each other, not needing her to tell us twice, grinned, and ran into our new home.

Roundhouse held my mother's fingerprints. Her art hung everywhere, including a crazy-happy sketch of Puddingstone in the hall. I guessed she meant it to be a hug from Boston, but the picture saddened me. The scent of her homemade lemon cleanser surrounded us. She sent us to Vermont with gallons of the stuff and the recipe (vinegar, castile soap, essential oil, and water).

Our real house smelled like a soup of cigarette smoke, jasmine incense to mask the cigarette odors, old coffee, the stink of kicked-off shoes, and the weird smell of the fabric used in Indian print bedspreads.

I sniffed the air as we closed the large glass-paneled front door and caught a whiff of old woodstove smoke, fireplace, and woolen blankets. Lavender drifted around us without an apparent source, though I could identify the fresh-cut wood smell from the carpentry projects Wyatt and Chuck had completed in the past months.

Off the long hallway was a warren of small empty rooms waiting for our mark.

The kitchen screamed for my mother's touch. Ridiculous amounts of groceries sat on the round table, waiting to be put away. Unwashed mugs with coffee rings were piled in the sink. I recognized the bags from the co-op where we shopped in Boston and wondered if I'd ever see that store again.

"I bet Diantha pretends she doesn't see the dirty dishes and makes us do them all the time," I said.

"That will be the first thing Diantha puts on our chore chart," Poppy said.

We rolled our eyes in unison. Poppy and I performed 90 percent of our actions in unison. We washed our hair in the same circular motion and, when shampooing, piled up our foamy wet hair into similar crazy styles. We'd moved from pretending we were sisters to acting like twins.

A pantry connected the kitchen and an oversized dining room. Wyatt and Chuck had knocked down walls, making four medium rooms into two giant ones.

Our massive new dining room table would fit fifteen without the leaves and at least thirty with them. Wyatt had built it with Quinn's help; they'd burnished the oak to dark honey and varnished it so smooth that the mice I heard scampering could use it as a skating rink.

A double doorway opened into the living room, the only room except the kitchen and dining room shouting a clear purpose. Three puffy sofas and four overstuffed chairs made the room look like a doctor's waiting room, but piles of pillows could turn the room into a perfect space for anything from dull meetings to building forts. A goliath of a mantel, longer than the one in Boston, held a single rainbow-colored peace sign. The grown-ups intended us to cover the length of plaster with millions of newly crafted ones.

As we climbed the stairs to the second floor, the sizable square landing showing many doors appeared. Poppy trailed as I sniffed a growing lavender scent.

We peeked into six bedrooms and the bathroom, noting a giant clawfoot tub, bare wooden floors, and a surfeit of iron beds of varying sizes until we reached the lavender source: here, in the most oversized room, where lavender buds filled a giant old-fashioned china bowl atop the narrow entry table.

We'd found Diantha's room. The walls gleamed with fresh violet-blue paint streaked with a faint yellow that seemed like the dawn rising. I recognized my mother's work. The patchwork quilt covering the bed matched the covers of the wall, as did a profusion of pillows. Across the simple long dresser were framed photos of Zane and Jacob, Diantha and Chuck's sons, along with a few group shots of the rest of us kids.

A midnight blue rug covered the floor, a phone sat on the nightstand, and a tall bookshelf waited for books.

We looked at each other, nodded, and ran to the room next door to claim it for ourselves and Henry. Being close to Diantha felt like the safest choice. Maybe she flipped between strict and crazy-lenient, but she was our grown-up.

Poppy and I slept holding hands in the metal twin beds we'd pushed together that night. Henry slept across the bottom like the puppy he pretended to be, and we rested our feet on him as though he were our very own St. Bernard.

No parent came up for three weeks. Diantha said we had to adjust to our new community before returning to being nuclear.

"Nuclear means mother, father, and kids—just that with nobody else," Poppy told me once we escaped to a hidden corner behind the barn, where we laid a gray wool blanket we'd taken from the house.

"But we weren't nuclear before," I said. "Puddingstone had seven kids and ten grown-ups."

"But we belonged to our parents."

"Who do we belong to now?"

Poppy squished her mouth in all directions, just like my mother did when thinking. "I guess we belong to everyone."

At that moment, I became more Ivy Puddingstone than Ivy Pascal,

Ivy with the many mothers, Ivy P belonging to all, belonging to nobody.

We were outside in the meadow. The grass rolled on forever and looked like I imagined heaven, but I wanted our cozy Puddingstone backyard with swings and trees small enough to climb. I missed the maypole that we'd incorporated into a thousand games of make-believe back in Boston. We'd pretended the pole was everything from a school where Poppy and I were the teachers—and Henry, of course, played the student—to the pole marking the bar in *Gunsmoke,* another show we'd secretly watched at Maura's house. Diantha promised we'd make a new one soon, but it would never be the same.

The gentle rolling pasture continued until it hit the rocky riverbank, where we could only go in pairs. Diantha had won that argument.

Poppy crossed her legs as though she were a Yogi. I tried to imitate her, but my legs were too long and didn't bend like hers. She tilted her head until it touched the scratchy blanket, then kicked her legs and stood on her hands. Her streaky maple syrup-colored curls piled on the gray wool, making a big puddle of hair. Our hair matched. We'd cut pieces off and put them side by side to prove it, but mine flopped down and never grew past my shoulders while her curls kept going and going until someday, we imagined, if she never cut them, they might reach her waist, like her mother's.

The day the parents had left, each whispered to their kids when they'd return. My nuclear parents said they'd be back on my birthday.

Two weeks later, when my parents called to ask what I wanted them to bring to celebrate my upcoming birthday, I chose hamburgers. In pre-Roundhouse times, the four of us used to sneak out to Mr. Bartley's Burger Cottage every time we went to see where Daddy once went to school.

"Oh, baby—a hamburger will get cold! How about a drawing pad and fresh crayons?" my mother asked.

We shared a crazy-big bin of crayons, but the boys had broken most of them, using them as tiny guns and miniature swords.

"Can I keep them just for Poppy and me? In our room?"

"Is that okay? Is there a sharing rule? What would Diantha say? I thought all the art stuff was for the community."

"Why can't Poppy and I be a just-us community?"

I swear I heard Mom's sigh from Boston, alerting me to her mood change.

The night before my birthday, I heard Diantha talking to my mother. I curled up outside the kitchen where we had the phone, holding my fingers to my lips anytime another kid got close.

I couldn't hear my mother's words, only what Diantha said to her.

"Annabel, honey, she'll be fine."

I guessed that *she* meant me.

I imagined Diantha nodding as my mother spoke.

"You can't leave your business with a deadline like that. It's only a few days," Diantha said. "Don't cry. Ivy will hardly notice. I promise. We'll do a million special things. Annabel, babe, stop crying, or I'll start."

She went on and on, telling my mother how fine I'd be, but I think my mother cried for a long time.

My mother called first thing in the morning to sing "Happy Birthday," promising we'd see each other the following week. She kept talking about the super important, meaningful, and significant event that prevented them from coming up that day.

"Something good has happened. Something wonderful. President Ford declared unconditional amnesty for every United States Vietnam War deserter and those who refused to serve. He calls them evaders; we call them heroes. You can't imagine what this means, Pudding. Daddy's work sponsored a gigantic party, and Sojourner Graphics designed the poster of the century!"

"You drew it?" I asked.

"We all had a hand in it. Wait till you see! I'm bringing one for your room."

"That's not my birthday present, though, right?"

"Silly. Of course not. We'll have a cake and ice cream and lots of presents. A ton of treats!"

I lacked the vocabulary or courage to say that the only treat I needed was her. I wanted to be as crucial to my mother as Sojourner Graphics and amnesty, the meaning of which was beyond my understanding. But she didn't ask if I understood, and I didn't volunteer my ignorance.

Instead, I mumbled words to keep her cheerful. My mother yearned for the joyfulness of life and goodness to fill me, and I didn't want to disappoint her.

My brother made our mother happy simply by existing. He was born with that knack; analyzing situations and then figuring out the best path forward became my role from the moment we stepped into Roundhouse.

Chapter 28

✿

Ivy

SEPTEMBER 1977

The Flavor of Carelessness

Either hell or heaven, most likely a bit of each, awaited me the day I turned eleven three years later. Birthdays in Vermont continued to be crapshoots, one of Zane's favorite words when describing anything to do with the grown-ups.

Disgusting, sticky late summer heat hung over the bedroom Poppy and I shared. We'd moved to the attic during year two at Roundhouse; our room took up half of the divided space on the highest floor. The ceiling sloped so sharply that even Henry bumped his head when he moved too close to where it came down. We'd begun Roundhouse wanting to be the closest kids to Diantha; now, we craved privacy.

Our attic room represented the worst of all worlds: hottest in the summer, coldest in the winter. Diantha stored suitcases, trunks, and a ton of unwanted junk on the other side of our room. Since the boys were too lazy to move stuff around to claim the space, Poppy and I felt safe from invasion in our third-floor sanctuary.

Plus, whenever we needed to clean our room, we just offloaded our mess to the other side.

Despite the trade-offs, our system was tight, and we loved the attic space. We sweltered in June, July, August, and most of September.

Summer meant sweating and bugs; by mid-October, we switched to wearing three layers in our room, but keeping our solitude was worth any discomfort.

We stayed alert, though. Diantha encouraged switching rooms whenever the mood hit, instructing us to "dialogue and negotiate," which the boys translated into "bullying and dirty tricks."

Now that all the boys except Henry were teenagers, our lives became a battle for privacy. Diantha sighed and said the hormones would soon choke us with Jacob and Mac fifteen, Zane fourteen, and Leo thirteen.

When Poppy and I refused to have Henry with us anymore, Leo took pity and invited my brother to share his room. Or it wasn't pity, and Suze or my mother bribed Leo with something. Or not. Predicting the mothers was a fool's game.

So far, we'd kept everyone from going after our space by whining about sweating and freezing, with Poppy's ability to terrify everyone with her tooth-baring feral expressions. But a room battle could still begin at any time; we never underestimated Zane's lust for might.

Childhood is for exploration! Such was Diantha's favorite saying, though, in her world, *exploration* included everything from seeing who could climb to the top of the power pyramid of power and then kicking off others to stealing anything we hadn't hidden.

Diantha repeated her phrase until I wanted to throw up. Her idea of freedom came with a list of unwritten rules three miles long, including facing a constant stream of vegetables, brown rice, and tofu. And carob. Did Diantha honestly think carob brownies, carob-flavored milk, or, worst of all, carob pudding had any relation to chocolate?

Having our school in the barn was the grown-up's idea of independent education. Three local communities ran the Putney Free Academy out of our barn—ours being one of the three. The other kids called Roundhouse "the children's commune," making us sound like a cross between *Lord of the Flies* (which Jacob had read aloud to us one chapter at a time) and what Jacob called us—*Peter Pan: The Drug-Soaked Edition*. Jacob had discovered he could dip into his father's pot stash.

"Happy Birthday, Ivy! Ivy, Ivy, bo-bivey, banana fana fo-fivey!" Poppy shouted when she opened her eyes. "Do you think your parents will come?"

We tracked our mothers and fathers as though they were rock stars, hoping for sightings, grateful even for news. I turned my head and wrinkled my nose at Poppy, electric moments after waking. Curls pushed out from every angle. When I stretched her coils, they reached almost two feet.

I shrugged as though my parents' appearance barely mattered. "Who knows? Are there any good marches going on in Boston?"

Poppy kicked off the sheet and crossed her legs. Sprite-like, flexible, and the master of cartwheeling across the meadow could only describe only a slice of her Poppyness.

"Mao Zedong died a year ago today," she said. "Jacob heard it on the radio. Maybe they're all flying to China for a memorial." With her forehead touching her knees, she bent and used her fingers to fluff out her hair. I envied Poppy's version of styling. If I did that, my hair just looked raggedy.

Poppy might only be half a year older than I was, but she acted a hundred years braver. She wasn't more intelligent, but she was far more willing to believe she was right about everything. Plus, she was cute enough to pull off being rude to grown-ups.

Adults chalked her cheekiness up to impishness; I'd overheard Diantha describe me as *dour*. I ran to the dictionary, where I read "relentlessly severe, stern, or gloomy in manner or appearance."

After reading the definition, I bit my tongue and held my tears, though I wrote in my diary, *why don't you give me something to smile about, Diantha?*

I prayed that Diantha read my diary, but I didn't think she cared enough. Her sons fascinated her, though. I bet even Jacob and Zane's farts made her smile.

Mac's thoughtfulness drew everyone to him, including Diantha, and Henry held the beloved baby position. Poppy charmed everyone, including Zane. Leo impressed us all with his creativity and was the best cook.

Dour me bored Diantha. That's what I believed.

Poppy threw her once-white, now dingy-oatmeal-colored stuffed monkey at me. I caught him, wiggled his multicolored butt at her, and tossed back my sad-eyed tiger. Our favorite stuffed animals, the ones we hid from the boys with the stealth of cat burglars, had become heart brothers, just as Poppy and I were heart sisters.

Poppy and I shared green eyes, our stuffies shared brass buttons in their ears that read *Steiff,* and both were gifts from our grandparents.

Poppy leaped out of bed. "Ready for the incredible celebration of being eleven?"

We cracked up, knowing what faced me. Fear underlay my laughter; hers held sympathy.

Our birthday-only painting greeted me as I clomped down the stairs; Diantha had awoke early and hung the picture in the same place as always, right where it would smack the birthday kid and everyone else first thing. Seven times a year, the dazzling circle within circles, the color of kiwis, strawberries, and limes, surrounded by screaming lemon-yellow rays that could pierce your skull, greeted us.

I wondered if my mother knew how Diantha planned to use this enormous piece of art when she'd painted it. Nobody argued much with Diantha except my father, but he paid too little attention to Roundhouse practices to bother.

After side-eying the colossal canvas, I made a wide avoidance loop and chanted prayers to be alone for breakfast as I headed to the kitchen.

Zane sat at the table with Mac, as inseparable a duo as Poppy and me. Like Poppy, Zane burned brighter than all of us.

Jacob avoided much of what went on by burying himself in books. Where Zane played his mother like a fiddle, Jacob seemed embarrassed by the privileges his mother allotted them.

"Happy Birthday, Barbie." Zane lifted his brown mug. He'd taken to drinking coffee after turning fourteen.

"Eff you, Spotty, I answered.

His nickname for me reflected Diantha's lectures upon discovering the Barbie doll my father bought. After suffering Diantha's wisdom about how Barbie embodied every sin against and by women, I'd held my doll ever tighter.

Spotty came from his habit of dabbing a mixture of zinc oxide and clay on his pimples and letting the white stuff sit on his face in crackly white circles all day. Leo had convinced him of the efficacy of the horrendous mix that he practically had to chip off his face.

Our morning enmity established, I grabbed a bowl from the dish drainer. The mugs, bowls, pots, and plates teetering on the high stack reflected our laziness in putting them away.

We no longer owned glasses; they'd all broken long ago. Mugs held all our drinks. They shattered less, plus we could provide an endless supply from the pottery we created at school. The color and shape of our coarse ceramics reflected the crafter's mood and talent. At the moment, Zane held a lumpy, squat gray horror Jacob had made on a day that he resented being at school instead of being allowed to read all day.

"Happy Birthday," Mac said. "I bet your parents will show up."

I shrugged to illustrate how little I cared and dipped into the granola we kept in a giant oversized mayonnaise jar.

We made the crunchy cereal in turns, and nobody missed their chance since it allowed us to sneak in extra honey, cinnamon, or vanilla, according to our preference. Today, we had a fresh Leo batch—a treat. Everyone else, including me, made the stuff with the flavor of carelessness, speed being our primary goal.

Granola-making slowed Leo, as he became our chemist and Betty Crocker, adding gourmet touches such as waiting to put in the raisins until ten minutes before the end. Only Leo's granola lacked burned or soggy oats, over-dosing with honey, or the overage of tongue-burning cinnamon endemic to the batches made by everyone else. Everyone else threw it all in and let the burning begin.

"Did you check out the sun, Barbie?" Zane's smile promised nothing good.

"Leave her alone." Mac waved Zane's words away. "Don't worry, Ives. There's just the usual."

"Did Diantha write her stuff yet?" I asked.

"Naturally." Zane laughed. "First up in the morning, last to bed at night.

Zane knew his mother. Diantha's standards meant strolling around the house and grounds to reassure herself we were alive, checking our chore charts, and refilling the cupboard with healthy ingredients that snarled 'Screw you,?' to our taste buds.

We used our secret kid meetings to complain about living in our screwed-up adult version of utopian childhood freedom—talking far from the ears of Diantha and any Puddingstone grownups who might be up for the week. They supposedly took turns parenting us when they came—less and less as we grew older—but mostly, they left raising us to Diantha and school, treating their turns at Roundhouse as little vacations from peace and justice work.

Freedom meant choosing from Diantha's array of what she wanted us to desire, which included almost nothing we actually desired. My gratitude toward my Aunt Kirstie, who sent me a package of magazines each month, was endless. I lusted for the Herbal Essences shampoo I saw in *Seventeen* magazine. The smell! The silky hair! The magazines might be a few months outdated, but what did it matter with us stuck out here?

The promise of hair heaven bewitched Poppy and me. We detested the natural shampoo concoction Diantha purchased by the quart in the hippie co-op in town, swearing the brown liquid smelled like the devil's behind. Last month, Poppy had begged her grandmother to send us good shampoo and cream rinse. Now, we had a secret stash of Breck buried under the sweaters in our bureau.

There's no way we'd leave our shampoo gold in the kids' bathroom where anyone could use it.

If we hiked five miles to Murphy's General Store, we could get Prell, but Poppy and I saved our stolen cash for new comic books and real chocolate. When the urge to break out struck hard, one of us would sneak into Diantha's wallet and remove a few dollars. We'd slip our new *Wonder Woman* comic down the front of our overalls and eat our Hershey Bars on the way back. Once home, we'd run up the stairs to brush away our chocolate breath.

Poppy and I craved candy so badly that sometimes we'd mix honey with butter and rough whole wheat flour, roll it into balls, and pop them like jellybeans. We craved spaghetti that didn't taste like cardboard and meatballs made from meat. I dreamed of the Cocoa Puffs we used to devour at Maura's house. I dreamed of having a regular mother like Joanne, Maura's mother who didn't make her kids eat tofu.

Most of all, I wished for books that weren't boring. I might be the second youngest in the house, but I was also the second-most-voracious reader. Our twice-monthly trips to the library couldn't satisfy my needs. Jacob let me read his novels, but they bored me to death. Still, he had stacks of them, being one of our two Roundhouse versions of Richie Rich. His sneaker-millionaire grandparents sent him and Zane approximately a million dollars a month. It was too bad that Jacob's taste ran to Tolkien and his imitators, though I slogged through them when desperate.

When I couldn't stand one more hour reading about Middle-earth, I snuck into Diantha's room to reread a Jane Austen or struggled through her *ways-to-live-right* books. She dedicated her shelves to everything written by Scott and Helen Nearing. I blamed the Nearings for half of the crap we put up with.

The Whole Earth Catalog, Women and Their Bodies, and Diantha's other favorites lived on her old-fashioned nightstand. One always sat atop the pile—*Liberated Parents, Liberated Children* had a dull yellow cover with black type. She'd scribbled notes next to the "types" the author laid out in the chapter titled "The Roles We Cast Them In."

In one of the margins, she wrote *poor Ivy is in danger of becoming the sad sack while trying to be the princess.*

Though I didn't understand the author's entire writing, I think Diantha missed the book's point. Either way, she believed the worst of me.

Underlined sentences marked the book seemingly dearest to her: *The Growth and Development of Mothers.* A child's drawing decorated the cover, which made no sense if this book was supposed to be about mothers.

Diantha had triple-underlined the words, *what is the answer to the age-old question, "Who comes first, me or my family?"* along with the author's statement: *I have decided it has to be me, and as I become a more mature "me," my family will derive the benefit.*

My childhood boiled down to knowing that all the adults in my life would underline that sentence and agree that Diantha had sacrificed herself for our safety and freedom.

Diantha had turned her life over to watch us. She seemed to have no life of her own.

After finishing my granola, I wandered back to the giant sun. Avoiding the words was impossible; the dreaded birthday beast approached.

Chapter 29

❀

Ivy

SEPTEMBER 1977

Signature Scents

Thick cloudy plastic with traces of erased grease pencil marks covered the giant birthday painting. A heavy black line down the center divided the plastic in two. On one side, Diantha had written *YAY!* She labeled the other side *Work Ahead!*

Today's messages awaited me.

Every birthday, Diantha moved the painting from the living room, brought out the plastic sheet, and tacked it to the wall above The Sun's temporary space. Writing something under each column was mandatory. We used the exercise to get back at each other for a year of pinching, snitching, and "liberating" stuff—we couldn't use the word *steal*, though that's what we did. No skill served us better than hiding things well. Cloaking, masking, and bold-faced lying made up the spine of essential Roundhouse skills. We stole the best of everyone's stuff, as though we were cat thieves in training.

At one time or another, we'd all tried to sweet-talk our parents into buying us a trunk with an unbreakable lock, but the idea insulted their fantasy of our lives.

Still, within the acres, we had built worlds of imagination; sometimes, we even fulfilled our grown-ups' Roundhouse dreams.

During our second year at Roundhouse, Poppy and I had built a fort worthy of Wonder Woman in one corner of a former hen house that bordered the deep woods. Jacob liberated old planks from the barn and helped us rig storage space. The shelves held magazines, a stolen plastic box filled with art supplies, and granola we regularly skimmed from the mayonnaise jar, though only Leo-made batches. But as time moved on, our allegiance switched to the barn. The barn might not be girls-only, but it was warmish in the winter and coolish in the summer.

The red barn provided magic. Even with our school sited there, we had plenty of hiding places that only we Roundhouse kids knew existed.

I thought the building must have been built by giants playing with wooden crates, haphazardly placing tiny, attached buildings and hidden rooms. We covered our most favored secret place with old rugs we dragged over from the attic in the house. Poppy painted flower murals over the splintering walls; Leo made a collage of old rusty tools. Zane had liberated an enormous pot from the kitchen, which Mac fashioned into our marshmallow roasting pan, figuring out how to build a fire large enough to toast without burning the place down. Jacob built a library.

We'd kept our secrets in that most hidden corner of the barn, the concealed platform beyond an area where people had thrown the old, broken, and unwanted for years and years. Secret stashes of candy, a growing mound of comic books, the teen magazines Diantha hated, and ones the boys hid in a box they shut tight with a stolen padlock.

As I approached the Birthday Sun, I wished I were in our secret barn space. Once I began reading, I almost scratched off the first layer of the skin covering my thighs. I started with Diantha's two-sentence evaluation; the maximum length allowed.

Yay: You're getting a handle on political analysis—keep reading my books!
Work Ahead: A slavish bondage to parents cramps every faculty of the mind.

—*Mary Shelley*

I knew Mary Shelley wrote *Frankenstein*, but now I wanted to discover who she was and why Diantha had chosen her words. Those words captured me. Diantha had the power to surprise.

Next came my brother's words, the boy who carried sunshine in his pocket.

> *Yay: I could live on your Bana H forever*
> *Work Ahead: Being happy!!!*

In the early days, when my brother cried for our parents every night. I made some banana bread with Leo's help and named it after Henry.

Poppy's words were as goofy as I expected.

> *Yay: You're honey, and I'm the tea; I'm butter, and you're the toast.*
> *Work Ahead: Sticking together like peanut butter and jam.*

Food obsessed us all. Ordinary people considered eating to be about nutrition and fun, but for us, our calories represented everything from love to rebellion to holding up a banner. Poppy and I devoted an entire wall of our room to forbidden ads we tore from the magazines I got from Aunt Kirstie, who sent everything from *Ladies' Home Journal*, a great source of food pictures, to *Life, Look, Time, Reader's Digest*—one Diantha especially hated, saying it represented the belly of the beast— and occasionally *National Geographic*.

Our montage included photos of SpaghettiOs, Dairy Queen, and Hamburger Helper. That one really drove the mothers crazy, so we put up a ton of them even though we'd never tasted the stuff.

When *Seventeen* magazine had first arrived, Poppy and I jumped up like Christmas had come early. Aunt Kirstie had bought me a direct subscription, as none of our Rhinebeck relatives subscribed. Roxanne, Diantha, Suze, and my mother hated the gift. They thought the magazine should be forbidden. Melanie laughed about it—Poppy's mother always took the kindest road. The other women were ready to go to the mat, which led to a Roundhouse meeting during one of the weekends everyone visited.

All of us kids had sat on the giant rag rug on the living room floor, propped on pillows in every color. The parents, whether by accident or not, sat by gender. The mothers and Roxanne argued about the narrow roles *Seventeen* would force on us: The makeup! The dating advice! The tight-fitted sweaters and short skirts! Surely Poppy and I would turn into tiny hookers if we read this magazine.

The men, for the most part, remained quiet.

Finally, Melanie rose. "We sent our children to Roundhouse so that they'd grow free. Does growing free mean growing only according to our exact beliefs? If so, exactly how are we different from our parents?"

And just like that, the argument fizzled. Nobody seemed able to hold in their head the idea that someone might be the prettiest *and* the smartest person in the room. Nobody gave Melanie much credit for being one of the most intelligent people in the group until she said something that reminded everyone.

You were only supposed to win one contest in this world, but I knew that wasn't true because of Poppy. Poppy could do everything.

I took a deep breath and read the next entry on the birthday board, the one I dreaded: Zane's.

Yay: You usually smell good.
Work Ahead: Stop being so damn stuck up; you're not as smart as you think.

Diantha must have told him to cross out the word damn, but I saw the letters through his slashes of dark lines. His mother only let him go so far, though she ignored how he circumvented the two-sentence rule by employing a semicolon.

Zane zigged and zagged. For Poppy's birthday, Zane had written. *Just stay cool.* He never treated Poppy carelessly. Last week, he'd snuck off to Murphy's and returned with a backpack filled with a copy of every comic book they carried. When he walked into the kitchen where we were all snacking, he gave us a chin-up nod and cocked his head to follow, a signal to meet in our hideaway. Our secret space was larger than the giant living room.

Zane shook his backpack until *Spider-Man*, *Superman*, *Wonder Woman*, *Star Wars*, *Justice League of America*, and *Captain America* covered an old army blanket. Then he nodded and tossed me a bag of my favorite, *Betty and Veronica*. That was Zane, trying at least once a week to prove he wasn't an ass.

When Suze had been here the previous week and noticed Zane zinging me, she offered comfort by insisting Zane and I would never be compatible. I was a self-sufficient, perfectionist, workaholic Virgo, while he showed every sign of being an impatient, tactless Sagittarius.

She added his good astrological qualities, but they slipped my mind by the next day.

Plus, she reminded me that being as tall as I was made people think I was older than my years.

I don't understand why looking older made people treat me worse, but people sure treated tiny Poppy better.

I couldn't wait for my mother to arrive, so I could stop trying to figure out everything in the world for at least a weekend. Mom had a way of making the world clearer.

Snob? How was I a snob?

I saved up dozens of questions between visits from my parents—scribbling them in my journal, waiting for the weekend when they'd answer anything I asked. Phone calls were never private, and I needed to be alone with my mother to ask the questions I needed answered.

After reading the rest of my Birthday Sun—ordinary birthday wishes dashed off to satisfy Diantha—I ran upstairs to get dressed for school. Poppy always grabbed extra time in bed because her morning meal consisted of one of her disgusting breakfast cookies—granola mixed with peanut butter and carob chips and then frozen—eaten in a minute on the way to the barn.

Now, having climbed out from her nest of tangled sheets, Poppy pulled her favorite so-called dress over her head. The blue fabric covered with tiny red and yellow flowers looked more like a nightgown than anything else, but Poppy swore it made a perfect dress. What might have been a thigh-length nightgown for a woman became an ankle-grazing billowing maxidress on her. She'd found the item in the local church thrift store, sifting through piles of clothes that smelled of all the former owners stewed together.

My jealousy took over as I watched the dress drift around her skinny body. We shared almost everything, but the blue dress was off-limits. Poppy deemed it her *signature outfit*, just as her mother's Muguet Des Bois perfume represented Melanie's signature scent. Each morning, Poppy took off the top of an old Muguet Des Bois tin. Sweet lilac smells filled the room as she dusted herself with a parsimonious hand. Poppy kept her jewelry in the light pink container and plucked out a bauble to wear each morning, moving through the day with her mother's memory continuously surrounding her from the chalky bracelet or necklace.

I pulled on one of my father's old T-shirts—forest green and swimming around me—and the same overalls I'd worn all week.

We ran down the stairs, raced down the path to the barn, and a minute later, we were in school. All I had to do was get through the next five hours, and then I could let go and breathe free, a comfort only provided when my mother appeared.

Chapter 30

❋

Ivy

Cover Your Whatsis

The footprint of Roundhouse's gigantic barn was twice the size of the house.

Maybe three times.

Wyatt, Chuck, and Quinn had walled off Putney Free School within it, along with members of the two other houses, Saorsa and Libertate. Each name meant "freedom": *Saorsa* was Gaelic, *Libertate* was Romanian, and those freedom lovers ran the school with input from our grown-ups.

Diantha described Saorsa and us as political entities; Libertate considered themselves agrarian-based. Perhaps that we had weeds and wildflowers made us partners, but certainly, it wasn't because of our success with farming. We yielded only stunted crops, which resembled our success with granola—very little. And like our Leo-made granola, only our tomatoes flourished. Leo loved tomatoes.

I hated visiting Libertate; Roundhouse's amenities made it seem like we lived in a palace compared to living there. Apparently, cleaning didn't fit into their political beliefs. Casual nudity very occasionally appeared at Roundhouse, and I wanted to puke every second that grown-up flesh appeared, but a state of undress was Libertate's norm.

After one afternoon of watching adult parts bob during a volleyball game, I avoided any and all visits to their place.

Saorsa was the opposite—I could stay there all day. They had an incredible library I could borrow from, food made by someone who loved the job, and Leesa. Leesa was kind, smart, liked me, and she made jewelry. She'd already taught me how to bend and polish copper and made me a bangle bracelet. Next, we were working on silver buckles; I planned to make one for my father.

Katie, a Saorsa adult and my favorite teacher, clapped her hands for the morning talk circle. "Grab your spheres, all."

Talking spheres had replaced *balls* after we had suffered through too many mornings of the boys' ball jokes.

The older boys sighed, Zane loudest of all, as we made our way to the giant once-beige carpet covering the rough barn floor. The rug and a rule against bare feet had come after too many embedded splinters required Diantha to dig in our flesh with an alcohol-soaked pair of tweezers and a fire-sterilized needle.

Zane sauntered over, tossing his green talking sphere into the air, trying to hit the unreachable rafters. "I bet they once used this place to hang people."

"Try to join us without terrifying the little kids." Peter, another Saorsa teacher, believed in freedom less than the other teachers.

Zane shoved Jacob to reach the circle before his brother and plopped down between Poppy and me, forcing us to separate. "Sorry, Barbie. I need some sisterly vibes."

"Bull." Poppy smiled with the swear, laughing as she tossed her hair.

"Morning thoughts?" Katie asked.

JoJo, the six-year-old Libertate candidate for enthusiasm king, rolled his sphere into the circle first. He ran over and threw a small package of store-bought cookies in my lap. "Happy Birthday! Peggy Lawton!"

"Wow! Thanks." My mouth watered. This trio of cookies, stacked together and wrapped in clear, crinkly plastic, was a top choice when we snuck out to Murphy's General Store.

Spheres kept rolling; presents kept dropping. Most gifts came from Murphy's forbidden food section. The grown-ups closed their eyes on birthdays.

By the end of circle time, I had a lapful of candy, another package of Peggy Lawton cookies, a worn *Supergirl* comic book, and a hardcover copy of *Call of the Wild* from Jacob.

Poppy, who'd waited to be last, rolled her sphere, inked with a million peace signs, right at me. "Hold out your hand and close your eyes."

When I obeyed, she slipped a ring on my finger, the metal cool against my skin.

"Wait a minute before looking. Let me count," Poppy said. "One, two, three, four, five, six, seven, eight, nine, ten. Okay! Open!"

The moonstone mood ring we'd swooned over in the May issue of *Seventeen* winked at me. I slipped it on, the silvery finish glinting around the jewel in the middle. "How did you get it?"

"My grandmother sent away for it. Look. The stone turned brown." Poppy handed me a piece of stiff cardboard where she'd written the meanings of the colors and bordered the words with twined flowers. Brown meant nervous and anxious.

Zane looked over my shoulder and read the color-key card. "Big surprise. You try it on, Poppy."

I slipped the ring off and handed it to her. After she slipped it on, the color lightened until it became blue. *Relaxed.*

Leo leaned over, took her hand, and then mine. "The color comes from the temperature of your skin. That's all."

"Killjoy," Zane said.

"Okay, kids." Peter clapped his hands. "Pick your stations."

Everyone wandered to their favorite subject corner. I drifted to the reading area as I stared at my ring, willing it to turn blue to show I could be relaxed.

Poppy picked up a paintbrush to continue making a border of the flowers, hearts, and leaves to set the school off from the rest of the barn.

Peter led a hunting safety session while Kate started a geography lesson. Three Libertate kids worked in the sewing space, stitching shapeless garments that resembled monks' robes. I'd do the same thing if I came from Libertate.

Nothing caught my eye from our school library, which leaned heavily on science fiction—Peter's favorite—and classics like Dickens to ensure we met Vermont's homeschooling standards, plus lots of movement literature purchased by Diantha. After opening and closing five books, I joined the tie-dyeing group.

Tie-dyeing was Putney Free School's cottage industry. We turned fresh white T-shirts into riots of color, transformed the monk robes made in the sewing group into swirling pinks and purples, and blasted white baby socks with every shade, making the perfect presents for hippie parents. Murphy's General Store carried them under the name *Putney Free Clothes*. We made and sold them as part of our math, economics, and business curriculum. We logged every time we finished a garment, signing up to receive the two cents per item or whatever we received.

Zane reached into a basket for a damp white T-shirt, folding and twisting it into a sunburst pattern.

"Get me some rubber bands, Barbie," he said as he tightened the rolled fabric.

I dropped a handful before him and then chose a pair of baby socks, the softest and easiest pieces to manage. I calculated how many tie-dyed socks I'd be forced to make before earning enough to buy a new *Wonder Woman* annual digest.

"You realize we're not even making minimum wage," Zane said.

I contorted the tiny socks into a free-form shape, planning a curve of reds and oranges. "How much is minimum wage?"

"Pretty sure it's $2.30 an hour."

The socks sell for $1.75 a pair. From start to finish, I can make about three pairs in an hour, and wrapping them takes about fifteen minutes."

Zane used a sponge to apply blood red to a shirt section he'd pinwheeled into shape. I kept my work easy by dipping one side of a pair of socks and then the other, letting the colors bleed.

"So, after Murphy's gets their fifty percent cut, and the school takes their forty percent for materials and overhead, what do we get?"

Math came easy; business numbers were doable in my head. Ten percent of my selling price came to eighteen cents, rounding up. For three pairs, I made less than sixty cents. And it took over an hour. "We're getting robbed," I said.

"Yeah." He picked up a new sponge for the screaming yellow. "I think that's our lesson for today. I'm gonna earn extra credit by starting a union. You in?"

We spat on our palms and shook.

The day turned out okay—my team won in softball—but I itched to see my parents. I expected them to show up before my birthday dinner. Birthday feasts were always a big deal, with us getting to pick our dinner. I'd asked for chicken parmesan this year, the dish that Grandma Camille always made when we visited Rhinebeck. I could almost taste the cheesy tomato flavor. I hoped my mother had remembered to ask for her exact recipe.

When school ended, Henry and I flew out of the barn, searching for the old blue Chrysler Grandpa Cooper had passed down to my parents when he got a new one.

"There's the car," I yelled to my brother, fast as always and passing me in a second.

"Hey, Ivy!" The deep voice came from the clearing where Diantha had hung three macrame hammocks we'd made in school. I reversed course and followed the trail to the machete-hacked area, smelling mint and basil from the nearby herb garden.

"Got something for you, birthday girl," Chuck shouted from where he swayed in the hammock.

I liked Chuck, who spent extra time explaining concepts we didn't understand—whether explaining checking accounts or why dogs die before humans. But like most of the grown-ups, he didn't wear a bathing suit when he swam. His hair, wet from the pond, shone in the sun. I squinted, so everything became hazy.

All of us kids, in an unspoken and one-hundred-percent-adhered-to agreement, wore T-shirts and shorts in the water.

Chuck held out a large box covered in what I recognized as my mother's handmade reusable cloth wrapping paper.

"Where's my mother?"

"She sent this," he said, offering the package with a big smile. "It's fantastic!"

"But where are my parents? I saw their car."

He rolled over to face me; I kept my eyes above his neck.

"Man, that water is great." He shook out his hair, sending water flying. "We should all go swimming."

I crossed my arms over my chest and jutted out my chin.

"Sorry, Ives. She's stuck at work, and so is your dad. I drove up to bring your present."

"Work?" My mother worked at the printing and art company she, Suze, and Rochelle ran. They were the bosses. Who could make her stay?

"A huge job," he added.

"Mao's memorial death shroud?" I asked.

"Huh?"

I dug my nails into my palms, one of my tricks against crying. "Throw it over," I said.

"Your mom worked her fingers off sewing this, sweetheart. She was heartbroken she couldn't come."

"Just throw it to me."

"They got an illustration and printing job from VSC."

"VSC?" Vietcong? I wondered.

"Vocation for Social Change. That's—"

Blah blah, peace, justice, save the world. "I don't care. Just throw the box over," I said through clenched teeth.

He sighed and threw the large box. I let it drop to the ground at my feet and sank into the scratchy grass. After untying the string holding the wrapping in place, folds of deep indigo, plum, and amethyst fabric stunned me. The softest material in the world caressed my skin when I touched the cloth.

I unfolded a blanket so lovely it might have drifted in from another galaxy. Constellations of silver stars rippled the shades of purple.

"Your mom said she made it from silk velvet fabric. And the underside is Egyptian cotton, which feels great against your skin."

I lifted a corner and saw soft violet-blue material.

Perfect stitches signified my mother's careful work.

Nothing in Roundhouse matched this luxury; nothing ever felt this good.

"Can I touch it?" Henry asked.

"Sure." I'd forgotten my brother's presence. I put the soft fabric on his lap.

He stroked the blanket as though it were a kitten. After a few minutes, I patted his arm and then took the quilt back.

"Do me a favor, okay? Run to the house and tell Poppy to meet me in the barn. And here, take this." I gave him a chocolate bar and a Cherry Tootsie Pop from my birthday loot. Poppy and I would gorge on the rest.

Once Henry disappeared, I dragged the blanket to the hammock where Chuck rocked.

"Your mother will be here tomorrow. I swear on my life. And your dad."

"Tomorrow's not my birthday." I squeezed my eyes against tears, crumpled the wrapping cloth, and threw it at the place I didn't want to see. Diantha stood a foot away as I turned away, hand planted on her hips.

What had I done now?

"For god's sake," she said.

I waited for her to name my sin of commission or omission. Diantha enjoyed categorizing our wrongdoings.

"Jesus, Chuck. Cover yourself." She threw a pair of swim trunks over the wrapping I'd tossed. "How many times do I have to say it? They're kids, just kids. They don't need or want to see your whatsis."

Chapter 31

✳

Ivy

NOVEMBER 1977

Santa Land

Queasiness bubbled when my parents took Henry and me to Santa Land in early November. They'd already brought too many presents and treats to Roundhouse. Spoiling us seemed wrong, as though they considered themselves grandparents. I wanted them to tell me to *stop pouting* and yell *slow down* at Henry as he raced in circles. I wanted my mother to tell me not to let the sun go down on my anger, just like Marmee told Jo in *Little Women*.

Santa Land? None of us belonged here, certainly not my mother, with her curly hair flying in the wind—she was the only mother around without a lick of makeup. Not my father, in his wire-rimmed glasses, wearing the Jewish version of an Afro. And certainly not Henry and I, dressed in what my Grandma Penny called our *schmattas*.

"Do they always have to wear rags?" I'd heard her asking my mother during a trip to see them in New York. "Would it kill you to get Henry a decent haircut?"

Surrounding us were children all hugged by neat happy sweaters, women in modest lipstick, and dads with well-combed hair.

As Henry relished riding the year-round Christmas trolley, shaking hands with Santa, and picking out candy canes for everyone, I imagined

Zane rolling his eyes. As my father and Henry went from animal to animal in the petting zoo, I scuffed through the brown leaves.

"Hey, Pudding, what's up?" my mother asked. "Is that too babyish for you?"

I shrugged and kicked up another pile of leaves.

"Daddy and I could split up next time. You and I can do something special just for us. Just for you. Where would you like to go?"

"Can we go shopping? For clothes? In Boston?"

My mother stopped before a bright red bench and sat, patting the space beside her. "You don't seem happy," she said after I plopped beside her.

I ran through all the things I could say.

I miss you.

Living here is hard. Sometimes it's even too much fun.

How could I explain the wearying aspect of always trying to be happy? When we weren't in school doing creative stuff, we ran around proving we were free. Our latest project involved collecting everything from old bike tires to splintered ladders so we could build a weird town in the woods.

I tried to explain my thoughts to my mother, forcing out some of the truth I kept inside as she nodded.

"Oh, honey." She took my hand when I finished. "I understand. My sisters and I loved Camp Wonder." She smiled at the memory. "They were some of the best times of our lives. But I missed Grandma and Grandpa so much it hurt sometimes. Being homesick is normal. I miss you, Pudding. We all do. We miss you like crazy pants."

Crying wasn't in my plan, but the tears fell. "If you miss us, and we miss you, why don't you let us come back?"

She drew me close and hugged me until I softened, melding with her until we became one—the way I wanted. My mother's tears wet my hair when she leaned her cheek on my head.

"I love Roundhouse sometimes, but sometimes I need to be alone. I need to be with you," I said.

Not responsible for making granola or worrying about Henry. I wanted to have experiences like my mom described at her camp, but just for three weeks and then back to normal. I watched a father and mother collapse on a bench across from us while their kids threw a ball around.

"I'm sorry." Her voice thickened. "I wish I could live here with you, but Rochelle, Suze, and I are busier than ever."

"I'll be so good. Henry will be perfect."

She hugged me, then leaned away and put her hands on my shoulders. "I'm going to come more often, Pudding. I promise. That will help, right? We're working on extraordinary projects right now— vital stuff. Roundhouse is going well for everyone most of the time, right? I miss you too, but you kids are doing great stuff, right? You all take care of each other. Diantha gives you everything you need?"

My mother sounded so desperate for my happiness that I couldn't resist giving her the gift. I nodded, and she squeezed my hand so hard it hurt.

"You're right. I guess I'm just homesick," I said.

"Think of all you can do here," she said.

"Like what?"

A toddler squealed, holding her mother's hand as they headed toward a field of sleighs piled with presents. This was a special once-in-a-while place, not for every day.

But my parents had sent me to a permanent Santa Land.

Mom tucked her sunny hair behind her ears as she bent her head to the side in thought. "There must be a thousand things. I bet there are a million places to make political murals. You can start a youth newspaper for the area and cover topics like civil rights. Your very own personal WPA project."

I started to ask about the WPA, as I didn't know what the letters stood for, but I stopped before the words left my mouth. As usual, my mother was describing *her* passions, and I didn't want another history lesson about Annabel's world.

"Sure. A newspaper sounds good. Maybe we can write about

segregation in Putney," I said. "You realize only White people live here, right?"

"Is that true?" She looked stricken. "Why do you think that is?"

Again, I shrugged. "Look around, Mom. I guess only White people feel welcome. Remember my kindergarten class picture from the Trotter? We had *so* much multiculturalism." Using my mother's favorite word was a deliberate choice. "Did you know this was a White person's place when you sent us here?"

Her mouth opened and closed twice as she struggled for words. "Jesus, Ives. I can't believe we never asked that question. Never investigated. We were too busy imagining how safe and free you'd be here."

Melanie arrived the following week and announced her plan to stay the entire month. She missed Poppy too much, she said. Having Melanie there meant I got lots of sideways mothering since she included me in everything she did with Poppy, but only a robot couldn't tell how much less intense her hugs were when she held me.

Melanie drank in Poppy like a bone-dry sponge-woman offered water, hugging her as though storing the Poppyness up for a long winter. With her mother around, Poppy's electric edges powered down. Managing life without being your own mother made every day easier.

I could spend days being joyful—one week, we wrote a play, designed costumes, and then acted it out for all three communes—and still cry myself to sleep. Seeing the softer side of Poppy convinced me we should be with our mothers and fathers because when you're little, parents are like your skin. All the bad things hit them first. Or they absorb them. Without my mother, everything scary or mean speared right into me. I had no wrapping without her.

A few days after Melanie arrived, as I sat at the kitchen table spooning peanut butter from the giant jar we refilled weekly at the food co-op, Diantha walked in like a woman on a mission.

"Not everyone wants your germs," she said without much conviction. We all ate just about everything straight from our zillion jars.

I scooped out one more spoonful, shrugged, and capped the jar. "Sorry."

For a sturdy woman, Diantha had delicate fingers. She sat beside me, tracing the wood grain with her finger. Rings decorated every finger except her thumb. Everyone had a soft spot for something—Diantha's weakness was jewelry.

Without a word, she removed her rings; trying on her rings was my weakness.

I slipped my favorite on my middle finger and held it out to admire the shiny gold. Diantha's wedding ring was unlike any I'd ever seen. Intaglio, she said, and a priceless Greek antique.

One by one, I tried on every ring, not one resembling the clunky silver pieces worn by most women I knew. Diantha wore gold and gems and loved talking about them as much as I wanted to listen.

She handed me a thinnish band joined with a round solid circle with a black design. "This one is from the sixth or seventh century AD. Do you remember what AD means?"

"After Christ. And BC is before." I put the ring on my thumb. Though she'd told me the design portrayed the Virgin Mary and Jesus surrounded by the heavens, I had to squint to imagine it—only the stars stood out. Diantha was the only adult who didn't add the word *fairy tale* to everything related to religion. The rest of the grown-ups thought they were educating us, but I loved the idea of heaven being real.

Diantha wove stories of Jesus, Mary, and Greek myths so many times that they'd swirled in my head into a portrait of Mary and Athena stretched out, drinking holy tea on fluffy clouds.

As I placed the rings on various fingers, Diantha talked. "My mother loved music," she said. "She sang opera when she thought nobody was listening."

"Why did she wait for nobody to listen?"

Diantha slipped off a battered gold bangle bracelet scrolled with flowers for me to try. "She never thought her singing measured up."

"Did it?" I pushed the bracelet high up my arm.

Diantha tucked her head to the right and stared out the kitchen window before answering. "I thought so. She sounded like an angel to me. She studied at Julliard, a famous music school in New York. But she only went for one year."

"Why?" I asked. "If she loved it so much?"

Diantha pointed to herself. "She got pregnant with me. And so, she married her boyfriend, my father, and that was that."

"What do you mean? That was that?"

"She had me, and then she had my five brothers. My father always worked, so my mother was always busy with us and the house."

"But you grew up rich, right?" I studied the gold strewn over the table, knowing she had boxes and boxes more. My Grandma Penny's jewelry fit in one box, and my mother still thought Grandma had too much.

She pressed her lips as though weighing her answer. "I did. But nobody in my family believed in nannies or babysitters. My grandma Yaya took care of us whenever Mom had to go somewhere. My mother ended up depressed in that low-key fifties martini way."

"That sounds tough," I said the words I imagined my mother might say. I didn't know what a low-key fifties martini way meant, but I didn't want her to stop talking.

"Hard for her, hard for all us kids." Diantha pretended to lift a glass to her mouth and drink. "She liked her nightly cocktails. She liked her cigarettes. And she liked jewelry. Lucky for me, that's the only habit I inherited."

I'd seen adults stoned, and I'd seen them drunk. Not often, but enough to hate it when they seemed stupid. I tried to imagine my mother always wearing her goofy high smile.

"That's why I bought this land and made Roundhouse happen. Women must help each other find their dreams."

"But how about you?" I asked. "What about your dreams?"

Diantha grinned with an openness I'd never seen. "Right now, this is my dream. Not for always, but for now." She leaned forward and whispered, "I'm studying everyone, including you, Pumpkin. I'm planning to write about all of this. And don't tell anyone about this, but maybe you can be my assistant."

"Really? Sometimes, I don't even know if you like me."

"Oh, sweetheart. Here's a secret—I don't know the singular right way to be a mother. Maybe nobody does. I've been hard on you because this world treats girls and women so hard. I want you to grow up strong. I'm not so worried about the boys. Men enter the world with three steps up. That's why we need places like this. So, we don't put all the burden on each woman's shoulders."

"But you're much nicer to Poppy. Don't you want her to grow up strong?"

Diantha picked through all her rings until she came to the tiny rose gold one she sometimes wore on her pinky. "Some people are born wrapped in a veil of confidence. Poppy's one of them. She'd shrug it off if I tried to strengthen her by boiling her in hot water. You? You need hardening, honey. I know you don't understand, and maybe I go too far sometimes, but I love you."

I wondered if Diantha had heard me crying and if she'd told my mother. "What does my mother think?"

Diantha handed me the tiny ring. "Wear this. And every day, when you look at it, I want you to remember this: Your mother loves you like crazy, but mother-daughter relationships are more complicated than those with their sons. And a mother's love can carry us, but it's often the men we need to inoculate ourselves against."

I nodded, knowing Diantha would be prouder if I looked the word up than if I asked her the meaning. I spooned up one more scoop of peanut butter when Diantha left the room. Everything I thought about Diantha's ways could be wrong. Or simply not correct. I kept twirling the ring on my middle finger, wondering what I'd tell Poppy or my mother about wearing this beautiful piece. And then the answer appeared like skywriting.

I'd tell the truth.

Part Four

❀

The House Meeting

Annabel

Life is very short and what we have to do must be done in the now.
—*Audre Lord*

Chapter 32

❋

Annabel

After Santa Land

Tears and angry words collided during the house meeting, a meeting unlike any we'd had before.

There were no jokes, no trays of homemade brownies, and no alcohol allowed, though Guthrie, Roxanne, Suze, Grady, and Chuck decimated two packs of cigarettes between them while Melanie, Wyatt, Quinn, and I choked.

"God damn it, we shouldn't be having this discussion without Diantha. Meeting like this is just fucking wrong." Chuck's anger showed in every breath he took. Three times, he'd walked over to the phone, and three times, Melanie had convinced him to sit down.

Melanie and I had surprised everyone except Guthrie and Wyatt with tonight's topic, hijacking the meeting from the purported discussion on ramping up our recycling efforts, Wyatt's favorite theme. He was obsessed with us being perfect, constantly reminding us that we needed to be examples. He cited his role in getting the City of Boston to implement a weekly curbside collection program. The city's first-ever residential recycling truck came up so often as a topic that we had to be careful that our rolled eyes didn't end up permanently out of place.

Melanie placed her hand over Chuck's. "I know you think we're being disloyal. But honestly, think of how much this concerns her and how much she'll have to say. We're not having a meeting with a solid vote. We're not making any decisions. We're in discussion."

"She should be in this discussion more than any of us." Chuck lit another cigarette from the house pack with shaking fingers. "Who else is as affected by this? Who else gave up as much?"

"All of us," I said. "All of us, except Roxanne and Quinn. Sorry, guys," I said.

"You're just telling the truth," Quinn said.

"Don't our children have equal rights with Diantha?" Melanie asked. "She gave up her job; we gave up our children."

The ache I'd felt since Henry and Ivy left had exploded into a crater of anxious longing. For the past three years, I'd piled work, meetings, and then more work and more meetings in the pursuit of burying that ache of losing my children. I'd told myself repeatedly that they were safer, happier, and better off in Vermont. Guthrie and I were both deeply involved in the horrors surrounding the busing crisis after the integration of Boston's schools was ordered—after the Black lawyer, Ted Landsmark, was attacked on City Hall Plaza by a White teenager holding a flagpole with the American flag, and rocks were thrown.

I was glad to have my kids far away, but I was also overwhelmed by guilt at participating in the integration process without having my school-aged children involved.

And then that guilt was overwhelmed by my fear and horror of using my children to make political points.

That led Guthrie and me to wonder if we were, in fact, no better than all the middle- and upper-class parents sending their children to private schools or moving to the suburbs.

And then all of that became no more than an emotional-intellectual brew of tangled thoughts when we'd visited the kids the week before. Even when Ivy had tried to cover her pain to please me—those efforts making me feel even worse—her misery leaked everywhere.

She needed me.

Henry needed me.

They needed Guthrie.

Melanie and I had spent hours in Valentina's kitchen the previous night, needing privacy away from the house, and many more hours walking miles at Jamaica Pond bundled against the November chill, preparing for this meeting.

Our hearts, minds, and guts knew the time had com for our girls to come home.

We knew Chuck would resist discussing the children returning without Diantha in the room—and he wasn't wrong—so we sprang the idea on him. Diantha's initial reaction would be resistance. Everyone knew that about her, but we also knew she could change once she had time to consider our ideas.

Melanie and I wanted our first attempt at the topic to be about the children, not Diantha's feelings.

I thought about our charged meetings about monogamy years ago—an issue that felt nearly childish in retrospect. The hours we'd chewed up about supposed sexual politics indeed were about no more than our raging hormones.

Once the children left, thankfully we never visited that topic again. I think all of us, especially the mothers, including Diantha, knew that if we made the radical choice to separate our children from their parents, it was incumbent upon us to be truly dedicated to the ideals that led to that decision.

We doubled down on working at the most feverish of paces.

At Sojourner Graphics, only a third of our clients paid the total cost of our services. We worked closely with the Haymarket People's Fund; we donated money from our company profits and served many of the organizations they funded. Haymarket had begun three years before, a remarkable trust fund initiated by the local young inheritors of fortunes who were aware of how the intense wealth disparity in America led to our panoply of social problems. Diantha and Chuck were early donors. At times Sojourner's client list seemed to include every group Haymarket funded; their list of recipients represented a who's who of social reform throughout Greater Boston. The recycling measures in Boston came about through the work of the environmental groups Wyatt worked with, and Sojourner provided every flyer, poster, and brochure they needed.

For months on end, our only social times were the pizza parties we had for ourselves and our staff on Wednesday afternoons when we brought in every pie made by Same Old Place down the street from us. We worked ridiculously long hours, perhaps because we recognized the price our children were paying for our commitment.

But after Santa Land, the price suddenly seemed too high.

Our balance was off.

We should be able to pay attention to our kids every day, not just in intense bursts that served neither them nor us.

"Listen, Chuck, this is an issue of the entire group. And certainly, we need Diantha in the discussion, but she'll have no more of a vote than any of us," Wyatt said. "We don't rule through who has the fattest wallet."

"But when did we start splinter group discussions?" Chuck asked.

"This isn't a splinter group," Melanie said. These are two mothers bringing up their concerns to everyone in the house—two mothers who don't believe we can wait until we're all in Vermont together."

"Why the hell not?" Chuck asked.

Guthrie stood as though his body held too much intensity to stay in his chair. "Because your kids are with their damn mother all the time and with their father a hell of a lot more than ours are. And because reality is fucking reality. If Melanie didn't bring this up here, we'd kick it down the road for god knows how long."

"Who's even complaining, other than some homesickness from Ivy?" Chuck asked.

"You know the kids are on strike, right?" Guthrie asked. "For better wages? And your son is leading the charge?"

"They're striking against the school, and I, for one, think it's great. What better way to learn about issues of class?"

"Jeez, Chuck." Quinn shook his head and laughed. "Do you suggest we make them do slave labor to learn about good labor practices? What's next? Feeding them spoiled food so they learn the failures of the Department of Agriculture?"

"Do the kids need to fall apart before we look at the best course for them?" Melanie laced her hands together.

Grady held up his hands for peace. "Does everyone agree that this is something that we should discuss? I'm concerned enough to want to put it on the table."

"And in a serious way," Suze added.

"How about this? We'll all be up in Putney for the week of Thanksgiving. Let's discuss it then, okay?"

"Do we give Diantha a fair warning?" Roxanne asked. "I don't want to blindside her."

Everyone turned to Chuck, who sighed in a way that told of a thousand pounds of tension.

"On the one hand, I don't want to keep anything from her. On the other hand, she's up there alone, and I don't think we should expect her to process this by herself."

Melanie brought her lacy shawl higher on her thin shoulders. "How about this? I'll take a few weeks off from work before Thanksgiving week and go up to Roundhouse. Let me talk to Diantha. Alone. That will make it easier for her. She won't feel like we're ganging up on her."

"Can we afford for you to take off three weeks?" Wyatt asked.

"I can't afford not to." Melanie laced her fingers.

Part Five

❄

Thanksgiving at Roundhouse

Ivy

Forgiveness is a gift of high value. Yet its cost is nothing.

—Betty Smith

Chapter 33

✼

Ivy

Seven Scullery Servants

Poppy and I squirmed on either side of Melanie at Sunday dinner. As Thanksgiving approached, we were all getting edgy and fretful, waiting for our parents and the coming rhythm change.

My hands itched to snatch a piece of cornbread from the overflowing platter sitting on the table as Jacob carried in a giant pot of chili, both made by Melanie. I loved cornbread—we all loved the stuff—and not only because it wasn't the dry whole wheat bread Diantha made us take turns baking. We all twitched, readying to make the grab. No matter how high the pile, we'd decimate the stack in minutes, but we couldn't take food before saying thanks—our version of giving grace as Grandma Camille and Grandpa Gordon insisted on at their table.

Even as we chanted our sweet thank you words, each gooier than the last as we showed off, competing to be considered *the best kid* by Melanie, our eyes darted, planning our attack to get the largest portions of the best offerings: the hot cornbread, the butter, and the most cheese to sprinkle on our chili.

Once Mac placed the final dish on the table, green beans, the nine of us joined hands around the glossy wood.

"Who wants to give thanks?" Diantha asked per our tradition.

Poppy spoke up first. "Me."

Diantha nodded. We didn't take turns; Diantha rewarded the loudest and fastest. Whether by design or accident, Diantha instilled a kill-or-be-killed survival instinct instead of teaching us cooperation or manners.

Poppy shook her glorious curls and cleared her throat as though about to recite the Gettysburg Address, something Peter had made us do at school the previous week. I waited for her to stand and take a bow.

"I give thanks to my mother for being here." She leaned against Melanie and smiled. "Every day, you remind me why I want to be a better person. That's it. I love you all very much. Let's eat."

Melanie beamed. I tried not to send out evil karma.

When Diantha uncovered the cornbread, everyone except her and Melanie reached out. Jacob, already six feet and with larger hands than his father, grabbed two pieces at once.

"Hey! Not fair." I raised my hand as though to smack his hand away.

"Look at the size of him," Diantha said. "He needs twice as many calories as you."

"So why aren't you and Melanie taking two servings?" I took a piece before nothing but crumbs remained.

Melanie placed a gentle hand on my shoulder. "Diantha and I don't expect a growth spurt anytime soon."

"I'm the smallest. Don't I need the most?" Henry had the shortest reach and held an extra-small portion of cornbread, a ragged piece with an over-crisped edge.

Diantha stood, filled Henry's bowl to the brim, and sprinkled a generous helping of grated cheddar on the slop. "Beans are the perfect protein, and protein grows muscles."

Melanie cut off three-quarters of her piece of cornbread. "Here you go, Henry. Consider this my contribution to the Let's Grow Henry fund."

I compared my mother, Melanie, and Diantha. Would I be a kind and good adult? A fierce creator? Talented? Rich? A fighter?

I pressed on the ring Diantha had given me, each tiny chip of ruby reminding me of my vow to tell the truth. I wondered if I'd have the guts to keep my promise when my parents sat at the table.

Two grown-ups sat among the seven kids, double the usual amount.

I decided that if the grown-up thought we were smart enough to mostly run our own lives, saying the truth shouldn't be so tough.

Melanie preparing the holiday dinner with us made the experience a thousand times better than the previous year when Diantha had spent the day ordering Chuck and us around like she had seven scullery servants.

With Melanie, the day became a glorious game. She pulled surprise aprons from a bag as though she were Mary Poppins. My mother had embroidered our names on one with an image of the spirit animal Suze chose to represent our inner self.

I prayed my spirit animal captured something pretty.

Melanie took a sheaf of papers from Suze, each piece explaining the meaning of our animals. After reading a few lines, she handed our paper to us with our aprons.

Jacob's apron, the largest, came first. "*Your spirit is the bear—representing strength and confidence. The bear requires solitude after he provides leadership,*" she read.

After trying to be teenage cool, Jacob tied on the apron, seeming proud of the lumbering brown and black stitched bear.

Poppy got an apron alive with teal, green, and royal blue. "*The peacock is the essence of beauty, offering lessons about self-love, integrity, and rebirth.*"

I waited as Melanie went through the remaining pile of papers and aprons, my envy of Poppy's beautiful spirit gnawing the entire time.

Suze deemed Henry's spirit "*The raccoon, a problem solver.*"

No one was surprised by the lion on Zane's apron or his words: "*Showing courage and strength in overcoming difficulties, this powerful animal also represents something 'wild' or difficult to control.*"

Zane laughed at the ladybug on Mac's apron, but I longed to have his words and image: "*The ladybug gives blessings. A master in the art of metamorphosis, she transforms from a hideous larva to a beautiful insect adorned with bright colors. Believe in yourself and dare!*"

For Leo, Suze chose the bee. "*Small but mighty,*" Melanie read. "*If the bee is your spirit, you are a creator in your own life and the life of others. The bee's symbolism has a long history of representing diligence, social consciousness, and spiritual development.*"

At last, Melanie handed me an apron with *Ivy* embroidered in purple and silver.

A turtle, head poking out just a bit, almost smiled.

Jealousy clawed. Poppy, the gorgeous peacock, spreads her magnificent feathers while turtle Ivy creeps and crawls.

Suze chose our spirits, so I shouldn't have blamed my mother. But I did.

Melanie caught my eye. "*Listen! The turtle is highly spiritual; she journeys toward wisdom, truth, and peace. She is compassionate, sensitive, and constantly checking in with her emotions.*"

"In other words," Zane said, "she's a crybaby, always worrying about herself."

"And you're a big bully lion, roaring around and biting everyone's head off," I said.

"Do you listen to anything, Zane? That's not what it said. You don't have an ounce of wisdom." Poppy wrapped the apron strings three times around her waist and tied a bow in front.

"Excuse us, Miss Essence of Beauty," Jacob said. Though he and Zane seldom acted like brothers, they never failed to pipe up when an insult came toward either. Tribal lines might change daily, but blood trumped everything, no matter how hard our parents tried to make things different. And we all knew it.

Chapter 34

❀

Ivy

NOVEMBER 1977

The Difficulty of Measuring Honey

O ur parents arrived for Thanksgiving in dribs and drabs. Unlike the days when we shared one and then two cars, now every couple had a car, though they acted a bit sheepish about it, always mumbling about jobs and schedules as though buses and trains didn't crisscross all of Boston.

"Why don't you just call it what it is?" Jacob had asked his father when he showed up with a used Dodge Dart, making him and Diantha a two-car couple. "The ethics of convenience."

"Hey kid, do you like seeing me or not? How can I get up here without a car?"

Zane shook Chuck's hand and then clapped him on the shoulder. "Welcome to the bourgeoisie, Dad."

Wyatt showed up first, coming two nights before the holiday, followed by my parents, Roxanne with Suze and Grady, and finally Quinn, who'd packed his car with slate for the crumbling roof.

Our Thanksgiving table held enough food to feed the entire town of Putney, as though the food would glue us together.

Everyone sort of dressed up for the holiday. Our so-called *schmattas* were dropped on our bedroom floors as we reached for clothes sent by our grandparents and aunts, including lots of hand-me-downs from cousins. Poppy and I wore matching long dresses my grandmother had sewn for us. Both were purple with tiny blue flowers and an apron sewn on from an empire waist—mine teal Swiss dot and Poppy's yellow and pink swirls.

Dinner veered between sweet and sickening as the parents vied for best absentee parent awards, falling over each other as they worked to show that they considered us unique and brilliant. The stuffing created by Jacob and Mac! The turkey roasted by Zane! The potatoes Henry and Leo mashed!

"Extraordinary pecan pie, Ives." My father rubbed his stuffed belly as he leaned back on the couch. We'd retreated to the soft sofas and chairs. He grabbed my mother's hand and smiled at her. "I can't believe you made it. Or that Grandma Camille shared her recipe. Don't tell her, but it tastes as good as hers!"

I sat straighter, basking in my father's praise.

"You did a terrific job, baby." My mother, squished between my father and Henry beamed, my brother leaning against her without leaving room for a molecule.

"The meal preparation was a master class in cooperation." Melanie shined with pride.

"But I made the pie by myself," I said. "'Nobody helped me. I didn't have to cooperate." Truth!

"Didn't I see Poppy measuring the honey?" Diantha smiled as she peered at me over Bowtie, who was lying in her lap. Even our dog seemed confused when the grown-ups dragged her between Putney and Mission Hill. Bowtie always headed straight for Henry when he arrived.

"That doesn't count." Stuffed though I was, I still sliced off another sliver of the apple cake Roxanne had placed on the living room table. Bakery-made. White flour. Sugar, not molasses. I couldn't get enough.

Melanie laughed. "You can't make a pie without measuring the ingredients."

Of course, Melanie—even nice-nice Melanie—stood up for Poppy over me.

"She just wanted to pour the honey," I said. "Poppy wants credit for everything."

Wyatt drew Poppy closer to him on the opposite sofa. "I think that if Ivy did everything except measure the honey, that counts as making the pie herself. I'd guess the hardest part would be the crust. Getting those squiggly things right."

Poppy twirled around and thumped her father in the chest with a pillow. "Have you ever measured honey? Do you know how drippy it is? Leveling it off takes forever."

Wyatt laughed. "I'm sure leveling honey is harder than anything I do."

"Harder than building the table?" I didn't want Wyatt's standing up for me to end.

Quinn held out his hands, palms showing. "Whew, since when has Wyatt been getting credit for that table? Who do you think spent six hours sanding that thing?"

"Tell him, hon." Roxanne blew her husband a kiss.

"I'm glad we got all that settled." My father rolled his eyes. "Speaking of amazing." He pulled a folded piece of paper from his pocket. "Someone just got an outstanding review and hasn't said a word yet."

My father squeezed my mother's shoulder, bringing a blush to her cheeks. He cleaned his glasses and unfolded the torn sheet from *The Boston Globe*. "I bought five more copies before I could bear to tear this out. Here's the headline: 'Radical Abstractions & Reality: Creating Political Change.'"

Before he could read the article, my mother pushed the paper down. "The review isn't for me. I only have one piece in the show."

"But you organized the whole thing," Roxanne said.

"Organizing or creating, which brings greater value?" Quinn gave his puzzled look.

"What do you think?" Roxanne tucked her legs under her.

Wyatt tapped on the coffee table he'd built with Quinn. "Couldn't have one without the other."

Grady leaned forward. "Political art? Writing? Sojourner Graphics, a collective serving the community? Legal aid? Organizing? Helping build the Fenway Health Clinic like Quinn and Wyatt did? Which of these serve parity most?"

Suze smacked Grady's arm. "Why isn't daycare front and center?"

My mother clapped. "Melanie and Diantha make more of a difference than anyone."

"If childcare is so important," I asked, "why are we here? Why did you get rid of us? Why did you want to get out of taking care of us?"

"Ivy!" Melanie looked like she might cry. "We never started Roundhouse to get rid of you!"

I hardened myself against Melanie's sad face. "If you love caring for children, why not take care of your own kid?"

"We didn't send you because we didn't want you with us. The working parents at Melanie's daycare center would have no options if she weren't there." My mother took a breath before continuing. "Dad works at least seventy hours every week on immigration issues so kids can stay in this country with their families. Grady rehabs bikes for kids in every housing development in Boston. Quinn, Chuck, and Wyatt are rehabbing homes for homeless families while also working at paying jobs. Roxanne, Suze, and I—"

I pushed away my dessert plate and glared at my mother. "We know, we know. You guys are the best thing since Rosa Parks. Let's crown you all the Official Saints of Puddingstone."

My father looked stern in a manner I'd seen but never felt directed toward me. "Stop being rude, Ivy. Now."

"Don't tell her to stop. You guys should listen." Jacob opened his arms to encompass all of us. "Ivy asked a good question. Don't you think it's a little weird that you sent us away to devote yourselves to daycare and poor children?"

Diantha banged her hand on the table. "Nobody sent you away, damn it. We brought you here. Look at you. You're all thriving."

"Why couldn't we *thrive* back home?" I slumped further down on a floor pillow and stuck out my feet.

"Isn't this home?" Annabel asked. "You've been here for three years."

"How come you want us to have a different home than you?" Henry ran his finger over the pie and cake crumbs left on his plate, not looking up after he spoke.

"Home is where your parents are," Mac mumbled.

"Sweetheart, we're here almost every weekend," Suze said.

My mother put her hand on her chest. "We have two homes—all of us—our country home here and our city home in Boston. Anyway, we can talk about this. I promise we will."

Nobody seemed to hear her last words except me. And my father, who put an arm around her. I felt a glimmer of hope that my truth might have been the smartest thing I could ever do.

"But we're always here," Henry said. "And you almost never come. And we never go there."

"That's not true." My father stood and began pacing.

"It is too! You only care about politics." My last walls fell away, and I let out all my anger. "Your children might as well be Peace and Justice. Those are your babies. If they're so important, why don't you keep us home so we can see what's going on?"

"We could help you," Henry said.

"Aren't you happy at all?" Melanie clasped her hands. "You're all doing amazing things."

"Can't we like things here but still want to be with our parents?" I asked.

"Personally," Leo said. "I like it here."

"What?" Grady asked. "You don't want to be with Mom and me?"

"Grady!" Suze glared. "He didn't say that."

"I'm only trying to lighten things up, babe." Grady reached for a cigarette and shook his head. "How did we get here?"

Poppy put her arms around Wyatt's neck. "Don't worry, Poppa. We're doing great here."

"Cause your mother's been here for like a month," I yelled.

My mother walked over to me and knelt. "Sweetheart, children need childhood. If it seems that Daddy and I devote too much to politics, it's not because we don't love you. We want you to grow up in a peaceful place while we fight for equal rights for women and civil rights. Fighting apartheid. But I hear what you're saying. I really do."

"Apartheid?" Henry asked.

My mother hung her head. "Why am I babbling? I should only be listening to you, not spewing platitudes."

As my mother's voice quivered, my father took over. "I'll explain apartheid in a moment, Henry. I'm sorry this hasn't been perfect. Political struggles mean everything, but not when you're a child. We need to meet about this. Soon. This week."

I jumped out of my chair, almost knocking it to the floor. "I don't want to meet. I don't want to talk anymore. Nobody listens to us. Nobody cares. I don't even know why you had us."

My mother stood and tried to put her arms around me, but I wrestled away. As I ran out, I heard her tears and Melanie offering counsel. "Shhh, don't worry, honey. I think having everyone here—the wonderful time we were all having—maybe it all got too overwhelming for a minute. We're going to work this out. I promise."

I stopped for a moment, wanting to hear what came next.

"All that sugar made us hyper," Diantha said. "The kids aren't used to it."

The chairs scraped, and then Suze's voice came again. "Let's calm down for a moment. Kids, how about you take a break? We'll do all the cleanup. After that, we'll regroup and talk everything out."

I bet Suze's real goal was getting us out of the way. Let the grownups drink more wine, smoke a thousand cigarettes, sneak a joint, and then they'd talk at us some more.

Poppy appeared next to me where I stood in the giant hall. She wrinkled her face, saying, hey, let's forget our fight.

I kicked the coat rack. "You were a jerk."

"I just wanted to stop the arguing," she said.

"You've been a creep since your mother came."

She stuck her face too close to mine. "You're just jealous that I have the best mother."

"Take that back!" I pushed my face so close to Poppy's we were almost touching. "My mother's just as good as yours.

Jacob and Leo appeared, with the rest of the kids following. Jacob put one hand on my shoulder and one on Poppy's, pushing us apart. "Come on. We got a surprise—something you'll like. Follow us."

Chapter 35

❀

Ivy

The Very Best Secret Spot

Jacob led us to our hidden corner of the barn, only accessible by dragging over a concealed ladder—our very best secret spot. Over our three years at Roundhouse, we'd lugged up torn pillows, old navy blankets, and our beloved giant steel mixing bowl— our marshmallow toasting bowl. That Diantha had never missed it testified to her wealth, I suppose. Missing a bowl? Buy another!

Oversized bottles filled with water leaned against shelves. We weren't stupid. None of us would make a fire without having water nearby.

I stomped around, narrowing my eyes at Poppy to remind her I was mad.

"Baby." She scowled and turned her back.

"Okay," Mac said. "Enough." He sounded like Suze, who dragged us to the table to talk things out. When that didn't work, she'd throw up her hands and say, "Enough!"

Zane fell into the only chair—a beanbag we'd liberated from the living room. "Let them fight. We can put bets on who wins. I call a dollar on Poppy."

"As though you have five dollars." Then I remembered that, of course, he had as much money as he wanted.

He reached into his pocket and pulled out a crisp bill. "Thanksgiving cash fresh from Grandpa."

I ignored him and walked around to face Poppy. "You shouldn't have taken my mother's side."

She shrugged. "We're not twins. Anyway, I thought you liked being with me all the time."

I wasn't ready to give in. "Can't I like being with you at Puddingstone all the time?"

Jacob put two fingers in his mouth and whistled for our attention. "Let's. Get. High." He held a baggie high and shook it.

I stared. "Is that pot?"

The boys snuck off to smoke pot plenty, but they'd never asked us to join them. And never Henry.

"You got it," he said.

"Henry's too young." *Me too*, I thought, but I'd never admit that.

"I'm only a year younger than you." My brother took a pack of matches from his pocket. "See. I'm ready."

"What are you doing with matches?" I held out my hand.

He tried looking tough, but it wasn't in him, and he handed them over. "In case we didn't have any here. I thought we would build a fire to toast those marshmallows we hid here."

"Good plan," Zane said. "We're gonna want those. Backup is always important. First, we get toasted, then the marshmallows."

We cracked up, Poppy did two cartwheels, and the awkward spell evaporated.

Jacob and Mac dragged the pillows into a ragged circle where we sat knee-to-knee close.

"Since this is your first time"—Jacob looked at Poppy, Henry, and me—"I'm going to show you what to do, and you're only allowed two tokes each."

The three of us nodded solemnly. We might fight and torture each other, but our circle of trust never broke.

Poppy leaned into me and whispered, "I'm sorry."

I wasn't ready to let go all the way, but I gave a slight nod of acknowledgment.

Jacob took a pack of matches out and lit the tightly rolled joint, taking a deep and appreciative pull. He was no rookie.

Poppy looked suspicious. "Where did you get it?"

Jacob held in the smoke, looking like a blowfish, and then whooshed out. "My father never keeps track of what he has. Every time he's here, I add a bit to my stash. Now. Watch and then do what I do."

He took a much lighter inhalation, holding it only for a moment this time.

The three of us nodded as though learning a new math equation.

"You understand?" he asked in a choked voice. "Not too deep. Not your first time. Promise?"

We made peace signs with our second and third fingers, as we did for all promises.

"Who's first?" Zane asked.

Poppy raised her hand, never afraid to go first in anything. She took a small puff and passed it to me. I held the sweet-smelling joint, terrified, but nevertheless drew it to my lips and inhaled until a coughing fit overtook me. My lungs burned as though someone had lit a fire inside.

"That was too deep. No more for you," Jacob said.

Still choking, I tried to argue.

"Nope." Mac shook his head. "You had the equivalent of two tokes. That's enough."

Henry did so well that it scared me. By their second drag, he and Poppy were experts, while I'd permanently ruined my lungs.

Within thirty minutes, we were scarfing marshmallows like they held the secret to life. Poppy toasted one golden layer at a time; only she had the restraint to toast, pull, and toast again repeatedly. The rest of us scorched the hell out of the outside, plucked it off, and burned our mouths eating the blackened sugar before sucking the gooey center from the stick. Patience wasn't our strong suit.

Once we finished toasting marshmallows, Jacob lay reading one of his beloved Hobbit books by the lantern we'd lit. Poppy, Henry, and I drew on the floor using chalk we'd stolen from the school art supplies while Mac and Zane played marbles.

"There's gotta be something else here," Leo said as he searched for marshmallows or candy that we might have forgotten.

"You got a serious case of munchies, brother," Mac said.

"I do, I do." He opened one cabinet after another.

"How do you know when you're stoned?" Poppy turned her head from side to side as though testing it.

"First, you look in the mirror." Zane wiggled his eyebrows.

"Why?" She shook her curls in her annoying new kittenish manner.

"Cause when you see that shit-eating grin on your face, you'll know."

Poppy touched her cheeks.

"Are you trying to figure out if you're smiling?" I puffed out my cheeks and then popped them.

She nodded and then laughed.

"Trust me," Leo said, opening another cabinet, "you're stoned."

Tranquility enveloped me. Like when I lay in the creek with the sun shining. If being stoned meant smiling and feeling this relaxed, I'd take up the hobby. I welcomed the fizzy fuzziness. Listening to Leo rummage around made a cheerful background noise like we were the kids from *Five Little Peppers and How They Grew.*

We could be the *Seven Stoned Peppers and How They Smoked.* I laughed aloud at my clever comedy.

"Hey, anybody know what this is?" Leo dragged an old trunk to the middle of the floor. "This lock is old, man."

"Where did that come from?" Mac asked.

"Way in back." Leo pointed with his thumb to the dark recesses.

"You thought someone hid food back there?" Poppy rolled her eyes.

"I never know what youse nudniks might do."

We laughed at Leo repeating the words his father used. "Hey, stop playing with my bike chains, youse nudniks," Grady would mutter.

Zane and Mac joined Leo, pulling on the lock, shaking it from left to right, and then back the other way.

"Nah. That won't work." Jacob dragged himself from the rug and crouched to inspect the battered metal. He pulled a few times, pushing the other boys away as they tried to wrest it from him. "This is old. I mean old, old. Leo, get something from the pile to bash it off."

Leo ran back to the tangled stack. I wondered if Wyatt, who worshipped ancient tools, knew hidden treasure might be in the mound of broken hatchets and rusted hammers. Briefly, I considered being the hero by getting him. He'd go wild, as though I offered golden awls.

I brushed away the fantasy. We seven stuck together; I'd never give up our best hiding place.

Thoughts spiraled in swirling colors as I fell back on the pillow. Was I high? I raised my hand to my eyes, peering at my mood ring. What color meant stoned?

My moonstone showed blue—a calm ocean copacetic blue. Finally, I'd found the secret of conquering anxious me. That would be my first line in tonight's diary entry.

"Got it." Leo ran back carrying an oversized claw hammer. "Be careful. The handle has splinters."

"Gimme." Jacob wrapped it in one of the pieces of cloth strewn around. Rags covered every surface, from the old napkins we used to get marshmallow goop off our hands to torn towels to wipe up egregious spills.

Jacob snapped the old lock off in minutes. He and Leo peered inside and then reared back for a moment.

"Whoa!" Leo drew out a rifle. "There's a ton of them."

Jacob leaned forward. "About five."

Mac and Zane joined them, leaning over the old wooden box.

"Shit," Zane cocked his thumb toward the house. "I bet they're planning an armed revolution."

"Who?" Henry asked.

"Don't be an idiot. These are ancient." Jacob ran a finger along one. "They've been here forever."

"Let me see." Henry tried to push past Mac.

I grabbed my brother. "Don't you dare touch anything! You want to get killed?"

Leo rolled his eyes and continued inspecting the rifle he held. "Jeez, Ivy. They're not loaded."

"How do you know?" I pulled Henry further back.

"Peter teaches us gun safety in hunting class. Nobody stores loaded guns."

Mac pushed the gun's barrel, forcing Leo to point it down. "*Our* guns are never stored with bullets. These could be different."

Poppy watched as the boys leaned in and took out more weapons. "We should bring these to the grown-ups. Or get my father up here."

"Right," Zane said. "Cause they'll let us figure out what this means. Shit, Poppy, we might have uncovered a secret war plan. I bet there's a manifesto on the bottom."

Minus Henry, who I kept tight against me, the boys began unloading the rifles, piling them on the floor until they'd emptied the chest.

"Hey, check it out." Jacob pointed and then pulled out a bunch of paper. "Look. Diagrams. Instructions. All sorts of stuff. We found a mother lode."

The boys acted as though they'd uncovered the secrets of the universe.

Leo lifted one of the guns and examined it, peering from tip to end. "This one is a Winchester."

Zane held up a pamphlet, comparing the picture to the rifle. "*Model 40. Winchester, the way you want it,*" he read.

The boys cracked up at Zane's dramatic reading, reminding me they were high.

"You guys are idiots," Poppy leaned over the colossal daisy she continued to paint.

I placed my hands on my hips. "Put them away. We have to bring everything to Wyatt or Quinn." The least likely grown-ups to handle this without yelling.

"In a minute." Leo held the gun as though hunting prey, peering through the sight.

"Is the safety on, man?" Mac's voice rose. "Don't be a jerk."

"It's not loaded. I checked." Leo swung the long rifle around and pointed it at his brother.

"I didn't see you check, moron," Mac yelled. "Put it down."

"It's too light to have bullets. You can tell. Peter taught me."

Mac headed toward him. "Right. Cause Peter's a fucking expert on ancient rifles."

"Okay, okay, give me a minute." Leo headed toward the edge of the second-floor landing and aimed at the open rafters. "Imagine the damage you could do with this baby."

He pushed away the hair hanging in his eyes and pretended to shoot. "Pow, pow, pow."

"That's enough." Jacob turned to Mac. "Control your damned brother."

"One more." Leo pointed higher, his finger on the trigger.

Jacob walked toward where Leo stood. "That's it, asshole." He stretched his arm and reached for the rifle; Leo avoided him by leaning far to the left.

The gun jumped with a force beyond what Leo could contain.

A shot exploded.

The wooden butt jammed into Leo's face, ripping open his skin and knocking him back. Blood ran from his cheek.

The roar of the bullet stunned and deafened me, leaving me hollowed. Shaking.

I buried my head in Henry's shoulder; he clutched my shirt so hard he ripped the flannel.

Muffled screams sounded through the pillow of deafness that had descended.

I slowly opened my eyes. Mac's mouth hung open in what could only be a howl. Sound couldn't penetrate the ringing in my ears.

Zane and Jacob ran across the room, their words inaudible.

Poppy lay on the ground like a rag doll.

Everything drained from my arms and legs.

Immediately, I knew I was to blame. If I hadn't started trouble at the table, if I hadn't told the truth, if I hadn't asked for more, we'd never have left the house.

"Get the fucking grown-ups," Jacob yelled.

Zane fell to his knees. He grabbed a dirty cloth and held it to the blood gushing from Poppy's neck. Row by row, the yellow flowers on her dress turned rusty.

"*Go*, Henry!," I screamed, pushing my brother toward the ladder. I ran to Poppy and sank beside her clutching her hand. "You're gonna be okay. You're gonna be okay. You're gonna be okay."

Part Six

❈

Grown-ups

Annabel

We have to take care of each other's children.

—*Ruby Bridges*

Chapter 36

✳

Annabel

The Farthest Entrance

F rantic screams pierced the windows. Guthrie was the first to reach Henry as we raced out in a ragged group, scooping my baby up as though he were five.

"Shh, calm down. What is it?" Guthrie held him as I ran my hands over my son, searching for damage.

"Are you hurt?" I asked.

"*Shot*! Come now. Come now. Come now." Henry panted between each emphatic word.

Chuck gripped Henry's shoulder. "What? What happened?"

"A gun? Did someone have a gun, Henry?" Guthrie asked.

Henry wrested from Guthrie's hold and rocketed toward the barn, which was at least a football field away.

"Call an ambulance," Guthrie screamed as he chased Henry.

Roxanne turned and raced back to the house.

"I'll get my bag." Diantha's breath came in ragged gulps before following Roxanne.

The barn seemed miles away. Mac waved his arms from the second-floor opening, one weather-beaten giant door swinging open. "Hurry."

As we headed to Mac, Henry shouted, "No! No! Follow me." He

took an unfamiliar path around the rambling buildings.

My heart dropped as images flashed. Guns. Blood. Broken children. Strangers attacking.

Ivy. Ivy. Ivy.

Guthrie followed Henry to an entrance I'd never entered. Nothing moved fast enough—not my feet, Guthrie, or time—as the nightmare wrapped tighter.

I arrived moments after Guthrie, racing in a maze of turns till Henry stopped and climbed a primitive ladder to a platform where Ivy knelt.

"*Daddy!*"

Ivy's scream lacerated me. But she was alive.

Guthrie flew up the rungs, and then I scrambled into the dim space, the children's screams and tears lacing together.

"*Quiet!*" Suze yelled when she reached the top. "Who's hurt?"

Guthrie called out. "*Here! Here!*"

I hurried and fell to my knees beside him as he leaned over Poppy, two fingers on her neck, moving from one spot to another, as Jacob pressed a dirty, reddening cloth onto the bloody jumble of rags already piled on Poppy's tiny chest. Footprints smeared and dirtied a mass of spilled yellow paint.

All the children closed in except Leo, crumpled in the corner between Suze and Grady. I looked for a moment until I saw his chest move.

"Give me room," Guthrie said.

"Mommy." Ivy's breath touched my hand as grabbed it to her mouth.

I wrapped myself around her. Henry held me from behind.

"Were you hit? Are you hurt at all?"

When my girl shook her head, I put her in Zane's arms. "For a moment, baby. Just for a moment. Stay with Zane."

Zane gathered her and Henry, taking them a few feet away, the three clutching each other.

I hurried to where the ladder met the platform lip. Wyatt climbed two rungs at a time, knelt, and held his hand to Melanie.

"Melly," I said.

She covered her mouth and ran with Wyatt to the giant daisy where Poppy lay.

They fell beside Guthrie and Jacob.

Melanie touched Poppy's waxen face and stroked her hair. "You'll be okay, baby. You'll be okay. You'll be okay."

When Guthrie shook his head the tiniest bit, Wyatt placed his fingers where Guthrie's had been.

An ambulance screamed from the road.

"They're here, baby," Melanie said. "You'll be okay."

Wyatt lifted Poppy's arm. He placed his rough fingers on her pale wrist and then under the edge of where her delicate jaw squared.

Diantha dropped beside Poppy. Our nurse. Chuck handed her a black bag.

For the third time in minutes, fingers went to Poppy's neck as Diantha pressed for a pulse. She put a stethoscope in her ears and pulled Poppy's T-shirt up, careful not to displace Jacob's hand holding the cloth that stanched the bleeding.

She took a flashlight and opened Poppy's beautiful eyes.

Jacob kept pressing.

Wyatt's eyes streamed with tears. He raised Poppy's hand to his lips and kissed each knuckle.

"*Nooo*!" Melanie fell to her knees. "*No, no, no.*"

Chapter 37

❇

Annabel

NOVEMBER 1977

Prayers are for Emergencies.

W e drove to Grace Cottage Hospital in two cars, Guthrie and Quinn at the wheel. They made the trip in record time and arrived within minutes of each other. We gathered at the entrance. Our ragged shattered group of ten walked into the quiet building with fear etched on every face.

Wyatt and Melanie accompanied Poppy in the ambulance.

Suze and Grady stayed at Roundhouse with a speechless Leo and a traumatized Mac.

And with the police.

Beyond all reason, I held onto the possibility of medical magic from the doctors, praying some miracles of modern medicine would bring the light back to Poppy.

Nurse Kathryn Dubois, who oversaw the waiting room, her name written on her badge in beautiful cursive, nodded as we walked in. Her cap and uniform were as crisp as she was soft and kind—she offered the children cookies and then poured coffee for the adults, murmuring sympathetic words, pointing out our luck that Grace Cottage Hospital had implemented a volunteer ambulance just one year before.

Henry squeezed my hand until it went numb, but I never let go.

Ivy climbed into Guthrie's lap as though she were five instead of eleven.

Nurse Kathryn Dubois watched over us, so comforting, with such a beautiful name—a name I'd never be able to stand again, a name now imbued with the grief and dread that showed in my shaking hands and Guthrie's shoulders rigid as a concrete slab.

Quinn took on the role of group communicator, thanking Nurse Kathryn for ferrying us snacks and getting updates from behind the door that led to Poppy.

The updates were that there were no updates as we sat there holding onto every shred of hope we could muster. Diantha was a nurse who'd not worked in years. I assumed her bag of supplies was woefully out of date—the hospital would have the miracle tool Poppy needed.

"Mama?" Ivy whispered from Guthrie's lap. She hadn't called me *Mama* for years.

"What is it, honey?"

"Mama. Do you know *Emergency!*"?

"Do I know what an emergency means? Yes, sweetheart. Emergency means a serious dangerous situation."

"No, no. I mean the television show *Emergency.*

I tilted my head in confusion. We had one old television in Puddingstone that we rarely watched, and there wasn't one at Roundhouse unless Diantha had secreted in a set. "I don't know that show," I said. "Why?"

"Don't get mad, but we watched it at Maura's house."

I nodded. Guthrie kissed the top of her head to let her know we were far from angry.

"Oh, Pudding. Of course, I'm not mad."

"People get saved in that show. Not everyone, but lots. Even one who got attacked by a bear. Do you think Poppy will get saved, Mama?"

Guthrie's eyes met mine. We blinked away our tears. He tightened his arms around Ivy until there seemed to be no room for anything but an angel of mercy between them.

"We can pray, honey. We can pray."

"That would be okay?" Ivy asked. "Prayers are for emergencies, right?"

Ivy twisted a rosy gold ring I'd not seen before around her middle finger. How had I never noticed such a lovely thing on her hand?

Wyatt and Melanie were unseen when we left—hidden somewhere in the back. Through Nurse Kathryn, they'd refused our solace—they'd turned from us when they entered the ambulance with Poppy and never looked back.

When we returned at three that morning, Guthrie carried Henry, and I led a stumbling, half-asleep Ivy into the silent Roundhouse.

"I don't want to be here, Mama." Ivy's voice rose with each word. "Please don't make me stay. Please don't make me go in the room."

The room meant the room she shared with Poppy. She *had* shared.

Poppy was gone, and I didn't know how Wyatt and Melanie could live with that. I didn't know the right thing to do for my Ivy. I didn't know how I'd manage, but I had her. Ivy and Henry were still with me.

Even with the millions of advice words my mother had offered since always, nothing covered this.

The house had twelve bedrooms, many barely bigger than a closet. Wyatt and Eric had carved some of the largest into boxy spaces just big enough for a double bed. We'd thought the kids would feel better knowing that each set of parents—including Roxanne and Quinn— had a permanent space. We figured the kids could go into our rooms and feel our presence even if we weren't there.

What stupidity and arrogance. Every second I hated us more.

"You'll sleep with us, honey."

"And Henry?"

"And Henry."

"And tomorrow we'll go home?"

"And tomorrow, we'll go home."

❊ ❊ ❊

I woke before the sun rose. I disentangled myself from Henry, wrapped around me on my left, with Guthrie beside him, hugging the edge of the bed, and Ivy on my other side. By some miracle, they readjusted their positions without waking, with Ivy throwing an arm over Henry in her sleep.

The scent of fresh coffee filled the kitchen from the almost-full bright red coffee maker. The Krups machine was one of the breadcrumbs pointing to Diantha's wealth, along with a handful of other splurges she'd made for the house, most of them in the audio category and worshipped by Chuck.

I grabbed one of the many clumsily made mugs and filled it, adding no milk. I needed the taste of a punishing black brew.

Lamp light shone from Ivy and Poppy's room.

Diantha sat on Poppy's bed, her eyes bloodshot, clutching Poppy's favorite sweater. One Melanie's mother had knit. Mohair. Such a difficult yarn to work with. But Poppy'd been worth it.

"I keep thinking how cold she must be," Diantha said.

I sat close beside her and put my hand over hers, and we were both now touching the soft sage-colored wool.

"Should we pack her stuff. For Melanie?" she asked.

I thought about how natural it was to assume Poppy belonged more to Melanie than Wyatt in death. How sad and odd, and, I thought, true. In the end, we belong to our mothers.

"What would *we* want?" My question hurt coming out.

"God help me, I have no idea." Diantha slumped onto my shoulder. "I failed them. Melanie should hate me. I hate me."

"I despise all of us," I said. "But we need to buck up. Our feelings are the last thing we should be worried about.

The short amount of time Diantha and I needed to pack Poppy's things almost broke us, but we kept going without allowing a single tear. A twelve-year-old girl didn't collect enough to make a life, but she had enough to break our hearts. With care, folding along every seam, we placed her clothes and treasures into Diantha's beautiful old family steamer trunk.

When we were done, I packed Ivy and Henry's stuff in anything I could find—backpacks, wooden crates, and even old shopping bags. I vowed to get Ivy and Henry out today.

Suze walked in and collapsed on the floor between where Diantha and I worked.

"How are you?" I asked. A ridiculous question, but what else could I say?

"Leo hasn't said a word. Not a sound."

Diantha fell down beside her. "Oh, honey. You must be a wreck."

"I'm a wreck, but at least I *have* Leo. And Mac. Melanie? How can she go on?"

I slid off the bed and sat on the other side of Suze. "I don't know. And I don't know what we can do for her. For Wyatt."

"I can't imagine they want to see me. The moment the police let us go, we're taking the boys to stay at my parents' house with us. My mother has already made arrangements for Leo to meet with a child psychiatrist." Suze's parents lived in Philadelphia, where her father taught at U Penn and her mother worked as a pediatrician at Pennsylvania Hospital.

She buried her head in her hands. "I keep telling myself that I'm lucky. I have two living children. The police believe Leo—they believe all of us. They believe it was an accident. A stupid, idiotic, shattering accident that will ruin all of our lives."

I rubbed her back as though she were a toddler. "Leo is strong. This *was* an accident. He will recover. I know it. He has you, Grady, Mac, and all of us."

Suze's back heaved under my hand as sobs racked her. "Melanie will never recover. Poppy is gone—that sweet fairy child, the light of Melanie and Wyatt's life. She's gone. And accident or not, my child took her out of this world."

I reached for words of solace, something I could say that might offer at least a moment's peace.

Diantha knelt before Suze, crying along with her. "All of us bear this. How did we never inspect every inch of this damn place? We can't bring Poppy back, but we'll help Leo. And you."

My stomach churned. Leo still hadn't uttered a sound. Ivy couldn't enter her room. Mac walked in circles around the house. Jacob hadn't lifted his head out a book, according to Diantha, and Zane simply slept or stared.

But those were the actions of our living children. Our Poppy had been wiped from the earth. Nothing in this world mattered except keeping our children safe.

I had no idea how we could go on.

Chapter 38

❉

Annabel

NOVEMBER 1977

Cops and Robbers

Grady and Suze took off with Leo and Mac for Philadelphia before noon. When I tried to hug Leo goodbye, I felt like I embraced a wooden scarecrow as he held himself rigid, even as he momentarily collapsed in my arms. Mac just kept patting Leo's shoulder as though a metronome attached them.

Once Suze's family left, the other kids could barely stand to stay inside the house, huddling on the porch until the temperature forced them into the hall. They begged to go home—meaning Boston, swearing they'd never enter the State of Vermont again. Diantha, Jacob, and Zane rode back with us that night, leaving Chuck to close up the house as best he could for the moment. Even in tragedy, someone had to ensure the pipes didn't freeze.

I worried we might push away our lives forever; I wondered if that's what we deserved.

I prayed today would be the most horrifying day of my life; I never wanted to experience a crueler one. Wyatt's father had come to get the dress they planned to bury Poppy in, her signature dress, Ivy called it. Melanie had told her father to ask Ivy so she would know which was Poppy's favorite. Neither Melanie nor Wyatt could bear to stay at the house.

Silence blanketed the house, suggesting three in the morning, though the clock showed eight. We were due at the chapel in Forest Hills Cemetery at nine, and services began at ten.

Burial would follow.

I buttoned Ivy's black dress up the back. She'd insisted we wear only the most traditional of clothes to the funeral. Guthrie's parents, who'd arrived in Boston the previous night, outfitted the children at Jordan Marsh. Ivy's stiff woolen dress resembled something an Amish girl might own, save the buttons running from collar to waist.

Guthrie placed a dark gray tie around Henry's neck. He began instructing our son in the art of a Windsor knot but stopped when Ivy frowned and silently completed the task.

When we gathered in our large Puddingstone entry hall, the shock of the formally dressed boys underlined our grief. Jacob, Zane, and Henry looked pallbearers. I wanted to rip off their suits. Guthrie wore the Brooks Brother we'd once fought over so bitterly. Chuck's suit almost held the imprint of a wooden hanger from the store where he bought it.

Pale Diantha clutched Jacob's hand.

"I have a car coming." She bit her lips. "My parents . . ."

Chuck placed a protective arm around her shoulders as her words trailed off. Zane squeezed his father's shoulder.

We understood.

Our parents were desperate to help; our hollowed children could barely leave our sides. We were zombies on autopilot.

Diantha appeared to be an apparition from a warped play, playing herself in an alternate universe. Seeing her thick dark hair twisted into a low bun, her curves contained in a black wool pantsuit, and wearing small pearl earrings made me want to fall to my knees.

Melanie and Wyatt, flanked by their parents, sat in the first row of the chapel. As we filled the pew behind them, Melanie clutched her father's hand hard enough to look painful. Sorrow rose like smoke and ashes. A black lace shawl covered Melanie's bent head, dulling her shining fall of hair.

Guthrie and I wedged our children between us. Ivy sat stick-straight with her hands clasped in her lap. When I tried to offer my hand, she tightened her body and further drew into herself. Henry slumped beside Guthrie. My parents were beside me; Guthrie's next to him.

I heard nothing the minister said. My thoughts rang too loud, my memories too sharp, remembered screams sanded away everything except flashes of Poppy on the barn floor.

Sobs sounded from the packed chapel. We cried for Poppy, Melanie, Wyatt, and our children. I brought Leo into my heart, praying he could heal.

Suze.

Grady.

Mac.

Shafts of weak light leaked from the stained-glass windows and touched on the rich Unitarian tapestry shawl lying against the minister's robes. When she finished, she bowed her head. "Let us pray for our child, Poppy." When she lifted her head, she nodded twice. "Zane Aetos has asked to say some words."

Zane shuffled out of the pew, kissing his mother before exiting. His grandparents drank him in as though he represented the elixir of all that was holy in this world.

When he reached the altar, he placed both hands upon the Bible and bent his head. At that moment, he appeared more of a man than a fourteen-year-old boy. His unruly, long brown hair had been tamed and matured. His grandfather had brought Jacob and Zane to a local barber—whether with or without their parent's consent, we neither knew nor cared.

We were grateful that our children could be folded in by their grandparents, absorbed by their love, and able to fall apart without worrying about their sadness. The adults of Puddingstone were too broken to be our best.

Zane ran his hands through his shorn hair and gripped the corners of the pulpit. "I planned to marry Poppy."

Ivy looked up.

"I never told her. I wish I had."

This boy speaking wasn't the cocky kid racing around Roundhouse. The most handsome. The one with the edge. The one Ivy said could be so mean, but still, the one who, when he appeared, made her fluff her hair.

Poppy had tried to teach Ivy to bend over then come up fast, using the wind to fluff her hair into a halo.

"Do I need to tell anyone how magnificent our Poppy was? Just seeing her brought joy. Poppy was radiant—like a sprite. My father said that the magic of childhood and the wisdom of the future glowed from Poppy."

Melanie curled around herself, looking as though trying to protect the tiny bit of remaining Poppy she held.

"I don't know why she's gone. Can we blame Leo?"

A gasp sounded at Leo's name.

Zane shook his head. "No. We can't blame poor Leo. We need to mourn his loss as well as ours. He believed he knew better than anyone." Zane paused, and then his eyes blazed at us. "All of us did. You taught us that we knew best. You convinced us we knew so much more than we did."

When Zane began crying, Diantha rose as if to help, but he put his hand up to stop her. "Jacob helped me write this. And my father. Because I wanted to give Poppy her full measure."

I held my breath as Zane worked to regain his poise. Seeing the suit hanging perfectly from his square shoulders showed me one of the men he might become—so many possibilities appeared. How would he grow into his family's fortune? Surety rang from him and Jacob; the safety of money had already woven a protective shield. Money might make them cruel or kind. Zane possessed both traits.

"Where lies the blame?" Zane then turned his eyes to the paper he'd placed on the lectern. "The belief in ourselves, a conviction that if we thought something, if we believed it, then it must be correct, put us in harm's way. We needed to learn the danger of that thinking. My father said we trusted in ourselves too much. He said the fault was theirs.

"We are children. Poppy was a child. We became arrogant children. We were too young to search for ways to build our lives."

Sobs from my chest hurt so much that I wondered where the pain would go. You could die from grief; could you die from shame?

"Jacob and I have talked with my father for many hours since Poppy died. My father is an honest man." He made an arc with his arms. "All of you consider yourselves truthful; you genuinely want to fix the world. You wanted to give us a better place, a healthier life. I believe that one hundred percent."

Zane gazed out at the first two rows, where the adults of Puddingstone sat with our families.

"But my father and my mother, Poppy's parents, Annabel, Guthrie, Suze, Grady, Roxanne, and Quinn, you believed in us too much. You thought that because you wanted a better world, so did we—that we'd spend our time at Roundhouse searching for the answers that would make us healthier in mind and body, free in ways that would make us strong, so we could make a better world.

"But we spent our time being kids; we snuck candy, stole from each other, and made hideaways. Like children do. We played cops and robbers, good guys and bad guys, all the time. And when we found hidden guns, the first thing we did was argue about them. We fought about who had the best answers. That Leo was wrong doesn't make him evil. Leo is nothing but good.

"We all hold the blame for that night—that awful night—because we thought we knew. We thought we were smart and ready for the world. We didn't know to call the grown-ups until it was too late."

Chapter 39

✷

Annabel

A Stuffed Tiger and a Monkey

W e stood beside the open grave in the silence requested by Melanie. She wrapped herself in her own arms, bent so low I worried she'd tumble in, her parents flanking her like sentries. Wyatt focused on the rushing water tumbling down the rocks above us, his parents' arms around his shoulders.

The previous night, Roxanne, Guthrie, Quinn, and I had discussed the wisdom of bringing the children to Poppy's grave. Guthrie and I carried our quandary to my parents. Letting Ivy and Henry witness their friend, their quasi sister, be lowered into the ground seemed cruel. Why leave them with that last image of Poppy?

My mother held my hands as we all wrestled with the question. "This tragedy has already emblazoned horror on them," she said. "Poppy's blood, the gunshot, their guilt. Poppy is dead. Seeing her laid to rest is the right thing. Think of the meaning of *being laid to rest.* The ceremony may bring peace."

Perhaps. Or maybe seeing the graveside ceremony would add to my children's nightmares. Being laid to rest was simply a kind way of saying buried in the dirt. In the end, Ivy had pushed the decision. "I need to be with her," she'd said. "Henry, too."

The waterfall overlooking the gravesite appeared angry.

Workers had dug away frozen brown grass to make Poppy's tiny grave. Her coffin rested on webbing that would lower her to the bottom of this final resting place.

Henry stood so close we had no delineation between us. He buried his head in my wool coat, refusing to face the grave.

Ivy, my child, my first baby, so blanched of life she'd become a statue of ice, clutched Guthrie's hand on one side and held a stuffed tiger and monkey in the other.

After the long forever minutes of quiet, the minister said a brief prayer. When she finished speaking, she invited the children to come forward if they wished. Each of them had an offering to send Poppy off to whatever heaven they imagined.

How had we offered them those fucking words? *Whatever heaven they imagined.*

What the fuck was wrong with us?

Ivy let go of Guthrie's hand, pushing him away when he tried to go with her. She stood at the grave's edge, looking so skinny and small in front of the open hole in the ground. When she sank to her knees, I started forward, terrified that she'd jump in, but Guthrie held me back.

I wanted to bury my face in his chest when Ivy went to drop in the monkey and the tiger, but nowhere on god's earth could I allow myself that comfort.

Ivy brought the ear of the monkey to her lips and kissed the brass button. She wrapped his arms around the tiger and squeezed them together, went to throw them into the grave, and then stopped. "I need them to stay together." The cold air was so still that we could hear her tortured whisper.

Before I could move, my mother stepped forward and sat beside Ivy, ignoring the frost covering the brown grass. My always prepared mother—how did she do it, how did I not?—unsnapped her black purse and brought out a red rubber band. She pulled off her leather gloves and asked something of Ivy, who nodded and placed the tiger and monkey in my mother's hands. Mom twisted the monkey and tiger into a tight embrace and then spoke softly to Ivy.

My solemn daughter took over for my mother in uniting the stuffed animals. My mother covered them with a snowy white handkerchief that I recognized as my father's. Ivy bound them forever together.

Only when my mother brought Ivy back to us did I allow myself to rest against Guthrie. The four of us formed a knot as Jacob and Zane gave Poppy their gifts for heaven.

We'd planned no formal funeral aftermath. Melanie and Wyatt didn't want to see anyone after burying Poppy.

No possible gathering seemed right. When Diantha, Roxanne, and I discussed whether to host folks at the house, our lack of desire to have people over—our friends and colleagues who'd crowded the chapel—became apparent in minutes.

"You know what would happen," I'd said when we discussed the question at the kitchen table. "Inevitably, we'd gather, talk, drink wine, smoke, and forget the kids."

"No. That's not possible. How could we?" Diantha gripped a mug of tea so tight I expected the ceramic to shatter. "Not at a time like this."

"Okay, maybe we wouldn't forget them, but we'd inadvertently push them away by our . . . whatever. Intensity. Grief. Everyone would be asking questions. We'd be drinking to paper over our guilt."

And shame, I'd not said. Shame and guilt washed over everything as though I'd pulled the trigger.

I caught Wyatt's eye as we milled around our cars, saying goodbye. He stood by his mother as the children hugged him one by one.

Wyatt's mother's sharp shoulders and narrow hips matched Ivy's. For one moment, I swore a ghost of a grandmother leaned over my daughter along with the apparition of a sister.

When cleaning Ivy's room, I'd found a curl from Poppy's hair resting in Ivy's treasured violet tin. I touched the hair Diantha had gotten for Ivy when she asked for it—I didn't know how Diantha managed such a feat—telling myself the similar color didn't match. Faint memories of chocolate came from within the metal, the remembered scent of Guthrie and me celebrating.

Ivy's eyes matched her grandmother's. Guthrie's mother's eyes. I was certain.

Melanie shook her head when we tried to hug her as they readied to leave. Her mother asked us to pack up all their things, placing Poppy's in separate boxes, and mail them to her home in New Hampshire. They were never coming back to Puddingstone.

I approached Wyatt after he guided Melanie to the car, closing the car without a sound, shutting away the image of her, collapsed, her head in her mother's lap.

"You've been strong," I said. "Who's helping you?"

"My father is a rock." He took both my hands in his. "Take care of Ivy. And Henry."

I nodded, blinking back tears, not wanting Wyatt to feel any need to comfort me.

Our eyes locked in our always unspoken agreement.

"Always," I promised.

Part Seven

✻

Mother and Daughter

Annabel and Ivy

Hold fast to dreams,
For if dreams die
Life is a broken-winged bird,
That cannot fly.

—Langston Hughes

Chapter 40

❋

Annabel

The Peacenik's Kids

Decades later, Suze, Rochelle, and I still shared a weekly pizza in the employee break room at Sojourner Graphics, though these days, we were more likely to explore nuances of aging than talk about the men in our lives.

With fifty in our rearview mirrors and our sixtieth birthdays looming, we could start on either of those discussions at any moment. Roxanne had left our collective to teach art at Boston University, a good thing since her patience with discussing skin care was thin, while ours was unending. If she'd still worked at Sojourner, she'd be rolling her eyes twice an hour.

Not being surrounded by too many ghosts—at least not more than I could manage—topped my thankfulness list. I credited Diantha, who'd found a way for us to stay close after Poppy died. Most of us moved to the Jamaica Plain area of Boston, known as JP, in 1978.

Wyatt lived in Western Massachusetts, while Melanie had moved to the other side of the country, as far as she could go without falling into the ocean.

Poppy's death had tainted Puddingstone. Grief and guilt gnawed everywhere we turned.

Moving was imperative, especially for Ivy, Henry, Jacob, and Zane, but most of all for Mac and Leo. Whispers had followed them down the street.

"Look! Those are the peacenik's hippie kids—the ones they sent away to the children's place."

"There's the kid who shot his sister!"

"I heard they tried to set fire to each other."

Diantha found places for all of us to live, sneaker money oiling the path. Our new house, right next door to Diantha and Chuck's place, was on a private road hidden in plain sight behind the post office. We didn't have Mike's Donuts, but the Same Old Place Pizza was two minutes away.

Guthrie and I missed Mission Hill, but in 1977, everything became about the kids, and JP bordered Mission Hill, so we lived in familiar surroundings while starting anew.

Real estate in many Boston neighborhoods had become gentrified and untouchable, but JP was still undervalued. Diantha plunked down a hunk of cash and bought two of the four houses on the unusual hidden road where we lived, only steps from Centre Street, where local shops lined up. One house had been for sale; one hadn't, but the next-door owners took Diantha's Godfather-style offer.

Now, the phrase *make them an offer they can't refuse* remained our code for tough times.

Diantha sold one of the houses to us for far less than the price she'd paid, required no down payment, and she held the mortgage. She found houses within walking distance from us, which she sold to Suze, Grady, Roxanne, and Quinn using the same deal.

We adored Diantha, though we still made fun of her behind her back. We called her the Marie Antoinette of the Movement, deeming *let them eat houses* her motto.

She and Chuck never sold Puddingstone, but they rarely went near the place. Valentina and Mary acted as caretakers, renting it out for dirt cheap to families in need,

We had the house, we had each other, and Valentina and Mary and Rochelle, and we got the kids through somehow. We never could make up for our mistakes, but we kept them connected, found therapists all around, surrounded them with love, and let them watch as much damned TV as they wanted.

Who knows? Maybe *Welcome Back Kotter* helped as much as the therapists. They hated *Little House on the Prairie,* watching the show only because Ivy loved making scornful comments and Henry wanted to make his sister happy.

Our house helped. Sun poured through the wavy old window glass, and the garden provided a bit of room to escape, but the boundaries were clear. The kids had rooms overlooking the weeping willow, where they hid from us.

Ivy's teenage years were not ones I'd ever want to repeat. Suffice it to say that her company afforded little pleasure to Guthrie or me—less to me. She was smart enough to get into the Boston Latin School, which just about guaranteed her a good education; I was wise enough to pretend that Guthrie and I had become aggressively and conservatively strict about things like curfews, makeup, and check-ins. This way she could rebel in ways that we actually didn't much care about.

Henry made up for Ivy by being so easy it made me guilty. So often the mellow child receives too little.

This year, I'd planted late summer flowers in profusion. When Guthrie went on about the August and September annuals being a waste of money, I tuned him out. I wanted to make the yard beautiful for Ivy's birthday, but once again, she spent it away from us. She'd avoided us on her birthday since leaving home for Pratt College in New York City, which then became her center for home and career. Now she returned only for brief visits.

I looked out the window as I poured a second cup of coffee for Guthrie and myself, seeing the dazzling sun shining on the bleached white deck and the rich blue sky, just as it had been the day I gave birth to Ivy, thirty-five years and five days earlier.

Butterflies flitted around the masses of black-eyed Susans, bringing needed pleasure as I ran through my day's schedule at Sojourner.

The deadline approached to have *The Drug Wars are the New Jim Crow* posters printed, but back-and-forth arguments between Prisoner's Aid and the Coalition for Prison Reform about colors prevented me from moving forward. I considered passing the task to Rochelle or Suze, allowing me to dig into designs for a local daycare center brochure. I'd reached my limit on playing referee.

As I carried two full mugs to the table, I tipped my chin toward the small television on the counter that I tolerated because Guthrie was likelier to take a turn cooking dinner while it played—but morning television depressed me. "Guthrie?"

He held up the morning *New York Times,* pointing to the headline: "For Early Risers, Morning TV is a Hot Market."

"And? Are you moving into advertising?" I poured milk over my granola, wondering, as I did each day, if the reminder of Poppy with every breakfast was worth the stabs of sadness. But, like everyone in our crowd, without fail, we bought granola from Leo's bakery, The Peacock and Turtle Bakery.

"The article covers the battle between CNN and Fox. CNN just poached an anchor, and I wanted to see—"

"I'll read about it. Please. TV in the morning?"

Guthrie lowered the volume. "Just for a few minutes. I need this to plan class."

I gave up the argument in face of Guthrie's invocation of his ever-inviolate work. Guthrie took the Law and the Media night class he taught at Roxbury Community College as seriously as his back-breaking legal workload. "The kids at Bunker Hill need knowledge and the ability to analyze more than any kid at Harvard" had become his mantra. Anything connected with Guthrie's work lived under mantle of holiness. Some things never change.

Guthrie's work, his devotion to his causes—Bunker Hill, studies about communities of color in Massachusetts bearing over twenty times the environmental burden of White communities, and his work at The Leaster Project—to release innocent men and women from prison and keep others from entering—consumed him.

"You get a pass for today, buddy, but that's it." I tucked the front section of the *Boston Globe* under my arm, picked up my coffee and bowl, and nodded toward the patio. He opened the door and leaned back, making it clear that I blocked his sightline to the small television perched on the counter.

Again I noticed the sun streaming from a sky so blue smiling should seemed mandated. I peeked at the antique rooster thermometer, which registered a hopeful 69. The weathered bird didn't fit with my bright colors garden, but Henry had rescued the piece somewhere in Rhinebeck, where he now lived, and restored it as a gift for me. I'd never throw away anything from either of my children.

My parents, both past eighty, kept busy. For my father that meant daily visits to the Cooper Family Repair shop, renamed when Henry became the new boss. My father frowned at some changes but took pride in Henry's work and devotion to the community. Like grandfather, like grandson, though in Henry's case, the volunteer time went to the horses, pigs, and goats who needed him at the Catskill Animal Sanctuary instead of church.

Jesus, Leo made great granola. This batch tasted like a gingerbread cookie made miraculously healthy. Leo changed the variety weekly, and since you never knew when a favorite would leave the rotation, I made a mental note to pick up more of this flavor on the way to work.

I laid the *Boston Globe* on the white table, using painted rocks to weigh the corners. My mother's new hobbies included this stone art. Of course, Camille being Camille, her pursuit quickly went from fun to making it perfect and selling them in gift shops throughout the Hudson Valley. We received her less-than-perfect ones.

The headline at the bottom of the fold on the front page read, "To Forgive is Design." The man who felt guilty about not protecting his daughter from rape and murder two decades before now pursued relief through forgiveness therapy, having talked to his daughter's killer on the phone and volunteered in prisons.

Thickness gathered in my throat as I read the article, thinking of the pain this man woke to each day.

Memories never leave; they snake around our tasks, work, lovemaking, and cooking and visit us in our sleep.

The first time I searched the internet, amazed by this new miracle of technology, I'd typed Clay's name in the bar.

I found nothing of meaning.

The first time I stored a document on a hard drive was a scanned picture of the original portrait I drew of him.

I still went to the library in every new city I visited to search the White Pages for Clay. I'd done it in San Francisco when I visited Melanie.

Melanie and I stayed in touch through handwritten letters. Electronic communication felt too immediate for her.

Wyatt and his younger wife were in Northampton, raising five children in a farmhouse and working on substantial hand-built furniture.

We might be scattered, but November 25, 1977, bound us forever.

I turned the page to find the continuation of the article.

"*Annabel!* Get in here now!"

Guthrie sounded frantic. The door slammed behind me as I rushed back into the kitchen, where he faced the television, his hands clamped on his head. "No, oh no, no," he repeated.

I stood beside him and grabbed his elbow. "What's wrong?"

He grabbed my shoulders and pointed me toward the screen where black smoke billowed from one of the World Trade Center towers in New York.

Chapter 41

❊

Annabel

Spending Emotional Capital

We tried calling Ivy endless times, but the jammed lines to New York City blocked us.

When Suze and Grady arrived at 10:50 a.m., twenty-two minutes after the North Tower collapsed, we fell into each other's arms.

Suze placed a bag of muffins and pastries from JP Licks on the table. "Have you heard from either of them?"

I shook my head.

Diantha and Chuck walked in moments later.

"Did you hear from Zane?" Guthrie asked.

Chuck shook his head. "Calls aren't going through. How about Ivy?"

"Everyone in the world is trying to call. Reaching the kids will take time." Guthrie spoke with decidedly false surety. He tugged at his graying beard every few minutes, a sure sign of worry.

"Henry and his family are fine. Worried, but fine," I said.

"The lines are okay in Rhinebeck. That's good," Chuck said.

Diantha sat beside Suze. "Jacob thinks the lines are just overloaded. I'm sure they're also trying to reach us."

"Absolutely." Suze took her hand. "Zane lives in Brooklyn, and

Ivy's uptown; they should be fine. "

"Her shop is downtown," I said. "Close. Too close."

Everyone knew this, but rising panic compelled me to repeat the facts until she called. Mike and Penny had given Ivy their uptown co-op, always trying to make her happy, even after they died. Guthrie had been surprised by his parents' move, but not me. They blamed us—mainly me—for the scars our children wore.

Ivy got the apartment and Henry got their summer house in Tivoli.

After Poppy died, Guthrie's parents spent their emotional capital on Ivy and Henry. In truth, I was grateful. Ivy could accept spoiling from her grandparents. Early on, she pulled away from our coddling, nurturing her never-ending blame.

We stayed in the kitchen for hours, nobody willing to move to the comfort of the living room television. Perhaps we needed to remain in upright, rigid positions to share some measure of the tragic discomfort of New York City. Of Washington, DC. Of Pennsylvania. Of our hometown, where we lost many locals. One of the crashed planes had taken off from Boston.

At one that afternoon, Jacob appeared with his small sons.

"Where's Corinne?" Diantha scooped the sturdy two-year-old to her lap, offering a chocolate chip cookie as though on automatic pilot. Chuck led the four-year-old to the toy corner, which Guthrie and I replenished regularly. We had to keep buying more; my husband couldn't refuse any child's request to take a doll, bag of Legos, or stuffed animal home.

"At the hospital. How come you're not there?" Jacob asked.

"Cause I'm here." She kissed her grandbaby hard on the cheek.

Diantha and Jacob's wife both worked at Mass General's ER. She'd introduced Corinne to Jacob, which should have heralded disaster, but Diantha showed an unerring sense for pairing people and had become an unlikely savant of matchmaking. Mac had met his boyfriend through Diantha as well.

"Are the kids all right?" Rochelle bounded into the kitchen, breathless, as though she'd run the five miles from Cambridge to our house. Her husband Paul and their daughter Alexandria trailed behind. I swallowed my instant jealousy at seeing Rochelle with Alexandria.

"Zane?" Alexandria asked. "Ivy? Did either one call?"

"We're still waiting to hear from them." Diantha looked at me. "Maybe we can turn the television off for a bit. I think it's too much for the kids."

Suze and I had a silent-eyed conversation.

Mine said *I need to keep watching.*

Hers: *humor her; she means well.*

"I'll move this set to the den—we'll make that an adults-only section." Guthrie shrugged in a quasi apology as he turned off and unplugged the small television. "You all know me."

We all knew Guthrie. He was always a news addict, but today, apprehension drove him. We all worried, but his fear ran closer to the surface. Everyone had changed the day Poppy died, but the effects were different. Guthrie blamed himself. As the first one on the scene, he could have, should have, or might have saved her.

If he'd run a little faster.

If he'd known first aid.

If he'd been more thoughtful and mindful of the possibilities inherent in an old farm, he would have searched every inch of the grounds looking for old guns—any guns. "What was wrong with me?" Each time Guthrie asked the question my heart broke again.

"Of course, guns would be on the property of any goddamned old house in Vermont," he'd said repeatedly. "How could I be so ignorant?"

"Why didn't any of us realize that?" I'd answer each time he got lost in self-hate.

My words only led to him pressing his lips hard and shaking his head. Eventually, I learned to simply hug him and make his favorite comfort food, his much-loved crazy combination of Kraft Mac and Cheese stirred with whipped cream cheese. Temptee brand if possible. I supposed every child of a working mother invented a ludicrous recipe during their hours alone.

Guthrie believed he'd been careless when we readied Roundhouse. Wyatt and Grady built tables and bookcases while I'd painted and decorated, Suze and Diantha planned a curriculum, Melanie wrote food plans, and Chuck created budgets. Why didn't he provide more than fucking kibbutz research? He should have been the safety officer.

Comforting him was impossible, but I believed what I said. We all should have taken that role further. We'd been so busy worrying about drowning that we'd forgotten to study the statistics of accidental gun deaths in rural states.

"And I called myself a facts and stats man?" Guthrie asked over and over.

Guthrie's need to track the news as we waited for word of our daughter and Zane's lives was no surprise.

When Jacob answered Diantha's ringing cell a little after two, we tensed like a single organism and then sagged in unison of relief at the sight of his smile.

"Zane's delivering food for firefighters with a Broadway group," he told us before returning to the call. "Stay safe, brother."

Jacob nodded and listened and then disconnected. "Sorry, Mom. Dad. He couldn't keep the line tied up. Everyone's waiting to reach family. And no, nothing from Ivy."

Our television vigil continued as every station played and replayed bodies falling from windows, planes crashing into towers, flames coloring the sky, the attack on the Pentagon, the smoldering remains in a field in Shanksville, Pennsylvania, and people racing from danger. Blame was already falling on Muslims; Muslims waved American flags to stave off an attack.

People stumbled, rising like apparitions from the attack zones.

Heroes rose from the dust.

I staggered between prayers, hope, and the sickening fear invading every cell.

❀ ❀ ❀

Hours later, Guthrie and I lunged when the phone rang, showing Ivy's name on the Caller ID. I stepped back and nodded at him. Ivy might be neither a Daddy's nor a Mama's girl, but her patience with Guthrie lasted longer. Even now, I could count on a sigh accompanied by "*Mom*" when I tried to offer advice.

"Hey, sweetheart," Guthrie said in a suspiciously throaty voice. "Are you okay? We've been so worried. I have you on speakerphone. Everyone's here."

"I'm okay." Ivy stopped and took a deep breath. "Did you reach Zane?"

Diantha came close. "He's out with a crew feeding firemen. Where are you, honey?"

Closeness grew stronger between Ivy and Diantha each year. Sometimes, when I got desperate after a long period of not hearing from her, I checked with Diantha to see how my daughter was doing.

"I'm helping people who walked from the site."

"You're at the shop?" I crushed and released the hem of my shirt.

"Of course, I'm at the shop." And then came the sigh. "I'm here at eight every morning."

"Did you have any damage?" Guthrie asked.

Guthrie's question somehow became a hug. "Oh, Daddy." Her voice broke. "It's okay, but there's dust and debris everywhere. People are like zombies."

"Can you get home?" Guthrie asked.

"Not really. No. The trains aren't running. But I'm safe here. I have a bathroom, a hotplate, and some food."

I thought of the television images. "What about the people outside? Where are they going?"

"I'm doing everything I can, Mom."

"I just meant—" I started to explain that I wondered what was happening with these wandering lost souls, but I knew she'd heard judgment. "Thank god you're okay."

Chapter 42

✿

Ivy

Wishing for Peggy Lawton

My hands shook hours after the planes hit the World Trade Towers. Explosions and sirens blaring still rang in my body—streams of people passed by my shop on their way to nowhere. I'd given away almost all my food; now, all that remained in the refrigerator was a frozen pizza to microwave for dinner in case I couldn't leave the shop.

I'd been outside for hours, standing beneath the exquisite sign my mother had painted. The deep indigo and silver letters spelling *Poppy's Jewels* seemed like a taunt to the gods. Where was the place for the bracelets, necklaces, and rings I'd crafted in such microscopic detail in a world where massive skyscrapers cascaded down? This place would barely register in the giant's fist of destruction.

Shop owners and residents formed a small knot on Church Street for most of the day. In the hours after the towers fell, we became a small tribe. The musicians living in apartments over our stores had an unending supply of beer. I, who always had coffee brewing, contributed caffeine. Nina, the owner of Vegan Bakes, provided a continual stream of dense banana muffins that reminded me of Roundhouse days. We fed ourselves along with the walking traumatized, everyone skimming only the surface of the terror. If we went deeper, we might disintegrate.

Finally, I went inside, dreading the idea of spending the night. According to the radio, neither trains nor buses were running, certainly not downtown where I had my store.

I tried calling my parents again, knowing they'd be a mess, thinking the worst. After Poppy died, we walked the earth waiting for something horrid to happen again. Anticipated danger joined us Puddingstone folk at all our gatherings; our uninvited guest RSVP'd every time. Zane and I discussed our hypervigilance ad nauseum at our monthly dinners at the mediocre Tad's Steakhouse—Puddingstone kids never lost their taste for forbidden foods.

For my birthday this year, Zane had taken me to White Castle and given me a box of individually wrapped Peggy Lawton Chocolate Chip Cookies. I wish I had them here now.

Our Puddingstone and Roundhouse bonds could have shattered. Instead, they became forged in steel. The only ones we never saw were Wyatt and Melanie.

I wondered if Melanie had filed me so far back in her mind I was inaccessible.

I wondered if Wyatt worried about me when a blizzard headed toward New York City or a heat wave slowed the city to half speed.

I wondered if he visited Manhattan with his new wife and four hundred new children when they managed to wrench themselves from their farmhouse. Maybe they came with him when he delivered one of his perfectly crafted tables to a banker on Sutton Place or brought one to a plastic surgeon's summer home in the Hamptons.

I wondered if he thought of me today when the blue sky turned black, and people fell from burning buildings. If he watched steel girders pancake to the ground on his television. I wondered if he owned one.

I'd wondered about Wyatt since Poppy's funeral when I gripped my father's hand so tight I half expected our skin to meld together, and a sneaky sense of being stared at had overwhelmed me.

Wyatt's parents stood on either side of him, just as Melanie's mother and father almost held her up during the burial. I remember asking my father why Melanie and Wyatt weren't next to each other; his answer had burned so deep that I could roll the scene like a movie at any moment.

"Neither Melanie nor Wyatt have anything to give. They're both too sad. So, they're leaning on their parents, who can be strong for them."

"Aren't they also sad?" All four of my grandparents wept endlessly for Poppy. I couldn't imagine their grief if it had been Henry or me.

"Of course. But parents can always muster strength from deep inside when their children need them. Right now, Melanie and Wyatt need their parents."

I had wondered if Melanie and Wyatt were still parents. I wanted to ask my father if parents got to keep being parents after their only child died, but I didn't want to make him sadder than he was.

Poppy's funeral had been the saddest day of my life. Thousands lost their mothers, fathers, sisters, and brothers with the towers falling, but even in memory, Poppy's burial felt worse. Guilt overwhelmed me with that thought, but though the idea was cruel, the funeral of one person you love can make you unhappier than the deaths of a million strangers.

Whenever death came near or tragedy loomed, I hurtled back to losing Poppy.

Wyatt's mother had stared hard that day. She studied me like a crucial test approached requiring her to memorize my every feature.

Did we resemble each other, Wyatt and me? When I visited my parents, I went through their photo albums page by page, stopping at two pictures. The picture that captured me first showed Poppy and me as we wrapped our arms around each other's shoulders. I never slipped it from the album to make a copy. I worried that if I possessed the photo, it would own me.

Roxanne must have shot the picture—only she had the camera

and skill to capture us in such sharp detail and drenched color. If you threaded our hair together, you'd be hard-pressed to separate Poppy's strands and mine. Back then, we called the color maple syrup. When I looked at the picture, I saw how our hair fell in the Grade A rich amber syrup range. All these years later, my hair had darkened to Grade B. Dark Amber.

In a photo of our extended Puddingstone family, Wyatt's hair is Grade A. My father, Guthrie, is the Grade B variety.

Poppy and I both had green eyes, as did Wyatt. And my Grandma Penny.

My parents had a picture of Wyatt's parents. They must have been visiting Puddingstone. Wyatt's mother's shoulders were square. Sharp. They made a perfect ninety-degree angle.

When I met Elijah, finally finding my love, one of the first things he commented on was my right-angle shoulders—a soldier's shoulders, he'd said.

My background intrigued him, same as with everyone I met, though he also came from the not usual. Both sides of his family had originally come from Iran; they'd lived there when it was called Persia. His father was Jewish, and his mother was Muslim; he looked pure Iranian. The line between Sephardic and Islamic families was thinner than most realized.

His background? My parents would love that. If genetics were up to them, God would shake the world like a snow globe.

Next, they'd find out he taught criminal justice at John Jay College and decide, without evidence, that meant he fought racism by turning out better police officers.

I almost rejected his courtship to avoid my parents' approval.

Most of all, I dreaded hearing my mother bring up Clay, the lost Romeo to her Juliet. I feared her comparing us as though Elijah and I were star-crossed, fighting the power solely by being together. I wanted to tell her I'd had a virtual United Nations of exes once I overcame my aversion to sex.

I punched Elijah's number and again got a message that translated to "no connection for you."

Going home to my apartment felt impossible, even if the trains began running. Going underground terrified me.

WNYC's continual news provided my background of barely contained panic as I called Elijah, my parents, Henry, and Zane in a never-ending loop.

Wyatt must know that Zane and I lived in New York City—him in Brooklyn Heights, me in a studio apartment on the Upper West Side. I'd sold my grandparent's co-op to fund Poppy's Jewels.

I wondered if Zane had any reason to be near the Twin Towers that morning. Maybe his agent had set up a fancy Windows on the World meeting. Perhaps yet another television executive was trying to tempt him from Broadway.

I imagined my terrified grandparents in Rhinebeck. I hoped Henry was with them.

Elijah was probably dialing me as often as I was him.

I locked the door so I could go into the back of the shop and calm myself with small chores as I listened to the minute-by-minute updates on the radio.

Starry light shined on gold, silver, and gemstones in the cases lining the front-facing part of my store—the space for customers; the scene looked as out of place in this new world as a ballgown in a war zone. I was grateful to slip into my cramped workspace. No velvet-lined cases or mood lighting were in the back, though I kept it as clean and organized as an operating room. The pricey items I worked with required tracking.

My anxiety grew as I sat at my workbench burnishing a made-to-order wedding band.

After another hour of trying to reach my family, Elijah, or anyone else, I felt like I might be the last person on earth.

Being alone was never my comfort zone.

All of us Roundhouse kids had the same problem: we constantly needed company and always craved solitude. We were walking contradictions.

Life was like a science fiction book of Jacob's I'd read at Roundhouse. The world revolved around cravings: salt led to needing sugar, followed by a hunger for fat and a longing for salt, a never-ending cycle that started repeatedly.

When I heard the doorknob rattle, instinct told me was to stay in the back and call the police—as though a single cop in New York City had a minute to check on a doorknob rattling.

Hypervigilance. Anxiety. Depression. I could name the symptoms of PTSD in my sleep. Each time I jumped, I reminded myself to breathe.

Sometimes, a cigar was just a cigar.

Every bulb in the front shined at the fullest wattage. Today was not a day to promote darkness.

I forced calming thoughts: A late wanderer from the disaster sought water. A bathroom. Food. I could share my frozen pizza.

The rattling now became continual knocks. I locked the door to the back workshop that held multiple thousands of dollars of inventory and then crept toward the front entrance. An outline of a tall male showed through the stained-glass window.

"Ivy!' sounded through the wood and glass. "It's me."

Me! *Me* means someone you know, someone you care for, someone who might make everything okay if only for the moment they held you.

I swung open the door and fell into Elijah's arms. We were the same height, five foot ten, and fit perfectly. Emotionally, we are opposites: I am a prickly pear; he carries a radar for all that needs fixing.

"How did you get here?" I asked without letting go.

He tapped one foot and then the other on top of my sneakers.

Aetos. Of course.

"Did you check on your folks?"

Elijah's parents lived in an oversized apartment on Cathedral Parkway, close to Columbia University, where his mother taught. Either way, walking here or there would be over an hour's hike from the John Jay campus on 10th Avenue, though in opposite directions.

"Mom and Dad look out for each other. And I'm sure my family has already gathered."

"But not the sainted son." Elijah's six sisters and father treated him like God's chosen one. His mother rolled her eyes even as she also doted on him.

He pushed me to arm's length while still holding on. "When I couldn't reach you, I couldn't breathe. I'd have walked ten times longer to reach you."

"Only ten? Is the thrill gone?"

He drew me back into his arms as I fought tears of relief and sadness. I didn't know what I had done to deserve this good man or how I had found someone who put me at the front of every line, but I fell to my knees each night in gratitude.

I honestly did this. Nightly prayer had become my habit.

"Food?" he asked.

"Frozen pizza."

"Excellent." He pulled a pint bottle of Jack Daniels, two cans of Coke, and a smushed Twinkies package from his backpack. He knew my taste for the cheap snacks I grew to love at Murphy's General Store. "Behold this perfect pairing."

"Are the stores open?" We walked to the back, where I kept the fridge, microwave, and a cluttered metal table that I could clear instantly.

"Many. Did you think everything in New York closed?"

"I thought the world was ending," I said. "I'm waiting for the subways to blow up and bombs to rain down. I was afraid to go to the bathroom where I couldn't hear the radio."

Elijah took two mugs from the short shelf, pouring a can of Coke and then a solid shot of Jack before in both placing them on the table. "Dutch courage. Sit. Drink."

I drank half the glass. "Is that phrase offensive? *Dutch* courage."

"My child of the communes. Do you know where those words supposedly come from?"

"No, but I'm sure a son of college professors will. Do tell."

"Work taught me the background. We learn about every possible offense there. One story says that English soldiers used Dutch gin to calm down during war as early as the sixteen hundreds. Another says—"

I cut off his explanation. Like my father, Elijah knew everything. "Do you think the world is ending?" I finished half my drink and tried not to cry.

He reached across the table and took my hand. "If so, I want to be next to you during each minute remaining on earth. I have two questions. First, will you marry me? And second, when will I meet your parents—all eight to ten of them?"

Chapter 43

❄

Ivy

Spaghetti Icicles

Handmade decorations weighed down my parents' Christmas tree—most of them brought to Boston by my grandparents. The attack on the World Trade Center had changed the world in ways enormous and small, including our family's inability to have Christmas in Rhinebeck this year.

My worried grandparents forbade anyone to fly. Only my parents, Henry, and I lived within driving distance of Rhinebeck. My grandparents thought celebrating at their house this year would be too sad. The rooms would seem empty without the usual numbers—us, my three aunts, their spouses, their children, their children's partners, six of the next generation, plus cousins from throughout the Hudson Valley.

Christmas there with our comparatively sparse group felt too weighted, so my parents hosted for the first time, with Grandma and Grandpa driving up the Taconic weighted down with Christmas decorations, presents, and Grandma's favorite butter in case they couldn't find it in Boston.

Grandpa Gordon took Elijah on a tree tour, naming the maker for each ornament. The only store-bought ornaments ever allowed were the ones Grandma's family had brought from Sweden.

"See this one?" Grandpa tapped a finger on a miniature gold-painted wire cage with a feathered bird inside. "Henry and Ivy made this together. Look at how the two of them combined their talents."

"For goodness' sake, Grandpa. We were teenagers, not child protegees." I rolled my eyes, though my smile belied my faux annoyance.

Grandpa waved my words away. "And this one?" He pointed to an intricate constellation of stars. "Annabel was only eleven when she made that."

I shivered. Any mention of the age of eleven brought what seemed like an autonomic response. My mother at eleven, crafting stars; me at the same age, watching a bullet strike Poppy. The endless memory of my nightmares—Poppy falling, tumbling, plummeting into a starry black sky.

"Lots of talent in this family," Elijah said.

Grandpa nodded. "Yup. Next year, when this country returns to normal, we'll be back to celebrating at our house. Then you'll see decorations, Elijah. We couldn't possibly fit everything in the car this trip."

Elijah's bright sweater, opposite anything he'd normally choose, could poke your eyes out with the reds, pinks, greens, and spangled bells. Grandma Camille had put her heart into this Christmas cardigan, her way of welcoming Elijah to the family.

"You'll love Christmas in Rhinebeck," Grandpa said.

"I look forward to it, sir. Ivy talks about your house like it's Valhalla. I'm sorry we couldn't be there today." Elijah knelt to admire a scattering of icicles made from raw spaghetti, which had been glued to a hundred-year hardness from a covering of glitter and Gorilla glue.

We made those the first Christmas after Poppy died, with Grandma and Grandpa using their fierce love to build a safe landing for us.

With a crowd of aunts, uncles, and cousins surrounding us, we'd opened presents, bit the crisp arms off Grandma's gingerbread cookies, and covered ourselves in the quilts covering every chair. Nobody had forced us to share our feelings. Our grandparents provided a secure landing, letting us be quiet automatons, clutching us even as we clutched new stuffed lambs, lions, tigers, bunnies, and kittens—mine a soft Siberian with blue eyes.

Their own sharp pain for us must have made them feel so helpless; perhaps they were trying to blanket our grief in a menagerie of warm-eyed fur.

My grandparents would have kept us with them in Rhinebeck forever if they could. They hated having their family far away. Grandma Camille squeezed my father's arm daily during every holiday visit to say, "Only you listened. You never took Annabel away like the others."

By others, Grandpa meant my aunts' husbands, who'd dragged them to California, France, and Alaska, according to Grandpa.

Just days before, someone had tried to smuggle a bomb onto a plane in their shoe. Now, Grandpa double-downed, justified in his judgment against flying as travelers were forced to remove their shoes to prove bomb-free feet, and Grandma hardened her opinion ever more of sons-in-law who spirited daughters away.

Before September 11, we waited at the gate for our families to arrive; now, only the ticketed and barefoot entered.

But soon, we'd be flying again. Eventually, everything becomes normal.

Living at a place where kids outnumbered the adults once shocked us. Then Roundhouse with its ratio of seven kids to one or two adults became normal.

And then, after Poppy died, the once-maligned nuclear families became our new normal.

Everything becomes normal. Even having seen bullets from an ancient rifle kill your best friend in front of your eyes. We became habituated to this new truth, shredding us from the inside out.

Soon, uniformed airline cops with guns and German shepherds patrolling the airport would be ordinary.

Grandpa and Elijah continued their tour, joining Henry and my father in the kitchen, where they morphed from discussing Christmas decorations to comparing the New York Giants to the New England Patriots. Their voices carried from the table, where they indulged the dessert Grandma was churning out as though the holy family might descend with empty stomachs in Jamaica Plain.

Mom and I read in the living room. I turned the pages of one of the dozens of magazines to which she and my father subscribed—everything from *Ms.* to *Vogue.* They'd picked up the habit while trying to repair our bodies and souls, treating us to anything they imagined we'd want. They remembered how Poppy and I liked magazines and ordered every periodical that wasn't pornographic or conservative.

After Poppy died, almost nothing was off-limits, from hot fudge sundaes to puppies, stuffed and otherwise, to watching unlimited hours of the newly purchased television.

When I'd asked why they weren't married like all my friends' parents—"Where are your rings?" I demanded to know—they wed in a quiet city hall ceremony.

Trips to Rhinebeck outside of holidays became frequent after Roundhouse, which meant baking, drawing, knitting, and hiking with Grandma; Grandpa built us birdhouses, doll houses, and furniture for the tiny people. He took us to work. I can still change the oil in any car.

Now, my mother rolled her eyes from the chair across from the couch where I sat as the kitchen voices grew louder. I nodded in acknowledgment of her comically frustrated expression. Mom and I hated how sports united men and recipes connected women. We couldn't fake caring about a single sport.

"Let's go to my studio. I want to show you something," Mom said.

My puzzlement must have shown. We never exchanged presents before Christmas morning, not even a tiny stocking stuffer. Grandma would say, "We're not that kind of family," when we begged for one teensy-weensy little gift. I still laughed, trying to imagine what kind of family that might be. Who were those crazy free people tearing the wrapping from boxes at midnight?

Henry and I inherited many habits from our Jewish, Catholic, city, country, communal, and always ethics-driven families. Now, I wondered what Elijah might bring.

"For once, no questions, okay?" my mother said. Evening light flattered her. Of course, almost everything complemented her no matter what she did. Lines showed, and silver laced her red-blond curls, but she still glowed with her halo of beauty. I'd accepted my sparer looks years ago.

We climbed the stairs to the attic, the space my mother claimed as her studio. Brushes, paints, oilcloths, pads, and easels surrounded us in soothing clutter.

"Come. Look." She took my hand and led me to the corner where she claimed the light was best. "I painted this for you and needed to show it to you when we were alone. It's almost finished, but I didn't want to rush to be done by Christmas. Don't tell Grandma I gave you an early present. If she finds out, say I made it for your birthday."

She uncovered the corner of a canvas painted with saturated oil paint, rare pigments my Aunt Kirstie brought from Tibet. Mom used the oils so sparingly that I feared they would dry up before being applied.

When the image came into view, cold shivers ran through me. Poppy and I, our arms wrapped around each other's shoulders stared back at me. The painting didn't mirror the photograph my mother had worked from somehow instead she'd built a dream from it. Enchanted faeries spoke through my mother's hand to bring our souls to the surface.

Poppy and I appeared as we'd been, entwined as only childhood best friends can be, sharing every thought, belief, happening, and detail of our lives. When we woke, we exchanged stories of the hours we'd missed while sleeping, offering each other our dreams. When we slept, we'd breathed in concert.

I stepped closer. Our hair, masses of streaky maple, mingled at our shoulders. Poppy's curls wound around my thick, straight strands.

Our happy shades-of-green eyes shone from our faces, hers flecked with amber and yellow, mine darkened with pine.

My mother had replicated the colors of the nightgown Poppy wore as a dress while imbuing them with an otherworldly quality. Where had it gone? I wished her parents hadn't buried her in it but instead given it to me, and then I was glad they hadn't.

My breathing quickened as I turned away. The posters lining the room illustrated my mother's unique style: dense, optimistic colors and slashes of electricity. In a few lines, she could capture the mood of any person.

My mother spoke against the forces of evil through her brushes and pencils. The signature *Annabel Cooper* on any artwork was synonymous with the voice of justice—I believed she could have been as famous as Frida Kahlo had she had the needed streak of ambition. But my mother never left the Sojourner Graphics cooperative. Workers ran Sojourner Graphics; her band of friends there were connected with iron thread. My mother never chose the glittering sole act that could have been hers.

Mom had stayed with her people. She never longed for the spotlight.

I sat on the floor and touched a flower painted on Poppy's dress. "Was it my fault? Poppy dying?"

My mother sank beside me. "Your fault? How could you ever be to blame?"

"Remember at the table? Thanksgiving?" I choked out one word at a time.

"Sweetheart. Pudding. What in the world do you think you did?"

"I started all the trouble. I was jealous of Poppy. I made such a big deal about her stirring in the honey, yelling about how doing that didn't mean that she helped with my pie. As though it mattered. Melanie defended her. But Wyatt didn't. Why did he protect me and not her? And then everyone began arguing about work, and I asked why, if Melanie's work at daycare was so important, you didn't value taking care of us."

"Oh, baby, how long have you been in the grip of this craziness? Please tell me you haven't been blaming yourself all these years?"

She squeezed my hand so tight that I cracked wide open. "I wrote every word in my journal," I admitted, "everything I recalled.

"Why?"

"I never wanted to forget the harm I caused. You don't remember?" I began reciting words I'd almost memorized:

Grady had said: *Political art? Writing? Legal aid? Organizing? What serves change best?*

Suze had said: *Why isn't daycare first?*

Mom had said: *Melanie does more than any of us.*

I'd said: *If childcare is so important, why did you get rid of us? If you love caring for children so much, why not take care of your own kids?*

I collapsed into my mother's arms, feeling her need to offer comfort.

"Oh, Pudding. All of us adults carried awful things from the barn. Mountains of guilt, grief, and confusion," she said. "All of us spend our lives thinking and saying mea culpa, and we each deserve a portion of the blame. But you kids? Not one of you was at fault. Not Leo. Not you. None of you. Lay that all on Daddy and me. We were the grown-ups in the room, even if we forgot to act like it. We were the bad guys."

I breathed deep enough to speak around the massive chunk of memories collecting in my chest and took my mother's hands in mine. Nobody would question our connection. We had the same long fingers and strange bumps on our middle knuckles. Our high cheekbones matched; our long legs made it difficult to buy pants, and we both burned in the slightest sun.

She smiled when I sat cross-legged across from her and placed her palms on my knees. "Don't hold things in, baby. You can ask me anything."

I stared at Poppy and me, our hair mingling, our gestures mirroring each other. Her shoulders and mine, both squared. "Is Wyatt my father?"

Chapter 44

❀

Annabel

Nobody Stays a Knockout Forever

The drive to Northampton a few weeks later offered too much time to think. I had too many uncomfortable thoughts and disturbing memories.

Dirty snow covered the wooded grass on both sides of the Mass Pike; the weather surrounded me with merciful gray. I wanted neither storm nor sun; damp and gloom matched my needs.

Decisions bounced like balls in a lottery drawing. After a lifetime of sharing every stray thought with Suze, today I had only my own opinions stuck in my head—I couldn't rely on discussion; Suze and I hadn't analyzed the meeting with Wyatt facing me. Not that she wouldn't understand. Or Roxanne. We lived that life together. But telling anyone but Guthrie would feel as though I'd doubled down on my duplicity.

The collateral damage of the Great Monogamy Debate of 1967 was bound to resurface, though I'd stuffed away every thought and possibility from that time like an unexploded bomb. Even now, I could scarcely consider the consequences of Wyatt being Ivy's father.

I'd shoved Wyatt into a deep crevice of my past, only uncovering memories during nightmarish rummages in self-loathing. Guthrie slept the sleep of the good and innocent while I tossed in my guilt.

Clues existed: Ivy's and Poppy's hair colors were so similar. But hadn't Guthrie's mother randomly observed during one long-ago dinner how my daughter's hair mimicked Mike's pre-gray hair, Ivy's grandfather, her genetic forbear. I studied old photos of my father-in-law as though the answer lived in each of his strands.

Wyatt probably suspected why we were meeting today. I'd said, "We need to talk;" no man hears those words without hearing, "We have a problem."

People say memories feel like "just yesterday," but the night Wyatt and I had spent together seemed like a thousand years ago, which struck me as odd. I'd only slept with two men in my life: Wyatt and Guthrie. If I included Quinn, my statistics would rise, but I didn't count that truncated evening. My still-on nightgown proved chastity when Ivy interrupted us—and since we were sane people, he'd left our bedroom.

Of course, Quinn's leaving might have been less about Ivy and more about Guthrie. Even the horniness of a man in his twenties couldn't withstand the straight man's fear of being in bed alone with another man. What would Guthrie and Quinn have talked about while lounging there? The Celtics? SDS? STDs? The Bomb Tossers softball team?

Had Wyatt confessed to Melanie? I doubted it. They'd been a quiet duo, peaceful people skating on beauty and do-gooding. Neither tried to win our noisy Puddingstone arguments, though both, perhaps by their habits of silence, could easily grab the moral high ground.

Melanie flashed brilliance when she chose to speak, but much of the time, she lived in and through her actions, directing her analytical mind toward action.

The last time I saw Melanie had been when Roxanne and I traveled to San Francisco to attend a conference on worker-owned businesses. Melanie invited us to her home, a small apartment as simple and spartan as she now appeared. Though nobody stays a knockout forever, Melanie, once our poster child for gorgeous commune women, seemed like she'd deliberately erased her physical desirability and burrowed into an ascetic life.

The three of us had shared only faint outlines of "where are they now" regarding the kids, revealing only the barest details. We stayed within the bounds of politics and careers, staying strictly *just the facts, ma'am.* She encouraged no more. Any word I spoke of my living children seemed cruel, though Melanie asked after both of them.

Our former Breck girl resembled a graying nun without the wimple. She ran through a synopsis of her life. She'd become a nurse, spent most of the eighties working with AIDS patients, and now worked in a renowned palliative care hospital.

When Roxanne and I left, in lieu of weeping, we downed whiskey sours in our hotel bar, staggering to our room only when the danger of authentic feelings passed.

I pulled up to the Friendly's in Florence, a quiet town near Northampton, where Wyatt lived. Though neither he nor I had anything to hide, I chose the anonymous chain restaurant with deliberation.

I lied to myself shamelessly.

We had plenty to hide.

Guthrie didn't know I was seeing Wyatt; my casual mention of a meeting in Western Mass could have meant a dozen possibilities. Meetings with far-flung political groups happened so often that Guthrie barely asked. For which I was grateful. Better a sin of omission.

Northampton's web of left-of-center connected agencies knew Guthrie, me, and, of course, Wyatt, who ran the local food co-op. Wyatt's wife, the beautiful Pia, was the center hub of Northampton's homeschooling network.

Wyatt waved as I walked through the restaurant door as though perhaps I wouldn't recognize him though it had only been a few years since I had seen him and Pia at Mac's wedding. I'd know that man if I hadn't seen him since 1977.

As plain as Melanie had become was as fine-looking as Wyatt

remained. Like many cowboy-type men, the years had somehow increased Wyatt's desirability as he closed in on sixty. There would be no disconnect when seeing him with his pretty, fresh-faced young wife and quartet of blond children. He was Hollywood-handsome still.

When he stood and bear-hugged me, I worked on not dousing him in an immediate shower of my anxiety and remorse.

"Annabel. You look good, hon."

I nodded, unsure if I believed him, mad at myself for caring if he thought I looked good, despite that I'd picked my cherry red sweater because it woke up my face and had raided my makeup kit that morning as furtively as Suze might smoke a forbidden cigarette.

We made small talk while drinking coffee and eating grilled cheese until the waitress refilled our cups and removed the plates. Then I dove in. "Do you know why I'm here?"

He swept back his still-thick head of hair and gave me the grin that once and still charmed me. "Does Guthrie know you're here?"

I shook my head. "No."

"Then I suppose unless you want to repeat our one-time time, you're here because of Ivy."

"Did you ever wonder?" I ripped the cover from a tiny plastic creamer and stirred it into my coffee.

"Sure," he said. "Sure. I wanted to snatch her at Poppy's funeral."

My blood stopped pumping. His honesty put me too firmly into his shoes. Of course, if he'd had two daughters, he'd want the live one back.

"So why are you here?" He leaned in to speak lower. "Why today?"

"I need you to take a DNA test."

"Why now?"

"Ivy. Something made her suspect." I didn't mention that *something* was staring at a picture of her with Poppy. "She deserves to know whatever the truth is about her genes. But remember, Guthrie is Ivy's father, no matter the results. Her only father."

I prepared a simple dinner that night, too nerved up to prepare more than a quickly broiled chicken breast with a side of canned peas—a nursery or sick room meal. We ate in front of the television, a habit we took up when the children left. When Guthrie had his way, we watched the news; if I controlled the remote, it was *ER* or *Will & Grace*.

Driving back from Northampton, I vowed to talk to Guthrie before the DNA results came back. It would be cruel to spring the news on him if Wyatt and Ivy matched. None of us would have a chance if I presented this as a fait accompli after the truth came.

Fear overwhelmed me, but we needed to talk before the results arrived in the mail. Even if the news confirmed Guthrie's paternity, we had to talk. The worry I'd carried for thirty-five years had become a barricade between us.

"Why don't we take a walk," I blurted as he cleared the dishes.

"A walk?" Guthrie seemed puzzled. Walking and talking wasn't our style. We were the couple who talked about taking more walks for our health, not the couple who followed through.

"We're in a January thaw." We'd watched the news that night. "Let's take advantage."

"I have a thousand papers to grade, baby. Maybe Diantha wants to take a walk."

I snapped off the television. "I don't want to walk with Diantha. I want to walk with you."

"What's up, Annabel?"

I sighed and let loose the words. "Put on your jacket," I repeated. "We need to talk."

Within two blocks, the supposed January thaw seemed more of a weather fairy tale than a forecast. We walked side by side, hands jammed into our pockets. I felt rather than saw Guthrie react as I explained our situation's basics.

Me. Wyatt. One night.

Ivy. Poppy. The painting.

His mouth and jaw moved as though trying to get my words down.

He was quiet for a long time, appearing to be having an enormous conversation in his head until he finally choked out a question. "When will the results come back?"

"End of this week, I hope." Today was Tuesday. "Beginning of next."

He nodded, a gesture I couldn't interpret. Did his nod say *okay, thanks for the information? Okay, and fuck you? Okay, and maybe I'll talk to you again when the results arrive?*

"Why didn't you ever tell me?" he asked.

I closed my eyes momentarily, seeking counsel from what I imagined my mother would advise. *Tell the truth, Annabel. There's no other answer.*

"I don't know for sure. I guess I didn't want to."

I sent a quiet apology to my mother as I wrapped the truth in gauzy modifiers.

"So why now? No bullshit, Annabel. I love you. I love Ivy, I love Henry, and I love our future grandkids. The only parents I have left are Gordon and Camille. We're staring down sixty. I'm never leaving you. But now you've dropped this bomb, and I want to know why. If I'm not the real father—"

"You're always the real and only father and—"

"Real? What a fucked-up word. And if that's true, if you believe that, I never had to know about Wyatt. So why did you keep it from me, and why are you telling me now?"

I pulled my scarf closer, the thick Irish wool bitter when the fringe flew in my mouth. My mother knit us one every year. By next winter, Elijah would own one. I glanced at Guthrie; he also wore his Camille-made scarf. His had no tassels, which was my mother's way of differentiating them.

We walked fast. The animal hospital, Angell Memorial, loomed. I wanted to pull my hand from my pocket and enclose Guthrie's in mine, but we hadn't come near the hand-holding stage of our crisis.

Ivy and Guthrie like to remind me, too often for my taste, how I tried to sail past arguments and problems; people being angry with me felt like a small death. I confessed to any sin to wipe away my children's or Guthrie's anger. How could I tell any of them this habit was born of my original sins? Wyatt and Clay.

I reached to find some semblance of honesty. A poster appeared in my head, my mother marching toward me, holding a sign aloft. *Speak the Truth,* the words screamed.

Political and personal goals are met so rarely.

I spoke into the icy wind. "You'll think this a weak-tea excuse, and it probably is. But it's the only truth I can offer. I never wanted to consider the possibility of anyone but you as the father of our child. Not for one moment."

I sensed his shoulders sag.

"I pushed the possibility so far back that I almost forgot. You are Ivy's father. Not just in the you-raised-her sense; I feel it in my gut." I didn't know if that was true, but I longed for that feeling. "Guthrie, do you remember the day I told you I was pregnant?"

He gave the smallest of nods.

"I fell in love with you that day."

He turned and looked at me for the first time since we began talking, his face conveying an unreadable library of words.

We stopped at a red light, reaching the gas station on the corner of South Huntington and Huntington, watching cars navigate the unused trolley tracks that still bisected the street. I stayed quiet until we were once again alone on the road.

"I'd loved you before, but never as much as when you rose to meet me that day." Tears I'd held back for blocks escaped. "I didn't want to be pregnant. I was terrified. And though I was so angry at you for saying I had to leave school, I knew it was true. But most of all? Telling you frightened me. A baby wasn't in our plans. Your ambition, your drive, and your determination could overwhelm me. And then, when I told you . . ."

The stream of tears began to garble my words. Guthrie handed me his handkerchief as I dug into my pocket, searching for a tissue. Guthrie, Clay, and my father were the only men I'd ever known who carried handkerchiefs.

"You turned into a father before my eyes; I watched our unknown child, boy, girl, whoever, enter you. You rose to the occasion instantaneously, you kissed both of us, and we became a family. And that's why I never told you, Ivy, or anyone else about Wyatt. Nothing would ever come between us if I could help it. I loved you before. But I fell head over heels for you that day."

Guthrie stopped. He leaned over, his hands on his thighs, gulping ragged breaths. We stood under the trestle bridge separating Boston and Brookline. In this dividing line, you left the gritty storefronts of Mission Hill and emerged into the greenery surrounding the Arborway and the high-rise Brook House apartments.

I touched his back lightly, my hand rising and falling with each troubled breath he took. "Are you having an anxiety attack?"

When he didn't answer, my panic rose. "Is it your heart?" Guthrie was fifty-seven. His father had died of cardiac disease. A heart attack wasn't impossible. I fumbled for my phone, ready to hit 911.

He shook his head and raised his hand to stop me, shaking his head and working to slow his breathing. Once his chest stopped heaving, he forced out a sentence: "There's something I have to tell you."

What he meant was *Annabel, we have to talk.*

Chapter 45

✻

Annabel

Social Tea Biscuits

A visibly shaken Guthrie was a terrifying sight. During even the worst of times, he held himself tight.

"What is it?" I wrapped his hands in mine. My words were stupid. *It* was me. "I'm so sorry. I gave you a horrible shock. I should have waited before telling you."

He shook his head. "No. That's not it. I mean, it is. It is a shock. Of course. Ivy is and always will be my daughter, but what do they say? Biology is destiny?"

A shot of panic fizzed in my chest. "If my mind were clear, I could explain—"

Guthrie held up a hand. "Stop. I'm trying to keep from spilling my guts, literally and figuratively, under the bridge. Let's walk home without processing a thing. Then let's have tea with brandy—or just the brandy. Then we'll talk."

"But I—"

He put a finger to my lips and took my hand.

My love felt fathomless, deep enough to stay silent as we headed home. I listened to my footsteps, the traffic, and the wind picking up as we retraced our steps.

"Tea?" I asked when we opened the front door.

"Tea," he agreed, "and the brandy, if we actually have such a thing. I'll be down in a minute."

We were not drinkers, but I kept a stock of offerings for friends and family: wine for Rochelle, Roxanne, and my family, rum and Coke for Mary, and vodka for general offerings. After finding out Elijah's preference, I bought a bottle of Jack Daniels. We had a scattering of liqueurs, among which was a pear brandy, which I assumed was close enough to what people poured in emergency tea.

I slipped off my coat, put the water up to boil, and then carried a tray with ginger tea, brandy, and Social Tea biscuits into the living room.

He gave the tray a wry smile. "Social Tea, eh?"

Guthrie's grandparents believed chicken soup cured; my grandmother, mother, and sisters considered dunking Social Tea biscuits in tea a nerve tonic. I shrugged. "Good news or bad, Social Tea always soothes," I said in my grandmother's singsong voice.

The pot of tea, a platter of Social Tea, and a pear-shaped bottle sat on the burled walnut coffee table we'd brought from Puddingstone. We ignored the old manila envelope he'd placed on the table, sat in the old tapestry club chair across from the couch, and splashed a bit of brandy in our tea. Silently, we dunked the dry cookies.

Guthrie visibly girded himself, raking graying hair, and then placing his hands on his thighs. "I practiced how to say this the whole walk home." He lifted the mug and took a long swallow. "I imagine I have a hint of how you felt an hour ago."

Guthrie had a secret child—I knew it in my bones.

But how? When? He rarely left overnight or went anywhere I couldn't reach him. An affair at work? I ran through the women at Leaster, at Bunker Hill. Maybe he'd filled the envelope with pictures of the son or daughter about to be revealed. Maybe they were ones the mother sent each year—ones he'd collected and kept in that old envelope for years.

Now I understood his pain about Ivy. Imagining him sharing a child with someone else just about killed me. Where did this son or daughter—were they grown up? still a child?—live?

Maybe he was leaving me. My confession had finally allowed him permission to run to his mistress.

"Sweetheart, this is hard to say."

"Say it, Guthrie. Whatever it is, rip off the Band-Aid."

Would he call me sweetheart if he planned to say *I'm leaving*? That seemed ridiculous. But then I remembered Mary telling me how long after she and her husband split, they kept their marriage habits, calling each other "honey." She offered her ex help with his parents; he asked her how the car was running.

Guthrie turned the large envelope round and round, drank the last bit of liquid in his teacup, and cleared his throat. "Clay is dead."

I tried to combine the words with the moment and have them make sense.

"You can stop looking for him."

I opened my mouth to ask why, how, and what, but nothing came out.

Guthrie knew I looked for Clay.

Guthrie knew Clay was dead.

"Maybe I should have waited to get past the Wyatt thing, but I couldn't stand seeing you beat your own breast, knowing what I had done."

"What did you do?"

Guthrie shook his head. "It's what I didn't do."

"Please stop talking in riddles."

He clutched the envelope, began to hand it over, and then stopped. "You can read this whole thing after I tell you . . ." He appeared to order his thoughts. "Mrs. Harris wrote to me—"

"Mrs. Harris wrote to you?" Visions of Mrs. Harris rose from the past. Her stern face, arms crossed against us as she stood on her porch in Greenwood.

"Remember when I gave Mrs. Harris my parents' address? I did it because I knew I might move around, but they'd stay put. Well, she wrote via my parents three years after we left Mississippi."

I added up the years quickly. Three years after we left, I was pregnant with Ivy or about to be.

"What did she write?"

He tipped the envelope toward me. "Do you want to read it?"

I shook my head. "After. Tell me."

He nodded. "Mrs. Harris always remembered us and how upset you'd been. She held on to my address."

Mrs. Harris's clean house would keep anything from going missing or falling into a corner. I imagine her tucking Guthrie's piece of paper in the oak hutch drawer where she kept essential documents.

"News of Clay's death reached her through the church."

"He died in 1968?"

Guthrie rose and came to sit beside me. "He died in '64 while we were there, but they didn't find his body until three years later."

"What? How? What?" I'm not sure why I acted or felt surprised. I always knew; I never wanted to know. Sadness seeped in.

"The Klan probably dumped his body in a river miles away. Mrs. Harris said they probably hung him first but didn't want to leave him there. Not with cops crawling everywhere. They—"

The images would haunt me forever. I held my hand up, unable to continue with thoughts of Clay until I was alone. "I understand. I'll read the letter. But . . ."

But what?

I stared at him. "You knew I was looking?"

He met my eyes. "I figured you were looking for him during all those visits to libraries to research art books every time we traveled. I felt awful because I knew his name would never show up. Mrs. Harris told me he used his mother's maiden name in Mississippi. He never wanted to get his family in trouble."

That's why his name never showed up in any microfiche.

"I saw you searching crowds at demonstrations. I knew you looked at that picture you drew. And then you painted Clay on canvas, making him even more permanent. I felt like we were living in a bad Willy Nelson song—he was always on your mind—and there I was. Jealous of a ghost."

I thought of the trio of dead boys. James Chaney. Michael Schwerner. Andrew Goodman. I never forgot them. Tortured. Murdered. Their bodies dumped like trash. They roiled around inside me, but it had been a story.

A tragic tale that added to the drama of my summer.

I hated myself for looking for Clay like some wounded fairy tale heroine all these years. The Romeo and Juliet of Mississippi. Swooning in private. I'd let our short romance overtake the greater meaning of Freedom Summer.

And I'd never faced the facts. Of course, Clay had to be dead. Or he didn't want me. What had I conjured?

"Why didn't you tell me? How could you let me keep looking? Making a fool of myself."

"I never thought you were making a fool of yourself, sweetheart." He tossed the envelope on the table and put his arm around me. "Don't ever think that. I didn't tell you because I was afraid."

I pulled my hands away, not ready. "Afraid of what?"

"Afraid that if you knew he was dead, the sadness and blame would rip you apart. Life was chaotic and scary for you when I got the letter. Pregnant with Ivy. Terrified of your life changing. You were so angry you had to leave school. I'd have done anything to keep you steady. Everything was so hard for you in those days."

"I didn't know you saw that."

He laughed. "Did you think you were invisible.?"

I twisted my mouth to the side and then answered. "Honestly? Sometimes."

He leaned his head back against the top of the chair. "I acted like it, didn't I? I can be pretty damn self-centered, huh? Too late for sorry?"

I shook my head. "I don't think sorry has a time limit. We're both in need. So why didn't you tell me after? Once the kids were older?"

"He was the love of your life. What if you mourned forever? What if you were sad forever? The longer I went, the longer I was ashamed of not telling you."

I didn't mean to, but I laughed. "Dear sweet Jesus, Guthrie, *you* are the love of my life. Clay. Clay was a star-crossed dream and nightmare, but I only knew him for less than a month. You, you were the one."

Guthrie raised an eyebrow. "Well, except for that one time, I guess.

I laughed. "Yeah. There was that. My walk on the wild side."

"You picked a hell of a time to walk."

"Listen to us, Guthrie. Listen to what we have. We can laugh at this moment. You've always made me laugh. You're the love of my life," I repeated. "Clay? I barely got to know him before he disappeared. Was killed. I made him into a god—the sainted one who got away."

Guthrie poured more brandy into his empty teacup. "This stuff isn't bad," he said.

"Perhaps we'll make our sixties the era of drinking."

He drizzled a bit into my cup and clinked his to mine. "To drinking."

"Living in the shadow of a saint must have been hard," I said.

"Trying to see whose eyes our daughter had must have been worse."

I stared at my husband. Both of us had worried about ghosts for so long.

Once upon a time, everything appeared possible. At eighteen, my possible meant fixing America. Exhilaration and pride merged into such a heady and potent brew I swore I shimmered in a physical manifestation of how going to Mississippi would change me and how I'd be part of transforming the world.

Peace and justice beckoned. I believed my destiny lay in Freedom Summer.

For decades, I'd either pushed away thoughts of Clay or lingered in his memories as though visiting a world of lost romance. One road led to avoidance. Avoiding the guilt I carried for causing whatever fate faced him. That path meant soaking in undeserved bathos. The other led to building fairy tales.

My guilt? I deserved that. Building a monument to the love of Clay and I had been a method to give myself the grace I craved. Guthrie's protecting me from the truth—whatever the reasons—played right into the game of Annabel and Clay as Romeo and Juliet.

I'd been naive to the point of simple-mindedness. Book-schooled but so inexperienced that before going to Mississippi, I thought sharing my frilly white bedroom with one of my three sisters represented a burden. Once there, my naivete stretched to believing that loving Clay was part of how I would save the world.

Instead, he died, killed by our romance. The Ku Klux Klan held the knife, shot the guns, and lit the matches in their hatred of him and our glittery young love, but SNCC supervisors had warned us against mixing it up romantically, spelling out in cold hard truth the suffering interracial romance would rain down.

But I was young, and he was young, and we thought the world revolved around us.

I'd committed sins of commission and omission. Most of all, I'd committed stupidity.

I envisioned my life in balance, with Clay and Poppy on one side of the scale and all the work I'd done on the other, and I had no clue about the tipping point. I'd keep working for good; I'd love Guthrie more honestly and be a better mother. With luck, I'd get to be a better grandmother.

And no doubt, I'd keep failing. But if I worked and loved honestly, from now on, I'd only fail with my eyes wide open.

And though I knew that only Guthrie could claim the role of Ivy's father, I needed to face reality.

I prayed for those lab results to be on our side.

Epilogue

❊

Ivy

Ghost Kisses

I inhaled the solitude of the empty kitchen.

Being alone in my parents' house was a rare luxury. I supposed I should be grateful for the constant company—COVID lockdowns forced so many people to become hermits—but some days, the sheer volume of people in our bubble stifled me. Between my parents, Elijah, our daughter, and our pandemic pod, I hunted for privacy as though tracking an endangered species.

Despite the spaciousness of my parent's home, my chances of being alone, truly alone, had been better in our Brooklyn house. There, Elijah would lock himself in his study to teach remotely. Our daughter had already lived on her computer—or anywhere away from us—since turning 13 three months earlier. I worked in a bedroom corner that I turned into a shop. At any given moment, I had a shot at privacy.

Since moving to Boston, stillness had become a rarity.

I peered at the stained newspaper clipping affixed to an index card, pondering whether I should triple or quadruple the "Cakes and Cookies" banana bread recipe.

I'd found the recipe in one of my mother's old notebooks. Before baking, I'd brought it to her studio for a reality check. She'd cut the recipe with pinking shears, stapled it to an index card, and then affixed it to the notebook paper with duct tape.

"Look," I said. "Not a lick of whole wheat, honey, or healthy oils. From whence came this?"

Her look softened from her initial annoyance at being interrupted. "Wow. That goes back. That's from my Confidential Chat collection." She ran a finger over the paper as though greeting an old friend. "Over fifty years ago. That doesn't seem possible."

By the time she'd finished explaining Confidential Chat, a mainstay of the *Boston Globe*'s "women's section"—and how Diantha had forbade serving the sugary, buttery white-floured, crusty-topped banana bread—there was nothing in this world I wanted to make more.

I quadrupled the recipe, deciding the banana bread would be my contribution to our Friday night Puddingstone dinner.

I was unsure if Elijah and I had escaped New York to help my parents or ourselves. We thought they needed someone to be there since they were well into their seventies, my father seventy-eight and my mother seventy-six. Elijah's sisters fought for the privilege of caring for his parents, so we were secure about his mother and father's safety. Henry, attached with unbreakable cables to his wife and three daughters, his animals, and his zealous commitment to keeping his family nuclear, wouldn't leave Rhinebeck.

He vowed to keep Cooper Repair open for the community, having expanded the shop to fix all the things one once would have tossed for an upgrade. Toasters. Lamps. Electric blankets. Old yogurt makers. Henry devoted himself to *fixing, not buying*! His mantra. He managed anxiety over climate change and his children's future one lawn mower at a time.

Weekly, he swore his eternal Zoom gratitude to Elijah and me for ensuring our mother and father wouldn't weather COVID alone.

"As though they'd ever be alone," I reminded my brother in each conversation. "They'd be fine without us. But you're welcome."

When we first arrived in Boston, we were quarantined in my

parents' finished basement, receiving our food as my parents handed it off on the top basement step.

When our isolation ended, my parents, those naive people who adored our daughter, embraced her as though receiving an offering from the gods. Elijah and I shared a look of relief.

Adoration of our daughter? Appreciation of Felicity was a challenging state for us to access these days. On the first day of the New York City lockdown, Felicity had stomped into her room, slammed the door, and communicated by text, suffering our company only when she wanted to ensure we knew which food she desired. Her dietary wants were a moving target.

Why didn't COVID hit when Felicity was ten? When she still found Elijah and me lovable? Now, a newly crowned teenager, our daughter exchanged hugs for giving us lists of demands. Before coming to Boston, she'd demanded we use her middle name—Camille—so "at least we could honor something other than happiness."

"And that's only temporary," she'd warned us. "I'm working on choosing my permanent new name."

So, good luck, Grandma Annabel and Grandpa Guthrie, I wanted to say as we emerged from the basement, lifted our masks, and handed over Felicity.

I mean Camille. Or any of the names making up the lists she scribbled, adding and subtracting daily. One day, she wanted *Daria*, meaning "the sea." Then, *Azadeh*, for "free." Or, her one-month favorite, *Ava,* for "voice." She culled them from Iranian girl names she'd found online. I discovered more ideas from the thousands of pieces of stray paper she scattered as she walked as though Felicity-Camille-Daria-Azadeh-Ava were a princess and we, the peasant servants, were meant to pick up behind her.

Grandparents willing to adore their newly teenage granddaughter were the best reason to relocate to Boston. Throwing in my parents' deck and backyard, life in Boston was palatial compared to hanging our heads out our Brooklyn brownstone windows.

Plus, we had our bubble.

Diantha's place next door allowed us another garden of delights. Chuck had died from a heart attack ten years before, but his beautiful planting remained. In April, masses of tulips reminded us of him, as did a cherry tree so lovely I almost wept when I saw the blooms.

"When your friends start dying, that's when aging breaks your heart." My mother had squeezed my hand as my father steered the car down the winding road in the new section of Forest Hill Cemetery on a trip to show me where Chuck had been laid to rest.

I'd stared out the window and then as I stood on the grass. Silent. Chuck could blow ghost kisses to Poppy from his grave to hers. I tried not to act like a sullen child, but my mother caught my thoughts.

"I'm sorry," she'd said. "Your heart was broken far too young, sweetheart."

Diantha assigned herself as Felicity's science tutor, my mother arranged space in her studio for Felicity's art classes, and my father set up a computer area fit for the genius our daughter and my parents considered her to be.

Growing up an only child in New York City, our girl thought we had deprived her of the dream childhoods she believed Elijah and I experienced. First, there were the idyllic circumstances to which she ascribed Elijah's childhood, surrounded by sisters, aunts, uncles, and cousins, all living within one block.

If Elijah lived in paradise, I grew up in Shangri-La. Not even the truth of Poppy's death denied her fairy tale. Nope. Poppy became Snow White. Nothing could convince Felicity that Roundhouse wasn't an idealized version of the summer camp she adored and the sleepovers her friends had every weekend.

I'd poured myself into motherhood—at times; I should have called it sacrifice-hood. I even visited Vermont for the first time since leaving at eleven. Felicity had been asking about *where Mommy lived with all the children* since she'd heard the story when my mother spilled the beans. Felicity was only five, but Mom's belief in utter transparency had grown stronger each year.

Henry and I advocated for keeping kids in the dark when appropriate, but we kept losing the battle of keeping our children innocent of the stranger parts of our early years.

Thus, when we asked Felicity what she wanted for her tenth birthday, and she said *going to Roundhouse, please, please, pretty please,* I stubbed my toe against the wall of forgetfulness I'd so carefully built.

Choosing between Felicity and me usually meant I went to the back of the line. I'd only held onto Poppy's Jewels after her birth because Elijah had insisted, saying, "You're not sending the baby to Siberia if she stays with my mother a few hours each day."

He was right. His mother considered having Felicity there a gift of time to imbue her with everything Persian and what she considered cultured in her battle to combat my parents' ways. "Your mother and father are so interesting," she'd say, using the word *interesting* as a synonym for *odd*.

Visiting Putney, Vermont, did not bring the closure and peace one might see in a fictionalized version of my life. I hated being there. Standing at the edge of the Roundhouse property made me shake so severely that I insisted on returning to the anonymous motel where we stayed.

When Elijah drove back to Roundhouse with Felicity, the current owners were not delighted to welcome visitors from *back then.* The shooting was no point of pride for them, nor was the history of what they called "that damned hippie house."

Two giant lines forming red circles, one inside the other, surrounded a pair of black rifles crossed at the bolts. Painted in the space between the circles were the words *We Don't Call 911.*

Elijah told me Felicity had stomped away, disgusted by the sign emblazoned on the side of the barn.

"How dare they?" Felicity said when they returned to the motel. My daughter's fury could scorch anything in her path. "They know about Poppy; I know they do. I'm glad you didn't see it. Never let Uncle Leo go back there."

Thus, for my daughter, my time in Roundhouse, along with Poppy, was ever more cast in goodness and perfection. She cast the new owners as devils trying to defile our beatified history.

Elijah and I supposed that building these idealized memories with sides of fiery indignation served Felicity well. We didn't want my trauma to taint her childhood.

Though I could live without the veneration.

I poured the last of the banana bread batter into the third pan for what my father called, jokingly and with pride, *Shabbos dinner*, and the rest of us referred to as *Puddingstone Night*. Here I was, about to become banana bread queen again—though here, unlike in Vermont, I could make loaves that weighed less than five pounds each.

Every Friday, we gathered at Diantha's—she'd inherited the extra-large dining room, each of us toting some dish we'd sweated over, threw together, or ordered from a local restaurant, depending on our moods. The one thing we could count on was leaving Diantha's with enough leftovers to hold us through the next day's lunch and dinner.

Damp air had frizzed, curled, or thickened everyone's hair except for Grady's—Suze's husband barely had any left—and Roxanne, whose silver hair hit her cheekbones in a perfect glossy blunt bob.

Mac carried in a salad with enough color to satisfy any nutritionist from the kitchen. His husband and twin daughters were building a castle from Legos.

Leo arranged the platter of baked goods that hadn't sold that day. Suze encouraged the practice for practicality, for zero waste, and because, as my mother told me, Suze and Grady never stopped treating Leo as though he bore the same fragility that had led him to barely leave his bed for a year after the shooting.

Suze and Grady still praised Leo's every move. I didn't know if they'd finally found the right therapist or if simply enough time had passed, but Leo had mainly recovered. Once Leo rose from the deep grief and depression that followed him through college and his years-long apprenticeship at a bakery in France, he'd devoted himself to keeping Poppy's spirit and memory alive. He resembled a monk without robes, dedicated to the practices he instilled at Peacock and Turtle. Leo hired only ex-prisoners, teaching and training them. Leo provided a stream of skilled bakers for shops through Boston. Starting in 2013, he used his connections to raise funds for Sandy Hook Promise.

If he had romantic relationships, we never saw any evidence.

He was able to safely be in our pod as he limited his business to having one employee baking in the back—sometimes him—and one on delivery duty.

Jacob's family couldn't be part of our bubble, breaking Diantha's heart, though she adopted Mac's children along with Felicity as hers.

Jacob's wife worked at Boston Medical; Jacob built computer systems for Aetos via Zoom while overseeing his teenage sons' line schooling. The four of them lived at the rambling house in Mission Hill. Puddingstone. Diantha had never sold the house on Alleghany Street. Over the years, she'd rented the place dirt cheap to families suggested by Valentina and Mary.

I wondered how Jacob managed to live there, imagining the roaming ghosts, until I stepped through the door after his first son was born. Jacob and his wife had cleansed the demons while keeping the sweetness, exchanging dark wood and layers of fabric for clean minimalism. They hung bright abstract art that had nothing to do with politics.

But Jacob kept the peace signs on the mantel. Seeing them immobilized me for long minutes.

Zane had a permanent room in his brother's house for when he visited, but he remained in New York when Broadway went on hiatus when COVID hit. Zane managed to be the most visible of our group to the outside and the most emotionally opaque to us. He never married nor brought anyone home for Diantha to meet—neither man nor woman. She told herself her son had married his work. I knew the truth of the rotating cast in his bedroom.

"Who brought wine?" Diantha asked.

Suze held up two bottles, one white and one red.

"Will that be enough, do you think?" Diantha put her hands on her ever-widening hips, beautiful hips that she flaunted more each year.

"Do you think she's planning her next career as a burlesque queen?" Zane had whispered to me at Diantha's eightieth birthday party.

I'd kicked him under the table and then whispered, "May we all have her sense of self like that when we're eighty. Your mother looks like a fertility goddess."

I missed Zane like crazy pants. He might be opaque, but only he gossiped without a guardrail. Suze was a close second, but as my mother's best friend, there were limits.

"You have this stupid wine conversation every Friday." My daughter assumed the face of someone held hostage.

Elijah patted her shoulder. "A child is a bridge to heaven, my darling Felicity."

"Stop it, Dad."

"I thought you wanted to get in touch with your Iranian roots."

"Not through your stupid Farsi sayings. And my name is Camille." She reached for the phone that usually lived in her jeans pocket and snarled. We'd forced her to leave it at home.

"Camille? Can you lend a hand?" Mac deposited his four-year-old twins in front of our daughter and dug into the canvas sack he carried on his shoulders. "Here we go. Crayons. Paper" He turned to me for a moment. "They're obsessed with tracing hands."

His husband knelt in front of the coffee table. "Guess what, girls? Camille is going to play with you!"

Even my grumpy daughter couldn't resist the ridiculous adorableness of Aimee and Michelle.

"I'll get a bottle of rosé from the basement." Roxanne whipped around, stopped, and looked at her husband. "I'll be right back, honey.

Stay with Guthrie, okay?"

Quinn nodded. His mind was fading, but his pure goodness remained. My mother had visited a gerontologist with Roxanne and Quinn when he first began acting confused. The doctor told them that personalities pare down to their essence when people are in these early stages of cognitive decline. In Quinn's case, that would be his kind soul.

"Ivy," my mother called from the kitchen. "Bring Daddy's brisket to the table. And then call everyone to dinner."

Brisket. My father morphed into his parents more each year while my mother became her mother—monitoring everyone, ensuring my father indulged in red meat no more than once a month, and nagging us to remain active during the shutdown.

My mother held out a china platter covered with gravy-covered meat. Grandma Penny's recipe, made with the prosaic ingredients of brown sugar, ketchup, water, and apricots, became magic after four hours in the oven. Grandma Penny used to make it every Passover.

"Careful."

"I got it, Mom." I smiled at my tone, hearing traces of my daughter. Or vice versa.

May you have a daughter just like you.

My mother never said it, but I swear I heard her bite those words back when I turned thirteen, and oh, how that curse had held.

I turned and saw my daughter on the overstuffed couch, turning the pages of *The Family of Man*, Max's twins snuggled on either side. Henry and I had turned the pages of that book so many times. In Mission Hill, in Putney, and here, in JP. Seeing the cover, the young person with their lips to a flute, a smiling companion behind—they could be female, male, it mattered not. The light of goodness beamed from their faces, as it did from my Felicity-Camille.

My girl would be fine.

I prayed.

A heavy damask cloth covered the table set with the crazy-ornate dishes Diantha inherited from her parents. She happily allowed us to scrape and cut brisket off the expensive porcelain Sèvres. Watching us puddle and smear ketchup around the elegant black, pink, and golden vermilion made her laugh.

Everywhere I turned, I saw the parents of the parents of Puddingstone.

Fifteen of us sat around the table. Twice as many if I counted the ghosts, the absent, and the missing.

Before we said thanks, I slipped my hand under the cloth and stroked the smooth oak table, remembering when Poppy and I first saw it.

"My father built this," Poppy had bragged. I'd been jealous. What could I point to representing *my f*ather? With all the leaves in, thirty could fit comfortably around that table. When the lockdown ended, we would fill every place. The wood still held the mirror finish, the dark honey color almost matching the sun streaks in Wyatt's hair, in Poppy's, in mine.

Wyatt wasn't my father.

That knowledge brought masses of gratitude. I didn't have to mourn Poppy again, this time as my biological sister. I didn't have to revise my relationship with my father, and though learning my mother's tangled worries had altered my connection to her forever, it was mainly for the better.

Now, after being locked down together for two months, I questioned, examined, and analyzed my family's constellations for everything, including cruelty and a lack of compassion. Cruelty was never my parents' sin, nor was a lack of empathy—perhaps I was the one who owned that tendency. Why else had it taken four decades and a pandemic to stop weighing the worth of my parents with my thumb on the scale?

Though I'd always put bad judgment on the con side of their ledger.

I looked around as my family—all my family—ate, laughed, and talked over each other. Snatches of conversation collided.

"Aimee, use your napkin."

"Let her be! You were just as bad at that age. Worse!"

"Did you hear that Rochelle's daughter locked down the contract for the health center's vaccine posters?"

The founders of Sojourner Graphics followed every bit of business chatter they could pry from Rochelle, whose daughter now oversaw the collective.

Conversations floated about everything and nothing.

"White sugar plays a role in ninety percent of arthritis cases."

"Ninety percent? Honestly, Roxanne?"

"The Boston Symphony hired Valentina's granddaughter."

"Has Mary's granddaughter had her baby yet?"

My mother raised a glass, and everyone quieted. "To Mary, Valentina, and Chuck."

Mary and Valentina had passed away a few years after Chuck. We let a silent remembrance of their memories pass over us.

"I need to fill two more boxes with canned food. Who's in?"

"Can I give you a check?"

Even during the pandemic, my parents managed to do miraculous things. Mom collected money for food—many thousands of dollars every week—for families without paychecks. And, of course, she drew: Cartoons to lift spirits, posters for struggling stores, and public health messages she had translated into a million languages. My father still practiced law, but only in- kind, concentrating on fighting executions and working against evictions and rent hikes.

The Puddingstone peaceniks still spread hope and care. Grady fixed bikes for free, Roxanne provided online art internships for college girls, and Leo would fight gun violence to his dying breath.

The list lengthened daily.

In the end, I joined the clan of good. None of my small staff at Poppy's Jewels came from art schools. Instead, I took a page from Leo and found talented people without the benefits that had been gifted to me from birth: women jailed for fighting against their abusers, kids caught for tagging who could use their eyes for magnificence on a smaller scale. I taught a free jewelry-making class at the settlement house near the shop.

My favorite lesson provided the secrets of making mood rings and passing along the mysteries of Poppy's signature pieces.

Even my sulky teenager worked for social change, leading her clique of girls on campaigns against bottled water. Perhaps there was a gene for do-gooding. Maybe doing good was our signature piece.

I imagined some people were put on this earth to tip the balance from evil to noble. And maybe these people were forced to carve out less for their kids.

But they tried, our parents. They parented us believing that with Roundhouse, they and we could have it all.

Poppy's death had ended Roundhouse. It had almost ended us. But the miracle was we didn't shatter.

Roundhouse, Puddingstone, and Poppy changed our lives. We worked our entire lives to balance our enormous loss.

What we, the children of Puddingstone, paid for our parents' dreams was higher than most.

Our parents' choices cost too much for all of us—for Wyatt, Melanie, and Leo.

But what miracles of recovery we became.

I silently prayed thanks to those around the table, the ghosts, and the missing.

May we always walk among the ethical, forgive trespasses, and find our core of humor.

I'd carried grief and anger into adulthood. Then, I brought my mother's wish to life and had a daughter just like me.

And thus, I recovered humor.

I met a man who kept his humanity even as he worked with prisoners and police officers; through him, I discovered my life held more luck and goodness than it did tragedy.

I'd been gifted a sweet, kind sibling through nature and blessed with six more through nurture.

My lesson became clear.

In the words of my Grandma Penny and Grandpa Mike's seders: *dayenu.* Have gratitude. What I had was enough.

Had the universe gifted me with no more than all these loving people at the table, it would have been enough. But I'd been given more.

Elijah, my treasure.

My multiple-names daughter wore the stamp of goodness even when hiding it.

Consider every path had been Grandma Camille and Grandpa Gordon's warning and hope.

Few of us reflected enough on our choices. My mother never thought a night with Wyatt would bring a lifetime of worry. Nobody contemplated Poppy's death at the end of the road to Vermont.

But my parents had surrounded me with a village of honorable people who tipped the balance to good. They repaired, fixed, taught, defended, created, and healed.

I smiled as my father placed another biscuit on my plate. He knew how much I loved Mac's baking powder biscuits.

My parents knew me.

My parents screwed up.

My parents were good people who neglected us in the name of freedom and strived for lives of honorable service.

I laced my fingers and held them to my mouth for a moment.

My five sets of Puddingstone parents chose a path that led to Poppy's death, and that choice would haunt us forever. But they also did extraordinary things.

They wanted to leave the world in better shape than they found it, and in the end, they almost managed to build a column of constant good, though their biggest failure nearly toppled it all.

Lately, my prayers have broadened. I prayed everyone could have moments of love and laughter that balanced out their inevitable grief ahead. I prayed that in Poppy's afterlife, she shined as spectacularly as she had on this earth. I prayed that if I screwed up—when I screwed up—my daughter's anger would never keep her from loving me.

At the very least, I prayed I'd meet disaster as well as my parents.

"You look so serious," my mother said. "What are you thinking?"

I reached across the table and took her hands. "I was thinking about everyone at this table. And about how much I love you, Mom. And how you and Dad did okay." I smiled. "By the time you grew up, you practically nailed it."

Was that backhanded praise or proof that I could not let go of the past? My mother looked grateful for my attempt at whatever amends I offered. I hoped to reach further into the state of forgiving but not forgetting. I never wanted to let go of Poppy. I'd always miss my sister of the heart.

I'd be forever thankful for this crazy quilt family with whom I'd been gifted.

Virtuous to the bone, all of them.

Acknowledgments

Author's Notes & References

Book Club Guide